Dear Deanne,

   May my written words
bring a message to your life.
Enjoy!

     Ruth A. Manieri

       Thank you!

The Myanmar Maneuver

by
Ruth A. Manieri

Bloomington, IN Milton Keynes, UK

authorHOUSE

AuthorHouse™
1663 Liberty Drive, Suite 200
Bloomington, IN 47403
www.authorhouse.com
Phone: 1-800-839-8640

AuthorHouse™ UK Ltd.
500 Avebury Boulevard
Central Milton Keynes, MK9 2BE
www.authorhouse.co.uk
Phone: 08001974150

First published by AuthorHouse 5/4/2006

ISBN: 1-4259-3232-0 (sc)
ISBN: 1-4259-3231-2 (dj)

Library of Congress Control Number: 2006904086

Printed in the United States of America
Bloomington, Indiana

This book is printed on acid-free paper.

To My Husband, the turtle collector
You are a Gem!

Significant Red

The RUBY is my personal gemstone.
This precious gem was meant for me alone.
Born in July on a hot summer night.
It is sure to bring blessings and delight.
Love, energy, passion, power and zest
Emit from its flawless clarity, at best.
The ruby stands for powerful feelings.
It's a "stone of courage" in all dealings.
This vivacious, fiery red rare stone
Shows irresistible brilliance in tone.
Second only to diamonds, it stands out
Revealing its beauty, without a doubt.
One who possesses a ruby is said
To have increased vigor to move ahead.
Feel fortunate being born in July.
For luck will be with you, on that rely.

- Ruth A. Manieri (July, 2005)

Chapter One
New York City

The Chan Continental Gem Export Company of New York City had its roots firmly established in Chinatown. Its real estate occupied an entire block. Mr. Lee Chang and his family were the proprietors for several generations. Mr. Chang's Great Grandfather began his business too far back for even Lee Chang to remember. If his own father and grandfather had not told their many stories over the years at family gatherings, Lee wouldn't know half of the facts. He was grateful he always listened attentively when the elderly spoke. It was all paying off for him now that he was a refined businessman himself having learned the gem trade from three wise men. He hoped that his son and grandchildren would someday follow his example and continue the tradition.

The Chan Continental Gem Export Company was a well-organized and established conglomerate highly respected by all in the gem trade. Over the years they managed to hire highly skilled and well-educated employees. Even on the executive level, they were lucky to have specialized men in their fields who were loyal and proficient. All of this made for a well-run company that brought in much profit and was allowing the company to continually grow and expand. They were always searching for new and up and coming lapidaries and gemologists who would be an asset to their company. Their standards were very high, but when one worked for the Chang Family, they were working for a very prestigious company.

One such employee who came into the company right out of college was Charlie Ling. Mr. Ling grew up in New York City and went through the New York public school system. When it came time for him to select a college, his first and only choice was GIA, the Gemological Institute of America, the New York Branch on Madison Avenue. It was a highly accredited school which was what Charlie's father wanted for him. While there, Charlie learned three basic and most important things: first, discover through research; second, learn thru education; and third, apply the learning through the Gem laboratory and instruments. He was instilled with the knowledge to ensure public trust in gems. He found out that the technical knowledge and integrity of a gemologist is important because of the rare and valuable gems he would be handling someday. While there he had access to the latest instruments such as microscopes, refractometers, Prism 1000 spectroscopes, and so forth. They were a far cry from the ordinary jeweler's loupe, though that was important to use as well. When he completed his schooling he received his Professional Gemologist Diploma and went to work for the Chang Gem Company. After several years, he added to his credentials by affiliating himself with the International Colored Gemstone Association, the Accredited Gemologist Association and the Gemological Association of Great Britain, all prestigious in their own rights. Charlie's job required him to travel a lot throughout the United States, to many gem dealers and jewelry stores. Eventually traveling to foreign destinations became part of his job description. Soon he found himself traveling to Southeast Asia, to Myanmar (Burma), which would turnout to be the first of many trips.

Charlie's family was concerned that he was too engrossed in his studies to think about looking for a lifetime partner. His father tried to encourage him to date but Charlie was preoccupied with learning his trade. He was determined to become established as a renowned gemologist before he could settle down with a wife and eventually a family. That was before he ran into Dena Wong in a restaurant one afternoon as they were both having lunch in Chinatown. Dena was a petite woman with gorgeous silky black hair and the biggest dark eyes he had ever seen. Her milky white complexion was stunning, especially in contrast with her beautiful luscious red lipstick. She had an attractively slim figure and was wearing a beautiful royal blue silk suit. Aside from this outward beauty, her perfume overwhelmed him and he could not wait to make her acquaintance. *I can't believe I am behaving like a school boy, he thought. I don't know what is happening to me!* He approached her as she was finishing her tea at the table in the corner.

"Hello, if I am not being too personal, may I ask you what the fragrance is that you are wearing?" Charlie asked as he bent over slightly toward the table.

"And who is asking?" Dena questioned as she picked her head up with a startled look. She was trying to seem uninterested though inwardly she felt quite flattered that someone was paying attention to her. *My friends always luck out with the opposite sex, she thought. Is my luck changing?*

"Oh, I am sorry for being so forward. I usually don't walk up to strangers and initiate a conversation. My name is Charlie Ling. I work in the city here in Chinatown at the Chan Continental Gem Export Company."

"Well, Charlie Ling, it is nice to meet you. I am Dena Wong. I am pleased to meet you." Dena extended her hand as if to offer a handshake. She didn't want to show any annoyance for fear of chasing this looker away. Her heart was actually thumping a bit. Her usual inner calm was shaken.

"So, what is the fragrance that has me mesmerized by its aroma?" Charlie insisted. Now he was showing his nervousness. His hands were sweating.

"Well if you must know, it is called *Love Spell*. My sister bought it for me from Victoria's Secret and I took a fancy to its scent. I can see it is also attracting other people's attention as well." Dena said with a smile. "Would you care to sit down? People are staring and that is making me nervous."

Charlie quickly slid into the booth, though very carefully and all the while keeping his eyes on Dena. It was, as they say, love at first sight. Her smile put him over the top. Her eyes were penetrating. He felt that he had found his one true love, his soul mate. *He was thinking that if he told his family about this they will laugh at him.* He felt this intense warmth just sitting next to her. *If this is what love feels like, then it is magnificent, he thought.*

"Love Spell; what a fascinating name! It seems to be casting a spell over me, so the fragrance is living up to its name. He could not help laughing at his own comment. I am so glad I decided to eat here today." Charlie said with a smile. "I would never have met you otherwise. I consider that a stroke of good luck. I usually eat in a local cafe right around the corner from my building, but today I felt like having something different. My morning at work was rather intense, so I decided to have an early lunch to air my brain a bit."

"I, too, am happy I came here today because I was really going elsewhere," Dena said. "I have already eaten, but would you like to have some tea with me?"

"A hot cup of herbal tea would be just fine right about now," he said as he blushed. "I don't think I could eat right now anyway." To divert attention away from his nervousness he said, "Let's open up those fortune cookies. I know there must be a good message in them for us. You open yours first."

"Okay, here goes." Dena broke open her cookie with one quick snap and smiled when she read her message for the day. "Mine says, *a love will come to you in a strange way. Be ready!*" Dena said with a gleam in her eye and a lilt in her voice. "Now, let's see what the day has in store for you, Charlie Ling," Dena chuckled with a delicate whimper.

"Are you ready for this? Mine reads, *don't take a new love for granted; it is a special gift.* Now I certainly cannot ignore this good advice, can I?" Charlie said with a lump in his throat. "I believe in fate; that I was meant to come here to meet you. Suddenly I have forgotten how tedious my workday was. You made all my stress disappear. You are my miracle worker!"

"I feel the same way. I feel like I have known you for a long time even though I just met you. You make a girl feel very comfortable, Charlie Ling." She knew she was being a little forward when she stretched her hand across the table to rest it on top of Charlie's. But she always acted on impulse, especially when she felt happy. She just knew this was right. She felt it! Her heart was telling her to act and she did.

"Thank you, Dena. You, too, are a very warm and trusting person, especially to a guy who just walked into your life unannounced." Charlie replied. He took both of her hands in his and held them tightly. They sat for a moment just staring into each other's eyes. *Charlie wondered if this was for real. He couldn't be this lucky; to find the perfect girl, the kind he wanted to marry someday. He knew his family was going to love this love tale.*

Dena broke the love trance with, "So, where did you say you worked?"

Charlie answered with a quiver in his voice, "Um, I work at the Chan Continental Gem Export Company." Not wanting to talk business, he quickly changed the subject. "I can't believe I have never seen you in here before. Where have you been hiding?"

"I wasn't hiding. I have been finishing school for a few years. I attended the Katharine Gibbs School on West 40th Street here in New York City. As soon as my education was completed I managed to get a job as a legal secretary to a new aspiring lawyer. The professional training I received from Katharine Gibbs made it easy for me to acquire a wonderful professional job even though I am young. And I always wanted to work here in the city. I didn't want to have to commute far away."

"Oh, so you are a legal secretary," Charlie repeated what Dena had just said. "That is so great! You are lucky to have found a job you enjoy doing. Nowadays it is hard to connect with a good job placement. I am happy for you." Charlie was hooked! His thoughts were racing even though this was his initial encounter with Dena. *I have to act quickly with this relationship not to lose this woman.* His heart was racing. He was stumbling over his words.

Dena asked, "Were you really having a bad day? You said before it was a tense morning for you. Don't you like your job?"

"Oh no, on the contrary, I love my job very much," Charlie said, coming back down to earth. I am a gemologist, something I wanted to be almost all of my life as far back as I can remember."

"Is that your family business? Did you follow in your father's footsteps?"

Charlie laughed at Dena's inquisitiveness. "My father actually gave me the inspiration for my career, but his field is a bit different than mine. He is an engineering geologist and is a professor at Columbia University here in New York in the Earth Science Engineering Center."

"My goodness, just what does he do?" Dena asked with much interest.

"He likes to think he is a caretaker of the earth's resources. His interest lies in the earth. He investigates soils, oceans, and atmosphere and looks for new sources of the earth's materials. On his desk he has a plaque that says, *for a geologist, life is a field trip."*

"That sounds like a very interesting job. Didn't you like to dig into the earth and its secrets?" Dena asked. `

"Not really; I wasn't interested in life on other planets, the effects glaciers have on oceans and climates, what makes continents move, or how mountains form. On the other hand, my dad loves the earth and how it works. He likes to think of the earth as his outdoor laboratory; he can reconstruct the past and anticipate the future. Yes, Professor Chin Ling is very popular among his students, from what I hear."

"Isn't working with gems something like working with the earth?"

"In a way it is, but it centers in on one aspect only, gems. I don't care about gathering data and interpreting it. That is too confining a position for me. My dad, on the other hand, likes the diversity of his earth science. He uses his knowledge to study rocks, soil materials and ground water. He is also a consultant for the state of New York when they investigate factors that affect structures like bridges, buildings, airports or dams. He is recognized for his knowledge of the geosciences. I am very proud of him."

"He is quite a man! Was he disappointed that you didn't follow in his footsteps?" Dena asked.

"Maybe at first, but he realized that I had to follow my own path in life. When he saw that I was serious about gems, he actually guided me in the right direction to pursue my career. I think he is proud of me now that I am a successful gemologist. Gems have always fascinated me and I went out of my way to learn all I could about them. Even when I was a young boy, I researched gems and wrote papers on them."

"Well, Charlie, I'm glad you succeeded in becoming a gemologist. It is a fine career. Do you travel a lot?" Dena kept probing subtly into Charlie's life.

"I'm starting to travel a lot more as my company sends me out of the country to inquire about gems from foreign countries. I find it very interesting. I recently returned from a trip to Myanmar in South East Asia. I must tell you about it someday. I don't like to make promises I can't keep, but I would like to take you there someday on a vacation, after we are married." They both laughed out loud at the thought of the forwardness of his remark. And, they never let go of each other's grip throughout the whole conversation.

The waitress brought their tea. Dena instinctively poured a cup for him first and then for herself. *Charlie was thinking about how sweet that was. She thought of him first.* As they slowly sipped their tea they exchanged a lot of work related stories. Before they knew it they were becoming fast friends. That was the first date of many to come for them. It wasn't long before they began dating officially. They were meant to be together. From that first moment in the restaurant, they both sensed what the other was feeling. They had more in common than they could fathom.

As the months passed they had continued to date and it wasn't long before they met each other's family and moved on to marriage. After about a year, Charlie and Dena Ling became Mr. and Mrs. and their families were thrilled. Since both of their jobs were in the city, they decided to get a townhouse where both of them could get to work easily. Their love was strong and they complimented each other in everything they did. Time went by and they decided to start their family.

A year later, Dena gave birth to their son, Daniel and a year after that to a daughter, Carla. Their family made them extremely happy. As the years went by they enjoyed raising their two children and managed to spend a lot of time with them. Daniel and Carla, in fact, were very much like their parents in their personalities. They enjoyed doing things together as a family and planned many activities and trips around their busy work schedules, just to do them together. Being born and raised in New York City, they knew just where and how to entertain their children. They had a wonderful childhood growing up there and they wanted their kids to have the same.

Charlie was becoming very prominent in his company and his boss was beginning to rely on him and his expertise and judgment more and more. Charlie's job began taking him away from home more frequently because he had to go on business trips both in and out of the country. But the money was outstanding so he wasn't about to complain. He and Dena adjusted to his travel routine. Once the kids were in school, Dena was working full time anyway.

As the weeks passed Charlie was working harder than ever. His boss approached him with a proposition to make another trip to Mayanmar. He wanted him to obtain some new gemstones and travel more extensively in Myanmar this time. Charlie knew that would mean leaving Dena and the children again, but he knew this trip would put him in excellent standing with his boss. He felt proud that his boss had so much faith in his judgment and that he recognized him for the experienced and efficient gemologist that he was.

When he got home that evening, he didn't know how to tell Dena that he would be traveling again, because he had just come back from a trip to California. That was only a week long jaunt but this one would be much longer because it was going to be out of the country and to a very far place again. He had been to Myanmar before a couple of times, but he knew it would be a tedious trip because of the distance. Southeast Asia was a very remote part of the world. There was never an easy way to tell his wife of an impending trip so he decided to just blurt it out. The minute he walked in the door, Dena knew he had something on his mind. She could always tell. Knowing he felt badly about leaving her and the kids again, she always initiated the conversation to make it less difficult for her dear Charlie.

Dena grabbed her husband in her arms and gave him a warm hug and a kiss. "So how is my handsome husband this evening after a long day of hard work? I hope you are hungry as I made one of your favorite meals." Charlie's face lit up and he smiled warmly as he returned the embrace and added another smooch.

"Oh you did, did you? As a matter of fact I am very tired, but never too tired to eat one of your gourmet meals," Charlie said as he wisped her with a kiss on the cheek again and again.

Dena laughed heartily as she always enjoyed his tantalizing displays of affection and welcomed them with a return sign of love. These acknowledged signs seem to be the glue that held their relationship together.

"Before we sit down to eat that delicious meal, I must get this off of my chest. I am sorry to tell you that I must go on another trip. This time it is to Southeast Asia again, that faraway place on the other side of the world. I know how much you dislike when I am very far away from home, so I always have a hard time breaking it to you. Even after all these years I find it hard to leave you and the kids even though it is for business."

Dena looked at Charlie affectionately and always tried to soothe him over. She said, "Don't fret, my dear. It is not forever. Of course, we will miss you a lot, but you must do this. Now, go get comfortable, I'll call the kids down here and I will have dinner waiting for you on the table."

With an uplifted heart Charlie said, "Honey, that's why I love you so. You always know how to make me feel better. With you and the kids by my side I feel that I can do anything. Thank you!"

Charlie knew he would be leaving early, so he was determined to enjoy his family and that special dinner that Dena cooked up. After they ate, they sat around for a while chatting about the events of the day. They watched some TV together and called it a night.

After a good night sleep, Charlie arose early, ate a scrumptious breakfast of soft boiled eggs, crispy bacon and rye toast and got ready to make his way over to JFK International Airport for his overseas flight. They said their good-byes and before he knew it, Charlie was on his way to South East Asia. He took a lot of reading material with him to get well-versed in the Myanmar culture. He was looking forward to seeing the enchanted land again. Though he had been there several times already there was always something new going on there. He knew this third world country was coming of age as it were, and he couldn't wait to see what new changes were made since his last trip there.

Chapter Two
Myanmar (Burma)

"This is Burma, and it will be quite unlike any land you will know."
-Rudyard Kipling (1898)

As the plane was making its final approach into Mingaladon International Airport in Myanmar, Charlie Ling pondered over some of the facts he learned from reading about Myanmar on the long flight from the United States. He was aware that Myanmar, the largest country in mainland South East Asia, was once called Burma, but since 1989 it is known as Myanmar. This beautiful country is bordered by the People's Republic of China in the north, Laos on the west, Thailand on the southeast, Bangladesh on the west, India on the northwest, with the Andaman Sea to the south and the Bay of Bengal to the southwest. *What a wealth of cultural influence these nations offered Myanmar, Charlie thought.* Glancing at some of his notes reminded him that the capital city, Yangon, a bustling city of activity, was formerly known as Rangoon. He was amazed that although it was considered a poor country it was actually called "The Golden Land" because it is rich in resources, especially gemstones and gold. The Myanmar people love gold! They use it extensively on their many pagodas, on accessories and even in their homes, if they are wealthy. He recalled seeing all the gold on the pagodas and buildings the last time he was there. The majorities of people are Buddhist and are very superstitious. Charlie knew that they are a friendly people, and he hoped that would be what he found again when he got there. As the plane was making its final approach, Charlie was captivated by the view from the air of the Bay of Bengal and other surrounding waterways. *What a paradise this is! I would love to bring Dena here, he thought. There is so much to explore and experience. The mystical charms of the East are so fascinating!* Charlie's thoughts were interrupted by the sweet voice of a stewardess asking the passengers to fasten their seat belts and upright their seat, as the plane was about to land.

When Charlie Ling landed at Mingaladon International Airport he realized that he actually arrived early, but he was glad because he had a lot to do. He was well aware of the main reason his company, the Chan Continental Gem Export Company of Chinatown in New York City sent him to Myanmar, to purchase some new precious stones. Charlie didn't mind the traveling. He actually got to enjoy that part of his job. But what distressed him most was leaving his wife and children for a long span of time. But there was nothing he could do about that as he needed the money to keep his family secure. So he tried to get use to traveling all over the world for his company. And since Gemology was his field of specialty, he rather enjoyed researching and seeking out precious stones. As he waited in the customs line he thought about what he would encounter here in Myanmar. He hoped there would be no major snags in his itinerary and that his trip would be profitable for all concerned.

Charlie felt the presence of the military at the airport when he went through customs and again when he got into town. It was obvious that the military was in charge of this country. As he waited in the customs line, he recalled what he learned after his first visit to Myanmar a few years back. Charlie read extensively about the history of the country. In the 1800's the British Empire invaded them and even until today, you can sense the British influence in their cities. He learned that after two Anglo-Burmese wars and a major revolution, the various Kings of Myanmar tried to resist the British encroachments and to modernize their country. Unfortunately the Myanmar society was drastically altered by the end of the monarchy and the separation of church and state. A new generation of Burmese leaders arose in the twentieth century from among the educated classes that were permitted to go to London to study law. These people believed that when they returned home they could improve their country's situation through peaceful protests and negotiations. This was a short-lived dream. During World War II the Japanese invaded Burma, expelled the British and declared Burma a sovereign state in 1943. At some time, one political activist named Aung San created his own political parties called Anti-Fascist People's Freedom League to govern the country. It was the defeat of the Japanese that brought in the new military administration. The military regime only saw Aung San as a traitor for his early collaboration with the Japanese. He was eventually arrested and U Saw, another activist engineered the assassination of Aung San and his entire cabinet. A new cabinet was formed and the Burmese acquired their independence on January 4, 1948. All of these wars and invasions left Burma impoverished and devastated. The years that followed saw many different takeovers, each one trying to alter or change the country's government and its political standing. A coup in March of 1962 led by a man named Ne Win, led to the arrest of government officials and the declaration that Burma was to be a socialist state. Good things started happening under this new regime for a while. In January of 1974 a new constitution was promulgated and resulted in the creation of a People's Assembly that held all legislative, executive and judicial authority. In the early1980's the economy grew as the government relaxed restrictions on foreign aid. By the latter part of the 1980's though, a rising debt led to an economic crisis. The country seemed on the verge of another revolution but the armed forces under General Saw Maung stepped in and restored order. The military government now under Prime Minister Saw Maung changed the name of the country to Myanmar in 1989. In the 1990's there were several insurgencies from some tribal minorities. There is still some tension in the government and among the various sects even till today. But all was calm and orderly in Yangon and everyone seemed peaceful and friendly in spite of the tight security. Charlie felt very safe and found the people friendly and helpful. Sometimes he felt that they were trying too hard to please.

Exiting the airport, Charlie found a lot of cabs waiting in line to transport tourists and travelers to their destinations in Myanmar. When it was his turn to request transportation, he hailed a cab and climbed in. He almost felt like he was home for moment with the cab ride. The drivers in Myanmar drove just as wildly as the New York cabbies. He thought the Myanmar drivers were actually more reckless as they don't have any traffic laws. As they drove along, Charlie, being a friendly guy, started to make conversation with the driver. He wanted to get his mind off of the roller coaster ride.

"Good Morning! I am visiting from America and I am going to be staying at the Dusit Inya Lake Resort on Kaba Aye Pagoda Road in Yangon. Please take me there."

"**Mingalarbar** (Good Morning!" the taxi driver replied. "It is a pleasure to take you, sir. Please make yourself comfortable and we will be at your hotel before you know it. It is not too far, maybe 20 miles. It will take us about fifteen minutes. That is one of our finest five star hotels in the capital city. It is situated on thirty-seven beautifully landscaped acres on the shore on Inya Lake. They tell me the view of the lush gardens and the mirror-like lake is spectacular from the windows of the suites. I have never stayed in there myself, but I believe those who told me about it."

Charlie interjected, "I am told they have a free-form swimming pool overlooking the lake, and that is almost like being on a peaceful and serene oasis. That I can handle, as I love to swim. And I sure could use some peace and quiet and some time alone. That pool sounds very inviting and I am going to try very hard to take advantage of it."

"Oh, they have a lot of activities for people who seek them. They provide tennis courts, a jogging track around the lake, a fitness center, with state of the art equipment, a sauna. Sometimes I wish I was a tourist so that I could enjoy a place like that."

Minutes later they arrived at the Resort. Charlie was anxious to check in as he wanted to get over to the gem dealer he came to town to see. However, he couldn't help but comment on the size of the place and the grandiose grounds of the hotel. "This is some place! The brochures I saw of it are right on the money! I can see why they call this the "Garden City of the East. Everything is so green and full of life; and very colorful. I think I am going to like this place."

"You are here at a good time of year," the taxi driver explained. "This being April, the month of the Myanmar New Year, we are celebrating *Thingyan*, the Water Festival which lasts for three or four days."

Charlie knew he should check in but he was curious about this festival, so he asked, "Just what happens at this Water Festival? I would like to know so I can be prepared for it if I take part."

The driver explained, "The festival is a well organized event. Four of the streets of Yangon are sectioned off and a vast queue of cars and Lorries and floats wait every year, to parade past the row of stands where they will be drenched with water from all sizes of hoses. The cool water is pumped from the Royal Lake and is very much welcomed by the revelers who linger long in the powerful jets shooting water at them."

Charlie was shocked. He asked, "You mean they actually throw or rather, shoot water at each other? They must get drenched to the bone."

"Oh, I assure you, they get very wet, but they love it. Since this lasts for four days, they are eventually half-drowned by the last day and ready to go home. The fascination wears off."

"Is that all there is to it?" Charlie asked. Do they do any other things to celebrate, or is that it?"

"The people do a lot more. They sing, dance and sway to music with their groups of friends as they enjoy the colorful floats and costumes some people wear for the occasion. Some of the local residents and their children plunge into the "rivers" of water as they pass their front doors. They say it is a delightful, refreshing shower."

"Is there any religious significance to it?" Charlie asked.

"Oh yes, the older people use these days as a time for religious activities. Some of them take part in a religious ceremony called *shin pyu*, a ceremony when small boys become monks for a time to learn to live a disciplined life. Their families actually make a procession with the boys riding elephants with golden umbrellas over them. It is a beautiful ceremony to see."

"Don't the boys object to this?"

"Not here in Myanmar. They are taught at an early age to respect their parents' decisions for them. It is a privilege to go to live in the monastery for a while. They don't like that they miss the fun of Thingyan or that their heads are shaved, but they are told that it is a special time of good deeds and contemplation."

"This is most interesting. I will have to tell this to my son back home. He will be shocked, I'm sure." Charlie said. "Maybe I can use this story as leverage when he misbehaves. I can always tell him I will send him to a monastery." Charlie and the driver had a good laugh.

"The nicest thing about the festival is the greeting. It is the custom of the Myanmar people to wish at this time of year for health, prosperity and spiritual tranquility to all friends, both far and near, in the coming year. That is our New Year greeting."

"That is wonderful. I think I really must take part in this festival. Perhaps I will go with the man I am meeting here on business if it fits into our schedule. I thank you for explaining the meaningful significance of the festival to me."

"You are doubly lucky coming at this time of year, as you will witness the bloom of the *Padauk*, the gum-kino tree. It is a big thing around here. After the first rain showers, it will burst forth with its tiny fragrant yellow gold flowers. This heralds the Thingyan Festival for us."

Even though Charlie was in a bit of a hurry now, he couldn't resist asking, "What does this flowering tree have to do with the festival?"

"For the Mayanmar people the Padauk tree is a symbol of strength and durability. Besides providing a splendid shade its hard wood gives out a high sheen when polished. A lot of furniture and flooring is made from it. It is even used in the rural areas to make cart frames, wheels and many other things. It is a very strong wood."

"I see that it is most valuable to you," Charlie said. "What about the beautiful yellow flowers? Are they used for anything special? It would be a shame to just let them stay on the tree."

"Those golden blossoms are what we Myanmar people love and romanticize about. Since these trees blossom only once a year and always in April, most trees turn golden overnight after the first showers of April. Regrettably many trees are damaged because people cut the branches off to get the flowers. The flower sellers in the markets do a brisk trade. People are eager to get the flowers to offer the first blooms to the Buddha either at the pagoda or in their home shrines. You are sure to see the young girls with coronets of the Padauk flowers in their hair or the more mature women with a sprig in a chignon on the nape of the neck. Our Padauk trees with their golden flowers have inspired many a poet.

Charlie knew time was flying but he had to ask, "Do you have any famous Myanmar poets? I am interested because my wife writes poetry."

"I am glad you asked because I am very proud to tell you. Our most popular verses are those of a seventeenth century poet king, Natshinnaung. He wrote the most touching sonnets, odes and lyrics that all Myanmar people hold very dear in their hearts. In them he writes about his enduring love for the much older widow of his cousin, Princess Datukalyar whom he had to woo for many years to win. Every time the Padauk bloomed he was far away from his love and that yearning to pin the golden Padauk on her hair inspired him to write his poems and romantic songs. I myself had a magical experience with the Padauk. Once when my family was traveling we came upon a route lined on both sides of the road with towering Padauk trees. The trees were in full bloom that day. I will never forget that moment when we moved through a road carpeted with fallen golden blossoms under an emerald and gold roof formed by the branches that meshed overhead to provide the shade and coolness. I wish everyone could have a similar experience with the Padauk at least once in their lives."

"Now I understand why the Padauk tree and its flower are so important to you. That is an awe-inspiring story that I will take home with me. My wife and children will enjoy it very much. You filled me with a desire to bring my wife here for that experience," Charlie said.

"I am glad you enjoy my stories," the driver said.

"It is nice talking with you but I think I'd better go check in as the day is flying by and I want to go into town. I would like for you to drive me to my next destination. Will you wait for me while I check in? I would like you to take me to Aung San Road? I have an appointment at the Zeya Gem Store there," Charlie said. "I believe it is located in the area of the famous Bogyoke Aung San (Scott) Market."

"Yes sir, of course I will wait, though it may be a little more expensive."

Charlie told the driver that cost didn't matter as his company gave him an expense account and he did not have to cut corners. That was one part of the job he liked. The perks were great! With that said, Charlie checked in, and was brought up to his elegant suite on the top floor. The room was just grand! He thought of his wife, Dena because she would have loved this suite with its private over-sized balcony and extra amenities. He wished she could have been on this trip with her. His memory escape was broken by the thought that the cab was waiting for him downstairs. He would have ample time later in the evening to check things out better and even find time to call Dena. He wanted to take advantage of all the hotel had to offer. *Why not treat myself to a round of golf while I am here,* he thought.

In a matter of minutes, Charlie was outside and hopping back into the cab. The driver waited as he had promised. As they rode along the beautiful countryside the taxi driver tried to make some pleasant conversation with his fare. "You ever visit our city before? You seem to know where you want go?"

"Oh yes, I have been here several times, but always on business and my visits were short. I never stayed long enough to enjoy your beautiful country. I would go to one place and that was it. One place I visited last time I was here was *The Karaweik at the Kandawgyi Lake.* One of the gem dealers took me there. That restaurant on the lake is magnificent! I learned that the boat with its double bow depicts the mythological *karaweik*, a water bird from Indian pre-history and its many-tiered spire. It is a fine work of Myanmar architecture. It was an unforgettable evening of dining that I enjoyed along with the outstanding dance performances accompanied by Myanmar classical music. That was an experience I will never forget! I did manage to also visit the Shwedagon Pagoda, the great cone-shaped Buddhist monument that crowns Singuttara Hill in downtown Yangon but I didn't have enough time to go through it thoroughly to appreciate its beauty. I am sure I missed a lot of things I should have sought out."

"The Shwedagon Pagoda is the most special attraction of my country," the driver said. "We are very proud of our Golden Pagoda. It holds a lot of history for us. It is our most impressive solid brick *stupa* (Buddhist Reliquary) that is completely covered in gold. It has been renovated many times over by our Monarchs over the years. The best time to observe its beauty is in the evening when the light of the sun is fading and the glow of the moon is appearing. The pagoda simply glows in all its glory at that time of day! Some people call it one of the Seven Wonders of the World. It is a landmark that is visible for miles. It is a cultural wonder where the eight hair relics of the Supreme Self-enlightened Buddha are kept from 2,500 years ago. People go in there not only to tour but to offer water, candles, increase (incense) sticks and flowers to the Lord Buddha. Ancient Myanmar architecture and artistic craftsmanship are there as well. There are four sphinxes, one at each corner. You will see figures of crouching elephants and men kneeling, pedestals for offerings all around the base. There are images of lions, serpents, ogres and spirits surrounding the base. On the walls of the first terrace you can see embossed figures of former kings. What is most intriguing, are the four entrances into the base. According to some legendary tales, there are supposed to be flying swords that never stop, which protect the pagoda from intruders. Some say there are mysterious tunnels underground that lead to Bagan and Thailand."

"Those facts I know. I made sure I browsed through a large portion of the Pagoda and its surroundings the last time I was here. I understand that the Pagoda has stood the ravages of time and inclemency of weather, and still looks majestic and somber," Charlie said. "I managed to speak with a monk inside when I was there who chatted with me for about an hour. He told me that everyone has many *klings* in their heads (worries). He said meditation is good. He told me to sit down, keep my body straight and my nose pointing forward and to listen to my breathing. He advised me to shut everything out which is difficult to do. As you do it slowly, you soon begin to feel calm. It was an exhilarating experience; one I shall never forget. I can still feel the sacred peaceful atmosphere of quietness. It certainly has a lot of history that I would like to read more about when I have time. Perhaps I will buy some literature about it while I am here. Maybe you can recommend a place where I can purchase a good book on Myanmar and its treasures."

"Oh yes," the driver said, "I know a very good book store in town. I'll write it down for you. No one should ever leave here without visiting the Shwedagon Pagoda in entirety. It is a heartening experience."

As they drove along the Inya Lake they spoke about Mayanmar and especially about the capital city, Yangon. Charlie was told that Yangon had a special aura about it even though it was a crowded, noisy city. Coming from New York City, Charlie found it easy to accept this city that was a mixture of old world charm and modern vitality. The construction of high rise buildings and five star hotels in the 1990's did not take away from its charm; and there aren't too many modern buildings in Yangon. In some areas of the city you can still see old British style buildings intertwined between modern-looking ones. The Myanmar government prefers to keep its historical look with its colonial architecture. You can even see old trucks and vehicles from World War

II still in use around the city; another hint of military rule. Yangon has a touch of modernism yet holds on to a lot of old world looks. *I guess that is what makes it such an exciting and interesting city, Charlie thought.*

"I know there is a lot to do during the day here," Charlie said to the cab driver, "But what do people do at night around here? The last time I was here I didn't get a chance to do too many evening activities."

"Actually the nights come alive here in Mayanmar, especially in Yangon. The boulevards are noisy with people selling foods and cigars among other things at their roadside stalls. You will find that out if you walk around the city in the evening hours. The people like to loiter around and just be sociable. We are known for our festivals and theater events. As I told you earlier, all of our festivals are related to religion and are glittering affairs carried on monthly. Every month something is celebrated here in Myanmar. So you are apt to experience one of the festival celebrations anytime you visit Myanmar."

They were nearing the area of the Bogyoke Aung San (Scott) Market in town. As they rode pass the various modern looking buildings, he visibly noticed what they talked about earlier; that Yangon also seemed to hold on to its old world looks. Charlie wondered what the Zeya Gem Store would be like. *Would it be a modern store or one that reflected the real Myanmar, with the ornate carvings and golden accents on it?* After several minutes, the taxi passed directly in front of the Aung San Market. "What a fine looking market this is!" Charlie uttered. "Why does it have two names?

"We are very proud of our famous market," the driver said excitedly. It is named after Mr. C. Scott who was the then municipal commissioner. But it is also called the Bogyoke Aung San Market in honor of a national leader, General Aung San who was assassinated in 1947. To a lot of Myanmar people he was a national hero, who loved his country and tried to improve it, while others thought he was a traitor to their country because of his activist activities. I think we hold on to the Aung San name as a sort of nostalgic touch. Tourists enjoy the market and we love their business. There are over two thousand stands and shops inside, selling a variety of things from groceries to handicrafts and antiques to the latest ware. It is easy to shop in there because it is built in a square shape, north, south, east and west, which makes it very easy to find things. You will find as you walk the long corridors there are shops of all kinds selling just about everything. We like to compare our Market to your malls in America, though I am sure our market is not as big. Each shop here has its own way of decorating and advertising to attract customers. One can never come out without having bought something."

"I may have to check that out later and perhaps buy some souvenirs for my wife and children. They always anticipate that I have something for them from wherever I go. I'm sure I'll find some unusual items, at least I hope so," Charlie said.

"Here we are! The Zeya Gem Store! As long as I have lived here I have never been in this store. That is probably because I have no need to buy gems as my family has some of its own. Most Myanmar families have family heirloom gems. Some are even old as they have been passed down through the generations."

"That is quite interesting," Charlie replied to his comment. "In my family we continue such a practice as well of passing down our precious things to our children for safe keeping. So we are not too much unlike you. I thoroughly enjoyed your company as we rode along and I want to thank you for the interesting and informative conversation. You made the ride enjoyable. Maybe I will be lucky enough to get your cab again while I am here in Yangon. Thank you! I will say Good-day, for now."

"**Thwame naw**!" (Good-bye)," the driver answered.

"Yes, my good man, **Thwame naw** to you," Charlie answered with a happy tone in his voice and the thought that he had learned a foreign word.

The ZEYA GEM STORE was situated at the end of the street so it was easy to find. Since it was adjacent to the Scott Market, it seemed to attract many tourists, those who were just browsing and others who had a keen interest in gems. The store was actually part of the downtown that formed a square with a railway just to the north. That undoubtedly made it easy for the Myanmar people and even tourists staying elsewhere to conveniently get to Yangon to shop and tour. The people came from all of the rural areas many times a week to do their shopping and other business in the city.

Charlie walked around the square for several minutes before going to the gem store. After several minutes of browsing, he finally came to the store he was looking for. When he walked in, the door tinkled with little bells to alert the proprietor that someone had entered. The store smelled of an aromatic herb that was quite pleasant. Charlie was impressed as soon as he walked in. He even heard soft harp music playing in the background. *Nice touch, he thought.* The display cases were made of teak with beveled glass fronts and tops. It sure gave one an appetite to browse. The light fixtures, of course, had a lot of gold accents, as gold is used profusely by the Myanmar people. It added brilliance to the overall decor of the store.

While Charlie ambled around checking out the display cases, he was approached by a gentleman who identified himself as Mr. U Khin Zeya.

"Mingala ba," (Good Afternoon) Mr. Zeya gleefully said. "May I help you?"

"Mingala ba, Yes!" Charlie replied. "I am here to purchase some of your gems for my company, the Chan Continental Gem Export Company of New York City. We understand that you are a government licensed establishment which is important to us. And your reputation stretches out over the oceans to America as being quite admirable. We know of others who have dealt with you and they have highly recommended your store and of course, you, Mr. Zeya. My company secretary actually called ahead to make an appointment for me with you. Did you get the call?"

"Yes I got that call and I was expecting you. I speak English very well, so it will be easy to communicate with you, Mr. Zeya said. We here in Myanmar speak English a lot. You are most welcome in my store and in my country. How may I help you, Mr......?"

"Ling, Charlie Ling!"

"Mr. Ling!" Mr. Zeya continued. "If you can give me an idea as to what you are actually looking for, I may better direct you and help you select some of my precious stones."

"Well, we deal in wholesale sales of our gems to jewelers all over the United States. So we must keep an ample supply of them on hand for the dealers and proprietors who visit our gem exchange in New York City. We always have to replenish our supply of gems. That is why my company sent me here today. I have been in Myanmar a couple of times before. But at those times I only visited Yangon once for a short time and then I traveled over to Mandalay. This visit is specifically to visit your store, Mr. Zeya. My company only comes to Myanmar for its precious gems. We are always satisfied with our purchases and have a need to replenish new ones constantly."

"Call me Khin, please, Mr. Ling"

"Only if you will call me Charlie."

"That is a deal!" Khin said. "The U part of my name is just used in front of men's names here in Mayanmar but there is no need to use it when speaking to me. They shook hands very warmly.

Charlie sensed immediately that Khin was a man who would be easy to work with. He seemed like he was his type of guy. He could always sense when a person was genuine and he liked Khin from the moment they started talking. Perhaps they would need each other someday for something or other. Maybe they would even become close friends and even introduce their families to each other. But Charlie thought that might be pushing it. For now he knew he had to concentrate on buying gems. So he asked Khin to start with the first display case and go around the entire store. Then if he didn't see what he wanted, maybe Khin would have some even more precious and rare gems in another location.

Charlie spent about five hours in the Zeya Store that afternoon. He managed to select a lot of gems, diamonds, emeralds, rubies, sapphires, etc. But he was still looking for some really rare looking ones and who better to advise him than Mr. Zeya. But as it was getting late, Charlie decided to make it a day and head back to his hotel. He felt that he had made a good start and his desire for obtaining genuine gems was truly peaked.

"Where are you staying, Charlie?" Khin asked.

"My company made a reservation for me at the Dusit Inya Lake Resort. It is a wonderful hotel and it has all the amenities I would want. I know it is actually a few miles from downtown Yangon, but that won't be a problem for me. Maybe you would like to have dinner with me some evening, along with your wife, of course. We will arrange for something later on."

Khin answered immediately, "That would be just wonderful! My wife, Myine, would enjoy dinner over there. She loves to go out, especially to expensive restaurants. I told her she must have been born under a golden star," he laughed. "She has wanted to go to the Orchid Café there as her lady friends were there for some affair and were raving about it to her. They have some high class al fresco dining on the outside terrace with a beautiful view of the lake. That really fascinates my wife!"

"Oh I know, Khin. My wife, Dena is the same way. I never have to ask her twice. She is out the door and in the car before me," Charlie snickered back.

"But first I must get business out of the way and off my mind. So I will be back tomorrow to continue my gem buying in your store, Khin. I can hardly wait to see your precious beauties!"

"I look forward to your coming," Khin responded. "And this time we will have tea and some lunch. So, until I see you tomorrow, **Thwame naw** (Good-bye)," Charlie.

"Thwame naw, (Good-Bye), Khin."

Charlie went back to his hotel room pondering all the events of the day. He knew he had a lot to do tomorrow with Khin Zeya, so he decided to call it a night. He ordered himself some room service dinner from the Inya Lake Grill, locked his case in the room safe, and decided to give Dena a call. He knew he would have a good night's sleep if he talked to her for a few minutes.

The phone rang in the Ling household for a while. Finally Dena answered it.

Charlie was so excited to talk with her that he forgot the time element.

Dena said, "Hello darling. I am so glad to hear from you, but do you know it is very late here? You must have forgotten for a moment that you are thousands of miles away on the other side of the world. But I don't really mind. It is so good to hear your voice."

"Oh, I am so sorry about the hour. I just had to talk to you. I had to hear your voice and tell you first that I love you very much. Then I wanted to tell you that I would be having a better time if you were here with me. I must bring you here someday. It is an enchanting country that I would like you to see. I am learning a lot about their customs and I would like you to experience them with me."

"We will have a chance one day to do that I am sure. But for now, concentrate on your business. We are all fine here at home. I'm glad you phoned and keep in touch even though the hours are so different.

I really don't mind. Now let me get back to bed. I love you. Good Night!"

"Good Night, my sweetheart; I will dream about you tonight. Give hugs and kisses to Daniel and Carla for me." Charlie smiled and felt better that he called.

In the morning, after a hearty room service breakfast, Charlie headed downstairs to get a cab back to the Zeya Gem Store. He was only minutes away from the square. He had thought of trying out the public bus system, but since he had his briefcase he didn't want to go roaming around in mass confusion with the throng of people rushing all around. Before he knew it the cab was in front of the store. Khin happened to be standing at the door when Charlie arrived.

"Good Morning, Charlie" Khin said. "I see you didn't dare chance a trek on the bus or in a trishaw. That three wheeled vehicle is an experience. I always feel sorry for the young boys who must peddle them. The weight of the people is a challenging chore for them. If you took the bus you probably wouldn't be here yet as it makes a lot of stops. I hope you managed to get some sleep as I will keep you quite busy today."

"I assure you, Khin, I am very rested and ready to get going. In fact, this beautiful day was making it very difficult for me not to do a round of golf. Maybe we can do that one day before I leave. Now, let me get back to business. I have a lot of examining and selecting to do. Shall we get started?"

As Khin was about to answer, a well-dressed Asian man walked into the store. Charlie noticed that Khin seemed a little bothered when he saw him. But he didn't say anything at first. The Asian man began to browse around and looked meticulously at everything. Khin noticed that he had a lot of jewelry on so he wondered why he was here again. Khin excused himself from Charlie and walked over to the man.

"Can I help you? He asked.

"Not right now," the man replied. "I am just looking."

Khin answered apprehensively, "That's fine. Let me know if I can assist you in any way. Feel free to look around."

"Thank You," the Asian man said politely.

When Khin returned to Charlie on the far side of the store, Charlie couldn't help but feel that Khin was bothered by something. Being nosy, he asked, "Is everything alright, Khin? You look a little nervous or something."

"Oh, it's nothing. I have been visited by that man several times before, but he never buys anything. And he doesn't talk too much. I just wonder what he is all about."

"Well, Khin, don't let him bother you," Charlie said as he patted Khin on the shoulder. "Let's get down to these fabulous gems of yours!"

With that said, Khin asked his female employee to keep an eye on things.

The two men sat down by the showcase displaying sapphires. Khin said, "Did you know that sapphires are said to have an air of mystery and intrigue about them? Some people like them and some don't. They are not for everyone, but some people enjoy possessing them. Are you interested in any of these?"

"Well, I would like to take a few back with me. I'm sure we have someone in the states who may be interested in them," Charlie said, "especially if it is their birthstone. Some jewelers like to make necklaces and earrings with sapphires also."

Seeing that Charlie was not too enthused about the sapphires, Khin moved on to the next showcase featuring emeralds. "Wow!" Charlie said. "What beautiful stones, Khin! I am going to have a hard time choosing. These are exquisite! What a radiant color of green! And the facets of the emeralds are so smooth and precise."

"Take your time, Charlie. Enjoy the beauty of the stones. The more you look, the more you'll see. Of course, I know you know that without me reminding you."

"Where do they find such exceptional stones, Khin? Your country is surely blessed with a rich source of gems! But where do they come from? That always intrigues me."

"Oh, we have a plenitude of gems Charlie, my friend," Khin answered. "Wait until you see my diamond collection! Some of them are magnificent! I have acquired some beauties over the years in the business." They glided over to the diamond showcase. Khin opened it and brought out several red velvet-covered trays with the most gorgeous diamonds. Charlie was in awe of the exquisite nature of the gems. He had seen many in his career, but none such as these.

"Now we are really talking gems!" Charlie said. "I don't know where to begin. Perhaps you can guide me along and show me the best way to look them over. Not that I can't recognize superb stones when I see them. Since these are part of your collection, I'm sure you know the flaws and perfections of each one."

The diamonds were outlandish, but it wasn't until Charlie reached the Ruby display case though that his jaw actually dropped. His eyes beheld some of the most extraordinary stones! All of them appeared to be the "pigeon-blood" rubies, the most expensive kind. Their colors were brilliant, far beyond description! *A poet wouldn't do them justice, he thought.*

"I thought the diamonds were great. But these rubies are stupendous! I certainly want a lot of these to take back home. I must have them. I have never seen such rubies in my life. My boss should be thrilled with this delivery."

"I want to purchase a lot of loose gemstones, Khin," Charlie said enthusiastically. "But I also want to acquire some of your fine jewelry. Your work is not only unique but you offer a variety of sizes in your jewelry pieces. That is what makes them so interesting. I love your style of setting stones, Khin."

"Well thank you, Charlie; I put my whole soul into my work. I want my work to reflect what my heart feels. I guess it is an innate talent I have."

Khin allowed Charlie to examine several more of his gems and jewelry pieces. Charlie bought some necklaces, bracelets, rings, pins and earrings that were already set by Khin Zeya into fine pieces of jewelry with some pretty gorgeous gems. But Khin noticed that Charlie was still a little apprehensive about what he was showing him.

Khin asked, "Why do you seem confused or have a look of uncertainty? I assure you these are genuine gems and you will have no trouble getting them out of the country."

"Oh it's not that, Khin," Charlie answered. "The gems you are showing me are flawless and of good quality. I am pleased with what I selected so far, but I was simply wondering if you had any larger uncut stones. We have some excellent lapidaries in our company who can make great use out of an uncut gem. They fashion stones into some beautiful shapes. They turn out quality gems. I don't know if they can equal your expertise but they may come pretty close to it."

"Well in my safe in the back room I have an assortment of a lot gems still uncut." Khin whispered. "Would you want to see them? I only show them to special friends of mine or people I can sense are genuinely interested in them. You'd be surprised how many phony buyers and con artists come through here. We have to be careful, you know."

"Why yes, I would really like to see those. And I totally understand what you mean about all types of people looking for and at gemstones. We get some weird characters in our city as well. Most are authentic buyers. But you can spot a phony when you see one."

"Pardon me," Khin said, "while I tell my girl I am leaving the floor."

When Khin returned and spread his uncut stones on the soft felt cloth on a display table, Charlie took a closer look at them. They looked next to perfect, but they were still not what he was looking for. There weren't many rubies in the collection. He saw plenty of diamonds, emeralds, sapphires and other precious stones. Though he wanted such gems, he was specifically looking for rubies, since they are rare and getting harder to obtain.

"Is there any place else we can go for some larger uncut rubies?" Charlie asked.

"Oh yes," Khin offered. "I can take you to Mogok, a famous town known as 'Ruby Land'. You will like it. It lies in the center of four mountains and is surrounded by lush green forests. In that town the people make their living mining gems and selling them. Geologists tell us that the rock layer of Mogok is one of the most natural rock layers of Mayanmar. The town of Mogok attracts the attention of many people because of its precious gems and of course because of its panoramic view. The scenery is simply magnificent! In Mogok the *HtaPwe* or Gem markets play a huge role in selling and buying stones. So there is a lot for us to see there. I have some time I can take off from my store, so I don't mind accompanying you there. Also, you are lucky that you came here at this time of year because we have the annual Gem & Pearl Auction and Sales in Yangon. It is held at the Myanmar Gem Emporium. Would you be interested in that?"

"Gosh, what a stroke of luck this is for me! That sounds awesome!" Charlie said. "That is right up my alley, as we say in America." What an unusual experience that would be for me! It is part of a gemologist's dream as far as I can see! I'll be here for several days so things should work out perfectly for me fitting those things into my schedule. But if for some reason I don't find time to go to the Emporium, I will have to do it on another trip."

"Very good," Khin answered. "First we will go to Mogok and transact our business with the ruby dealers. Then, when we return to Yangon and time permits, I will set us up to take part in the Gem Auction. Is that agreeable to you?"

Charlie, bursting with enthusiasm, said, "That sounds great, Khin. Thank You! Let me know when all the arrangements are finalized for our trek up to Mogok. When we return, you can fill me in more about that auction."

"Okay, Charlie," Khin replied. "By the way, how do you feel about getting together this evening with my wife Myine and I for dinner. I wouldn't want you to dine alone. We would like to take you to our favorite restaurant in Yangon. I'm sure my wife will love that idea. She loves to go out to dinner."

"Thanks for the invitation," Charlie said. "That sounds wonderful for two reasons. One, I will get to meet your wife, and two; I will have a chance to try some of your Myanmar delicacies, under your guidance, of course. I always like to try new restaurants with their ethnic foods whenever I travel. I will put myself in your hands. I can't wait to meet your wife," Charlie smiled. *He thought of Dena again and wished she was at his side.*

"I have a dark blue jeep Cherokee, so look for us at the hotel circle."

"That's perfect," Charlie said. "I'll be waiting for you in the lobby, watching out the swivel door for you."

A few hours later Charlie was waiting anxiously in the lobby of the hotel by the door so he could see when Khin and his wife arrived. When they pulled up Charlie ran out to meet them and hopped into the back seat.

"Good evening!" Charlie said.

"Mingalarpar," Khin and Myine said jointly. "This is my wife, Daw Myine Cho."

"I am pleased to meet you." Charlie said. "I am curious why your wife has a different name."

Khin answered proudly, "Just as we use a U in front of men's names, we use Daw in front of all women's names. All wives keep their own family names here in Myanmar. They do not take the husband's name as their family name as wives in most other countries do."

"That certainly clarifies matters for me. Thank you!"

"Are you ready to taste some Myanmar cuisine?" Khin asked. "We have chosen one of our fine local restaurants. We hope you will like it. We like to go there because it is not a noisy, busy place like some of the larger restaurants here in Yangon. I hope you are pleased with our choice."

"I am not a fussy eater," Charlie said. "I know I will be satisfied with whatever place you choose to take me. So, where are we going?"

"We will be dining at the *Green Eggplant* on Inya Road here in Yangon. Myine and I love to go there. We will have a wonderful dinner, I am confident of that."

When they pulled up in front of the GREEN EGGPLANT, Khin parked valet so that they didn't have to walk too far. The sign out front was actually cute. It was a giant-sized green eggplant with the name of the restaurant embossed in gold down the center of the eggplant. It made for a very appealing introduction to dining there.

After they were seated by the window overlooking the town square, Khin, Myine and Charlie ordered some wine to toast and enjoy with dinner.

"*Korhai chokdee*!" ("Good Luck"), Khin said lifting up his glass.

"Cheers!" Charlie responded cordially.

"Okay," Charlie said. "Help me out with this menu, Khin. What do you and Myine like to eat when you come here? Why don't you order for me? You know better than I what the best dish here is."

Khin said, "Actually there are a lot of different ethnic foods here in Mayanmar, but our food has an identity all its own. You will see when I order. It will seem like you are eating Indian, Chinese and even Thai food all in one. Yet our food is not as hot as Thai, or a spicy as Indian, nor does it resemble Chinese cooking much, except in stir-fry."

"Coming from New York, I have eaten just about everything." Charlie said. "I like to try different things especially in places where I travel. I am always happy to try a new food oddity."

"Well, let me see," Khin said. "I think we will start off with "mohinga" which is a light curry-based fish soup first. Our salads are pretty much like yours in America, so you can order any one you want. Then, since we are known for our noodle dishes, we will try the stuffed Inle fish with fried Shan noodles, fried gourd, and cabbage and of course, the famous *green eggplant*. That should be sufficient until dessert time when we will indulge in fried bananas and banana pie with our tea. There is always fresh fruit too. Do you think these foods will satisfy your taste buds, Charlie?"

"By all means they will, Khin. They sound delectable. You and Myine surely know how to dine! Let the feast begin!" And so they ate heartily and had some pleasant conversation.

After dinner, Charlie, Khin and Myine walked around the grounds a bit and chatted about their families. Charlie told them about his wife, Dena and her career as a legal secretary. She worked in Manhattan for a lawyer whom she adored. He explained that his kids, Carla and Daniel were very dear to his heart. They were entering their teen years but they still had great respect for their parents and did not rebel too much as most teens do. They were attending the public schools in New York and were excellent students. Charlie said that he and Dena were proud doting parents.

Myine and Khin shared Charlie's love of family. Khin said, "Myanmar families are very close and the children are highly respectful of their elders. We actually do a lot of activities together as a family unit. Love and respect, rights and responsibilities are the foundations of a Myanmar family irrespective of our religious background. We hold this tradition dear. But, we also make humor a very important part of our family life. We like to look on the lighter side of life. We have a popular song here called *Hpay Gyi Ko Chit Tai* (We love big Daddy). I don't know how it is in your country, but here in Myanmar we think a father melts quicker than a mother when a child sheds a few crocodile tears. A mother usually sees through the children's foibles and fables and when she picks up a cane the children are apt to run crying to father."

"Your customs are not unlike ours, Khin. My children do the same thing with us. Dena is the disciplinarian in the family. I am less strict and my children know that they can come to me with any problem or share all their joys as well. They know I am, as we say, a "softie," and I will give in to them almost every time."

Myine added, "Aside from the emphasis on discipline and morality, we do have a lot of fun as a family unit. Our children are taught at an early age to fuss over their parents. When Khin arrives home from work, my daughter, Sein, runs to the bedroom to get her father's *pasoe* (his evening garment), to change into. My son, Mya, immediately has a cool glass of water or juice waiting for his father. Sometimes they are overwhelming with such attention, but we allow it so as not to disillusion them."

"Do you eat your meals together?" Khin asked.

"As a matter of fact, we do. My wife and I have always demanded that our family sit down together at meals so that we can share all our thoughts and keep a close family bond."

Charlie said. "My kids like to tell us jokes and quips that they have heard in school. We do a lot of laughing together. We in fact do a lot of things together as a family. We believe in family in a big way. Thank goodness, we have good children who are obedient most of the time. Our children like to share their daily experiences about school, friends and other things that interest them. We consider ourselves lucky in that regard."

"There is a lot of chatter and banter at our table as well," Khin said. My kids like to mischievously let cats out of the bag about their mother scrimping on meat and groceries so she could buy the latest *batik*. They get on my case as well if they smell my tangy breath when I come home after I have stopped off for a nip or two on the way home with my friends, much to my wife's annoyance," Khin laughed.

"Our family values are not too different as far as I can determine," Charlie added.

"I was wondering about something I have seen on the faces of your young girls and women. They seem to have a mud or makeup of some kind on their faces. What is that?"

Myine answered, "Why that is *thanaka*, a fragrant ecru-colored paste that they use as a sunscreen or a firming and cooling cream. All the women rub thanaka on their faces. The powder is an adornment on their faces. It is very soothing for the skin. It is from the bark of a small tree that grows here in Myanmar. They beat it on a rock into a sort of goo and then apply it as a makeup. Here in Myanmar it is almost a sign of beauty to wear it. We all wear it now and then, especially in the sun. You can buy it in a lot of stores here as it is plentiful and not too expensive."

"I guess it is like our women wearing powder and blush and other cosmetics. Except that our women don't necessarily get cooling sunscreen protection from it as yours do. I will have to tell my wife and daughter about this. They will find it amusing and fascinating at the same time," Charlie said. "In fact, I am going to buy some for my two girls."

Khin added, "Perhaps you have seen the men chewing *betel*. They chew it and spit it everywhere, which is not very nice. But here in Myanmar it is tolerated as it is an old custom. Our streets are stained with red sputum as a result of this practice. I was squeamish at first when I was growing up, but I got accustomed to the sound of *Harkkepuiii*, and the clearing of the throat. The men who chew betel actually get high on it. I have never tried it and don't intend to. It is a gross habit. But the men here enjoy it."

"Back in the states, some men use chewing tobacco instead of smoking. And it is the same principle, they chew and spit. A lot of our baseball players chew it. I never tried it myself nor do I intend to. I don't even smoke." Charlie offered.

"Is baseball your main sport?" Khin asked.

"It is one of our sports," Charlie answered. "We have many others like football, tennis, basketball, golf, soccer and hockey. We have too many sports in the states. One never knows which to follow or take an interest in. But our stadiums are always full of spectators for all of the games played. Americans are big sport fans. It seems to be a huge part of our culture."

"Here in Myanmar, we have a cane ball game called *chinlon*. The ball is made of strips of cane that are woven into balls about four inches in diameter with about twelve pentagonal holes. The ball is very light but resilient, not very expensive and lasts quite a while. It reminds most tourists of your football because it is played with the feet, head, shoulders, elbows and knees, except for the hands. But there is no goal to shoot at nor are there a fixed number of players. It can be played by one individual or by a team in a circle. The object is to catch and keep it as long as possible in the air. It used to be played without shoes but nowadays they wear canvas shoes. For men, chinlon provides an opportunity to show off their physique with their tattoos. I guess you would call it a macho thing."

Charlie thanked Khin and Myine for a delicious dinner. He was thoroughly enjoying the conversation with them, and he told them how much he enjoyed the Myanmar treats. But as it was getting late, Charlie mentioned that he was quite tired. Since they had a busy few days ahead of them, he asked them to call it a night. So they drove him back to the hotel. He gave them a warm handshake, as it was a strict Myanmar custom not to hug in public.

Khin poked his head out of the car window to give Charlie a few more tips. "I will see you in the morning around 7:00 A.M. so we can get an early start for Mogok. It would be wise to take an overnight bag with you in case we decide to stay an extra day. You'd be surprised how much time you can spend seeking out gems. Also, it is cooler in Mogok because it is 3800 feet above sea level so you might want to wear a light jacket. Take comfortable walking shoes that you don't mind getting dirty. Don't forget your sunglasses. We have a bone-jarring trip ahead of us through farmland, jungle and villages. Our roads are not the most comfortable to ride on, but the scenery will be fascinating. If it were not for the rubies and sapphires that are abundant in Mogok, it is unlikely that any humans would live there. Instead you would find the tigers and leopards which now roam further in the hills."

"The way you talk, it reminds me of the Gold Rush days in America, where the rich and hopeful combined to create the kind of town where one best leaves the children home."

"No, Mogok is not like that," Khin explained. "There are some people with big dreams just as there are people down on their luck whose dreams never panned out. For the most part, you can see people with a deep respect for that which nature provided. Both the town's residents and foreign visitors can move about day or night in complete safety. Can you say the same about New York City?"

"In some areas, yes, but in most places one has to be cautious in New York or any city."

"I had better get back to my room and get ready for tomorrow. Thanks for the suggestions for the trip to Mogok, Khin. I will be ready and waiting for you downstairs in front of the hotel. And Myine, it was a pleasure to meet you. You are a delight! Thank you for everything. Give your children a hello for me, even though I haven't met them. Perhaps I will get to meet them before I leave for home."

As Charlie was entering the hotel he heard a loud screech in the street. He ran back out to make sure it was not Khin and Myine in trouble. They were fine. However, someone mentioned that an Asian man had been run over by a car. Charlie found that coincidental. So he went closer to see what he could find out. Khin and Myine also ran over as they had not left the hotel grounds yet. Khin and Charlie looked at each other after checking out the body of the man. They could not believe what they saw! The body was that of the Asian man who was frequently coming into the Zeya store. He was killed instantly it seemed because his head was crushed.

Charlie finally said, "Khin, that's the same guy! Can you believe it? I wonder what he was doing around here! It almost seems that he must have been spying on you or tailing you. I hope that doesn't make you uncomfortable again."

Khin answered, "I cannot imagine what he wanted from me. I don't know him, never sold him anything, in fact, never spoke much to him. Oh well! And you know something, Charlie; no one will ever know what this is all about because here in Myanmar accidents or incidents are not investigated. That's just how our military regime operates here. They will clean the accident up and see if he has any family or friends with him. If not, they will bury him somewhere and that will be the end of it. Well, I will say good night again!"

"Don't worry Khin; this is probably nothing to concern yourself about. Good night to you as well. Get a good night's sleep because I intend to keep you very busy and active." Both men laughed.

Chapter Three
Bangkok, Thailand

Bangkok, the "city of angels," was a mixture of aromas, sights, and visual delights influenced by a combination of European, Chinese and Indian cultures. This bustling city was split in two by the Chao River (River of Kings) and had its share of gleaming glass towers rising toward the sky. The high rise buildings, home to many top companies, straddled the main streets and towered over banks, restaurants and other businesses. This made for a very hectic financial district. One could see buses, taxis, and tuk-tuks running in all directions with crowds of people using them. These vehicles caused a lot of traffic jams and pollution. A *rot dtit* (traffic jam) is a fact of life in Bangkok. Walking through the streets in the hot humid weather in Thailand was not the chosen form of getting around.

The city was even more exciting because of the Bangkok Transportation System's famous "Sky Train." This unique overhead rail system, built in 1999, snaked throughout the city of Bangkok and proved to be cost efficient for the daily commuters and an easier, carefree way to travel in this congested city. Its routes were so complex that a person could ride from one end to the other taking people to and from the Siam Center, a major retail area. Of course there were other important stops along the way for those who chose to make them. The Sky Train provided a welcomed alternative to driving in the crowded streets below. Since a lot of international cultural or social events came to Bangkok, the Sky Train was used a lot. In spite of all the congestion, the Thai people are the friendliest of any major capital city. Surprisingly they tolerate city challenges and still remain fun-loving and easy-going.

The limousine was traveling rather fast through the streets of Bangkok. As it sped along toward the downtown area, juggling the traffic snags, the car phone rang.

"*Chai krap ka*? (Yes?)" Mr. Nicro answered. "What is it? I told you not to call me unless it was important."

"*Man sam kan* (It's important)! Well, I think it is," the voice on the other end said. "Ms. Chandra Sholara is calling you from Myanmar."

"Yes, my dear, what news do you have for me?" Mr. Nicro asked.

"We have lost our contact here in Yangon, Myanmar. He was just accidentally run over by a car and he is dead. He must have been running in haste in or out of the Dusit Resort Hotel and was not paying attention. He was struck by a cab that was leaving the hotel driveway rather fast."

"*Mai kao jai!* (I don't understand!)" How did it happen? Didn't he see the car coming?"

"*Mai chai*" (No!) The people drive rather crazy here in Yangon. They don't follow normal traffic patterns and laws. He must have been preoccupied with your affairs and his own and he wasn't being careful."

"Will there be a police investigation?" Mr. Nicro asked concerned.

"I overheard some people talking there would not be one as the military regime doesn't bother with those trivialities, as they call them. They consider such accidents incidental." Chandra replied. "Since our man has no family to speak of, I think it best to drop this and not give the Mayanmar authorities anything to be suspicious of."

"I guess you are right. Did you manage to talk to our man before the accident at any time?"

"About an hour before that, he and I met. He still didn't find out too much, but was getting ready to go to Mogok, as that is where Mr. Zeya, a gem store owner, was taking some American gemologist. Do you want me to take over?"

"I guess you will have to now." Mr. Nicro said.

"*Kao jai!*" (I understand)," Chandra replied.

"*Korp khun!*" (Thank you) Chandra.

"***Mai bpen rai***" *(You're welcome!)*

"By the way, where are you staying in case I have to contact you?" Mr. Nicro asked. "I hope it is to your liking."

"I am staying at the Hotel Nikko Royal Lake on Natmauk Road in Yangon. It is in an exclusive area and offers an ambience of a haven in the city. My suite is in one of the wings that face the Shwedagon Pagoda, so I have a wonderful view. I am very comfortable, thanks to your generosity."

"***Sa wat dee,***" (Good Bye) Chandra said sweetly.

"***Sa wat dee,***" (Good Bye) Mr. Nicro said as he closed his cell phone.

The phone disconnected and the limo kept speeding toward its destination. The Sky Train was zooming above the expressway as people were making their way toward the city. Most Thai people used the sky train because it made it easier to get around the city. Bangkok was a bustling city and a major gateway to a lot of trade. The limo paved its way toward the downtown business center where the World Trade Center was located between Silom and Surawong Streets which ran parallel through the city, dividing it in half.

Mr. Nicro and his entourage exited the limo and proceeded into the Trade Center to the elevators. When they arrived on the twenty-fifth floor, the elevator opened up to a plush office reception area. The office arrangement was circular in design and the modern shaped furniture added to the eye appeal. After passing up the receptionist and the secretaries, they entered an office that overlooked all of Bangkok. This was the city office of Mr. Nicro's company, the Unique Asian Wood Products Company. His company specialized in fine wood work, especially those carved from teak. Woodcarving is one of Thailand's traditional handicrafts. An artisan might work for six to eighteen months on one sculpture. Each piece is unique and is one of a kind. Mr. Nicro built his little empire up from scratch. He started out with a small shop and managed to grow into a huge corporation. His teak pieces were valuable and known for their durability. Anything made from teak is said to be able to withstand all kinds of weather. So if the prices are exorbitant they are surely worth the price.

Mr. Nicro checked for messages, but for the moment there weren't any, either on the fax or his e-mail. The four gentlemen sat down around the conference table to discuss their concerns. He then addressed his three assistants, "Our business is doing very well, gentlemen. According to the Market our shares have increased by ten per cent. It seems the tourist trade has picked up here in Bangkok which is certainly giving us a shot in the arm."

One of the men asked, "What about your teak turtle situation? Did you ever find out anything about the break-in in your main factory office? Did you get any leads from the police investigation?"

Mr. Nicro answered, "I am sorry to tell you that we did not obtain any information on the teak turtle sculpture that is suppose to be somewhere in Myanmar. My contacts have been trying to obtain some leads as to where it is since it was stolen from my store along with other precious pieces. As you all know, it was originally made by one of my artisans for a friend of mine who owned a gem business in Mayanmar. After my friend died, his wife thought I might want to have it back in his memory, so she sent it back to me. I really cherished the turtle and I was devastated when my main shop office was robbed and it was taken. I have been trying to find it ever since. I cannot imagine why someone would want the turtle as I had so many other more valuable teak pieces, though they did take some of them. I had a few leads that it made its way back to Myanmar. One of my men heard that a Mr. Zeya who owns a gem business in Mayanmar was supposed to have seen it somewhere. That's why I had my Asian man sort of spying on Mr. Zeya. I thought maybe he would overhear something. Now I will have to rely on other sources to see if any information turns up. I told my other lead in Myanmar to keep track of the movements of Mr. Zeya for now."

Mr. Charnwit, one of the other men in the circle said that sounded good and that he should let time take its course and see what happens. "Let's see what your man in Myanmar comes up with. Hopefully he will stumble on to something."

Mr. Nicro said, "It's not a "he", it's a "SHE! Ms Chandra Sholara is quite adept at what she does. She is my most trustful employee and a very efficient spy. I can rely on her to accomplish any task I give her. Actually I think she will be more successful at finding the whereabouts of my turtle sculpture. Maybe being a woman has its advantages. I have no doubt that Chandra will turn up something. I must give her some time to regroup and re-start the search."

One of the business partners asked, "How did you come to have a woman in your employ? Where did she come from?"

Mr. Nicro offered without hesitation, "Chandra comes from beautiful Pattaya here in Thailand, with its lovely sweeping bay. Her family owns some sort of lacquerware business there. Since it is only ninety minutes by car from there to Bangkok, it is convenient for her to get here when I need her. I met Chandra when I traveled there for a vacation at the resort on Pattaya Beach. She lives in a luxurious condo in the city, several blocks from the beach. She was looking for an exciting job that would allow her to travel a bit. So I hired her on the spot. She has been with me for several years now."

Mr. Nicro said, "So now! Let's go over to the *Vertigo Restaurant* at the Hotel Banyon Tree in downtown Bangkok and have some dinner. The view overlooking Bangkok from the rooftop dining room is magnificent. I will treat you all to some roasted duck over rice, mussels in curry and fried fish with ginger. At least, that is what I enjoy there, but you may order whatever you like. Of course, you may indulge in some fresh fruit and dessert afterwards as well. I wouldn't want you to talk about me." They all laughed!

"Miss Bianta, please ask my driver to bring the limo around to the front entrance." Mr. Nicro asked. "We will be leaving in a few minutes for dinner at the Banyon Tree. If anyone calls or faxes come in for me from Ms. Sholara, please forward them to me immediately before you leave. Thank You!"

Ms. Bianta said, "Would you want me to remain beyond my quitting time, as this seems important to you?"

Mr. Nicro answered, "I'll leave that up to your discretion."

Within minutes the Nicro Group made its way to the elevators and into the limo. As the car cruised along, they discussed some other matters of importance relating to their Unique Asian Wood Products Company.

Dinner went well and everyone seemed satisfied with what they had eaten. On a lighter note, the men engaged in a long conversation about the elephant problem in the city. It is not unusual to see an elephant walking through the streets with their *mahout* (caretaker), panhandling trinkets to make a living. Years ago the elephants were valuable because they helped with the teakwood timbering business hauling logs up hills and through narrow paths. Both captured in the wild and born in captivity, elephants were joined with their *mahout*, usually for life. It is getting more difficult to find caretakers for the elephants even though the domesticated elephants are controlled by the Ministry of Agriculture. When timbering was outlawed by the government, there was an excess of elephants around. Many people continued to do logging illegally and worked at night to avoid detection. This put the working elephants in harms way as they stepped on land mines and even suffered from the drugs the caretakers gave them to work longer.

"Mr. Nicro, being an animal lover and an intense admirer of the elephant, said, "Tourism actually provided a haven for our elephants. Elephant camps, like the *Mei-Ping Elephant Camp*, provided a better life for our left over elephants. In these camps they provide tourists with elephant rides and their performances generate enough for their food and care. And the mahouts are happier as well. The tourist donations and admission fees help these camps exist."

As Mr. Nicro was about to order dessert, his cell phone vibrated, as it was on mute.

"*Chai krap ka?* (Yes?) This is Mr. Nicro speaking."

The voice on the other end chimed in with, "Hello, this is Chandra Sholara, Mr. Nicro. I just wanted to fill you in with some minor details so that you can keep abreast of my whereabouts. I figured I would try to pick up where my partner left off. The last thing I knew from him was that he overheard a Mr. Zeya in the gem store make a comment to his employee about some teak sculptures a friend of his had in Mogok. I will keep an eye on Mr. Zeya, who is traveling around these days with a Chinese-American gemologist. When I know anything more of importance, I will call you. If you don't hear from me it means I haven't found out anything more."

"That sounds good, Chandra. Thank you and keep me informed. And, an envelope is waiting for you at your hotel at the front desk. I know how you like to shop. I hope you buy yourself something very special."

"*Korp khun mahk* (Thank you very much), Mr. Nicro. Good Night!"

Chapter Four
Myanmar

The next morning Khin was at the hotel bright and early as he promised he would be. Charlie, of course, was anxious to get started. He had all of his gear and his overnight bag with him. He looked like a genuine prospector.

"Are you ready to journey out to Mogok's Stone Tract, the legendary Valley of Rubies?" Khin asked. "We have to ride for a while so sit back and enjoy the scenery. I brought my binoculars along, so feel free to use them when you want. There are some fantastic views of the mountains as we ride along. Fasten your seat belt as the roads we will be traveling on have many hairpin turns as they wind through the mountains."

Khin took the road close to the shores of the Bay of Bengal northward toward Mandalay before veering off in an easterly direction to Mogok for a seventy mile drive. He wanted Charlie to see some diverse wildlife. He explained that most of the surrounding islands are covered in rain forest. He said, "Instead of seeing people on the beaches, you are more likely to see turtles and other wildlife, especially in the evening hours. For years visitors were not permitted to come to this area and disturb the wildlife and its pristine beauty. But now the government allows some diving groups, with a license, to enter the area. Our military government is very strict and does not like its laws and regulations violated."

"We are getting closer to the "city in the clouds, Mogok" Khin said. "Did you know we are a land of many legends? Would you like to hear one special legend?"

"That would be delightful," Charlie said.

Khin, happy to talk about his country, explained, "Well, the legend says that at the beginning of time, a giant serpent named Naga, laid three eggs. From the first came the King of Pagan, Pyusawati; from the second, the Emperor of China; out of the last egg, all the rubies. That's why they think so many rubies are found in the Mogok region of Mayanmar (Burma). Who knows how much truth there is to this legend?"

"That is quite interesting!" Charlie said. "I'm sure you have many more legends to relate. I enjoy listening to you."

"I have another bit of trivia for you. The famous Ngamauk Ruby descended to Mindon Min, the last King of Burma. It then descended to Mindon's ill-fated son, Thibaw, with whom it remained until that day when the British army took him prisoner in the summer-house of his palace in Mandalay. From that day to this the famous jewel has never been seen again. There are a lot of stories that circle about it, but none of them are newsworthy."

"Your history is most interesting, Khin. I will have to read up more about it when I get back home. I find your culture fascinating."

"We are almost at the tract where you will find many dealers. Just stay close to me and I will steer you in the direction of my friend who works closely with the *Burma Partners*. I think he will give you the best assortment of high quality rubies at the fairest prices." Khin said.

"Who are the *Burma Partners*?" Charlie inquired.

"They are a firm that will be very helpful to you as they can authenticate a completely natural stone for you since they are affiliated with recognized laboratories such as the American Gemological Labs I and the SSEF of Switzerland. The Burma Partners always provide a certificate from a lab supporting their authenticity check."

"Here we are," Khin said. "Take all your gear with you because I'm sure my friend will want to show you a bit of the mining process before he shows you his magnificent array of gems."

Charlie and Khin made their way over to the Schwei Nei (Gold Sun) Gem Store. As they were about to enter Charlie noticed a poem on the wall plaque by the door. It read: *The glowing ruby shall adorn; those who in warm July are born. Then will they be exempt and free, from love's doubt and anxiety.*

What a nice touch for an entryway! Charlie thought. Dena would love to hear that since she is the poet in the family. And, as irony would have it, she was born in July. Charlie took a few minutes to copy it down for her.

As Charlie and Khin browsed around the store, they saw two pictures in gold frames showing famous rubies. One showed a picture of the *Anne of Brittany Ruby,* a famous ruby that is housed in the Louvre in Paris and another one showing the *Edwards Ruby.* A plate at the bottom of that frame said: *Named in honor of Major General Sir Herbert Benjamin Edwards.*

While engrossed in the famous ruby pictures, Charlie and Khin were approached by Khin's friend. "What can I do for you two gentlemen? Oh my goodness! Khin Zeya??? What a great surprise! What brings you out this way? I haven't seen you in a long time. It has been way too long." The two men shook hands. It was not the Myanmar custom to display outward affection.

"Charlie, I would like you to meet my friend, U Shein Sanda, the owner of this fine establishment."

"It is nice to meet you." Charlie said. "What an odd name you have! What does it mean?"

"Well, actually Shein means *reflection* and Sanda means *moon.* Perhaps my mother knew that one day I would be selling beautiful gem stones that reflect the beauty of the earth," Shein chuckled. "What can I do for you?"

"I am in your country on business trying to obtain some of your fine gem stones for my company back in New York. I already purchased many of Khin's fine work and some of his precious stones, but I was looking for some bigger, uncut ones that our lapidaries back home could work with. Our lapidaries are some of the most skillful artisans in the world. They are well educated and adept at their trade. My company distributes gem stones to many stores and companies across the United States. So we like to have an ample supply of them on hand so these men and women can unleash some of the beauty of the gems with their topnotch skills. Khin told me you were the man to see. So here we are!" Charlie said.

"I see! It is always nice to have visitors from other countries in our stores, but it is even better to see old friends. Welcome to Mogok! I hope I can live up to Khin's expectations of me. Before I take you out to one of the mine areas to show you where these beautiful gems come from, take a look around my store. Meanwhile I will get ready to join you," Shein said.

As Khin and Charlie looked at all of the displays in the store, they also noticed that Shein had quite a few other things for sale. There were a lot of teak sculptures in the showcases along the back wall. For a little store, there were a lot of valuable items in it. There were even some lacquer boxes with heavily embossed gold designs etched on them

"Did you find anything interesting, Charlie?" Khin asked.

"Yes, I did. I have been admiring this teak turtle. Take a look at this, Khin. It is so unusual!"

Khin said, "Oh I had seen that turtle when I was here last time. I thought it would have been bought by now. But I guess it is waiting for the right person to come along. The last time I saw it, I told my own store employee about it, as she is Oriental. But she didn't have the money to even make an attempt to buy it."

"Well, I think I might purchase this for my wife, Dena. I know she would love to have it as turtles, for us Chinese, are a sign of longevity, among other things," Charlie said.

"Well then, by all means, ask Shein what he wants for it." Khin said.

When Shein came back into the store from the back, he saw that Khin and Charlie were over by the sculptures. "I see you are interested in my teak collection. What piece in particular is your eye on?"

"That turtle is so unusual! The carvings on it are phenomenal! May I have a close look at it?" Charlie asked.

Shein unlocked the case and placed the turtle in front of Charlie. When Charlie touched the turtle he felt inspired by its beauty. What workmanship! The *scutes* on the top protective shell were carved so intricately that Charlie felt as if they had a message to tell. Shein told him to look closely underneath at the *plastron*, the bottom. It had twelve oddly-shaped spots that ran from the neck to the tail and on eight of the spots there were unique symbols of some kind imbedded in the teak. It had four toes on each hind leg that were emphasized by deep cuts into the teak.

"I can't get over the size of this piece of teak!" Charlie said in awe. "Do you happen to know its approximate measurements?"

Shein answered, "I believe it is about twelve inches long and eight inches wide and about six inches in height. I only know that because I did measure it myself at one time. I, too, was amazed at its size. The craftsman must have had an intriguing time designing and carving it. Do you know something that I find interesting about it? It is rather heavy for a teak product, but I chalk it up to being a thick block of teak inside."

"Now I really must have this turtle! How much do you want for it?" Charlie asked.

Shein looked into his books and then looked up at Charlie.

"Two thousand dollars, American cash, of course," Shein said.

"Would you settle for eighteen hundred?" Charlie asked sheepishly. "I must have this for my wife."

Khin looked at Shein as if to say give it to him, and Shein nodded an okay to Charlie.

"You are a clever man, Mr. Charlie Ling. You have a deal!" Shein uttered. And all three men laughed heartily.

"Okay, leave it here in my store until we return from the mines. You know it is not permissible to take teak items which are considered antiques out of Myanmar without the proper licenses. I don't want you to have to pay a lot of duty or be asked unnecessary questions about it. So I will have to hide it in the gems and rubies that you buy. I can pack it so that it looks like only gems are being exported. Customs officials never open up gems that are exported if they are sent with authentic credentials and certificates. And as I am a reputable dealer with the right connections, I see no problem with this business transaction. I am able to maneuver my gems anywhere at anytime."

"How are such valuable gems and such packed, Shein?' Charlie asked inquisitively.

"We use professional art packers and shippers. First we call in a "packer" who packs it in wooden crates with inner insulation. The merchandise is evaluated by a professional and then it is placed in a sturdy and stable container. Then the "shippers" take over. All of the overseas shipping crates, whether small or large, must have an affixed stamp indicating the wood-packing materials were heat-treated and fumigated for infestation. Otherwise customs can open, inspect and seize the package or return it. An insulted crate will allow the piece to slowly acclimate to the extreme temperatures in the cargo areas of planes. These specialists we hire know customs requirements and are knowledgeable about proper documentation, correct insurance values and accurate descriptions of the actual merchandise. An insurance broker confirms the objects in transit by the client's master policy prior to departure. It is always wise to get this confirmation in writing. I like dealing with these people as they do all the hard leg work for you. You can purchase insurance from the shipper for one-time shipments by having an appraisal done ahead of time, having photos of your merchandise and getting a condition report. It is a good investment to protect your high-value pieces."

"I think we should get going. Time is flying and we have a lot of ground to cover," Khin said.

The three men left in Shein's all-terrain jeep and made their way toward the mines in the mountains. In about ten minutes they arrived at a very busy working mine. Men with shovels and carts of different sizes were going up and down and in and out of various sections of the mine. As they stepped out of the jeep, Shein told Khin and Charlie to follow him down the path to get a closer look deeper into the mine and its operations.

"I will give you a guided tour, as I have done this many times before for my special customers," Shein said. "You will find some hard-working men down here. It is every Myanmar man's dream to find the ultimate gemstone. Years ago working in the mines was very dangerous, but in these modern times the miners use up-to-date machinery and equipment. You will see for yourself as we move along from area to area."

As they walked Shein continued his tour speech. "I don't know if you are aware of this, but the Ruby belongs to the "conundrum" mineral group, the red variety. The genuine ruby is a fiery-red gem which is why people call it the gem of hot summer nights and beautiful red sunsets. The ruby is extremely rare and one of the most valuable gemstones in nature. Its breathtaking color, excellent hardness and irresistible brilliance make it the *King of Precious Stones*". Most rubies have minor inclusions, which are like fingerprints, which prove their authenticity. Inclusions reveal the beauty and individuality of each stone."

"If Americans knew these attributes of the ruby, I'll bet they would sell more engagement rings with rubies rather than diamonds," Charlie laughed.

"I imagine that is so!" It is funny you mention that," Shein continued. "It so happens that the ruby carries a lot of power with it. By that I mean that it is said to possess the ability to rekindle a love which has waned. It is said to be the most passionate of nature's gemstones and the rarest. I'm surprised that you, being Chinese, Charlie, do not know that your ancestors, the Oriental people, treasured the ruby as the most precious gem. It was once considered to be a powerful amulet."

"Oh, my grandfather used to tell me stories when I was young. And I do remember him saying something about rubies. But that was so long ago that I had forgotten. And, sometimes I thought my granddad was just telling me stories." Charlie replied.

Khin interrupted the conversation with some remarks. "I do know rubies are mined throughout Southeast Asia, but I understand that Myanmar produces the highest quality stones. Some say you can actually tell when the rubies are from the Mogok area of Myanmar because due to an accident of nature, the Mogok Rubies possess great beauty in their natural, untreated forms. Rubies from some other parts of the world are heat treated to bring out their color and clarity. Not so with the Mogok rubies. Nothing about them is man-made. They are truly rare and naturally beautiful."

Charlie said, "I heard that natural rubies are becoming quite rare. Is that true, Shein?"

"That is so. However, the Burma Partners still have the ability to buy at a good and ample source for a wide range of gems in various cuts, sizes and clarity levels. Man is always looking for stones that are rare, have vivid color and good internal characteristics and that are pretty near perfect in proportion so that they can be cut easily. As I said earlier, our miners are always searching for that one 'Masterpiece of Nature'."

"What about the colors of the rubies, Shein?" Charlie inquired. "Does one shade of red take preference over another?"

"Definitely," Shein responded quickly. "Our rubies are found in many shades of red, but the *pigeon blood red* is the most sought after because it is the rarest. However, to some people it is just a matter of what they prefer to look at. Let's start heading back to my store. I can better show you there how to best choose a ruby."

Having seen what the mining process entails, the three men headed back up the path and returned by jeep to Shein's store. They were pretty tired from walking around the mine sites for some time. Shein offered them some tea and a light lunch of fish and noodles. Afterwards they were ready to continue their quest for some fine rubies.

"Now that we have rested a bit, are you ready to continue examining my rubies?" Shein asked. "I have plenty to show you and a lot to tell you about them. And, I want to see how much YOU know about the gems you buy, Charlie."

"Oh, so you are going to put me to the test, Shein?" Charlie laughed. "I assure you I have studied gems extensively and I am more than qualified to select fine ones. But when I am out of my own realm and treading strange new waters, I am open to suggestions."

Shein invited his two visitors to come and sit with him at his magnificent octagonal table covered in black felt. They each took a cushioned swivel chair and made themselves comfortable. Charlie was getting all psyched up for this, as this WAS his field of expertise.

Shein began, "Let me start by showing some of my prized rubies. First look at this 7 MM. Antique Cushion cut top red ruby valued at $7,599.92. It has nice crystal clarity and is 2.19 carats. This next one is 9X6.8 MM Oval Cut, 2.25 ct., with a very slight inclusion and is priced at $2,783.92. Next, a 7.5 X 6.5 Octagon Cut Top Pigeon Blood red ruby, 3.03 ct. priced at $688.29. These are just a few that I have cut already. Oh, and this one, a 15.5 X 12 MM Heart-shaped, 12 ct. found in the Mogok tract, asking price $15,599.00, is one of my most valuable rubies. Being affiliated with the Burma Partners helps me to get my hands on some of the best rubies, Mogok rubies. Although our rubies are becoming increasingly rare, Burma Partners is able to buy at the source and always has a wide range of gems in various cuts, colors, sizes and clarity levels. So, if you tell me your exact needs, Charlie, I can better select stones for you. I have cheaper ones as well. Here is a round, 1.06 ct. one for $289.00. This next one is actually a pair. Check out these two heart-shaped rubies for the price of one, 1.45 carats at a cost of $398.00. Finally, this brilliant cherry-red Heart ruby of 1.02 carats is $498.00."

Charlie was full of awe. Being a gemologist he had seen many fine gems, but none that could compare to these Mogok ones. He asked Shein, "Do a lot of gemologist and collectors come here for their gems?"

"Well, to be honest with you, Charlie," Shein responded, "We have all types of people coming here. Some come to buy gems as an investment and hope they increase with value with time; others buy gems to resell them at a higher price to make a profit for them; while a few collect gems simply because they are addicted to gemstones. Some people just like to own rare things and are delighted when they find new stones to compliment their collection."

"I suppose you are right, Shein," Charlie said. "Nowadays people do strange things."

"But to answer your original question, we don't get many people of your caliber out here, Charlie," Shein said. "This is a country far off the beaten path and most people will not travel out this far."

"That is interesting," Charlie said, "as I would think a person would travel far and wide if they knew they could obtain an object of rare and exceptional beauty and value."

"Do you cut all of your own gems, Shein?" Charlie continued.

"I have been an expert lapidary, very skilled at cutting and polishing my stones since I was very young. I inherited my business from my father who was a very skilled lapidary. It is in my blood I guess. All the people who work for me have been trained in my secret method of cutting, as most lapidaries protect their family secrets and only pass them on to their apprentices. When lapidaries cut a gemstone they try to make sure it doesn't look too perfect because then it may look fake. Our cutting is done in two steps. First the stone is rough cut. The final cut is taken using sapphire or diamond powder in order to polish and cut it. Aside from that, there are also two styles of cutting. One is CABOCHON, the old way of cutting; the other is FACETED, which makes symmetrical surfaces on a gemstone."

"My friend Shein is quite an educated man in his field," Khin interjected. "Tell Charlie about your background."

"Oh, I don't like talking about myself, but since you are friends, I will share some of my personal background with you. You see, at first my father hired a private tutor to teach me the basics of the gem business. He wanted me to be knowledgeable and know what I was talking about when people asked me questions. He worked very hard and long hours so he could afford to send me to Yangon University. Because of his sacrifice I was able to study both the international gem market and the precious gems themselves. I excelled so well in my classes there that one of my professors arranged for me to travel to Thailand, Hong Kong and Mandalay and even England to observe other gem dealers and mines and so forth. I can say I got a well-rounded education. That is what I attribute the success of my business here in Mogok today to. I'm only glad that my father lived long enough to see me graduate and take over his business, his dream."

"That's quite a story," Charlie said. "He must have been so proud of you."

"That he was...that he was." Shein repeated.

"I won't interrogate you then, Shein," Charlie said. "Family secrets are family secrets. So let's leave it at that! I think we should get this business finalized so we can start getting ready to make our way back to Yangon. I would like to use Wells Fargo to insure the safety of my merchandise. Do you recommend anything else of importance that I should follow through with?"

"Shein offered, "The Burma Partners will arrange that for me through your Wells Fargo Company in the United States. As soon as plans are finalized, along with the necessary vouchers our government requires, I'll give you a call at your hotel to inform you when your packages are en route to the states. Oh, and your company will have to pay for the merchandise C.O.D. when it arrives. So, my friend, when you are ready to leave for home, your merchandise will already be well on its way. And be assured that your special gift will be enclosed somewhere in the packing."

"Thank you so very much, Shein, for everything." Charlie said, as he shook Shein's hand warmly. "You made my gem buying adventure delightful. I thought I knew everything about gems. But most gemologists know that it is a fact that you never know everything. Working with them is always a learning experience. There is always something new to find out about gems. But since I have visited you and your famous gem town, Mogok, I learned how much I don't know. You are a wealth of information! I'll be seeing you then, Shein. Hope we meet again. Who knows, maybe I will have to come back again to Mayanmar one day or should I say, I will make a point of coming back here with my wife for a pleasure trip only."

"That would be very nice. Perhaps I can make a trip down to Yangon and meet up with you and my friend Khin someday in the future."

An hour after Charlie and Khin left a woman walked into Shein's shop. She was browsing around when Shein approached her.

"Can I help you?" Shein asked.

"I was admiring your gems and your teak pieces. I am vacationing in Mayanmar and I was told by some of my friends in the gem and jewelry business to visit Mogok for the best gemstones. I see you have a wonderful display! But I am spellbound by your teak pieces. I didn't expect to find them here," the woman said. "I come from Bangkok, Thailand where teak is used extensively. In fact, I work for a man who has a large teak woodworking business. So I am enjoying your collection."

"It's funny you mention that, madam," Shein said. "I just sold a piece to a friend of mine from Yangon." Don't tell me you are interested in buying one also? This would be a lucky day for me. Sometimes I go months without selling anything. Then all of a sudden business picks up, like it is today."

"Oh?" the woman looked inquisitively. "I don't know if I will buy anything, but I certainly will take a closer look at your sculptures, as I love teak and appreciate its value. "What did you sell, if I might ask?"

"The piece was a fine turtle sculpture that the Chinese man wanted for his wife. He said something about it being a symbol of "long life" to the Chinese people." Shein answered.

What a nice present to buy for one you love!" the woman said. "Well, let me see now...do you have any small pieces of teak sculpture? How about that little oblong box in the corner there? How much do you want for it?

"That is only $50.00," Shein said."

"Let me take a closer look at it. Yes, I think I can find some use for it back home. I'll take it," the woman replied. "I can use it on my desk for something and it will be a memento of my trip to Mogok in Mayanmar."

On the way back to Mayanmar, Chandra Sholara was dialing her cell phone!

Charlie and Khin made the drive back to Yangon. They were engaged in some light conversation to past the time. Khin started in on one of his stories. "In 1505, which I know is quite a long time ago, an Italian merchant named Ludovico di Varthema visited Burma and was the first European to report the wealth of the Mogok rubies to the western world. He said the sole merchandise of the Myanmar people are their jewels. And of course, he was also the first Westerner to become rich by dealing in gems from Burma. Today it is not so easy to become rich in the gem market, but every year hundreds of gem dealers from all over the world gather in Yangon for the annual 'Gems and Pearl Auction and Sales" which is held at the Myanmar Gem Emporium in Mayangone."

"I am always amused with your stories, though I know they are quite factual," Charlie said. "Someday maybe I will have some extra time to sit with you and exchange stories about our cultures."

When Charlie and Khin finally arrived back in Myanmar it was early evening. Since this would be Charlie's last night in Myanmar, he asked Khin to meet him later in the evening for a farewell dinner at the hotel. Khin was grateful and said he would be there around 7:00 P.M.

"I know I said I would take you to the Gem Market while you were here, but we took longer than expected in Mogok so we will save that for another trip." Khin said. "That should give you an incentive for returning to Mayanmar."

At dinner that evening Charlie and Khin exchanged friendly conversation. Khin wanted to know more about Charlie's wife, Dena.

"Does Dena work, Charlie or is she a homemaker? I know my wife, Myine, basically stays home to care for the house and our two children, but sometimes she helps me out in the store just to break the monotony. She is actually very knowledgeable about gems and jewelry and can handle herself very well with customers."

"Well, Khin," Charlie answered, "Dena holds a full time job as a legal secretary at the Gardina Law Firm. She is a very qualified secretary and has good credentials, having gone to Katharine Gibbs School in Manhattan. She lucked out with a great boss who treats her like family. So she is happy with her life. Since our two children, Daniel and Carla are in school full time it is good for her to be busy at what she enjoys."

"That sounds like a success in the making!" Khin said. "I wish her all the best of luck in her career."

"Thank you, Khin. I'll be sure to tell her that. And, will you please tell your wife, Myine, that I said good-bye until we meet again, which I hope is not too far into the future?"

Afterwards Charlie thanked Khin for all his help and told him he would keep in touch with him as much as possible. He asked him to visit him if he ever came to New York City. Khin shook hands with Charlie and thanked him for the invitation.

Chapter Five
U.S.A. - New York City

Early the next morning Charlie left for Yangon airport for his flight to Bangkok which would connect to his flight to Paris and then on to New York. He had a lot of traveling to do and knew his precious cargo would be safe with the Burma Partners handling things for him. This peace of mind would make for a pleasant, carefree plane ride home.

After what seemed like an endless trip home, Charlie arrived at JFK International Airport. The company limo was waiting to take him right to the Chan Continental Gem Export Company. Although he was rather tired, he was anxious to see if everything arrived intact and curious to know what his boss, Mr. Lee Chang thought of his purchases. So he pushed the thoughts of jet lag aside and decided to give it a go.

"Well I've returned, Lee. Did you manage to open up our beautiful gems and take a look at them? I hope they are to your satisfaction."

"Charlie, you more than pleased me. In fact you outdid yourself in selecting some of the finest gems I've ever seen in my life. That was one trip I didn't mind paying for. You are to be commended."

"Thanks, Lee. I really enjoyed myself and picked up a wealth of information I can use in this business. My contacts were fantastic! My trip to the Mogok Stone Tract was a lifetime dream for a gemologist. To see first hand how the gems are actually mined is a masterful hands-on lesson. Those people have come a long way with their mining techniques, Lee. Nowadays they are using a lot of modern equipment to dig down deeper into those mountains. The area is quite a place to see. Every gemologist should travel there at least once in a lifetime to see this wonderful place. When my friends and I were coming over the mountain to Mogok which lies in a valley surrounded by mountains, all I could see was a city that looked liked a fairy tale. Quaint white pagodas were towering over the city. They looked so clean and perfect dominating the area. From the height we were at it was absolutely breathtaking."

"Maybe I will go there with you someday." Mr. Chang said.

"I wouldn't mind that one bit, Lee. Myanmar is a wonderful vacation place as well as a business interest for us," Charlie said. "You would love the country. There is a lot to see and a lot to do. Though a lot of the activities there are quite different from ours, they are quite interesting and most intriguing. You can always find something to do there. They even have some great golf courses. The country has a long way to go to catch up to us, but they have come a long way. Some people say that *Myanmar is pagodas and pagodas are Myanmar. You cannot separate one from the other.* I found the pagodas I have seen to be wonders that we here in America could not equal in extravagant beauty and spiritual aura. One can learn a lot visiting these pagodas. They are in every city, in every town, and in various shapes and sizes. It is worth a trip there just to see these wonders of the world. At least I consider them to be such. One is more magnificent than the other. I haven't even seen a third of the pagodas that Myanmar has. Maybe someday when I go back with my wife I will visit more of them. Each one has its own story to tell."

Lee said, "You are really well versed about this Myanmar, Charlie. I can see the country has a hold on you of some sort. The several trips you have taken there, has left their mark on you. But that is a good thing, I think."

"Yes, Lee, I sort of love that country. It kind of grows on you. Maybe it is the warmth of the people. I found them to be extraordinarily friendly. In spite of all their struggles throughout their history, they have kept their image of friendliness."

Lee Chang could hear the enthusiasm in Charlie's voice. To keep his upbeat spirit he said, "I found this additional package in our order. The label on it says: FOR CHARLIE LING / PERSONAL. So I put it aside surmising that you must have bought something for yourself."

"My trips are never complete unless I bring home something special for Dena, you know! My two children, Daniel and Carla must be sitting outside my apartment building awaiting my return."

"I know that. So go on home and we will talk in a few days. Take some time off to recoup yourself. You had a busy, hectic week in Mayanmar, I'm sure," Mr. Chang said.

As the taxi made its way through the streets of Manhattan toward the Upper East Side, Charlie relaxed and thought of his family. His suspicions were correct. Daniel and Carla were outside on the steps relaying with their cell phones to Mom upstairs that Dad had arrived. When Charlie got out of the cab, they ran to him, smothered him with hugs and kisses. Even as teenagers they were not ashamed to show their love for their dad. They hurried inside, grabbing Charlie's luggage and extra packages.

Dena was waiting anxiously for her husband to come home. When he walked in the door, she leapt into his arms. The kids left them alone for awhile so they could exchange their affection. They knew their father would call them down when he wanted them. They were just relieved that he was finally home with them.

"How are you my darling? You look tired but have that look of satisfaction on your face of a well-spent trip."

Charlie could not wait to tell Dena all about his trip. Even though he was exhausted, he was very anxious to share his experiences with her. "The Myanmar pagodas and scenery are simply magnificent but they cannot surpass the living monuments, the Myanmar people. I have the smiles of these friendly, peaceful people engraved on my heart. I must take you there someday. I want you to meet Khin and Myine Zeya and their children. You will like them."

"How was the weather there?" Dena asked.

"Myanmar has three seasons. From March to May it is very hot; the rainy season lasts from June to September; and the cool season is from October to February. Since I went in February I lucked out with some good weather. It was somewhat cooler in the mountains in Mogok, which is where I went to buy some real rubies."

Dena was curious about the people. "So how are the people in general?"

Charlie could not help but pour on the compliments. "They come from many ethnic backgrounds, each with a heritage all their own. I found them to be a most enchanting people! I never saw such a happy race of people. Everywhere I went I was treated so warmly and kindly, even when they didn't know me. They are excellent hosts, too. U Khin Zeya and his wife, Myine treated me to dinner and helped me enjoy some of the Mayanmar delicacies. Your ears must have been ringing because I was talking about you a lot."

"You must have felt very much at home, I think," Dena said. "And I was worried about you. I knew you would make new acquaintances."

"I hope you always worry about me and miss me, my dear," Charlie answered affectionately. "I especially missed you, my dear Dena, when we were having our pot of tea. It is a Mayanmar custom to while away an evening with their friends over tea. They are a rather humorous people also. They like to tell jokes and amusing anecdotes and exchange legendary stories. It was really a wonderful traveling experience; one of the best places I ever visited. On my two former trips there I was in too much of a hurry to enjoy anything pleasurable. This time I met great, unforgettable people everywhere I went."

"What do you have for me, my dear Charlie?" Dena asked. "You always bring me something very special that you've thought out with your heart."

"Well first, I want you to read this poem I copied from the doorway of a gem store in Mogok. I just thought it was so beautiful. And since you are my favorite poet, I just had to copy it for you. I knew you would appreciate its meaning. I hope you keep it forever. And secondly, I think you are going to be very surprised with this gift, Dena. It is something very unusual and VERY special. I can not wait to see your eyes when you look upon it."

"Let me see it, Charlie," Dena pleaded. "I cannot wait another minute."

As Charlie uncrated the turtle and released the insulated bubble wrap, the turtle was ready to get unveiled from the final soft bag. Dena's eyes grew larger with each step Charlie took.

"Wow!" Dena said excitedly. "What a magnificent piece! Where did you ever find this? You really outdid yourself this time, my dear. I just love it! My goodness, where shall I put it? Where will it be safe?"

"It was bought in a very special part of the world in a little town named Mogok in Myanmar. I bought it in a gem shop there. I could not resist buying it for you as it was so exquisite a piece and looked so valuable. And, it is a sign of long-life, which I wish for you, my love." Charlie said.

"Thank you," Dena said, as she kept kissing Charlie. "What is it made out of? It looks like wood and a very expensive wood at that."

"It is made of teakwood from Thailand. It was handmade and hand carved from the intricate etchings that are on it. Someone took a lot of time creating this beautiful sculpture. Now tell me," Charlie asked, "where are you going to put it?"

"I think I am going to put it on the credenza behind my desk in work as it will overlook my whole office and bring me good luck. As we Chinese believe, the turtle's magic unites heaven and earth. Some of our ancestors said that the turtle carried the world on its back and therefore it was an example of great patience. Heaven knows in my job I need a lot of patience with the clients we deal with, that sometimes ruffle your feathers, as they say. It is too nice of a piece to hide. It was made to be on display," Dena said.

"Okay then, my love, you put it wherever it brings you the most happiness. That is what I intended it to do for you. And since this is our tenth anniversary of marriage, I wanted to give you some extraordinary gift."

Daniel and Carla came downstairs when they heard their mother shout out in surprise when seeing her gift. They were astounded at what they saw! They knew their dad had bought something very special, but they could not believe the beauty of this turtle. They always liked when their father displayed his love for their mother.

"Now that your mom's gift is out of the way, you two kids deserve something extraordinary for being so patient." Charlie said. "For you, my son, I have purchased this jade gemstone with the hope that you will do something wise with it. I chose it from many that I saw, with the help of a wise gem dealer in Myanmar."

"Thank you, Dad," Daniel said. I know this must have cost a lot and I will treasure it and save it for my future."

"Carla, my sweet blossom, for you I have this magnificent sapphire gem. I hope you will see its beauty as I see it and keep it always so that you know how much your father loves you."

"I love you, daddy", Carla said. "I will cherish it forever and maybe when I am older I will have it set into a necklace for myself."

With that done, they sat down to a wonderful dinner that Dena had prepared for them. The conversation centered on Charlie's trip until Dena interjected that her boss had finally made the grand move to New Jersey. The Gardinas had been looking for a home somewhere in Jersey for quite a while and they finally stumbled on the house of their dreams.

"Is Nick moving his law firm also?" Charlie asked.

"Oh no, he said he has the bulk of his business clients here in the city so he has to remain. He will have to do some commuting everyday, but he said it will be well worth it. I'm glad of that, as I love my job and wouldn't want to move somewhere else or travel far to work."

Daniel interjected some comments that were on his mind, "I don't know, maybe it would be nice to get out of the city and into a Jersey suburb. A lot of my friends have moved there and they seem to be very happy in their new suburb surroundings."

"That is a relief for your mother, Daniel," Charlie said, "but you are entitled to your opinion. When you are older, YOU can move to New Jersey if you like." They all laughed. "Let's finish our dinner and call it a night."

Myanmar

The phone rang at the Unique Asian Wood Products Company in Bangkok. A call was coming in from Myanmar. Ms Bianta answered the phone and quickly learned that the call was an important one for Mr. Nicro. She interrupted Mr. Nicro's board meeting with her phone relay.

"Chai Krap Ka?" (Yes), what is it?" Mr. Nicro asked.

"Miss Chandra Sholara is on line two for you, Mr. Nicro."

"Khop khun" (Thank you!) Mr. Nicro said. "And hold all my other calls."

"Excuse me gentlemen," he told his board members, "I have to take this call."

"Chandra, what have you found out?"

"Well, I tracked this Mr. Khin Zeya and his Chinese American friend from Yangon to a small mining town called Mogok. I lay back for quite a while pretending to be a tourist as they were gone for quite a while. When they returned to the Golden Sun Gem Store, they stayed there for a long time. Finally, after they left, I walked into the store pretending to be browsing. Anyway, to make a long story short, I found out that the proprietor sold a teak turtle piece to the Chinese American man. I made my way back to Yangon, but lost them in the shuffle. What do you want me to do next? I have a feeling the American man is about to return to the United States."

Mr. Nicro said, "Lie low for a while, maybe for several weeks. Enjoy your vacation a bit more. There is a lot to do in Myanmar. Maybe you can go to one of their festivals. They are always very joyous. But be very observant to the activity around you. If you go into town, see if you can find out more about the American gem dealer; maybe about where exactly the man lives. Ask around. Maybe that Mr. Zeya knows something. Maybe you can go in his store and make some inquiries. Or perhaps if you listen well you might overhear him say something. You know what to do Chandra my dear. Use those sleuth skills of yours."

"I will try my best, Mr. Nicro. I don't know how long it will take me to find out anything, but I will call when I have something of importance to tell you. Thank you for letting me remain here in Myanmar, at your expense. You do not have to coax me to take advantage of this wonderful place. Maybe I will take a few day trips to some other towns nearby to do some shopping. Good-bye, for now." Chandra said.

After several weeks passed, Chandra made her way over to the Zeya Gem Store. She was determined to find out something because she hated loose ends. Now she was getting impatient at not knowing anything. She felt that she had to make a more aggressive move in her probing. She entered the store as a woman just casually looking around at beautiful things. Khin's employee approached her and asked if she could help her. Chandra had a sophisticated look and knew how to handle herself. That is why Mr. Nicro kept her on his payroll. She was invaluable when it came to getting a problem solved.

"May I help you, madam?" the worker inquired.

"I am on vacation and doing some shopping for myself. I went to the Aung San Bogyoke Market and to some other markets in Bagan and Inle Lake. But I was advised to buy my jewelry in Yangon. I was looking for a beautiful ring for myself but I don't know what kind of gem I really want. Can you make some suggestions?" Chandra asked.

"Perhaps it would be best if you spoke to the owner, my boss, Mr. Zeya. He is on the phone with someone at present. Would you like to wait?"

"Thank you," Chandra said with a sound of satisfaction in her voice. "I'll keep browsing to see if I find anything to my liking." While she waited and pretended to look around, she couldn't help but overhear Khin talking to someone. She, in fact, maneuvered herself over to where she could more adequately hear what was being said.

Khin, speaking rather loudly, said, "It has been several weeks since you left Mayanmar. I was wondering when I would hear from you again, Charlie. How are things in Chinatown in New York?" There was a short pause. "Was your merchandise intact? Did your wife like the turtle?" Khin paused to await Charlie's response, then continued with, "I'm glad to here that! Thanks for letting me know that all turned out well for you. Please continue to keep in touch with me. Good-bye, my friend."

Chandra's ears stood up. What a break! Finally she had a lead, or at least, she thought so. What she would do with it was another story, she thought pensively.

After he hung up the phone, Khin came out to greet his customer. "My employee tells me you are interested in purchasing a piece of my fine jewelry. What can I do for you madam?"

"Oh, hello, I am Chandra Sholara, visiting from Bangkok. I am interested in purchasing a gemstone ring for myself but I am uncertain as to what stone I want. Can you offer any suggestions?" Chandra asked.

"Why of course I can. Step over here and I will show you my ring showcase." Khin said.

An hour went by and Chandra finally made a selection. She chose a most striking oval cut ruby set in gold with some diamond baguettes on the sides. Khin sized the ring for her and place it on her right ring finger. She settled her account, thanked Khin for his time and help and praised him for his beautiful gemstones and jewelry pieces. She could hardly wait to exit the store as she now had something of value to tell Mr. Nicro. She left and went immediately back to her hotel.

It was almost 7:00 P.M. in Bangkok, but Chandra knew she had to call Mr. Nicro. She called him directly this time. There was no time to waste.

"Hello?" Mr. Nicro said. "Chandra? Do you have any good news for me, my dear? Did you find out anything? I am so anticipating some GOOD news from you."

"As a matter of fact I do have good news for you and I did find out something significant, Mr. Nicro. I learned that your turtle is now in New York City. To be exact, it now lives in Chinatown where the American gem dealer lives."

"No kidding? How in the world did it get there?"

"My eavesdropping in the Zeya Gem Store paid off. I was lucky enough to overhear a phone conversation between Mr. Zeya and the Chinese American man," Chandra said. "How great is that?"

"That was outstanding work, Chandra. Now I want you to go to New York. Stay in Myanmar at your hotel until I send you a couple of men to accompany you to New York. Then I will give you further instructions," Mr. Nicro ordered.

"Fine," Chandra said. The phone call disconnected.

℃

Chandra found a lot to do in Yangon while she waited for her help to arrive. She went shopping, of course, as all women like to do. One day she even tried out the *thanaka*. She bought a small container and when she got back to her hotel, she put some on her face. She liked the feel as it was very soothing. It felt so cool that she left it on when she went down to the pool for a few hours. The store keeper told her many people use it as a sunscreen. She found out that they were right! It worked better in the sun than any sunscreen she had ever used. Chandra even discovered that it was quite a cleansing agent for her skin as she washed it off. She planned on getting more to take home.

Later that evening Chandra stumbled upon a festival going on with a marionette show by one of the pagodas in Yangon along the river. Hundreds of people came with their carts full of wares to sell and to camp under the tamarind trees. The most interesting barge that was on the river side was the one carrying the marionette troupe. Chandra was enthralled at the number of people that filled the festival ground. She walked from stall to stall buying some earthen-ware, and some cane baskets. She noticed that the festival had all the trimmings of a fair with ferris wheels, merry-go-rounds and the marionettes shows. It was a realistic open air show. Chandra found the marionettes quite fascinating. She approached one of the puppeteers to see a marionette more closely. She learned from him that the marionettes were hand painted with a mixture of lime and talcum powder and water. This becomes a kind of dough. Then tamarind seeds are heated for five hours, crushed and brought to a greasy cream. The two doughs are mixed together for painting the character's faces. The man told her it takes about ten layers to obtain a lasting painting. Chandra wanted to know what the tattoos meant. The man explained that the Burmese believed the tattoos protected them against blows of misfortune. The Burmese people use to cover themselves with them and symbolically reproduced them on their puppets as well. He told her the story of the Venetian merchant, Nicolo Di Conti, who came to Burma in 1435 who said: "All inhabitants, men and women, decorate their flesh using an iron point that paints them in an indelible manner. Thus they are painted for the rest of their days." The puppets themselves were decorated with sequins and glass pearls.

"What about the strings that move the puppets?" Sandra asked. "There are so many. Do they get tangled?"

The man continued to explain, "The marionettes were hung by ten to twenty strings. The strings were essentially white so that they remained invisible. The strings were solidified, protected against moths and dipped for several days in the juice of the *Te* fruit, a local tree whose acid allowed disentangling the strings easier. The five main strings, called "life strings" were tied to the shoulder, spine and the temples."

"Your stage is unusual. There is not much scenery on it. Why is that?"

"We keep the stage bare except for a green branch stuck in the middle and a *kadaw-pwe*, which is an arrangement of two bunches of bananas and green coconut on a tray decorated with flowers wrapped in green banana leaves."

Chandra asked, "Is there a significance to this display?"

The man added, "Yes, the *kadaw-pwe* means an offering of respect and it is an important item in any Mayanmar celebration both in family circles and in public. One thing about the Mayanmar marionette show is that its strength lies in the lyrical beauty and the epic grandeur of the dialogue which is rendered in song, arias, recitatives and commentaries in rhymed prose supported by the orchestra.

"How many people does it take to operate the marionette?" Chandra asked.

"Usually it takes two, one to recite or sing and the other to manipulate the strings in coordination."

"I know in most plays that I have seen back home, there is always a king and queen or a prince and princess. I notice you have a king and queen."

The man was amused with Chandra's interest. He said, "There is a saying that no play is complete without the royal court scene with the king and his ministers, but it is a fact that the scene is boring to the audience. It is, however, considered auspicious to open the play with this scene. In the colonial days, it was a reminder of Myanmar's sovereignty which had been lost. The glorious music of the orchestra and the song in praise of the king and his realm awakened nostalgic memories in the old who passed them on to the young. And don't miss the *hna-par-thwar*, the duet dance which is the love scene. You may get tired from the length of the show. Our marionette shows seem to go on all night. The Myanmar people love fun, music and entertainment and they are content with nothing less than whole night entertainment."

"Well I will stay as long as I can," Chandra said. "I know I will enjoy the show after your explanation of it. Thank you for all your information and for being so nice."

Chapter Six
New York City / Three Months Later

When Nick opened his office door his jaw dropped and he was quite upset. His law office was a mess. Papers were strewn all over the place, things were broken, desk drawers were open, and cabinets were ajar with their contents on the floor. He felt very disheartened.

The Gardina Law Firm was part of a brand new twenty-eighth floor skyscraper in Manhattan. The sixteenth floor was more than enough space for a small law firm. Nick Gardina always dreamed of having his own firm. After he finished Law School at Fordham University on West 62nd Street, he knew he would remain in the city. Throughout his college years he had spent many an evening in its various restaurants, at its theaters, attended many sports events, and of course dated a few respectable women. Trying to block out the fact that there was a mess in his office, Nick started to daydream for a few moments about how he met Giovanna. Thoughts of her always soothed him over.

He pondered how he often went to Lower Manhattan to the South Street Seaport. He loved to take in the view. It was a place Nick went because there was a lot of history there and a lot to do and see. It seemed to have the lure of romance for him. He would walk the bumpy cobblestone streets to Pier 17. The Maritime Museum was one of his favorite places because to him it reflected New York's past glory as a port town. He loved to look at the fleet of ships that were there for tourists. The four-masted, 347-foot cargo vessel, the "Peking" that sailed the world in 1911 fascinated him.

The view of the Brooklyn Bridge was awesome! Of course, the boardwalk allowed one to take a leisurely stroll and even sit on a bench and have an outdoor fast food lunch. While walking along he always enjoyed the street performers known as "busters" who performed a variety of music from classical to Dixieland bands.

Since Nick was so drawn to this place, it was almost inevitable that he would meet his life partner there. He would often go into the three story pavilion where all the shops and restaurants were. He perused the shops many times, but today one in particular caught his eye, The Ragalo (Gift) Boutique with its beautiful yellow rose embossed on its sign was a spectacular attraction! However, it was not the shop but the woman in the window that captivated Nick. Although he didn't need anything in the boutique, he knew he had to go inside and at least look like he wanted something. He had to meet this woman with the dark hair and warm brown eyes.

As Nick entered the store he pretended that he was looking for an item for his home. Though he was in his early thirty's, he was feeling like a school kid right now. The woman approached him and said, "I can see you are very interested in our lamps from Tuscany."

"Not exactly," Nick said. "I just wanted to see what you had in this little boutique that looked so appealing from the outside. And the real truth is that I wanted to make your acquaintance. My name is Nick Gardina. I have a law firm on the Upper East Side on 63rd Street. I often come down here to enjoy the Seaport."

"It's nice to meet you, Nick. I am Giovanna Fiore and I am the proprietor of this shop. I have been here for a few years. I am surprised I have never bumped into you around here or on the pier."

"I know we are both working, or at least should be working, but may I take you to dinner tonight here on the Pier? After I close my office I can come by your boutique and pick you up after you close for the day. What do you say? I know I am being quite forward, but I really want to take you out."

"I would like that," Giovanna answered. It is not everyday that a good looking gentleman walks into my shop and asks me out to dinner. You have a date. I will see you later then."

That was the beginning of a long future for Nick Gardina and Giovanna Fiore. They tied the knot a year and a half later.

Nick's daydreaming was interrupted by a loud voice and a door slamming. He jumped a bit but came back down to earth. "What in the world are you doing, Dena? Stop slamming the door."

"Good Morning, Boss," Dena said happily. "What's wrong? You look like you've seen a ghost! Did you have an accident on your way to work? What is it? You are scaring me! Her boss was never curt with her. He was the most easy-going man she knew.

"I'm sorry I was so abrupt with you, Dena, but I am a wreck. My mind wandered into a daydream and I was blocking out all of this. But look around. What do you see? Is this our neat little office with everything in its proper place? Someone ransacked our office last night. I don't know how they got in, but I guess thieves have their ways. They didn't seem to take too many things of value. I see a lot of surface objects missing. I haven't had a chance to check the files to see if they were tampered with."

"I can't believe this, Nick!" Dena said looking bewildered. "This can't be happening around me again. Don't you remember that Charlie and I had our home broken into a few weeks ago? We thought the thieves were after gems that they thought we had hidden somewhere since Charlie is a gemologist. But nothing was taken as far as we could tell. Our home was just ransacked and messed up. And you know it really shakes you up to know strangers got into your home and that they were even INSIDE your home looking through your things. This break-in seems awfully coincidental to me! Did you call the police yet?"

"Yes, they are on their way. I can't understand what anyone would want with my little law firm. But then again, this is New York City! Don't touch anything until the police do their investigation and try to get some fingerprints or evidence or whatever it is they look for. They should be here any minute now. So sit tight!"

"What in the world is this all about?" Dena wondered out loud. "Do you have a disgruntled client? Did you antagonize someone lately?"

"I haven't the foggiest idea what this is about, but I hope it will be resolved soon. I did see that two hundred dollars I had in my middle desk drawer is missing. It was left open. That's how I know it is gone. That will teach me to lock things up."

"Yes, but you know when someone wants something, they find ways to even get into locked drawers, so don't browbeat yourself about it." Dena said.

The elevator opened and two of New York's finest detectives appeared. James Graci and Linda Mc Bane were partners in crime for about ten years and had seen just about everything. They introduced themselves, identified their precinct, showed their badges and got right down to business. Their team of experts followed and came up right behind them on the second elevator.

"Please stand back or have a seat while my team checks the scene out. We have to scan for prints and other clues. I hope you two didn't touch or move anything. This may take a while," Detective Graci blurted out.

"Dena asked, "Would you all like some coffee? I have some freshly brewed Kona coffee."

"Thank you!" Detective Graci said. "That would be nice. I did miss my morning coffee break when your call came in. So, yes, I would enjoy a nice hot cup of java with just milk, no sugar. My crew will take it the same way. They usually follow me at everything, even my coffee choices."

"Okay, I will be right back. I won't be disturbing anything as the coffee is in the next room," Dena said.

"Can you tell me how they got into the building, detective?" Nick asked.

"Thieves have their ways. I see that you do not have an alarm on your offices. They undoubtedly picked a few locks, maybe even broke them somehow. My men will determine that after they investigate your place."

After an hour or so of examining the rooms, Nick's office and Dena's secretarial area, the police came up with a few prints and said they would run them through the system. They asked Nick and Dena to try and make a list of what they thought was missing and might have been stolen. They would be back again tomorrow sometime to give them a report of any findings.

Detective Mc Bane said, "It seems like they came up through the back of the building because the doors back there were pried open with a crowbar or some strong tool. Your office door lock was picked. I don't think they were too professional as thieves; they were kind of sloppy. We'll be in touch with you soon about the prints." With that they left by the freight elevator.

Nick and Dena looked at each other and let out sounds of relief simultaneously. They felt a little uncomfortable now that they knew someone was spying on them or invading what they thought was their safe environment. They were both staring out the huge skyscraper windows into the sky.

Nick interrupted this temporary lapse in time with, "Okay, Dena, I don't want you to worry or be afraid to come to work, enter the building or work here alone. I am hiring a security officer and maybe a receptionist so that you are never alone here. Will that make you feel safer? Besides, our firm is growing and you could use some help around here."

"That sounds soothing, I must say. Although I don't really feel afraid, I think it is best to do as you say. It is always better to think ahead. Thank you, Nick!"

As the hours rolled by, Nick and Dena took inventory of the office and its contents. Nick was missing money and desk things, but his files seemed to be untouched. Dena on the other hand had a mess. Her desk was all torn apart, most of her personal desk items either taken or broken.

After a while Nick heard Dena cry out. "Oh my!" Dena shrieked. "They've taken my precious turtle, the one from Myanmar that Charlie gave me just a short time ago. It was supposed to bring me GOOD luck. So much for that! I can never replace it. What in the world would they want with my turtle? Unless they realized it had great value. What a strange item to steal from us!"

Nick came running over to Dena. "Calm down! Things can be replaced with other things. At least we were out of harm's way when the thieves broke in. I would rather them take things than take YOU!" Nick said.

Dena was crying. "But, you don't know how much trouble my husband went through to get this for me. He is going to be heart-broken, not for himself, but for me. He knows it held a lot of meaning for me."

"Well, let's allow the police experts to do their job. Maybe they will find it!" Nick said.

"I guess you're right, Nick. Thanks for the consolation! But I don't know how I am going to break this news to Charlie. He is going to be furious, I think."

℘

Chandra and her two companions felt victorious with the acquisition of the turtle and other incidental things they confiscated in their break-in spree in the Gardina Law Office. They were in a limo trying to get to the airport as quickly as possible. They decided to take a flight out of La Guardia Airport instead of JFK International just to change their travel patterns somewhat.

Chandra picked up the phone and dialed Bangkok, Thailand.

It was very late in Bangkok. The evening silence in the Unique Asian Wood Products Company Offices was broken by a telephone ringing rather long and loud. Finally someone answered.

"Hello, this is Mr. Nicro speaking."

"I'm sorry I am calling so late, Mr. Nicro, but I think you won't mind when I tell you some good news," Chandra said.

"I have been waiting and wondering what kind of progress you were making for me, Chandra." Mr. Nicro replied. "So, is it good news?"

"As a matter of fact, it is. The incident went rather well. It was quite easy to get into the building. There was no alarm system to contend with and we were able to move about freely."

Mr. Nicro, being an impatient man, asked, "Well, did you get my precious sculpture?"

"Yes, we did, Mr. Nicro, and it seems to be in perfect condition. The woman had the turtle displayed on the top of her credenza behind her desk. It was easy to spot."

"How did you ever find it?"

"First we followed Mr. Ling home to see where he lived. We had to wait a few days though to make sure they were all out of the house. So after the two children went to school, and Mr. and Mrs. Ling left for work, we made our move. But as luck would have it, the turtle was not there. So then I thought that maybe Mrs. Ling took it to her place of business or somewhere. So we waited again another day, and followed her to see where she worked. To make a long story short, we hit pay dirt. She is an employee of the Gardina Law Firm. From then

71

on it was easy to make our move after a little planning. After closing time we entered the building through the back door, pried it open and made our way up to the law office. We checked for alarms and luckily there were none."

"How are you planning to get out of the country with it?" Mr. Nicro asked. "That might be a problem."

"Not to worry, Mr. Nicro. We packed it in a separate carry on bag with a false bottom. We are on our way to the airport as we speak. Everything should go smoothly now. We just have to be careful going through customs." Chandra replied.

"Be careful and cautious as well, Chandra."

"We will not take any chances or call any attention to ourselves, Mr. Nicro. So rest easy and we will see you soon."

As the limo arrived at the airport, Chandra and her two companions started to gather their belongings for a quick and easy entrance into the airport. The driver left them off at the curbside check-in. There was quite a crowd gathering outside so they had to wait their turn. They put their baggage down and proceeded to wait in line. They were making small talk about how long the trip would be and how good it would be to go home to Bangkok for a while. They were wishing they didn't have to change planes several times to get home, but that was not to be. As the line moved forward toward the ticket counter, Chandra bent down to grab her precious cargo.

"My bag is gone!" Chandra uttered. She was frantic and starting to panic. She was trying not to be too loud so as not to call attention to herself and her companions.

One of the men said, "Weren't you keeping an eye on it? How could you be so careless? Look around, maybe it is behind us. Check the people out also. Maybe someone picked it up by mistake. Was there anyone around you with the same kind of case?"

Chandra cried out softly, "I do not believe this! How could I take my eyes off my special bag? Mr. Nicro is going to be so angry! Let's look around a while. Maybe we will see someone carrying it. Perhaps they picked it up by mistake."

After about a half hour of searching through the airport crowds, even at all the various airline ticket lines and gates, they still found no one carrying a case that resembled their missing baggage.

Chandra dialed Bangkok again, this time using Mr. Nicro's cell number.

Mr. Nicro answered almost on the third ring, "Hello, what is it? I just spoke to you a little while ago. Are your travel plans changed?"

"I know, Mr. Nicro. I don't know how to tell you this but someone stole my special bag with your sculpture in it as we were waiting in the check-in line outside at the airport. I should have been more careful especially knowing I was in New York in a busy airport. I am so sorry. We looked everywhere we could to see if someone picked it up by mistake. There was no sign of it. The person who took it was very slick. What do you want me to do now?"

"I think you have done enough for one night and I do not think you will get any leads as to my turtle's whereabouts for some time or maybe ever. I want you and the two gentlemen to come home now. Good Night," Mr. Nicro said as he quickly ended the call.

Chandra hung up and told the two men the instructions Mr. Nicro gave her. They proceeded to board their plane for home. "Mr. Nicro is not very happy with us. I do not look forward to facing him," Chandra said with sadness in her voice. "I have never let him down before. This may be the end to a perfect job for me. I think my career may be over."

The two men tried to comfort her but she was very distraught over her misjudgment.

Chapter Seven
High Bridge, New Jersey

Living in a small town had its advantages. Everyone seemed to know each other whether they lived on the same street or took part in town activities and local church functions. There was always some interest to captivate everyone.

Located in the rolling hills of Hunterdon County in Western Jersey, Upper Main Street in High Bridge, New Jersey was a long action-packed thoroughfare. People of different ethnic backgrounds settled down there to raise their families and forge their lifestyles. The Main Street neighborhood offered various types of interests, from parks and small shops and boutiques to church activities and school related happenings. What better place to settle down to make roots than Main Street, U.S.A.!

The Safenski's were one typical family of Polish extraction who made their way to High Bridge. Krystyna & Kazimierz were both from Brooklyn, New York. Their families settled in the Bensonhurst section of Brooklyn. They both came from average sized families with two siblings each. They met in high school and remained together even through college years. After their wedding and honeymoon they decided they wanted to move to "Jersey". They followed realtors from one town to another until they fell in love with Main Street in High Bridge, N.J. As they toured through the downtown to check out the area they found a plaque that said: *High Bridge was named for a 1,300 foot long, 112 foot high bridge built by the Central Railroad Company across the South Branch of the Raritan River. It was too costly to maintain and was eventually filled in with an embankment, leaving a double-arch culvert by which the river and Arch Street passes through. The township was formed from Lebanon, Tewksbury and Clinton Townships.* That was interesting enough for them to make them want to settle there. They seemed to feel comfortable in this rural community they stumbled upon.

It was there in High Bridge where they found two homes, side by side for sale, one Victorian style and the other a Tudor, both with style and nicely landscaped properties. After careful consideration, Krystyna and Kazimierz focused in on one special house that they could call "home."

The stately Victorian home was just what Krystyna wanted in a house. A spacious foyer opened up into a magnificent Great Room. Her attention was caught by the stacked fieldstone fireplace with its ornate oak mantle and sprawling stone hearth. As she stood before it, she could picture many happy times and memorable moments around it with family and friends. The huge, updated kitchen took up the whole left side of the home. Krystyna loved to cook, especially her Polish specialties like pierogi and golabki, so she knew that was one room that would elicit appetizing aromas and lure a family around its table. The breakfast nook was nestled in an alcove graced by a huge bay window that overlooked a lushly adorned yard with an in ground L-shaped swimming pool. The right side of the house had a magnificent Master Bedroom Suite and bath with a Jacuzzi in the corner. French doors opened onto an oval-shaped deck surrounded by evergreen trees for privacy. The winding staircase twisted upward. Upstairs would be perfect for her upcoming family because it had three bedrooms and three full baths, plus an additional room that could be used as an office or hobby room. Krystyna was excited about the home. It had so much potential for her to dabble with. Being a homemaker came naturally to her and she could hardly contain her eagerness to start filling the house up and decorating it. Krystyna's hobby was antique hunting, so she knew dressing up this Victorian would be easy, yet challenging. Another feature of the house that made Krystyna happy was the huge basement. She had an enormous amount of antiques to store there.

By profession, Kazimierz, or Kaz as he liked to be called, was a custom's inspector at Newark Liberty International Airport. His job was to check cargo and visitors entering the United States and enforce the import/export laws and regulations of the federal government. He even had to do agriculture inspections at times. He actually enjoyed searching for contraband because that was important in preventing illegal drugs and imported merchandise from being smuggled into the United States. He felt successful at his job when he was able to seize some contraband.

Kaz was also an innately gifted and talented painter and carpenter and knew a lot about masonry and electricity, thanks to his father who was a successful house builder. So if there was any reconstructing to be done on the house, it would be easy and definitely inexpensive.

While Krystyna and Kaz worked on their new home in the passing months to set it up and decorate it, they wondered why the adjacent Tudor house was vacant for a long time since they moved in.

Krystyna asked, "Why do you think this beautiful house is still not sold?"

Kaz responded with, "Krystyna, **pilny swoich interesow**. (Mind your own business). In time someone will buy it."

Krystyna laughed when she said, "**Moze ten dom jest nawiedzony.**" ("Maybe this house is haunted!")

"Krystyna, where do you get such ideas, Kaz retorted back. "Pay attention to your own home! I think the reason it is still not sold is because the asking price is rather steep." With that said, they came back to thoughts of their own home.

Now and then Krystyna found herself staring out her kitchen window to check out the empty Tudor. Occasionally she would see people going and coming. Several Realtors stopped by to undo the lock box on the front door to let potential buyers in. Whoever owned the house, kept up the maintenance. A lawn man would come by weekly to manicure the lawn and property. Krystyna even noticed that an electrician was changing some outdoor lights. Krystyna mentioned to Kaz that on one occasion she saw a young man walking all around the house and property. Yet as time passed, still no one bought the house.

Lo and behold, about six months later, Krystyna spied a couple checking out the Tudor. They seemed to be about her and Kaz's age. One always wonders about neighbors when one buys a new home or resettles in a new town. Will they be friendly? Will they like me? Will we like them?

❧

Giovanna and Nick Gardina were no exception. They loved life and people and sentimentally knew that when they found their home and town, it would be their home forever. On one of their realtor excursions, their hearts skipped a beat! They couldn't believe their eyes! There on Main Street in High Bridge stood the two-story house of their dreams! The Tudor with its towering turret and side, roof-covered carport reminded them of the villa in Tuscany, Italy where they honeymooned. The white stucco two-story, ten room house was beckoning them to come in. It didn't take them long to make up their minds. This was their house! A feeling of warmth enveloped them.

It was early spring when Giovanna and Nick Gardina moved in next door to the Safenski's. Krystyna was relieved to see that her "haunted house" would be vacant no longer. The Tudor was coming to life! The Gardinas moved in and began to change their house into the "Gardina Look"!

"Kaz, **Jestem barzo szczesliwa** (I am so happy), "we have new neighbors!" I can't wait to make their acquaintance," Krystyna said excitedly!

"**Chico (quiet),** don't be so nosy; give them a chance to settle in. Then we will invite them over for an evening visit," Kaz said.

After several weeks, one afternoon, Krystyna walked over to the Gardina's. When the doorbell rang, Giovanna answered it promptly. As soon as she opened the door, Krystyna blurted out, "Welcome to the neighborhood! My name is Krystyna Safenski. My husband, Kaz and I live next door in the Victorian. Here are some crusciki I made for you. They are one of my Polish goodies. I hope you enjoy them."

"Oh hello! I am so glad to finally meet you. My name is Giovanna and I live here with my husband, Nick. I am so very happy to meet you. My husband will be glad to meet you as well. These look like our

Italian funnel cakes, but I am sure yours taste far better. Would you like to come in for a minute?"

Krystyna instantly said, "Yes, I'll come in, but only for a moment. We were wondering who would move in next to us. This house was vacant for quite a while and I kept telling Kaz that I wished someone would move into it soon. We are so pleased to have you for neighbors. We would be so happy if you and Nick would come over for an evening visit tomorrow about seven o'clock so we could all get acquainted."

"I'm sure Nick would be glad to come over with me tomorrow evening. Thank you for inviting us. We will see you tomorrow then around seven. I am so excited!"

Krystyna's heart jumped because she was anxious for them to get together. After all, it was a long time that they had no neighbor. She couldn't wait to get home and tell Kaz.

It didn't take Krystyna and Giovanna and Kaz and Nick too long to get acquainted. Before they realized it the Safenski's and the Gardinas began their lifelong friendship. Even though their professions differed immensely, they seemed to have a lot in common.

Giovanna was an interior decorator by profession so she would have no trouble sprucing up her home. She could make a room come alive with anything from unusual furniture to a small insignificant knick-knack. She graduated from the Antonelli College in Cincinnati, Ohio with her diploma in Interior Decorating. She was a natural working with furniture, lighting, wall treatments and interior accessories. Being an inquisitive person, she loved to browse through stores, flea markets and garage sales to see what unique articles she could find to add some pizzazz to a room. Giovanna found her shopping adventures intriguing whether they were done in malls, fine stores or simple country stores.

Nick began his law practice as soon as he finished college. He managed to set up a small firm with an ongoing business at home but he also maintained a profitable law office in New York City with an efficient staff. His busy practice gave him little time for home and family. So he left it up to Giovanna to keep the home fires burning. She was excellent at that and managed to combine being a good homemaker while keeping her husband as her main interest.

Little by little, as summer changed to fall, the Safenski's and the Gardinas socialized off and on and got to know each other rather well.

Though fond of each other, they still respected each other's privacy. Before they knew it, the winter months set in.

The Safenski's were blessed with a new little life, their first-born on December 24th, Christmas Eve. They barely noticed how cold it was that winter because they were so preoccupied with their new arrival. What a wonderful gift their newborn son, Stefan Anthony was, especially being a Christmas baby! They felt very blessed to have a healthy baby and a son. Kaz wasn't too overjoyed at having to drive in a snowstorm to the hospital, but when he saw his son, his heart melted, just like snow. He knew that Stefan would be the apple of their eye and he was already planning all the activities he would like to do with his son. *He was imagining playing soccer and baseball with him. He even relished the idea of taking him on the Columbia trail section of Patriots Path, the State's longest mountain biking and jogging trail; when he was older, of course. Mountain biking was one of Kaz's favorite pastimes besides golf.*

The following year the Gardinas had a very special reason to be thankful. On Thanksgiving Day, they were gifted with their first child, a baby girl. Francesca came into their lives at 7 pounds and 4 ounces and she had the most beautiful head of dark hair, just like her mother's. What a delight she was for them; and what a precious gift! Nick loved his little sweetheart and he wanted to protect her and give her a happy, full life.

With each passing year the Gardinas and Safenskis felt like they were more like family than friends. Even their children were compatible and always got along. In spite of all their busy lives they managed to make time for outings and visits together.

⁋

Krystyna, being a restless woman, who needed to be on the move, tried to get out shopping at least once a week. She would check out the newspapers for the upcoming yard sales in the area and select a few that might be of interest. After she situated Stefan in his car seat in the mini van she would get on her way. Her enthusiasm made it easy to rummage through all the unusual items she came across. She had an eagle eye and knew a good thing when she saw it. Most of the time Krystyna shopped alone, that is, except for her son in tow. She always had her stroller handy. She was very lucky that Stefan was a good baby and didn't fuss too much. That made her sprees more enjoyable.

As Krystyna and Giovanna's friendship grew with each passing year, they found that they had one exceptional thing in common - shopping! Whether they went to the mall, rushed through the supermarket, breezed through a yard sale or visited antique dealers, they enjoyed each other's company and never seemed to be at a loss for words. They valued each other's judgment and would exchange their opinions on almost anything freely and openly.

One day Giovanna asked Krystyna to go with her to the open-air Golden Nugget Flea Market in a neighboring town of Lambertville. "This is supposed to be a huge outdoor bargain sale!" Giovanna explained. "Someone told me there are sixty antique shops which are right up my alley. They have plenty of collectibles too which I'm sure should interest you. Who knows what we may find?"

"I'm game," Krystyna replied. "You've got my interest peaked. Let's head out early tomorrow. I'll pick you and Francesca up around 9:30 A.M. We'll take two strollers so that we will be able to walk around with ease."

"Fine, Krystyna! I look forward to an adventurous day," Giovanna answered excitedly. "We always have such fun and inevitably end up coming home with a few choice items. I love a good bargain and the challenge of searching for it! See you tomorrow at 9:30 A.M. sharp!"

On the cool summer day, Giovanna and Krystyna, with their kids beside them, set out for the Flea Market to do some serious perusing amidst other people's treasures. Their husbands, of course, sometimes thought they were wasting their time. Krystyna said with a chuckle in her voice, "Kaz always laughs and says, "Krystyna, **kochasz ludzi graty.** (You love other people's junk)! Will you ever bring home anything worthwhile?"

Giovanna added, "Well, Nick usually asks, Vanna why do you want old things? Go out and buy new, updated things. We certainly can afford them. I would just laugh and say Nicko, you have no sense of adventure. It is the thrill of the hunt that Krystyna and I love. It brings so much satisfaction when you find a precious item that can be re-used, rebuilt, or refurbished to fit into your home - somewhere. Someday we may come across something valuable." They both ended the conversation with laughter and were on their way.

The two women arrived at the Flea Market about 10:30 A.M. and began to make their way through the maze of vendors' tables. There were plenty of dealers displaying their wares with the hope of selling some of their treasures. Krystyna and Giovanna ambled on from stand to stand in endless pursuit of something. After a short while of browsing, they came upon a stand with all kinds of exotic items. One thing in particular caught Krystyna's roving eye - a leatherback turtle replica which looked hand-carved by a fine craftsman. It had quite an artistic effect to its appearance. Krystyna, being an antique expert and having seen many valuable collectibles, immediately noticed an oddity about the turtle. She began to examine it closer. Her thoughts were running wild! *This had to be made by one fine artisan as the workmanship was simply intricate.* On the top protective shell odd-shaped scutes or plates were carved. When she turned it over she was mesmerized by the markings on the bottom. They looked like hieroglyphic symbols or something. She could not believe the workmanship on this turtle! *What a piece of wood,* she thought!

"Giovanna, look at this turtle! It is so magnificent!" Krystyna shouted.

"Wow, Krys, let me have a closer look; this is something else! Look at those designs and lines. It is quite heavy, too. I can't begin to fathom how anyone could conceive of and carve such a magnificent piece of sculpture."

"Oh Giovanna, I must buy it! I simply have to have this turtle!"

"Go for it, Krys. It seems to be calling out to you," Giovanna smiled. She was feeling so happy for Krystyna.

Krystyna hollered over to the vendor, a middle-aged man who was watching the two curious women. "Good afternoon. I am interested in the turtle you have basking here in the sun. Can you tell me something about this turtle sculpture? Where is it from? What is it made of? What do the markings on it mean?" Krystyna barely came up for air.

"Slow down lady. Give me one question at a time. I am not going anywhere. You have my undivided attention." He paused for a moment to allow time for the woman to calm down. "Now, let's start from the beginning," the vendor said politely. "First of all, I bought it from a vendor at a flea market in upstate New York several months ago. I thought it was rather odd and that I would make a little profit with it."

"Where do you think it is from?" Giovanna asked.

"I don't have a clue! I didn't particularly care where it was from. I just knew that it was an attractive item that maybe I could sell for a profit. I like rare things. I seem to attract people to my stand with them. I have a lot of luck selling what I consider exotic things."

Krystyna's curiosity was launching. "Do you have any idea what all those carvings are or what they signify? They certainly add a lot of interest to this sculpture."

"Like I said, madam, I don't have an interest in markings and gouged out symbols. They do not interest me at all. I simply find an article that I find unusual or that I consider might be rare or one of a kind."

"I wouldn't call them gouged out symbols. They are far too beautiful to put them into such a category," Krystyna said with annoyance in her voice. She thought for a moment, *this man hasn't a clue about this turtle. I must rescue it.*

"So, can you tell me how much you are asking for this turtle?" Krystyna questioned.

"Yes, of course I can, madam. The asking price is $245.00."

Valuing Giovanna's opinion, Krystyna asked her what she thought, even though she already suspected that it was more valuable. "What do you think, Giovanna?"

"I think it is a little too high."

Krystyna turned back to the vendor and inquired, "Is there room for negotiation here? The price seems a bit steep for a flea market item." She wanted him to come down even though she knew it should be priced higher.

The vendor looked pensively for a few seconds, rubbed his chin and finally blurted out, "I can come down a few dollars."

"Are you saying only a few dollars?" Giovanna asked.

The vendor replied, "That's about right!" He looked away for a moment pretending to be disinterested in making the sale.

The two women looked questioningly at each other and in the same breath said, "It's not worth it. Thank you anyway." They then turned on their heels and started to walk away, with their strollers rolling on before them.

The vendor held back for a few moments, as the shoppers walked away a bit. He was a little annoyed with these two ladies at this point. *Everyone wants everything for nothing these days, he thought.* In a sheepish voice, he called out to them, "Wait, ladies. I will come down to $225.00 even." He wanted to make this sale, especially after all the explaining he had to do.

Giovanna and Krystyna looked at each other a bit puzzled. Giovanna nudged Krystyna with her elbow and gave her a sly wink with one eye. With a quick reply Krystyna said, "That sounds good to me. I'll take it."

Giovanna intercepted with, "No taxes and we'd like it wrapped up."

In a whisper, Krystyna said, "Aren't you pushing it a bit? It IS basically a flea market!"

The vendor, wanting this sale, muttered, "I'll go along with your request as it is a delicate sale. I can honestly say though, you didn't make my day! You are two tough ladies. I hope this turtle brings you good luck because I certainly don't feel that it brought me any. I practically gave it away," he grumbled under his breath.

Krystyna and Giovanna took their precious purchase and sauntered off feeling satisfaction from a deal well maneuvered. They didn't walk too casually at this point for fear that the vendor might change his mind. The deal was done and payment made, but they were taking no chances. They pushed their strollers along at a quick pace and were anxious to get back into their car and out of there.

As they walked back to the car, Giovanna said, "With a little TLC and some polish you can resell this piece and maybe double your money. Or better yet, it would be an excellent antique with which to start your antique business you always talk about."

"Yes, I know," Krystyna said. "But I think I want to research this piece a bit and try to find out where it was made and what it is made out of. My curiosity is getting the best of me. I want to know what those markings mean, if anything. They must have meant something to someone, perhaps to the person who carved it. Do you think I have a chance at finding out anything? Wouldn't you want to know these things? Or do you think I am getting carried away with this?"

"I don't think this is silly or a wild goose chase at all! Giovanna said. "It sure wouldn't hurt to try and find out things about it. It might prove to be a learning experience for all of us. The worse that could come of it would be that you ended up keeping it for yourself."

As they continued to walk toward their car, Krystyna clutched the turtle close to her bosom as if to shelter and protect it. She had one hand on the stroller and the other wrapped around the turtle.

"Now that's a little ridiculous, Krys," Giovanna snickered. Don't you think you should put that turtle into that big tote bag of yours?" Then she added, "How about lunch?"

Krystyna dropped the turtle into her canvas bag and placed the bag into the stroller pouch. She felt that she had a rather successful day shopping.

With their kids in their little booster seats, they lunched at a small café in the Commons. The Commons was what High Bridge called its downtown area, where everyone gathered to do their business, shop or take advantage of the wonderful restaurants. Afterwards as they silently rode home with their purchase secure in the car, the two women glanced at each other and burst out laughing. "Kaz is really going to think I am a foolish spendthrift," Krystyna blurted out, "he always tells me I bring home other people's "junk." But I really don't care what he thinks. I know a great purchase when I see one."

"Let him have his cynical fun, Krys. You know a good thing when you see it. If it gives you some small pleasure to own it, so be it. Besides, Kaz should have more confidence in your ability to secure good antiques. He is a customs inspector. I'm sure he sees some pretty strange articles coming in and out of the country. He should be use to you bringing home things. You told me many times that you have a cellar full of antiques and collectibles for when you open your store someday."

"I certainly do have quite an assortment of antiques that I have been accumulating over the years. I even acquired some of them before I even met Kaz. Some of my things are quite expensive. For instance, I have a circular pedestal table with leather inlay valued at $4,200, an armoire with a beveled mirror priced at $1,575, a gorgeous oak roll-top desk valued at $2,100, a magnificent redwood étagère for $725. I also acquired some pieces of lesser value like an oval mirror for $280, a marble pedestal for $500, a teak music box for $255 and a blue Tiffany lamp for $395. And that is not mentioning all my nostalgic items. So he knew what he was in for when he married me. He knows I am obsessed with my collection of rare and odd things. He doesn't really mind though. He tells me to pursue my dreams and do whatever I want with them. I'm sure he will stand by me when I really do get serious about opening up my antique store someday."

"That's nice to hear, Krys," Giovanna said. "I guess we are both lucky to have understanding and considerate husbands. Not too many women are that fortunate."

As months went by Krystyna started to pay more attention to her "turtle fantasy." She was getting Kaz nervous with her obsession with this turtle. Kaz, being an inspector and interested in wood making, decided to take a closer look at the wooden turtle to see what was captivating his wife so much. After examining the turtle Kaz had to agree with Krystyna. This was certainly an odd one. It almost appeared as if it was once alive. He laughed to himself. As he looked at the protective shell it seemed to be covered with unusually-shaped scutes. When he turned it over he noticed that the bottom or the plastron was assembled very deliberately into eight even shapes with some very odd symbols on them. The person who made this was on a mission for sure. As he was about to put the turtle down where Krystyna had placed it, he heard a knock on the back door.

His neighbor, Nick, was at the door. "Hi, Kaz. I hope I'm not interrupting you. Do you have a few minutes to spare? I don't want to bother you."

"Sure, come in, Nick, You never bother me. I actually welcome the intrusion. I need a change of pace right now," Kaz replied. "I was just examining more closely this turtle my wife purchased recently and I couldn't help but notice how much weight it was. But I must get away from it for a while, because I am getting engrossed in it like my wife."

"Let me feel the weight of it, Kaz," Nick requested. He took hold of it very carefully and turned it over and back. "You are right. This is a rather heavy piece. Its looks are deceiving to the eye." Nick handed the turtle back to Kaz who placed it carefully on the mantle where Krystyna had placed it.

"You know, Kaz, I noticed that you do fine carpentry work. I have some space in my New York office that needs some expert refurbishing. Before I contact an outside contractor, I was wondering if you would be interested in taking a look and giving me your opinion. I have been putting this project of mine off for far too long. I think it is about time to finish it."

Kaz asked, "What exactly do you have in mind?"

"I would like either a library or a private conference room with detailed bookshelves and some fine furniture in the extra space I have there. Maybe you can give me your opinion of several other things I would like to change or add as well." Nick explained.

Kaz was thrilled with the request and said, "I'd be delighted. Not that I can promise you my undivided attention, as I do have a day job you know. What is the time allotment you were thinking of? I really only have weekends for extra projects."

Nick continued, "Give me a day when you can come into the city with me so I can show you my office and the area in question. Money is no object. But I'm sure that you will keep my best interests at heart."

Just then, Krystyna interrupted with, "Okay guys, do you want to eat supper tonight?"

"Okay, Okay! Give us a break! We are talking about something important," Kaz said.

"I'll talk to you again about this Nick. I'll let you know when I have a free day. Good night!"

"**Buona sera**, (Good night), you two"

"**Buon Appetit**! (Enjoy the meal)"

"**Do widzenia**!" (Bye, see you) Kaz replied laughing. "And **smacznego!**" (Good appetite) Kaz added. Both liked having fun with their ethnic replies. Krystyna always got a kick out of their odd word exchanges.

The next morning, Krystyna called her friend, Giovanna to ask her advice about opening an antique shop. She couldn't sleep all night after Giovanna planted the seed in her head. She was all fired up about it and ready to start her pursuit of her dream.

"Good Morning, Giovanna. You got me all fired up the other day about my desire to open a shop of my own. I was toying with the idea of opening an antique shop in my garage. I already have quite a few things that I've purchased over the past few years. I think I have enough to set up shop and get started with my own business."

"Well, Krys, if it were me, I wouldn't want my shop in my house. I think it would be better to look for a store somewhere in town in a good spot. I know you are trying to be economical but I don't feel that is the way to go with this. As a matter of fact, I saw a small store for rent on the boulevard the last time I was in town. I think it might be perfect for your shop. It seemed to have a good location to me. A lot of people were passing around it. I think you should have a look at it. You might be pleasantly surprised."

Krystyna getting excited said, "Oh, Giovanna, would you go with me, please? I kind of like your idea. I don't want to tell Kaz about this until I am sure it is the right place. Besides, he is going to ask me what I propose to do with our son, Stefan. But I already have that part figured out. I could hire a nanny for him or put him into nursery school. In another year he will be five years old and ready for kindergarten. But I have put that in the back of my mind for now. So, will you go with me?"

"Okay, tomorrow I'll pack up Francesca and meet you at your house. By the way, are you planning on asking me to work with or for you, or would you like me as a business partner?" Giovanna questioned.

"Well, as a matter of fact, I was definitely going to ask you to be my partner, but I wanted to see if I could get the business started first," Krystyna muttered. "I think we will work well together and work wonders in our business."

"I am so glad to hear that, as being in business would be right up my alley, Krys," Giovanna answered. "I think we would make a great team!"

"Leave things up to me for now. I'll talk to my husband and get back to you about further details," Krystyna said.

The next day before Krystyna left the house she knew she had to tell Kaz about this venture of hers. So she just came out and told him after breakfast. She figured it was better to be direct rather than beat around the bush, as it were.

"Kaz, Honey, I want to run something by you." Krystyna was pacing back and forth from the sink to the table in a nervous state.

"Oh, my goodness! When you call me "Honey" I know it is something big," Kaz said. "Anyway, I thought something was bothering you for a while. You have been very fidgety of late, if that is the correct word to described your actions. Ever since you bought that turtle you have been acting very pensive. Okay, sweetheart, **O co chodzi?**" ("What is it?").

"Kaz, it is nothing serious, it is just...it is just...that I have to ask something of you," Krystyna stuttered as she bent over to kiss Kaz on the forehead.

"You know you can always come to me with anything, Krysia," as he used his pet name for her. **"Choc tutaj!** (Come here!) Sit next to me and calm down. You are a nervous wreck! Now, what is it?" He hugged her tightly as she sat down next to him.

"Well, Kaz, remember when I talked to you when we were first married about opening an antique store? Well, the time has come for me to do just that! I have plenty of things to start out with and besides, the "stuff" we will finally get out of the basement and attic should make you happy. You always say I am cluttering up the house. There, I finally said it!"

"Okay, **"powoli!"** (Slow down!) Hold it! Take one thing at a time! If this is going to make you happy, then I will not stand in your way. I will give you a chance to make a go of it and I will back you up one hundred per cent. I know what a gifted dealer you are and will be. I always told you to follow your dreams and I knew this day would come. Now, tell me everything from the beginning - slowly. Relax; you know I am always on your side."

Krystyna felt relieved at last and explained that she had thought about opening a store in their garage. But Giovanna's advice was that one should not put a business in their home.

Krystyna continued, "Giovanna saw a store for rent downtown on the Commons that would make a perfect shop for my antiques. I would like to go and check it out. I also hinted to Giovanna that I would want her to be my business partner."

"So far I like what I am hearing. You sound like you thought this out in great detail. I think you should pursue this change in careers at this time in your life, Krys."

"Okay then; I am going down with Giovanna in a little while to check out this store she saw. If it looks good I would want you to come with me the following day and look it over to see what you think," Krystyna said.

"Okay," Kaz answered, "You go with Giovanna and look the store over while at the same time checking the area out around it. Then I'll go with you and we will see about this 'dream of yours'. We had better inform Nick about this as well since his wife will be involved directly with your business."

"I'll tell Giovanna to explain it all to Nick. I don't think there will be a problem. Giovanna is pretty much her own person and Nick allows her to do her thing."

Krystyna kissed Kaz and thanked him for believing in her. She told him she would make him proud and be a successful business woman.

Krystyna and Giovanna drove downtown in record time. It is a wonder they didn't get a ticket for speeding. Their enthusiasm was getting the best of them. When they stopped in front of the store, they got so excited. It really looked like the perfect spot for her business. Unfortunately the owner was not there then so they had to go home a little disappointed. They did, however, walk around the building to see how big it was from the outside. To their surprise they found a large parking area in the back for their customers to use. Then they spent several minutes peeking into the front window to see how the inside looked. It was all they had hoped it would be – so far. When they got home they told each other that they would keep in touch.

It was late afternoon when Kaz came barreling through the kitchen door. Krys couldn't wait to corner him. When Kaz saw his anxious wife he said, **"Co robimy?"** (What are we up to?)

Krystyna was very excited. Kaz could see that by her demeanor. "Kaz we went down there today, but the shop was closed at that time. But we looked around the outside and peered into the front window. I think this store will work for us. Since we couldn't make contact with the shopkeeper, I thought maybe you and I could go down now and see if it is open. I know you are tired, but what do you think? Could you force yourself to come with me? I am feeling so anxious about this. I don't want to let the opportunity slip through my fingers, as they say."

"Okay, okay, my love, let's ask Giovanna and Nick to watch Stefan and we can go and check YOUR place out," Kaz said affectionately. "In fact, maybe Giovanna would want to go with us, since she may be your partner. Nick will watch the kids. Or maybe we will all go together. Let's go over there and see if they are in agreement with a quick run downtown."

"I am so lucky to have you for a husband, Kaz. You at least listen to my ideas and give me a chance to spread my wings," Krystyna said with much affection in her tone of voice. "I am so excited about this!

I cannot tell you how much I love you for this trust you place in me. I will make you proud. You will see!"

After hearing all the details, Giovanna and Nick loved the idea and decided to join the Safenskis on their jaunt downtown. This was another turning point in their friendship. Not many friends will stop what they are immediately doing to help out another friend. But Krystyna, Kaz, Nick and Giovanna were more than friends; they were close like family members.

So, they dressed the kids and off they went. When they got to the town they got a parking place right in front of the store. That was their first sign of Good Luck! Kaz liked the location because it was right in the center of town where there would be a lot of pedestrian traffic. It seemed to be a safe area and the street lights lit it up well. They all checked it out from the outside again and seemed pleased with their findings. The men were glad to see the back lot paved. That was a plus!

Kaz said, "I think your store has the workings of a potential success story. So far, I like what I see. What do you think, Nick? You are the legal mind in our midst."

"Yes, I kind of like this place. It has a certain warmth about it. But we have to find out all the particulars about the building, the rent, the insurance, etc." Nick added. This will happen all in good time. And if it is meant to be, everything will fall into place."

The minute they went inside, Krystyna and Giovanna fell in love with their surroundings. There was a beautiful entry way leading to a store that stretched out long and far back about the length of two living rooms. A semi-circular counter extended around the right side wall about in the center of the room. There was ample floor space for her antiques and a lot of wall space for other items. Krystyna lit up with excitement as she already had her mind racing with ideas to decorate and spruce up her shop. Giovanna was ecstatic!

The owner came out from the back as Kaz and Krys and Giovanna and Nick walked in further. The children were following along behind not touching anything.

"What can I do for you fine people?" the owner asked.

Kaz answered first, "Well, we are very interested in renting your store. My wife and her friend are thinking of opening up an antique store which they have always wanted to do. Your store seems to be quite perfect for them. We've checked out the outside; liked what we saw and also like the inside very much. Can you tell us what the monthly rent is?"

"The rent is $1800 a month, not counting electricity use. You can paint; decorate it up with drapes, blinds or whatever you wish. It has a new hardwood floor which I just had installed. That should be to your liking," the owner said.

"That sounds reasonable," Kaz said. "Give us a day or two to talk this over. I'll give you a deposit to hold it for us. Would that be okay?"

"Fine!" said the proprietor. "I will await your reply."

Kaz wrote out a check for $500 to hold him to a possible deal. "Good day to you," Kaz said and they all left.

Since they were in town, they decided to go to one of the local restaurants and have a quick, casual supper together. They were able to chat more about their new business venture and weigh the pros and cons a bit more. It proved to be a very insightful evening.

As they rode home, the women couldn't stop chattering about their new-found store. They hardly came up for air. But the men allowed them their happy venting time and let them explode with enthusiasm. They, too, were extremely happy for them.

☙

The Commons, as downtown High Bridge is called, is a laid back area with all the essential stores and businesses a town should have. The High Bridge Library, Town Hall bank, restaurants, stores and other buildings completed the town's main street. Most events that took place were usually at "The Commons." People who lived there understood the significance of "The Commons." It was THE gathering place for anyone who was part of this town.

A Saturday morning in the late summer in High Bridge is just grand. The summer sun, though still very hot, seems to cast long shadows hinting of autumn's arrival. The leaves just slightly begin to change color as if teasing Mother Nature. This county of Hunterdon in New Jersey is a wonderful rural section of real estate!

Krystyna woke up first in the Safenski household as she was an early riser. As she looked outside the leaves were beginning to fall from the huge oak trees. She went down to the kitchen and began preparing a delightful breakfast for her family. Kaz was awakened minutes later by the aroma of freshly brewed coffee. In a matter of seconds he was in the kitchen to enjoy his first cup.

Kaz greeted Krystyna with a cheery Good Morning as he sipped his coffee.

"Dzien Dobry, Kaz!" (Good Morning, Kaz), did you sleep well?" Krystyna gave him a sweet kiss.

"I did. In fact it was one of the best night's I've had in weeks. It must be the fall weather coming close. I always sleep better in the cooler weather. The smell of the falling leaves gives me a very nostalgic feeling. It also revs up my appetite for some of your homemade baked goods. What did you make for breakfast today?"

How do homemade apple walnut muffins sound? It is one of my own recipes and I know you will like them as they are loaded with cinnamon which you love."

"Bring them to me, my dear. I knew I smelled something delicious when I was coming down the stairs. You never cease to amaze me."

Krystyna said, "I'm glad you had a good night's sleep because you said you were going to talk to Nick. So at least you will feel well-rested. Why don't you call Nick now? It is after nine o'clock and they are usually up early."

With that said, Kaz began to dial the Gardina home. The phone rang several times and Kaz was about to hang up when someone picked it up. It was Giovanna and she sounded quite chipper.

"Buongiorno!" (Good Morning")

"Buongiorno, Giovanna. It's Kaz. I was wondering if I might talk to your husband for a few minutes. Is he up yet?"

"Are you kidding? He is already washed and dressed as we speak. He had his breakfast and is now raring to go. Let me get him for you."

Several seconds later Nick was on the other end of the line. "Hello, Kaz! I hope all is well with you. What can I do for you?"

"I wanted to pick your legal brain a bit," Kaz said.

"I thought you were calling to tell me you had some time to go into the city with me."

"Well I do have this weekend free, so we could do that, if you want. But first let me run a few things by you," Kaz said.

Nick obliged with, "Go right ahead and ask away."

"You know my wife wants to open the store and have Giovanna be her partner. Could you help us out with the legal stuff?"

"Yes, of course I will," Nick added. "Giovanna was trying to explain that to me last night, but I was so tired that I pretty much tuned her out. I'll do whatever I can to help; you know that."

"Well, I want to know what to do about the lease for the store, theft and fire insurance and anything else I should be aware of," Kaz said. I'd like your opinion and your legal assistance. Since they are going to be partners in this endeavor I think we should talk about this."

"I'll tell you what. Why don't I pick you up in a half hour? I have to go into the city to my office for a while. We could talk as we drive into the city."

"Great, Nick. I'll be ready. Thank you!"

As the men drove down the Turnpike Nick told Kaz he was glad he asked him to represent the women, and there would be no cost. He would look over the lease and advise him on how much theft and fire insurance to get. Kaz was grateful and relieved that he had someone he could trust and rely on. It was nice to have a lawyer for a friend.

The Gardina Law Firm was uptown on Third Avenue and 52nd Street. Nick rented the entire 16th Floor. Kaz was impressed with the location and very surprised when he walked off the elevator into a plush office. The reception area was painted in a cornflower blue with a lot of silver accents around the room. The crown molding around the ceiling created a sophisticated atmosphere. The hardwood floor with an octagonal accent rug in the middle of the floor completed the décor.

"This is quite an eye catching entrance, Nick!" Kaz said.

"It took a lot of time and effort but I finally have it the way I want it. Giovanna helped a lot. You know decorating is her field. She enjoyed having a free hand at purchasing whatever it took to make this come to fruition. Can you imagine a woman having free reign to buy anything she wants? Those two, Krystyna and Giovanna should have a blast setting up their new store. Dare we trust them with our money?" Both men laughed.

Nick continued, "Follow me down the hall into my office area. The office on the left is my secretary's, Dena Ling. Mine is across the hall and is much larger in size. The conference room I want you to work on for me is at the end of the hallway on the opposite side from my office. Come on. I will show you the project I want you to tackle for me."

"I know you were robbed a while ago. You know, Nick, it is hard to fathom how thieves got into this building and into your offices. They have guts even attempting to break-in in this part of town!"

"Thieves have ways, Kaz, as they have proven here." Kaz followed Nick down the spacious hallway. "Here is the room I want you to update for me. What do you suggest? Look it over and give me your honest opinion. Now I need YOUR expertise, my friend."

Kaz looked around and saw that the room had a lot of positive possibilities. The huge skyscraper windows made for great atmosphere for a conference room for guests and clients. He told Nick that on the wall opposite the windows he would construct book shelves, open ones and closed ones, and maybe even include a built-in a wet bar. He suggested buying an oval mahogany table with plush arm chairs for comfort, enough to seat about 12 people comfortably. Nick was taking to Kaz's suggestions.

"I like what I am hearing, Kaz. You have great ideas. I knew you would do well by me. I would like to have a hardwood floor as I have in the reception area with another area carpet under the conference table."

"Do you need a safe built in anywhere? That far corner would be a great spot for it."

"You know, Kaz, after the robbery I was telling Dena that I should have some safer place to store my files and valuables, especially if we are on vacation or out of town on business. I purchased a large safe from the Data Media Safe Company. That costs about $11,500, but I feel that is money well spent. I also told my secretary that I would hire another person as a receptionist so that she is not here alone, so I am looking for someone."

"The far corner looks like a good spot for your safe. That won't be difficult to do, Nick. I can do the carpentry prep work and then you can fit the safe you buy right into it. It should blend in perfectly with the wall. I can always fancy it up for you with some decorative woodwork.

"I never thought I would need a security system, but now I am considering adding that as well. I have contacted several companies to get estimates on burglar-proofing my office. So before you start your work, Kaz, I will have that installed. Then you can come and go at your leisure to do your work."

"Everything sounds okay with me. We will go into more detail regarding the kind of wood, paneling and door hardware you prefer. Your style and your preferences are important to complete this job well. Living next door to each other has its advantages, as we can talk things over as we need to."

With that settled the men left for home. But Nick detoured to Little Italy for some Italian food. They had a great lunch. These two men were so opposite in nature yet their personalities clicked. They enjoyed a fine Italian meal and of course some Italian pastries for dessert. Nick had his favorite "Baba" while Kaz indulged in a cannolli. They even stopped by Ferrara's, a famous pastry shop in Little Italy, to pick up some Italian specialties for their wives and children.

❧

When Kaz walked in the door back in High Bridge, Krystyna couldn't wait to find out what kind of office Nick had and how he could help them with their legal things. She was a human question box.

"Nick is going to represent us when we take over the store. So now we can rest easy that all will be on the up and up. He will look out for our interests and check out the insurance, and fire & theft angles for us as well. And he is more than pleased that Giovanna will be your business partner. He feels you two will work well together. By the way, what did you do all day while I was gone, Krys?"

"Giovanna and I took the kids and went to the Commons to walk around a bit. It was such a beautiful day that I couldn't bear to stay inside. I thought Stefan could use the fresh air. We passed by the store and the rental sign was off the door. Do you think we can give the owner an answer soon, maybe tomorrow?"

Kaz said, "As soon as I finalize the details with Nick's help, we will call the owner and set up a meeting to sign the lease. Then we can get the insurances settled and you can start decorating and setting up shop. We have a lot of work to do, you know."

"I know that!" Krystyna retorted. "I have so many wonderful ideas for that store, Kaz. I cannot wait to get in there with Giovanna and start setting it up with our special touches. With my ideas and her professional decorating ability, we should be able to set up a fine shop, one we can all be proud of. This is going to be so exciting!"

"You'll be in there before you know it. Have you thought about what you will name the store?"

"We were tossing around a lot of name combinations, but the one Giovanna and I came up with is, "Safe-Gard Fine Antiques". What do you think of that name?" Krystyna asked. "It is made from both of our last names, SAFENSKI and GARDINA. Since we will be partners we thought it best to have a name that would please us both."

"That sounds pretty original. It kind of grows on you as you repeat it. I like it! We will have to register the name so it becomes official. I guess I will call the store owner tomorrow and tell him we will definitely be renting the store," Kaz said. "Nick and Giovanna should be alright with that decision. I think Nick has all his paperwork done for us."

How do we register our name?" Krystyna asked.

We have to register the name with the U.S. Patent and Trademark Office. Nick and I were talking about that last week. He said to go on line on the website www.uspto.gov because it can be filed quicker that way."

"Krys asked, "Is there anything special they have to know because I will go over it with my partner, Giovanna."

"Nick said, you have to sent them a description of your trademark, tell them when or how it is used, and tell them what classification your business should be registered under. Then they will want a drawing of some sort of your trademark name and, of course, the registration fee of $900.00. That should do it."

"That doesn't sound too complicated. I'll tell Giovanna about it and we can proceed with the registration. I am getting really excited now, Kaz. I am going to start gathering all my antiques I have stashed away in our attic, basement and garage at home. I must clean them all up and get them ready for display. I know Giovanna will help me; so it shouldn't take me too long to get organized. Do you think you and Nick can transport all of the antiques I have in our Explorer and Nick's van? Some of my furniture pieces are rather large and expensive and have to be handled very carefully."

"We should be able to manage ourselves," Kaz answered, as long as you trust us with them."

"You know I trust you implicitly. Now, I know you had something to eat in New York with Nick, so I didn't prepare any dinner. I fed Stefan earlier so he is okay. I will eat something light and then maybe we can have some coffee and dessert."

"**Dziekuje!**" ("Thank You"). That would be fine, Krys. I'll freshen up a bit and make a few phone calls, one to the store owner and the other to Nick to tell him to finalize things for us."

The store owner was thrilled to hear from Kaz. He knew they were fine people and he was glad to get the store rented. After Kaz hung up the phone, he immediately used his speed dial to phone Nick and tell him the store was officially rented and it now belonged to their wives. All that was left was for the four of them to go down to the store tomorrow and transact the necessary business.

Chapter Eight

The Safe-Gard Fine Antique Store of High Bridge was on its way to opening day. Kaz and Krystyna and Giovanna finalized the deal with the store owner with Nick at their side for reassurance. Everything went well and now they were ready to begin decorating and filling up their store. Kaz spent many nights and weekends building new shelves and display cases, hanging new light fixtures, and so forth, while Krystyna with Giovanna's interior decorating skills, designed the storefront window display. Giovanna suggested purchasing a multi-colored octagonal area rug for the floor in front of the center counter as an accent piece. Krystyna loved the idea! They both felt that it would add to the ambience of the store and focus the attention on the center of the store where most of the expensive items would be placed. Things were shaping up and it wouldn't be long now before they could have their grand opening.

"I think we are almost ready to start bringing my antiques from the house, Kaz," Krystyna said. The sooner you and Nick transfer my antiques, the sooner Giovanna and I can start placing them and pricing them. It is going to take us about two weeks to get everything set up and ready for opening day. Maybe you can start this weekend."

"What do you plan on doing with your son, my dear?" Kaz asked warmly.

"I already signed him up in the Little Genius Nursery School in town. Giovanna is also putting Francesca in the school. I'm sure they will be fine. I have done my research on the school and it comes highly recommended. They are both very bright for their age and I think they will do well. We will take them in every morning from 9:00 A.M. to 12 Noon on our way to the store. When they are dismissed we will be there to pick them up and bring them to the store for the afternoon. That should work out alright. We certainly can keep an eye on them the rest of the afternoon. With the large back room we have in the store, we can bring some of their toys over and that should entertain them. Besides it will only be for one year; then they start Kindergarten."

"I guess that will be okay," Kaz said. "We will try it out and see how things go. If they become bothersome, maybe Nick and I can pitch in. Before we know it they will be starting elementary school. I'm going to go now and pick up Nick and start transporting your antiques."

It took the men about ten hours to pack up the van and Explorer and move everything from the house to the store. They had to make several trips. Kaz was glad to see all the stuff Krystyna had accumulated over a few years vacating the house. Now he would have more room for some of his things.

The Precision Sign Company was finishing the installation of the awning with the store name embossed on it just as Kaz and Nick arrived with the last load of antiques. They were impressed with the design and royal blue color of the awning. Against the bright white exterior siding, the awning was made even more attractive by the fancy lettering they chose for the name, *Safe-Gard Fine Antiques.* The sidewalk sign they ordered and designed themselves for the front was a scroll-shaped placard with a gold key slanted across the center that fit in perfect with the town's motif and with their store name idea of safeguarding their merchandise. The women were proud of their creation and of their trademark they put on the placard, a key, to signify safety and security.

"The sign looks great!" Nick said. "The girls did a terrific job, as I knew they would. I know they put a lot of thought and planning into it and the result shows their hard work."

Kaz replied, "Those two work well together and manage to complete everything they start. They have such novel ideas! We are lucky to have talented wives, don't you think?"

"I must agree with you there, Kaz. We are two lucky men!"

Everything was falling into place rather nicely. Krystyna couldn't believe there weren't any problems of major importance and she was grateful. With all the things finally in the store and set up all that was left to do was add some finishing touches. They would add some fresh floral arrangements for accent, put some potpourri around, and maybe light a fragrant candle on the counter. Their ideas were limitless so you could expect anything to pop up for the Grand Opening.

Giovanna and Krystyna were busy arranging things in the store, using their decorative talents, and applying their final touches. They were so glad Stefan and Francesca were behaving as they always did when they played together. The two mothers didn't have to worry about the two tots.

As evening drew near, the finishing touches were nearing completion. The store looked terrific! Every piece seemed to be placed well and the sophisticated accents provided by Giovanna, like the hanging drapery in the storefront window and the silk floral accents in the showcases added a warm ambience to the store. The two women took one last look, hugged each other and burst out crying from happiness.

"Can you believe we did this?" Krystyna asked.

"I knew we would. It was just a matter of when, where and how." Giovanna said.

"Thank you for making that special place for my 'lucky' turtle sculpture in the showcase behind our counter. It will surely bring us good luck, as it seems to have done so far," Krys said. "I am glad it has a central place where everyone coming in can't help but notice it."

"Do you know something?" Giovanna replied. "I think you are right. I attribute our good fortune to that turtle of yours. Now I am glad you insisted on purchasing it, even though at the time I thought you were overdoing it a bit by coddling it and studying it."

"Do you know something, Giovanna? I somehow feel that I am not finished with that turtle yet. I am still mesmerized by the markings on it and its overall style."

The two friends laughed and agreed to meet again tomorrow to talk things over and decide on a Grand Opening Day.

Sunday morning in High Bridge was always first and foremost a holy day, one in which most families went to church, whatever their house of worship might be. Just as they did every Sunday since they met, the Safenski and Gardina families met at the eleven o'clock Mass at St. Joseph Church. They always started their week off with God's blessing upon them, because they still held tightly to their roots and their upbringing. Afterwards the two families made their way downtown to the High Bridge Café to enjoy a hearty brunch and pleasant conversation. They were lucky their friendship clicked right from the beginning when they first moved next to each other.

"Before we have our Grand Opening I think we should do some advertising." Krystyna said. "I want to put an ad in the Hunterdon County Democrat Newspaper in the Special Features Section."

"Giovanna added, "I think the Local News Section *Around the Town* would be another part of the paper to consider. Since we are residents of the town with a new business that should enhance the town, I think a lot of people will take notice."

"That is all good and well, but I would also put a blurb into the business section as well," Nick offered.

"Isn't there a local magazine called the Hunterdon Life that features new businesses and upcoming events in the town?" Kaz asked.

"You are right, darling," Krys added. "I have seen that magazine in the beauty salon a few times. I usually peruse it to see what is currently going on in town. So I am sure a lot of other people do the same."

Kaz said, "Well, I think you should do all of those things. The more advertising we do and the more exposure we get, will benefit our grand opening and our business."

Giovanna interjected, "Krystyna and I will get right on that tomorrow. We want to have the grand opening before the school year begins while the town is still into end of summer activity. A lot of people shop here at this time of year."

Krystyna was getting really excited. As they drove home she was talking like a chatterbox. Kaz had to stop her and quiet her down. He didn't want to squash her enthusiasm. He simply wanted her to be calm and think things out carefully. Krys got the message and started winding down a bit as they arrived home.

The next morning, Giovanna called Krys with the good news that she wrote down some information for their advertising adventures. Krys was all ears and told Giovanna that she too was up quite late penning her thoughts as well. They decided to go down to the store and make some calls to the papers and magazine. Giovanna mentioned that Nick suggested they try to get an ad on the internet also. He said there was a sight called www.finestantiques.com. This ad campaign of theirs was turning out to be very interesting and challenging and they loved every minute of the excitement. After some phone work, the appropriate contacts were made to place all the ads in on time. The women even contacted a local TV station to see if they wanted to cover the opening. It looked like the grand opening was going to get off on time, with no glitches.

Now all that was left to do was make a guest list. Besides the media advertising, they had to sit down together and make a list of people like the mayor, the city council members, other local business entrepreneurs in the town, and their own family members and friends. Before they knew it the invited guest list was about two hundred in number and counting. They loved every bit of enjoyment this was bringing! This was a labor of love.

The Grand Opening

Two weeks later on a beautiful Saturday in High Bridge, the Grand Opening Day had finally come. Krystyna, Kaz and Stefan arrived first around 7:00 A.M. Several minutes later Nick, Giovanna and Francesca came. A local caterer from High Bridge was hired to bring hot and cold h'oredouveres, soft drinks, desserts and coffee and tea for their guests. The Party Time Place was providing the decorations like balloons for the kids, and the paper goods with an autumn theme, even though it wasn't quite fall. The women even purchased small key chains with their store name engraved on them to distribute to all guests and visitors as a memento of the day's festivities and in keeping with their 'key' theme.

Before they realized it, it was time to open the door. Hundreds of people filed in and out of the store all day long to celebrate the Grand Opening of the Safe-Gard Fine Antique Store. Most were impressed not only with the store's appearance and its wonderful merchandise, but also with the warm and friendly reception they received. Sharing the goodies that were offered made for great hospitality. This kind of atmosphere was sure to jump start a tremendous business venture for

Krystyna and Giovanna. So many people they knew came by to support them, but there were a lot of strangers there as well. Their advertising campaign paid off, as was seen by the throngs of people coming in.

In mid-afternoon, Charlie and Dena Ling arrived, as they were invited guests of Nick and Giovanna. Nick had to invite his secretary and her husband. Krystyna and Kaz finally got a chance to meet Dena and Charlie Ling. They had heard so much about them from Nick and Giovanna. Nick brought them over to Krystyna and said, "I would like to introduce you to the most efficient secretary in the world – MINE – Dena Ling and her husband, Charlie."

Krystyna replied warmly, "It is so nice to finally meet you both. Nick often talks about you when we are together."

"I hope it is all good things he talks about," Dena said.

"Yes, he definitely says only praiseworthy things," Krys said. "Now that I've met you, I can see why he considers you a close friend as well as a loyal colleague."

"Thank you," Charlie and Dena said simultaneously. "We are so happy to have been invited to such a wonderful event!" Dena added. "This must be so exciting for all of you!"

"Feel free to browse at our antiques. I hope you enjoy the day with us. Help yourself to some food, too," Krystyna said. "We have catered some wonderful appetizers and such."

Dena and Charlie walked around the store and were enjoying the excitement of the day. Dena was one to take a close look at things she found interesting. She appreciated old and preserved things. Her family, too, had a lot of heirlooms that were passed down from generations. So she knew the value of some of the pieces.

The crowd of people kept flowing in and out of the shop. Krys and Giovanna were thrilled with the response. Everyone seemed to be enjoying the day. They also were happy that they sold several big pieces as well. The day was turning out to be profitable in more ways than one. The media even showed up in response to the ads and they were getting more coverage than they ever expected.

After about an hour, Krystyna heard some loud excitement in the center of the store. When she walked over to see what it was about, she saw Dena and Charlie staring at the wall behind the main counter. Giovanna and Nick ran over as well.

"Is anything wrong, Dena?" Krys asked nervously.

"What is the matter, Dena?" Giovanna inquired. "You are as pale as a ghost and you are shaking!"

"I can't believe what I am looking at! At first I thought I was seeing things," Dena said dumbfounded. "That TURTLE, in the showcase, may I take a closer look at it?" Her eyes were tearing up and she could hardly see. Charlie offered her his handkerchief.

"I don't see why not," Krystyna answered. "Why does it interest you so much? And why are you so upset?"

"Well, you see, it looks like the one that was stolen from me a while ago. My husband, Charlie, bought a turtle sculpture for me on one of his business trips to Myanmar, formerly called Burma in Southeast Asia," Dena replied. "Nick can tell you how attached I was to it. I had it enthroned on my credenza behind my desk in my office for all to see when they came in. It was what I thought was 'my lucky charm'! You see it was my tenth anniversary gift from Charlie, so it held a lot of sentiment for me. And now to see it here, of all places, is a real shock!"

Nick chimed in with his comments. "Gosh Dena, can you believe this? Talk about fate! Maybe some of our other things that were stolen from the law office will show up here or close by. How in the world did it end up here?"

"Let me get it down for you. By all means, take a closer look at it," Krystyna said. Krys went behind the counter and reached up, opened the glass case and took down the turtle carefully. She slowly lowered it to the hands of Kaz who passed it over to Dena.

Dena looked at it very thoroughly, flipping it over several times. She rubbed it tenderly as if to say, *I've found you!* Then she said with a quiver in her voice, "Charlie, I think it is MY turtle! There are no two teak sculptures that are alike usually and it doesn't look like a replica. How did it ever get here? And what are the odds of me getting to know these people here in High Bridge? This is a small world indeed."

"Please take your time, Dena," Krystyna said. "Maybe you can tell us a thing or two about it. I have wondered about it since the day I acquired it. It has intrigued me from the moment I set eyes on it, just as I see it has its hold on you as well."

Charlie couldn't contain himself. After checking it out he said, "I believe this is the teak turtle I purchased for my wife in Myanmar last year. I would know it anywhere, as I studied it very intensely before I bought it. The markings on it are so unique and very unusual that it definitely is the ONE I bought. There is not another like it anywhere." He continued to coddle it as if it were a precious pet.

Krystyna then said, "I have a lot of questions about that turtle for you, but I have no time today because of our Grand Opening. Would you be willing to come to our house tomorrow? Since it is Sunday, I presume you can come. Nick and Giovanna will bring you over. We will have an early dinner and discuss THIS TURTLE!"

"We would like that very much," Charlie said. "I am anxious to tell you what I know about it and eager to find out how you happened to get it. First I must calm my wife down as she is very excited right now. I will fill you in on everything I know." Charlie walked over to the beverages and got a cup of tea for Dena. He knew how hot tea always soothed her.

"Great!" Krystyna said. "Kaz and I will be looking forward to having you over our house. You may bring your children if you like. I know they are older than ours but if they want to come, they are welcome."

"Thank you, we will definitely be back to see you tomorrow then," Dena said. "But for now, don't let this spoil your day. Let's continue to have a good time and browse through your fine things. I know you will put the turtle back in its spot for safe keeping. I kind of like the way you have it enthroned on that special shelf behind glass." Dena chuckled a bit.

The Grand Opening was such a success that they hardly noticed how fast the time went by. Before they knew it, it was six o'clock and time to close up. They had made some great deals and managed to sell a few larger pieces. So it turned out to be not only an exciting day but a rather profitable one. They knew they would have to replace some of the items that were sold with some new pieces eventually. But they didn't mind because they knew that would mean more antique hunting and bartering. The day was a big success! Everything usually closed at six in High Bridge. The Safenskis and Gardinas straightened up as much as possible and decided to go home. They closed up the shop and started for home, quite exhausted. They undoubtedly would have a lot to talk about later on about the day's festivities. They were just happy their Grand Opening drew the huge crowd. Their souvenirs and goodies seemed to have been a great attraction; a perfect touch. They were feeling appreciative of the wonderful people that stopped by.

The next morning following their usual Sunday attendance at Mass in St. Joseph Church, the two families met for their weekly breakfast rendezvous in town. After they finished, Krystyna and Giovanna left the kids with their husbands and made their way down to the store. They were anxious to get down there to clean up some more. Even though they all pitched in the night before to tidy things up after the parade of visitors stopped, they still wanted to refresh the whole store with their magic touch. They were both meticulous housekeepers. They also wanted to secure the turtle for its ride back to the house. They decided not to keep it in the store until they settled the matter about this turtle.

On the ride home, the women decided they would both make some things for the dinner they would be sharing with the Lings. Giovanna wanted to make lasagna and bring the Italian bread. Krystyna thought she would make filet mignon on the grill with side dishes of salad, asparagus and roasted peppers in bread crumbs. With an added touch of some wine, the meal was complete. Dessert was never a problem as Krystyna was a great baker and always had something on hand or she could whip up a fresh dessert in no time. They discussed the fact that they wanted to get the meal over with early so that they could have more time to talk about the turtle sculpture with their guests.

Charlie and Dena arrived at the Gardina home about two o'clock in the afternoon. After a quick hello, Nick and Giovanna walked them over to the Safenski house. When they rang the doorbell, Stefan dashed for the foyer to be the first to open the door.

Stefan kept the door a little ajar as he peeked to see who was there. Nick looked through the crack and saw Stefan. "Hello there, young man," Nick said. "Are you going to let us inside?"

"Stefan, let our friends into the house. You know Nick, Giovanna and Francesca," Kaz said. "All of a sudden my son is shy. Go figure!"

When Kaz and Krystyna got to the door, they welcomed Nick and Giovanna and their good friends, the Lings.

Kaz announced, "Come on in; we are so happy that you came. We will sit in the family room for a while and indulge in some of Krystyna's appetizers and my famous cocktails. Krys has been busy preparing some things we hope are to your liking, like sliced kielbasa and some small Reuben sandwiches and even some homemade egg rolls. And she makes a great Margherita or Martini, if that is to your liking. Or there is always wine to tempt you."

After an hour of exchanging small talk, Krystyna said that dinner was ready; so they all went into the dining room where a feast was awaiting them. Everyone enjoyed the meal and the conversation so much so that, they didn't realize that two hours had passed. Charlie and Dena Ling seemed to fit right in with the Gardinas and Safenskis. Krystyna thought they would wait until a little later for dessert. She asked them to move on into the family room where they could talk. The kids were under control, as they were playing on the sun porch.

The two full sofas were on either side of the cocktail table next to the fireplace. Two odd recliners were off to the side. They all took a comfortable seat and got ready for the big discussion. Krystyna started the conversation as she moved the turtle onto the cocktail table for everyone to see. "I think we should start with you, Charlie, if you don't mind. You were the first one to see the turtle and I'm sure you know a lot about it."

Charlie replied anxiously, "Yes, I do know some things but not as much detail as you might think. I was on a business trip to Myanmar. My contact there, a man named Khin Zeya, turned out to be a wonderfully well-versed man and very cordial and helpful to me. He took me to some exciting places, the most special one being an actual gem mine called the Mogok Stone Tract. Not to bore you too much, I will get to the point. While in Mogok, I also visited his friend, Shein's, Gold Sun Gem Store. His friend did not only have gems for sale in his store but he had quite a collection of teak sculptures. Teak is very plentiful in Myanmar and from what I was told, any authentic teak sculpture that is made, is one of a kind, hand crafted by a skilled artisan. That is what makes them so costly, aside from the teak itself."

"That is fascinating!" Krystyna said. "I suspected that the wood might be teak, but I wasn't exactly positive."

"Did you notice anything peculiar about it, Charlie? Kaz asked. "What drew you to it?"

Charlie answered, "The fact that it was so unusual and had intricate carvings on it made me want to examine it closely. And I did just that.

I also thought it was quite heavy for a teak wood piece, but that idea faded due to other conversation. I looked it over quite well and then decided to buy it as Dena told you, for our tenth anniversary. Since the turtle symbolizes longevity, we Chinese people consider it a good luck sign to have it in our possession to bring us a long life."

Nick asked, "Charlie, tell me something? Did you inquire about any of the markings on the turtle? Did this Shein fellow know anything specific about it?"

"Not really! He just knew that it was actually made in Thailand but that it was probably owned by someone in Myanmar. He thought that was why it was in his country, but he didn't chase after facts about it."

Nick continued, "How did he know it was made in Thailand?"

Charlie explained, "Shein showed me a Thai company symbol on the turtle's foot which was pretty microscopic in size, not visible to the eye without a magnifying glass. It said **UAWP**, whatever that means. Shein had no idea what it stood for, just that he suspected that it was Thai because he had seen it on some other teak pieces that he acquired directly from Thailand."

"This is mind boggling!" Giovanna said. "I am so captivated by all of this! I want to know more and more, don't you? I don't think I will rest until I know all about this turtle."

Kaz asked, "Did you have trouble getting this out of the Myanmar country? I know it must be a third world country with a lot of government regulations. Since I am a customs inspector, I know those kind of things are hard to export."

Charlie answered sheepishly, "Now that I know you are a customs inspector, I am not sure I should tell you what I did to get it out of the country. You might think I am either very clever or very stupid."

Kaz replied, "I am sure you have a good reason for whatever you did, Charlie. I am not here to judge you. I consider you a friend. Don't let my job status get in the way of you being open and honest with us. Please?"

Charlie said more relieved, "Thank you for that. I want you to know I do not do illegal things usually. But this man, Shein advised me to ship the turtle incognito within my company's gemstone delivery. He said as long as I had the papers of authenticity from him for it, he wouldn't worry about declaring it or showing it and so forth. The military government of Myanmar does not look favorably upon people taking their teak or precious antiques out of the country. So to avoid a problem, I took Shein's advice to let him pack it for me securely. All went well so no one detected anything. The customs agents at the airports in Myanmar or Mandalay do not open gem stone exports too often. I was lucky because they let my shipment go right through. That is because of Mr. Khin Zeya's and Shein's reputations. They are highly respected in Yangon and Mogok in Myanmar and always have the proper documentation for their shipments."

Krystyna spoke up, "Well, we certainly know more about our turtle now than we did before. And I am sure there is a lot more we are going to learn about it as the days and weeks go by."

Dena asked, "How did you women get the turtle in your possession?"

Giovanna answered, "We are both antique enthusiasts and we spend a lot of our free time frequenting antique stores and flea markets. One day we went over to the Golden Nugget Flea Market in Lambertville and we were browsing around as usual when Krystyna spied the turtle."

Krystyna continued, "When I saw the turtle I just knew it was something of value. We both examined it as closely as we could under the watchful eye of the dealer who was selling it. He didn't seem to know too much about it. He said he bought it from some dealer in North Jersey. We bartered with him for a while and he finally sold it to us for two hundred eighteen dollars, which I now think was a huge mistake on his part. I don't think he knew the real value of the turtle. For that matter, obviously we didn't either!"

Giovanna added, "You are absolutely right, Krystyna. If he knew how valuable it was he never would have had it up for sale. I'm sure of that!"

"Most people do not know about things like that," Charlie said. "Unless you are a dealer of foreign antiques or precious things or sell such things for business reasons, you would not know much about it."

Kaz said, "I see all kinds of items go through customs in Newark. People buy the oddest memorabilia and souvenirs sometimes. And most of them have no idea how valuable some of their purchases are."

"Why don't we take a closer look at the turtle now to see if we can notice any unusual markings on it that we overlooked before?" Nick suggested.

Krystyna added, "That is a good idea. At this point we seem to be at a standstill as to its origin among other things. Let's go over to the dining room where the light is much brighter. Maybe if we all put our heads together and open our eyes a bit more we will come up with something of worth."

As they sat around the table, they each took their turn at taking a closer look at the turtle as they passed it around. Kaz had put some magnifying glasses on the table that he had, hoping they would make it easier to see something that the naked eye missed.

Kaz said, "Well, I see the small initials on the foot with my magnifying glass. They are the initials that Charlie's friend, Shein said were there, **UAWP**. Perhaps we could investigate further to find out what they represent or what company they might stand for."

Charlie answered, "That might be easier to do than we think. I can contact Mr. Zeya in Myanmar and ask him if he thought of any companies in Thailand that might have those initials. Maybe he can find out for us what those letters exactly mean. I'm sure he can call around to some of his business colleagues. One of them should come up with the right answer."

"At least that would be a good start," Dena said.

"There seem to be some very odd looking signs or symbols on the bottom of it," Krystyna said. "I have looked at them many times and have not been able to decipher any of them. They are really peculiar!"

"I, too, often take a look at the symbols and cannot figure out what they mean or if they actually mean anything at all," Giovanna said. "Maybe they are just a design the artisan etched into the teak wood."

Krys added, "Maybe Giovanna and I can do some research on the Thai and Myanmar alphabets in our High Bridge Library. Perhaps that would put us on the right track. Who knows, maybe we will decipher some spy code or something!"

Kaz laughed and said, "Now Krystyna, don't get carried away with this!"

"You know," Charlie said, "I have a feeling you might stumble on some good information by doing that. So I say, by all means, go for it."

Kaz interrupted all this enthusiasm with, "Well, I don't know about you people, but I am craving a little dessert. How about it Krystyna?

Maybe we should have our cake and coffee now; later on we will chat a bit more. I think we all need a break from this intense work."

"That sounds great to me as well," Nick chimed in. "I can smell that dessert you have hidden somewhere, Krystyna. I have been sensing its aroma since I arrived earlier. You know me and my sweet tooth!"

"Alright, you guys. I know when I'm outnumbered. Take our turtle friend into the family room and I will set up the table for dessert," Krystyna said.

With that the couples all went into the other room to sit and socialize a bit to get their minds calmed down and off the turtle. The kids came into the room as well and were playing with all sorts of toys and games. Krystyna gave them their dessert on little snack tables so they could keep playing while they had their sweet treats.

Several minutes later Krystyna had the dessert ready to serve. She called everyone back to the dining room where they could enjoy some lemon meringue pie and chocolate layer cake. They all were about to satisfy their taste buds after their mouths were watering from the aromatic scents of home baked goodies.

While they were engaged in conversation, the kids were occupied in the family room. In fact, they were quieter than usual. Kaz went to check on them. When he peeked into the room he saw them playing with the turtle as if it was their pet. So as not to startle them, he watched them for a few minutes before he walked in to take the turtle away from them.

Kaz then said, "I see you are having fun with the turtle. I'm sorry kids, but that is not a toy for you to play with. Bring it over here to me, Stefan."

When Stefan picked the turtle up he almost dropped it because he was nervous with his father's tone of voice. He thought he was being reprimanded. Kaz ran over to him and grabbed it just in time. As he put his hand over Stefan's, they both had their hands on the turtle.

Stefan said, "Daddy, did you feel that? Something moved on the turtle just now when you grabbed it."

Kaz answered him, "Not really, but I did hear a click or some kind of a noise. Did you break it?"

"No Daddy," Stefan said. "We were just playing with it and pressing those funny marks on the bottom and when you asked me to hand it to you, I heard a noise."

"Let me take the turtle to the grownups now. You and Francesca go play and finish your dessert."

When Kaz walked back into the room he looked a little flushed. When he explained what had happened in the other room everyone's interest got peaked again.

Nick said, "What do you mean, you heard a "click?""

Kaz replied, "I'm telling you, I heard some kind of a noise when Stefan handed the turtle to me. He said he and Francesca were pressing the bottom spots on the turtle right before that. They were playing some sort of game using the turtle as their pet. I thought maybe they broke it when I heard the rattle, click, or whatever it was. But they assured me they didn't drop it or break it."

This is becoming very complicated," Giovanna said. "Why don't we do some pressing and probing ourselves? There is something very strange going on here. In fact, it seems a little mysterious. I think this turtle is trying to tell us something."

"It's a LOT mysterious!" Krystyna said. "This turtle reminds me of the Rubik Cube Craze of the 1980's "

Nick got into the conversation now as he was very interested in these puzzling things. "I remember that Rubik's Cube, too. I actually did research on it when I was in school. I know very few people have ever been able to solve it on their own. Most of the solutions were done by groups of people putting their heads and ideas together. That puzzling toy created a lot of interest back then."

"Tell us something about the Cube, Nick," Kaz added. "Maybe it will give us a clue as to what to look for with our turtle."

"Give me a minute to collect my thoughts. I kept a file on it in fact. Just wait a while; I'll run over to my house and see if I can find it fast. I'll be right back."

When Nick returned he continued, "Well, I found my file. I know the Cube was invented in the 1970's by Enro Rubik, a Hungarian obsessed with 3-D geometry. He even got his students and colleagues obsessed with it. The Cube mania spread after a German doctor name Tibor Laczi discovered it and took it to the 1979 Nuremberg toy show. But people in those days showed little interest in the Cube. It probably confused them because they couldn't solve it. It was extremely hard. A mathematician named David Signmaster, brought it to public attention outside of Hungary. His interests in it lead to an article about it in the Scientific American Magazine. It sort of caught on and found its way to the states for while. People would spend hour upon hour trying to solve Enro Rubik's puzzle. It was a doozey! They would examine it, flip it around, press it, push it, probe it; you name it, they did it! I did it! It could drive you mad at times. I never came close to solving the mystery of it, but it always fascinated me. This dilemma of yours with the turtle reminds me a lot about it; brings back some memories."

Kaz said, "Well I think we should do all those things. We have to get serious about this turtle. Let's press, probe, push, shake; do whatever it takes. With all of our heads together, we should be able to find something out."

Charlie took the turtle, turned it over and stared at the symbols with intensity. He pressed them different ways, but nothing happened. "We have got to find out what these symbols mean! Look at this one carved on the top shell by the neck. It is another kind of symbol, almost like a word, **hpwin**. Now what does that mean?"

Nick said, "I think we had better get started on that research. Charlie, maybe you should copy those symbols down on paper and show them to your friends in Myanmar."

"I am going to call Khin Zeya first thing in the morning and tell him to expect a fax from me with these symbols and markings," Charlie said. "Dena and I will be leaving now, but we will stay in touch with you every step of the way."

With that said, they all bid each other good night!

The next day, Giovanna and Krystyna decided to go to the High Bridge Library before they opened the store on Monday morning. When they arrived, the librarian was just opening up. She commented on how anxious they were behaving and how early they were there. They ignored her comments and her look of annoyance and followed her in. They could not wait to delve into the books and computer files to see what they could find out. The History books were in the back section so the women went immediately there and found a large table on which to spread out their books and make room for note taking. Giovanna got her hands on the Encyclopedia Britannica and started to search for Myanmar and Thailand. Krystyna began with the card catalog in order to located specific books on Southeast Asia. Krystyna searched the shelves to locate the books she wanted, brought them to the table and began reading. Both of them knew this was going to be a long drawn-out affair but they were determined to proceed. Several books had quite a bit of information about Mayanmar or Burma. They both managed to find the alphabet symbols used in Myanmar and in Thailand which they figured would be good to start with. They made a lot of copies of facts they found that might be helpful and took a lot of notes. Giovanna even went to the language references where she found the Awesome Library in Thai. She thought that was going to be helpful until she saw how complicated and complex the language symbols were. She immediately closed the book. Krystyna found some basic facts about the Myanmar and Thai languages. She looked over at Giovanna and said, "You know something Vanna, I am going to try and contact the University of Yangon in Myanmar. It said in one book that I was reading that it has one of the oldest and famous libraries in Asia."

Giovanna answered, "That might be quite difficult because I think you really have to have the name of a person to contact; no one will give you the time of day otherwise. How about if we ask Charlie Ling to ask his friend to go out on a limb for us and pay a visit to the Yangon University Library for us? He already said he was intending to contact his friend there."

"That is the best idea you've had today. I am going to do just that. Any little bit we do will be a help I'm sure."

Since it was getting late and they had to open up the store, they decided to stop for now. Krystyna checked out the books she had because she still wanted to read up more about Mayanmar and Thailand. The two women left the library with a lot on their minds.

Once they opened the store and got things in place they sat down with their coffee and their piles of books. Krystyna said, "Gosh Giovanna, this is quite a situation we've gotten ourselves into. I think you are right in suggesting we contact Charlie Ling and ask him to help us out."

"I know Krys, but I think we should still keep on researching. Maybe we will stumble onto something. The symbols of the language of Thailand that I saw didn't match at all. Nothing even came close. This is a little tedious and frustrating, isn't it? Deciphering the alphabets of Thailand and Mayanmar is becoming quite a chore! Some of the

Myanmar letters looked a little close to the ones on the turtle. That is a plus! Maybe we should have researched the numerical symbols as well. What makes it even more difficult is that we haven't a clue as to what it is we are supposed to be looking for."

Krystyna added, "When we close up the store after five o'clock we can go back to the library for a while. Kaz said he would pick up the kids from school so we don't have to worry about them. We're making some progress so maybe we should continue while our thoughts are fresh. I think we are getting on the right track."

"I think I would rather go home tonight with all this information, feed our families and then maybe meet at your house to talk about this with our husbands," Giovanna said. "I think they are curious as well and would like to know what we have found out so far."

"That's a good idea," Krystyna replied. "Maybe while we read about this and look it over together, we will make some progress. Having the turtle close by will be helpful as well."

Dinner went well in both households. Krystyna and Giovanna made easy meals so that they could get to work with their investigating. Giovanna got to the Safenski house around seven thirty. Krystyna was finished with her evening chores and was anxiously waiting for her. Their husbands decided to watch the kids and get them off to bed so that the wives could do some work on their project.

"Okay, where do we start?" Giovanna asked.

Krystyna answered, "I think we should meticulously compare the alphabet and numbers with the turtle's symbols, one by one. It will take a while but we should be able to come up with something. At least I hope so."

After about an hour of making comparisons in both the Thai and Myanmar languages, the women were getting nowhere. As patient as they were, they were getting a little frustrated. No alphabet symbols seemed to match any of the symbols on the turtle; they moved on to the numerical symbols.

"I think it must be a number puzzle of some kind." Krystyna said. "Let's try to match them up and see what happens."

They continued to work at this matching game. They worked a while with the number symbols of Thailand, but to no avail. Nothing was a match!

Nick and Kaz listened intently at everything the women were saying and they tried to closely examine the turtle as well.

Finally Giovanna said, "It looks like we are making some headway with the Myanmar numerical symbols. Look at this, Krys. Some of these number symbols actually look like a match. They aren't exact, but they are close in shape."

"Oh my goodness; I think we are on to something here, Vanna." Krys said. "Let's see if we can match them all. This should not be too difficult."

Two hours later, they had eight perfect matches. The symbols stood for the numbers 0,1,4,8, and 9 and some were used more than once.

"Let me see them," Nick said. "You know, I think you are right. They certainly do look like numerical matches. I think you are on to something at last."

"Yes, but what do the numbers mean?" Kaz asked. "Do they follow some sequential order? Do they stand for something? Charlie must do his part now, I think."

"I agree with you, Kaz," Nick said. "We must talk to Charlie and ask him to get his friends to come to our assistance. At least we made some progress though. I feel like we accomplished something, don't you?"

Krys had one more thing on her mind. "Before we finish, let me have one more look at the turtle. My son said when he was pushing the bottom of the turtle he heard a click. That intrigues me! It may be nothing, but I think we have to pursue that aspect as well."

Krystyna proceeded to press away. She heard a click now and then, but nothing else happened. The noise seemed to be coming from inside the turtle. She said, "Maybe something is broken inside. Maybe our kids dropped it and are afraid to tell us."

"You know something, Krys?" Giovanna said. "We must find out what those letters mean by the turtle's neck also. They must have something to do with this puzzle, if that's what this is. Whoever made this was ingenious and very mysterious for a reason, I think."

"This is so baffling, yet so amazing at the same time," Krystyna said. "What in the world have we stumbled on, Vanna?"

"I don't know, but whatever it is, I am determined to pursue it to the end. I feel like Jessica Fletcher or the Snoop Sisters, don't you? I just hope we can be as good detectives as they were." They all had a hearty laugh.

"There is one more thing we have to consider, I think," Krys said. "I was also wondering about Dena Ling. Do you think she will want the turtle back? After all, it really was hers before it was stolen. She has been most gracious throughout all of this and I think we must approach her about her feelings and thoughts."

"Let's not worry about that now," Giovanna said. "We have more important things to consider. Besides, she has been more than gracious about the whole thing. Let's see how things go."

The two couples said their good nights and the Gardinas walked across the lawn to their home. Krys and Kaz locked up and went to bed.

Chapter Nine

Charlie Ling's phone was ringing quite early. He suspected it must be Khin Zeya from Myanmar. He was right on the money!

"Good Morning! Ling residence," Charlie said.

"Hello Charlie! It is Khin from Yangon. I hope I am not calling you too early. I wanted to get back to you as your message faxed to me yesterday sounded so urgent."

"It is not that it is urgent; it is just very important to me and several of my friends. Did you manage to decipher any of the symbols or words or whatever they are?"

"First of all, those letters **UAWP**, stand for Unique Asian Wood Products. It is a company from Thailand that specializes in teak products of all kinds. So perhaps that turtle was made by an artisan in that company. I can contact them for you to see if I can find out anything, if you want me to," Khin offered.

Charlie answered, "I would be so grateful if you could do that for us, Khin. The information might lead us to who made it or for whom it was made. So you can go ahead and inquire whenever you have time. Oh, and one more thing, our wives asked if you could possibly go to the Yangon University Library to see if the Myanmar symbols they found on the turtle are authentic. They said it has the reputation of being one of the finest in Southeast Asia."

"I will do all I can for you. But what is going on with your wife's turtle, Charlie? Is something wrong with it? Why are all these questions surfacing about it?"

"It was stolen from my wife's office after she had it for only a few months. A while after that it found its way to an antique shop owned by my wife's boss and her friend. I will have to explain the whole affair to you at another time when we can talk at length."

Khin continued, "As far as the single symbols are concerned, I know they are Myanmar symbols for numbers. I hope that helps you out. The word **hpwin** means "OPEN. But I will look further and do some of my own research into this for you. Maybe I can come up with some help for you to solve this puzzle."

"Just having you as a first hand Myanmar contact is a blessing in disguise! Khin, thank you!" Charlie said. "I am lucky to know you and we are grateful for your help. That might be the breakthrough we needed. I will let you know of any further progress we make as soon as I know something further. Thank you very much!"

"Let me know if I can do anything else for you. I'll be in touch with you soon to find out how things are going. Give my regards to your wife and family."

Charlie replied, "And you say hello to Myine and your children as well. So long for now!"

Charlie couldn't wait to call Krystyna and Giovanna to tell them what he had learned from Khin Zeya. The minute he hung up from Khin he was re-dialing Krystyna.

The Safenski household was stirring with movement as everyone seemed to get up early. "Good morning! Krystyna, speaking."

"Hello Krystyna, this is Charlie Ling. I'm sorry I am calling so early, but I have some good news for you that I'm sure will make you very happy."

"By all means, Charlie, tell me. I am always ready to hear good news."

"My friend, Mr. Zeya in Yangon, Myanmar called me this morning. After examining the information I faxed to him, he had some very good news for us. The symbols are definitely Myanmar number symbols. How is that for good detective work?"

Krystyna was overwhelmed with emotion. "That is wonderful! What great news! Giovanna and I have been racking our brains trying to figure these symbols out. What a breakthrough this is for us! I am so grateful, Charlie. We have to get together again some day to probe into this discovery of ours. I cannot wait another minute to get into this. Would you and Dena be free this weekend? We all can meet at my home again and have dinner and get down to our mystery work. How does that sound to you?"

"I think we can make it, but I will check with Dena. If you don't hear from me, that means we are coming. If all is okay with her, we should be there around five o'clock"

"That would be fine," Krystyna said with much exuberance. "I will get the others together and we will have a great evening, I'm sure."

Several days of waiting were more than Krystyna and Giovanna could handle. They were so excited that they could hardly wait for Saturday to arrive. Krys, with Kaz's help prepared another terrific meal. This time it was a Polish menu that started off with an appetizer of hot slices of kielbasa (Polish sausage) with horse radish garnish. Krystyna outdid herself even while making this quick dinner. The pork loin (pieczen) with honey sauce was complimented by her special potatoes baked with eggs and cream, mushrooms in sour cream, Polish beets, and (mizeria) sliced raw cucumbers in sour cream. The meal was topped off with a dessert of (sernik (cheesecake).

When they all sat at the table, Kaz said aloud, *"Smacznego!"* which meant, Enjoy! Nick added his toast of *Bon Appetit*, while Charlie interjected with *Fu-lu-shou*, meaning may you have longevity, prosperity and posterity. With this League of Nations sitting together and sharing a meal, how could they not have good luck and enjoyment?

An hour and a half later, the friends made their way into the family room to see what leeway they could make with their turtle mystery. Kaz placed the turtle on the cocktail table for all to see as they began their discussion.

Charlie began relating his conversation with Khin Zeya. "My friend was very helpful in deciphering our symbols. He said they are Myanmar numerical symbols. Now all we have to do is try to figure out what they mean or what they stand for. That leaves more research for you girls. Maybe Dena could go along with you to the library this time. She is anxious to help in some way. They say two heads are better than one. But I think three heads will unravel this mystery."

Giovanna answered very enthusiastically, "That was incisive work, Charlie. I hope you thanked your friend for us. I think Dena, Krystyna and I will be heading over to the library next week sometime. I'll call you and Krystyna to set up a time."

Charlie interrupted once again. "My friend, Khin is not finished with this yet either. He is going to go to the Yangon University Library like you asked to see if he can find out anything more about the numerical symbols. I forgot to tell you that Khin also knew what that word **hpwin** meant. It means "OPEN" in Myanmar. I think that is going to be very helpful to us in the long run. It was put on that turtle for a reason, I'm sure."

"Yes, I think we are becoming quite astute detectives now," Nick offered. "Now if we could only find out what that clicking was all about, that would be a big plus also, I'm sure."

"We will get to work with that aspect of our "case" as soon as we try to find out what role these numbers are playing in our puzzle." Krys said.

The following Monday was the Labor Day holiday. In High Bridge, the town always kicked off the day with a small parade after which people had lunch and browsed through the shops. Krystyna and Giovanna decorated their Safe-Gard Fine Antique Store in red, white and blue streamers because they wanted a patriotic theme. As Krystyna was hanging the American flag on the outside by the doorway, she got a brainstorm. She went rushing inside to tell Giovanna about her insight.

"Giovanna, I just had a thought when I was hanging up our flag. Maybe those number symbols stand for dates or for some historical event in the country of Myanmar. It is worth looking into, don't you think? From what I learned so far, the people of Myanmar are very history minded and base a lot of their events on a celebration of one kind or another."

"You always get crazy brainstorms, Krys. What kind of dates? Do you mean like historical dates, birth dates, or what?"

"That remains to be seen. We will have to find that out. But at least it is a thought to start with. I can't wait until the weekend to delve into some of the Mayanmar history and culture. Do you think Dena would come out tomorrow to help us?"

"I'll give her a call. Maybe she can take a day off from work," Giovanna said. "I think we can close the store for one day. Since we were open on Labor Day we should give ourselves a day off tomorrow."

When Dena heard of their recent findings she was more than anxious to go to Jersey and get to work. She said she would be at Giovanna's house around ten o'clock.

The next morning, the women set out on their mission. They arrived at the library early and got down to researching Myanmar and its history. Several hours later they sat down together at a long table to decipher their factual information and sort through everything they thought might be important. They were on a mission and there was no stopping these women!

Krystyna asked, "Do you think we should start by researching important dates for Myanmar holidays and special significant days there?"

Dena answered first, "That sounds logical to me. If we can find some dates important to the Myanmar people, maybe we will get faster results in deciphering the symbols. At least I hope it is dates we are supposed to be looking for."

Giovanna added, "I'll go along with that idea."

"Okay then, let's get busy researching any dates that we think might be important or have some special meaning for the Myanmar people."

Giovanna found out that Myanmar had a constitution written on January 3, 1974. "That seemed like a significant day to me. What do you think? I also learned that November thirteenth is National Day in Myanmar; December twenty-fifth is Christmas just as it is here. Finally, I found out that March 27th was Day of the Army, a national holiday with parades. If we feel any of these dates are likely to be important to us, I will research them further. I was simply choosing dates at random."

"They all sound significant. It's possible one of them may be the one we are after; but let's digs further," Krystyna said. "What did you come up with, Dena?"

"All the dates you mentioned, Giovanna, sound like they might hold a lot of meaning, but I think it will depend on how we interpret them. Well here are a few I found; on July 19, 1947 the people of Myanmar celebrate Martyr's Day in memory of some General Aung Sun, who was murdered defending his country. I also found out that Myanmar has been under military rule since September 18, 1988 and Mayanmar broke away from the United Kingdom on January 4, 1948 and formed the Union of Myanmar. These are all very historical events to the Myanmar people, so I copied them down."

Krystyna continued the discussion with, "I found these dates: Peasant's Day is March 2, 1962; their Water Festival is celebrated from April thirteenth to the seventeenth, which is like their New Year Day; July eighth is the beginning of Buddhist Lent; March tenth is Dry Season Celebration, a national holiday. There are so many possibilities that we've uncovered so far. For a small country, they sure do a lot of things and everything has some kind of special meaning for them. I don't know how you feel about this, but I think we have our work cut out for us."

"Why don't we go back to the store and sit down with our turtle and start checking the dates against our numerical symbols?" Krystyna asked. "Maybe looking at it will give us some inspiration."

A few minutes later the women were back at the store and busy at work. They made a shorter list of the special dates they found and began comparing them to the symbols on the turtle's plastron (bottom). The date that finally matched all of the symbols was January 4, 1948, the Myanmar Independence Day. They felt very satisfied with the results of their efforts. Their hard work was paying off.

"Can you believe we narrowed the symbols down to one date?" Dena cried out. "What a chore that was! I'm glad it wasn't a lengthy one, too. I don't think I could take this kind of pressure for a long span of time. It would drive me crazy."

Krystyna said, "Somehow I felt it had something to do with patriotism in a way. Our Independence Day is very significant for us so why wouldn't theirs be for them? I never thought we would come up with anything so quickly."

"I can't wait to tell Charlie what we've found out," Dena said. He may have some additional insight as to the significance of this day. He's spent enough time there."

Giovanna said, "Let's go to my house this time and we can have supper together and fill in our husbands with the information we successfully obtained. They will be happy and proud of us, I'm sure. Dena, don't forget to call Charlie, too. I think he will want to be there as well."

"Yes, I must call him and also tell him to notify Khin Zeya that we have cracked the code. I am sure Khin will be happy to have that information. I know Charlie will be pleased."

Giovanna had a chance to show off her culinary skills this time. She, with Krystyna and Dena's help, managed to turn out a delicious Italian meal. A cold antipasto was the first course; the second course was Fettucini Alfredo, followed by a main course of Veal chops, eggplant parmesan and sliced tomatoes with mozzarella. Dessert was Tiramisu, one of Giovanna's favorite specialties. Once dinner was over with, they made their way to the spacious Gardina living room.

Krystyna began the evening's discussion. "We managed to narrow down all of the dates to one in particular, January 4, 1948, the formation of the new Myanmar Union and the end of its occupation by the United Kingdom. All of the numbers in that date match the symbols on the bottom of the turtle. January is the first month of the year that is one; the weekday is the fourth, so we have a four; the year is self-explanatory, one, nine, four, and eight. So what do we do now?"

Nick said, "The person who used this date must have been a true Myanmar patriot. He must have had his reasons for using them on the turtle. Now it is up to us to find out the reasons since we have the turtle in our possession. I think we should do as our children did and try pressing those numerical symbols in some kind of sequence according to the date and see what happens. So, let me have a go at it."

Krystyna handed Nick the turtle enthusiastically. Everyone watched as he first looked intently at, turned it over and then started moving his fingers gently over the bottom of the turtle.

Nick pressed 1, 4, 1, 9, 4 and 8. Nothing happened. He said, "Of course I didn't expect anything to happen so easily. I'm sure the person who created this puzzle didn't want to make it too easy to get it to do anything. This is actually very ingenious! The person was brilliant! I was pressing the symbols in exact sequence of the date as we read dates. Okay, who wants to try next?"

Charlie reached over to take the turtle from Nick. He cradled the turtle in his palm, felt the smoothness of the teak and rubbed his fingertips over the symbols. In his mind he had a plan and tried his way, adding a zero to the month and day, 01, 04, and then leaving the year as is; 1, 9, 4, and 8. *Naturally, he thought, I knew it wouldn't be this easy for me either.* No clicking was heard by anyone. He said, "I really thought my zero theory was going to work. Oh well, so much for wishful thinking."

Kaz asked to have a go at it next. "I am going to pick up on your theory and place a zero before each and every number, 01, 04, 01, 09, 04, and 08." He meticulously pressed the zero and then one, moved on to the zero and four, and got faster as he continued to press zero one, zero nine, zero four and zero eight in sequence. Not a sound was heard; no clicking as he had hoped for; and nothing moved in any way. They were all getting frustrated as this was taking a while and getting them nowhere.

Krystyna said, "Rome wasn't built in a day. We need to be patient and stay with it no matter how long it takes. Let us women have a try. I was thinking about something while you men were trying your methods out. When I was researching in the library, I found that a lot of dates in Myanmar were written with the day first, then the month, and finally the year. Let me try it out." She pressed 4 for the day of the week, then 1 for the month of the year, and finally the year itself, 1, 9, 4, and 8. Nothing happened. "So much for my idea," she said very disheartened. "We can't give up though. We must keep trying everything we possibly can. We have to exhaust every aspect that we know about. We were all kids once. Maybe we have to start thinking like a kid solving puzzles. Remember when we use to have those square slide puzzles with the numbers all scrambled in them. We had to slide them around in the square until they were in sequential order. It was challenging but we did it!"

"Krystyna, those were childhood games," Kaz retorted. "What connection does that have to this? Let's be realistic here."

"Don't get so hot under the collar, Kaz. We are all feeling a little frustrated with this. I am simply trying to offer a simple solution to a very complex situation. Anything is worth a try at this point."

Kaz said apologetically, "Maybe you are right, Krys. You may be on to something. I shouldn't be so judgmental. I'm sorry."

Giovanna asked to try next. She poked at the bottom in the same sequence that Krystyna used, but added the zeroes again, 04, 01, 01, 09, 04, and then 08. As she did so, they all heard a lot of clicking going on. Their nervous energy made them all burst out with laughter.

They clapped, slapped each other a high five and jumped out of their seats! When they calmed down, they all decided unanimously that they should do the same thing again but slower and listen to the clicks. They were finally on to something! As they hovered over the turtle, this time Dena had the honor of pressing the symbols on the plastron. She felt honored that she had a turn at this. *After all, she thought, this was originally MY turtle. I want to help solve the mystery of my lucky charm.* She wished with all her might as slowly and painstakingly she pressed the date in the same order and sequence that Giovanna used 04, 01, 01, 09, 04 and lastly, 08. They all heard things clicking faintly inside as she pressed the numbers, but nothing else really happened. The turtle was clicking away as if he was trying to say something to them all. They all got befuddled at this point.

Krystyna broke the silence that came over the friendly group. "What in the world is going on here?" Krystyna asked in wonderment. "This thing is clicking away as if it is talking to us, yet nothing moves on the outside. All the clicking seems to be from the inside. The sound reminds me of a cricket's chirp. Whoever made this was quite a genius! But I wonder if the person really wanted anyone to get this opened, if that is what is supposed to happen. Maybe we are getting carried away with this. Maybe it isn't really a puzzle or something to solve. Perhaps the artisan made it to make sounds for his grandchildren while they played with it. I must say I am stumped. I don't know how all of you feel about this."

Charlie was thinking about his friend, Khin Zeya. "You know folks, there is an awful lot of clicking going on here, but that seems to be all there is. Wait a minute!" Suddenly Charlie got a little excited. He jumped up, grabbed the turtle, in a gentle but aggressive sort of way. "I just thought of something. Didn't my friend say that the symbol **hpwin** means OPEN? Well, HELLO? We haven't even considered it nor looked at it as maybe being a part of this puzzle. We all seemed to have forgotten about that symbol on our turtle friend's neck."

Dena added, "You know, Honey, I think you might have a very positive and important point here. I think we should keep it in mind as we move on with this. I don't think it was carved on the turtle meaninglessly."

Kaz added, "I agree. You may think me a little silly, but I want to follow up with my wife's earlier theory of remembering when we were kids ourselves. I would like to give the turtle to my son, Stefan again and see how he handles it. Maybe by watching Francesca and him play with it we can figure out what they did that we are NOT doing. It is worth a try, don't you think?"

"What have we got to lose?" Nick said. Ask him to come in with Francesca and let's watch them for a while."

Stefan and Francesca began to play as they did before, but they were nervous as their parents were watching. They were having fun though and even gave the turtle a name, *Slowpoke*. That was certainly a fitting name for him, the grownups thought, as they listened in on their fun. Before long the grownups heard shouts from the kids. They ran in to see what the commotion was all about. They watched as Stefan probed and poked. After a few moments Kaz went over and asked Stefan what he does to make the clicks. He showed his father that he presses the bottom spots while he holds it by the neck. Krystyna was afraid the kids might break something so she told Kaz to take it from them.

When the parents got the turtle back, they proceeded to take turns pressing the combination and pushing. When it was Krystyna's turn, she pressed 04, 01, 01, 09, 04, and 08. The way she was holding the turtle, her thumb was close to the neck. She inadvertently pressed the section marked with the symbol **hpwin** by the head with her thumb. That proved to be the right maneuver! All of a sudden there was a louder click and the turtle shell sort of loosened up from the head back to the tail. It was almost like watching the trunk of a car pop open or the hood of a car as you popped it open from the inside. It actually just opens a bit and waits for you to lift it up. Krystyna gently lifted the round turtle shell and was able to flip it upward carefully as if it was on a hinge. They all stood up in shock and gave out loud gasps! They were hugging and hollering and high-fiving and crying, all in one. It was as if a pressure cooker was being allowed to let its steam out slowly after reaching its boiling point.

"This is amazing! Krystyna said. "I knew this turtle was unusual! But I must say, I surely never expected this!"

"What is happening here?" Giovanna uttered with surprise. "I cannot believe what I am seeing!" Who would have thought our turtle would come alive?" Giovanna laughed from nervousness.

"My turtle is lucky after all!" Dena said happily. "Somehow I knew in my heart it would leave its mark on me or someone!"

Charlie couldn't contain himself. "When you think about it, it didn't take us too long to figure out the puzzle. I think it is because of Nick's plan of using group theory, if that is the correct term. We all put our heads together and it seems to have paid off for us."

Nick, Kaz and Charlie were shocked beyond measure. They just stood back and observed all that was happening. They were letting the girls have their enjoyment. After several minutes, Charlie asked to have a closer look. As they all stood around him, he lifted the turtle up, looked underneath and then placed it back on the table. As they all gazed with delight at their prize antique, they watched as Charlie lifted something out from inside of it.

"What is that, Charlie?" Dena asked. "It looks like black felt. Oh my goodness! Our surprises are not over yet. What do we have here?"

Giovanna's interior decorating skills kicked in when she said with a smile, "That is not felt! THAT is VELVET! Black velvet usually means something expensive is in your midst; at least that is what I think."

"Let me see, please, let me see?" Krystyna asked excitedly. She couldn't control herself. "This is fascinating! I have never seen anything like this before in my life! What is it that we have found? What have we gotten ourselves into?"

Charlie added hastily, "There is something hard inside of the velvet. Look! It's a black silk bag! But it is not a plain black bag. Look at the brocade design woven into the silk. I remember Khin telling me that the people of the Inle Lake region of Myanmar weave some of the finest silk in the world. From the feel of this silk, I am certain that it is from Inle Lake. He told me the young girls there weave and fashion the silk from tiny thin threads. What deftness and skill they must have to produce such beautiful material! If you look very close you can even see some very fine gold threads running through the fabric. My goodness! This is another example of the innovative spirit of the people of Inle. Those people never cease to amaze me!"

Dena said, "Oh look, Charlie! There is a design embroidered into the silk on one side. I can't make out what it is. Let me see it a little closer." After a few seconds Dena said with certainty, "It looks like a Buddha. Yes, it IS a Buddha. How significant is that?"

"It probably was sewn into the bag for blessing and luck," Charlie said.

"Look Charlie, it is tied with gold corded tassels," Dena said. "Let me untie the tassels."

"Be careful, Dena," Nick said, "in case it is something breakable."

When Dena undid the corded tassels, the bag loosened. Charlie helped her spread the bag open and then he put his hand inside. What he came up with was so incomprehensible that they were all speechless! The men never thought they would see the day when their wives were at a loss for words. This discovery was so unexpected that they were caught off guard.

"What do we have here?" Charlie asked, almost stupefied. "I believe it is a gemstone of some sort! Get something soft that we can place it on, Krystyna. A good magnifying glass would help as well. I wish I had the tools of my trade with me. I will have to rely on my eyesight for now.

Krystyna hurried back with a large piece of felt that she kept around for household purposes. Giovanna helped her spread it out over the coffee table. When Charlie placed the gemstone on the table they all tried to take a closer look. One at a time they eyed the gem and were in total shock.

"I don't know where to begin explaining this," Charlie said. "I have seen many gems and some of the world's finest recently but never one so exquisite. It has to be very rare and extremely expensive."

"Can you tell us anything about it, Charlie?" Kaz asked.

"Well, it is one very vivacious ruby as far as I can tell," Charlie replied. "It most likely is a Mogok stone since it is pigeon blood in color, one of the most sought after rubies."

Giovanna said, "Its color is breathtaking!"

"You can see its irresistible brilliance with the naked eye," Charlie continued sharing his expertise with his friends. "I don't see any visible inclusions which should add to its unique beauty. If there are any hidden inclusions, those will add to its authenticity. If I had my ultraviolet lamp here, you would be able to see the different shades of fluorescence it emits. However, the best way to view it is in daylight."

Dena's curiosity could not be contained. She asked, "How many carats do you think this ruby is, Charlie?"

"Oh, I don't know exactly. I would have to take it into our shop and have the expert lapidaries study it for us. There is one thing I can tell you though, it is one very valuable, maybe even priceless gem."

Nick was interested in the cut of the gem and said, "It appears to be oval in shape. The person who placed this ruby in that turtle must have cut and faceted it to fit just perfectly inside the oval turtle."

"Charlie added, "The oval is the most common cut used. But the cut doesn't give it value, the carats do."

Krystyna, not being able to stay silent, then said, "It looks like we have a lot more researching and inquiring to do, more than we expected. We thought the turtle was the mystery. Now it seems we have more problems on our hands. I would like to know who actually made the turtle or who the owner was."

"You're absolutely right, Krys," Nick said. "I think finding the original owner will put us on the right track of learning more about the ruby. I hope it is not a stolen one. We certainly don't need that kind of trouble."

Being totally enthralled by all of this Charlie said, "I think I can help out here. I am going to ask Mr. Khin Zeya to contact that Unique Asian Wood Products Company in Bangkok, Thailand. Maybe they will give us a heads up as to who made the turtle or why it was made at all. First thing when I get home this evening, I will call him as it will be a decent hour to call over there."

Everyone agreed to let Charlie do some inquiring with his Myanmar contacts. Meanwhile, they had to find a safe place for the ruby. It was unanimously agreed by all that it should be held for the time being in a vault at the Chan Continental Gem Company. They had excellent security for such gems.

That evening when he got home Charlie placed a phone call to Myanmar. "Hello, Khin. It's Charlie Ling. Hope all is well with you and your family."

"Thank you for inquiring as to our welfare; we are all just fine. What's going on? Is anything wrong, Charlie?"

"We all cracked the code of the turtle by comparing the markings on the bottom of it to the symbols for Mayanmar numbers. Our wives did a lot of research and with all of us working together we cracked the code the artisan used. We heard all these sounds inside the turtle. When we pressed the symbols in just the right sequence the shell popped. Then I remembered that word **hpwin** meant "open." When we pressed that part of the turtle by its neck it unlatched itself. We were able to flip it up gently."

Khin interrupted Charlie. "What are you telling me, Charlie? You actually were able to open up this turtle. Was anything inside?"

"Khin, you are not going to believe this! Inside was this soft black velvet bag with golden tassels around it and a small intricate Buddha stitched on the bag. It almost looked like a fine minute tapestry. Someone took a lot of pains to stitch it in gold, orange and green colors. It was magnificent."

"So was the bag empty or was something in it?" Khin asked.

"Khin, you would have been in your glory. Inside the bag was the most brilliant oval ruby I have ever seen. Even I could not appreciate its beauty at first because I was dumbfounded. We all were! With all my expertise, I was speechless! After we all calmed down, I took a magnifying glass and examined it as best I could. It appeared to be flawless. It is definitely a pigeon blood ruby and I think it must be an old family heirloom. Whoever placed it in that turtle for safe keeping, surely wanted to protect it."

"All I can tell you is that Mayanmar families do such things all the time. They place or hide their gems in the most unusual places. I, myself, have my family gems securely hidden away. But most families pass on to their children or other family members, information about their heirloom gems and where they are hidden so that they remain in their family."

"I can understand that, Khin. I probably would do the same."

"So what are you going to do now, Charlie?" Do you need my help?"

"Yes, I was wondering if you could try to locate the owner of the turtle, maybe by contacting the company that made it. That might give us a lead to the owner or the artisan or to who put the ruby inside."

"Thank you for trusting me with this information," Khin said. "Give me a few days, maybe even a few weeks and I will see what I can do to help you out."

"Just be careful and please do not tell anyone what we found inside. That information could cause trouble for us I fear."

"I'll talk to you soon, as soon as I do some poking around. Let me see what I can find out from this end. Give my best regards to your wife. And, Charlie? Don't worry. We will resolve this somehow."

Chapter Ten
Bangkok, Thailand

A week later, Khin Zeya, wanting to help out his friend in America, decided he would travel in person to Bangkok, Thailand on a business trip to pay a visit to the Unique Asian Wood Products Company. Prior to going though, Khin did his research in locating just where that company was. He learned that the actual company was on the outskirts of Bangkok, but that the company maintained offices in downtown Bangkok in the Trade Center. Now that Khin narrowed down the location, he was able to make the trip with certainty. He e-mailed the hotel and booked himself a small suite in the Shangri La Bangkok Hotel on the banks of the Chao Phaya River. It was only thirty minutes from the airport and had convenient access to the business and shopping districts. More importantly, it was adjacent to the Sky Train which he was familiar with. That would make it easy to get around the city.

Khin arrived at Bangkok's airport in the late morning. He didn't want to arrive too early as check-in time was 2:00 P.M. He first took a cab to the hotel and checked in. As he was in Bangkok on many other occasions, he was quite familiar with the Sky Train. He knew it was the fastest way to get downtown, avoiding traffic snarls and mass congestion. He was always mesmerized by the hectic activity of the city of Bangkok. It was more complex than that of Yangon in Myanmar. Khin arrived at the Trade Center and entered the spacious lobby with all its marble and brass appointments. He made his way over to the directory on the center wall to find out what floor the company he was seeking was on. Obtaining that information, Khin proceeded to walk over to the eight elevators. He chose one and lifted off to the twenty-fifth floor. When the elevator door opened, Khin saw an exquisite area with a receptionist at a circular mahogany desk.

"Good Morning, Miss!"

"Good Morning! I am Miss Bianta, the receptionist/secretary. How may I help you?"

I am Mr. Khin Zeya, a gem dealer from Yangon in Mayanmar. I was wondering if I could speak to the owner of your company or maybe the CEO."

"What is this in regard to, if I may ask?" Miss Bianta said.

"It is actually a very important matter," Khin said. "Someone I know recently came into the possession of a teak turtle sculpture that we think was made by your company."

"What makes you think it is our product?"

Khin replied, very certainly, "We found a company logo on it and traced it back to you. It is compulsory that I speak to someone of importance in this company."

"One moment, please," Miss Bianta said. "Have a seat and I will arrange for you to meet with Mr. Nicro, the owner. I believe he is in today."

A few moments later, Mr. Nicro appeared from a back office. "Good Morning, Mr. Zeya. My receptionist tells me you are inquiring about a teak turtle sculpture. I assure you I am very much interested in this. Come with me to my private office."

The two men entered the plush office of Mr. Nicro and made themselves comfortable in the sitting area by the window where they could speak casually and frankly. Mr. Nicro initiated the conversation. "Tell me Mr. Zeya; are you in possession of this sculpture?"

"Not exactly," Khin answered very definitively. "A friend of mine has it and has asked me to find out what I can about it as he lives in the United States. You see, my friend, a gem dealer, was visiting me a while ago in Yangon to obtain some gems for his company in New York City. While here, I took him to see the Mogok Stone Tract. He purchased the teak turtle at the Golden Sun Gem Store for his wife. When he brought it home and gave it to her, she decided to take it to her Office for luck. In the interim there was a robbery at the law office where she works. The turtle was stolen along with other things. By a stroke of what she considers *luck*, she and her husband were invited to the Grand Opening of an antique store in High Bridge, New Jersey where her boss resides. One of the owners of the store is her boss's wife. I know this may sound complicated but my friend's wife saw the turtle there at the antique store. Can you imagine finding it again in an unassuming place after it was missing for over a year?"

Mr. Nicro said, "That is quite a story! That turtle has been traveling quite a bit for a slow fellow." He and Khin laughed at the quip. "Tell me, how did the antique store acquire the turtle?"

Khin told him the two women store owners found it at a Flea Market in another town in New Jersey while they were shopping for antiques. Seeing that it was so unique, they were determined to own it. So they purchased it from a dealer who obtained it from some other dealer in another part of the state.

"Well, Mr. Zeya, that is amazing! I will be honest with you only because I find this so bizarre a tale. I had an artisan in my company carve that turtle for me. It was a gift for a very dear friend of mine in Mayanmar, a Mr. Kyi Lin Win."

"Where in Myanmar does he live?" Khin inquired, very interested.

He used to live in Yangon, where he owned a prestigious gem and wood sculpture store," Mr. Nicro said. "He passed away a few years ago. After his death, his wife sent it back to me to hold in his memory. She said it was his wish that I take it back and cherish it, as he did. You are not the only one with a story, Mr. Zeya. You see, I treasured that turtle because it was very rare and because it always reminded me of my dear friend. He had it for many years. After he died and I got it back it looked like it had changed somewhat. It looked a bit different than I remembered it."

"In what way was it different?" Khin asked with much curiosity.

"I found it to be heavier than I remembered and it had Myanmar symbols carved on the plastron and one single word carved on the top by the head. I assumed that because my friend was a craftsman he decided to carve his own heirloom symbols onto it for his son. But I never scrutinized it too much as I was distraught over the loss of my friend. So I just put it in a special place in my main store office."

"I am puzzled as to how it got back to Myanmar," Khin said.

"Unfortunately it was stolen from my store during a local robbery. I was never able to track it down until recently when some of my employees happen to hear of it being purchased in Mogok. I had my people try to trace it, but to no avail," Mr. Nicro said with a bit of disillusionment.

At this point Khin sensed that Mr. Nicro was holding back in his explanation. He almost felt that he was hiding something from him. But Khin decided not to pursue the conversation in that direction.

Mr. Nicro concluded with, "I decided to stop my pursuit of the turtle when I learned that it was out of the country, never knowing at the time that it was actually in the United States. I knew that I was out of my own territory and that it was useless to continue a search. So tell me, who owns it now?"

Khin said, "It is owned by the two women who own the Safe-Gard Fine Antique Store in High Bridge, New Jersey. Since they cannot talk to your friend, I think they will probably want to talk to his widow to see if she can tell them anything about those symbols."

Now Khin was the one holding back information, but he somehow felt the turtle's contents had nothing to do with Mr. Nicro. He didn't appear to know that it even opened, let alone that it had something valuable inside. It was time for him to leave. He thanked Mr. Nicro for his help and bid him farewell.

Mr. Nicro said, "I hope my turtle finally has a permanent home and that it doesn't cause anyone any trouble."

If Mr. Nicro knew the new contents of it, there might be a problem or he might put his friends in harm's way. So Khin was careful not to say anything and decided not to go any further with the situation.

When Khin got back home to Yangon, he immediately dialed New York. Charlie was home and was more than happy to hear from him.

"So what did you learn?" Charlie asked with much anticipation.

Khin explained that Mr. Nicro, the owner of the Unique Asian Wood Products Company in Bangkok was the original owner of the teak turtle and that he commissioned one of his artisans to hand carve it for a friend as a gift. The friend, a Mr. Kyi Lin Win, lived in Mayanmar and was a noted gem dealer and wood carver. His friend died and the wife sent the turtle back to Mr. Nicro as a memorial keepsake. But

Mr. Nicro had no idea what Mr. Win did to the sculpture. He said he knew there was something different about it but that he couldn't figure out what it was. Suffice it to say, that Mr. Nicro is no longer interested in the sculpture. He was just relieved that it was found and is in good appreciative hands," Khin said. "He said he will no longer pursue it and he is calling off any of his employees who may be still trying to track it down."

Charlie thanked Khin and told him he would be in touch again soon. In the meantime though, he asked Khin if he would try to locate the widow, Mrs. Win or the son.

"There are a lot of families with the name Win in Myanmar but I will try to narrow your search down by checking out wood and gem dealers in Yangon first when I return home. If I don't have any luck in Yangon, I'll move on further. My wife and I are due to take a vacation trip to Mandalay and other surrounding cities that we haven't seen in a while or at all. So I will mix my pleasure trip with a little business for you, my good friend. I will be in touch with you as soon as I return from my vacation, Charlie. Hopefully I will have some good news for you. Give my regards to your wife and family."

Chapter Eleven
Yangon, Myanmar

The next morning Khin checked out at 12 Noon and took the first flight out of Bangkok for Yangon. As he made the flight he tried to map out a plan of action to take on where to start looking for Mrs. Win or her son. He couldn't wait to tell Myine all about his trip.

When he got home he sat down and told Myine about Mr. Nicro and his Asian Wood Products Company and how his artisan was commissioned to create the teak turtle. Myine was shocked to learn that the turtle actually spent most of its life in Yangon in the possession of a Mr. U Kyi Lin Win and his family. She was rather shocked to hear that the widow of Mr. Win returned it to Mr. Nicro after her husband died. She thought it rather strange that the family didn't keep the turtle in the family as an heirloom.

Khin said, "Since Mr. Win had his gem and woodcraft business in Yangon, I figured that would be the best place to start searching for information."

Myine said, "The name Win is a very popular name here in Myanmar. It shouldn't be too difficult to locate where his business was. Maybe some store owner will remember him and his family or at least know something about them."

"I sure hope you are right, Myine. Tomorrow I am going to the Bogyoke Scott Market to begin inquiring. There are plenty of dealers and store owners there and I'm hoping to get lucky."

"I will go with you. One of our proverbs says, *two heads are better than one.* I think I can be a big help to you. So we will get up early and get this so called investigation underway."

When the amber Myanmar sun came up in the morning, Khin and Myine found themselves at the Bogyoke Market. Rather than waste time today they decided to check out all the gem dealers and woodcraft artisans first. Stall after stall was a dead end. No one seemed to know of Kyi Lin Win.

"You know something, Myine? I think we have to know a little more about Kyi Lin Win; maybe the name of his business or perhaps his wife's name. We seem to be getting no where. I am going to place one call to Mr. Nicro to see if he remembers the actual name of Mr. Win's store. So let's return home for a little while so I can contact him."

When Khin got home he called Mr. Nicro's company. Miss Bianta, the secretary put him through immediately.

"Hello, Mr. Zeya, how can I help you?"

"I was wondering if you might remember the name of the store that Mr. Win owned in Yangon. Having that information would be very helpful to me in locating his widow."

Mr. Nicro thought a moment and then said, "I believe it was something like the *Thiri Thuza Gem and Craft Store*, or the *Thiri Thuza Fine Woodcraft and Gem Store*. Don't hold me to the exact placement of the words. I do remember the Thiri Thuza words though. In fact Mr. Win's wife's name was Thuza. I distinctly remember that because he always referred to his wife as his angel. He told me Thuza means "angel" in the Mayanmar language."

Khin replied, "Well, *thiri* in Myanmar means gold and *thuza* means angel. So maybe it was the Golden Angel Wood and Gem Store or something similar. You have been a big help and I am grateful. I have my work cut out for me. I thank you, Mr. Nicro; your information should give us a better lead."

When Khin hung up he explained to Myine what Mr. Nicro said. She was kind of elated with the information and thought they now had a better chance of making a little headway.

After a quick light lunch, Khin and his wife returned to the Bogyoke Market and continued asking around about the Win store using the words, thiri and thuza interchangeably with gold and angel. After several hours walking through the market of over two thousand stores, they were quite tired. When they were almost ready to call it a day, they entered one last shop. It was a *panbu* (sculpture) store that specialized in producing figures and floral designs made of wood and ivory. The proprietor happened to know the Win family from a few years back.

"I knew a Mr. U Kyi Lin Win when I was a young man. My father use to deal with him and barter over Mr. Win's wood products. He made some very fine teak pieces, I remember. In fact, I think he also dealt in gems."

Khin asked, "Would you happen to know what the name of his store was?"

"Let me think now. Hmmm! Yes, Yes, it was the Thuza Gems and Woodcraft Store; no, the Thiri Thuza Fine Gems and Woodcraft Store. If it wasn't worded that way then I am pretty close to whatever it was named. Does that help you out?"

"Khin answered, "You are a big help, sir. Would you happen to know where in Yangon he had his store? An address would be doubly helpful to me."

As a matter of fact I do because it was in the neighborhood I grew up in. I lived over on Ahione Road and the Win store was on Pyay Road on the People's Park side. My father use to take me in there all the time with him to buy things for his own store. I remember seeing a lot of sculpture pieces and a second side store with gems and jewelry. He had a son who helped out in the store and went to school with me. His son was always interested in stone sculpture. His wife use to sell lacquerware in a side room as well. I remember that she was very artistic as well. She use to paint beautiful pictures right there in the store as she waited for customers to come in."

"Oh, one more thing," Khin asked, "you wouldn't happen to know the son's full name, would you?"

"Let me think a moment. His name was, Sanei Win

"Thank you very much for your help. I can't tell you how indebted I am to you. I will tell everyone about your little business here in the Market when they come into my Gem store. At least I can repay you that much."

Khin and his wife went home feeling elated with their findings. At least they were getting somewhere. The names would surely lead somewhere.

The next morning they were off again, only this time they had a specific destination in mind. They drove over to Pyay Road where they were told the Win store had been a few years ago. When they got there, there were several stores on the block across from the park, exactly like the young man described. So they wandered in and out of the stores hoping to stumble onto something that would help them. Out of all the stores, there was only one woodcraft store there. The owner said he bought it from the previous owner's widow.

"Do you happen to know the widow's name?" Myine asked politely.

"Let me see, the owner said thoughtfully. I think it was Daw Thiri Thuza. Let me check my books to make sure I am giving you the correct names. The name must be on my bill of sale."

Several minutes later, the owner came out from the back of his store, to verify that he was correct with the names he had given them. "The store was called the Thiri Thuza Fine Gems and Teak Woodcraft Store. It seems that the store was named after the wife of Mr. Win."

"You were very helpful and I am in your debt. I wish you good luck in your business."

While exiting the store, Myine said, "Khin, I think we finally have a small breakthrough. We had almost forgotten our own custom of the wife keeping her own name. How could we forget such a thing?"

"That's just it, Myine, we are not thinking. We must be more attentive to what we are doing. I am certain that this information is a huge breakthrough. It helped us to see the importance of our names. Now all we have to do is try and find Daw Thiri Thuza, Mrs. Win. Since the man said she sold lacquerware in the side of the store, perhaps she is still selling it someplace else."

"Myine answered, "Lacquerware establishments will be next on our agenda then."

The next several days, Khin and Myine went through the phone directory to find the locations of all the lacquerware shops in Yangon. There were quite a few, but in time they felt they could check them all out. So over the next week or so they inquired in all of the lacquerware stores they could find. Daw Thiri Thuza (Mrs. Win) was in none of them nor had anyone known of her.

Khin said thoughtfully, "I have a feeling Daw Thiri Thuza is no longer in Myanmar. Maybe she lives with her son somewhere. We haven't checked him out yet. What do you think we should do now?"

Seeing that Khin was somewhat distraught Myine said, "I think we should take our planned vacation now and go to Mandalay and maybe Inle Lake. That is where we were going to go in the first place before all of this happened with your American friend. Remember our old Myanmar proverb: *Never think of knowledge and wisdom as little. Seek it and store it in the mind with small particles of dust, and incessantly-falling rain drops when collected can fill a big pot.* Let's not get discouraged, Khin. We have learned a lot so far. In fact, I believe we have learned a lot in a short while. So let's use our minds to sort out what we know and apply it to future ventures. Every little piece of information is useful and we will find out more as we go along. Now, start planning our vacation."

"You are always so wise and practical, my dear Myine. I am going to book us a nice trip to Mandalay. From there we will see how things materialize. I know you like to travel and shop so I will make this trip pleasurable for you even though we will be on a special mission."

Chapter Twelve
Mandalay, Myanmar

"O the Road to Mandalay,
Where the flyin fishes play,
And the dawn comes up like thunder
Outer China 'crost the Bay!"

Excerpt from the poem, the Road to Mandalay by Rudyard Kipling

Khin Zeya wanted to be true to his word to his friend so he booked a flight to Mandalay for Myine and himself. To drive it would take fourteen hours to get to Mandalay from his home in Yangon, so they decided to fly instead. He figured that would be the best place to start his search for Kyi Lin Win's widow. He thought Mandalay would be a good jump-off point for the cities of Bagan and Inle Lake as well. He was traveling with his wife Myine as this was to be vacation time for them as he well knew. She loved to travel so she would not get tired of hopping around from place to place. She realized that Khin was on a mission for his American friend and she was willing to help him as much as she could.

They arrived in Mandalay rather early and they would not be able to check into their hotel. So Khin rented a jeep at the airport and they made the twelve minute drive into downtown Mandalay. Khin picked a fine hotel so that Myine could enjoy all its amenities. After all it was their vacation.

The Sedona Hotel Mandalay had a great location in the heart of Mandalay; one just perfect for them. It had fantastic views of the Mandalay Hill and of the Royal Palace. One good advantage was that is was only a short distance from the center of town. Since they could not check in yet, Khin rode around the city a bit to get some bearings on where he would like to take Myine.

Mandalay, Myanmar's second largest city seemed more like a big village to Khin. It still had a lot of dirt roads and small shops. Khin rode along the Irrawaddy River where he and Myine could enjoy the surreal vista of the Sagaing Hills and the white inverted cones of the pagodas pointing up to the sky. What a magnificent site to see; white against lush green hills and blue skies! They knew that white rather than gold was the predominant color of the temples in Mandalay. Khin parked the jeep and they continued their tour on foot. Years ago you would only see bicycles being ridden up and down the narrow streets of Mandalay; now cars were becoming the mode of transportation in the city. He didn't think he would locate Mrs. Win here but it was worth a try. If anything, he might get a lead somewhere or from someone. There were a lot of stores here in Mandalay so he had to seek and ask.

Khin was aware that Mandalay was a cultural and religious center for Buddhism; he also realized that it was a great commerce center. Gold leafs that were handmade, woodcarving, and cheroot (cigar) rolling made it look like a huge Oriental bazaar. You could feel the Chinese influence with all the increased activity. Of course, this was to Myine's liking as she loved to shop and browse and spend money. As they walked along they offered some alms to the young red-robed Buddhist monks who begged for their morning food from the village people. Myine and Khin were use to that custom as they did the same thing back home in Yangon. The Myanmar people had great respect for their monks.

After walking around for a while, Khin decided to go back to the hotel as they wanted to spend a few minutes refreshing themselves. They arrived at the Sedona Hotel and got themselves settled into their comfortable room. Afterwards they decided to go back to town to see about having some lunch. Khin thought he would give Myine a treat so he rented a rickshaw to get around the narrow streets. It was relatively cheap, about $3 American.

"Khin, this is delightful, "Myine said. "I remember riding in one of these when I was a child. My father brought us here to Mandalay on a long boat ride and we stayed here on what was supposed to be a family vacation. I remember having a lot of fun. What memories this brings back to me! Riding in this rickshaw is surely a treat for me. Thank you!"

"I'm glad it brought back some pleasant memories for you, my dear," Khin said. He held her hand as they rode along, taking in the sites.

They stopped at Mandalay Hill which is the best place to look out over the city. They passed the two immense statues of lions which guard the holy hill. It was impressive to walk through them. Since it was quite a hike from bottom to top, they took the elevator to the top to take in the panoramic view of the Old Royal Palace and Fortress, the Irrawaddy River and the Shan Hills in the distance. From the top they could also see the site of the war casualties in the 1945 battle between the British and the Japanese. This was all part of their Mayanmar history and heritage so they were enjoying this. They had almost forgotten how beautiful this city was until now. The scenery was breathtaking! They leisurely strolled down stopping at several of the sacred places that were there to visit. When they reached the bottom they decided to take that much anticipated break for lunch at one of the fine cafes.

After the refreshing lunch Khin wanted to go back to the shopping area to see if he could make some inquiries about Mrs. Win. He knew her husband was a craftsman and a gem dealer so he thought that's where he would start. One shop he saw was the Yoma Yadana Arts & Crafts Producers Co. He and Myine went in to look around. As Myine bought a few things, Khin asked one of the sales people if he ever heard of Kyi Win. That was the first dead end for Khin. They moved on to another shop, the Aung Myanmar Souvenir Shop. He approached a couple of women standing at a counter, again asking if they ever heard of Kyi Win or Mrs. Win. They looked at him rather strangely; wondering why he was asking. He sheepishly tried to explain that he was inquiring for a friend. The women chuckled as Khin thanked them and went to look for Myine. When he found Myine he told her he didn't think this was where Mrs. Win settled after her husband's death. He felt like he was grasping at straws, as they say.

Several days later after touring downtown and visiting places they wanted to see, they left Mandalay for the town of Bagan which was about an hour and ten minute flight. They decided to fly instead of drive so as to save time. They only planned on spending one day in Bagan.

Myine wanted to see Bagan as that was one city she never visited. Bagan was more of a pilgrimage center but it was known for its lacquerware. Khin thought he would take a chance and ask about Mrs. Win there. He thought maybe she was connected with the lacquerware business in Bagan since she had such a shop in Yangon in her younger days. He had nothing to lose by checking it out. Myine saw the nice shopping area with numerous shops. They went into the Shwe La Yaung Lacquerware Shop, the Golden Bagan Lacquerware Shop and the Chan Thar Lacquerware Work Shop. Despite all their efforts and the eager helpfulness of the store proprietors, they found out nothing of importance. Before evening set in they headed for the airport for the hour flight back to Mandalay.

After they landed at the airport in Mandalay, they picked up their jeep and drove back to their hotel for the night. They planned on leaving for Inle Lake which would be the last part of their vacation tour. The Inle Lake region would have more for them to do so they planned on staying there several days.

The bright morning sun came up early over the mountainous background as Khin looked out of his hotel window. He and Myine packed up, took most of their belongings to the jeep and then had a hearty breakfast in the hotel dining room. They had packed a smaller suitcase for a two or three day trip to Inle Lake. It was only a twenty minute plane ride from Mandalay to Heho Airport in Inle Lake. They planned on leaving their jeep at the airport until they returned.

Khin and Myine enjoyed the flight and before they knew it they were walking out of the plane and into the Heho Airport. The hotel they chose to stay at was a forty minute ride from the airport. For the first part of this trip they hired a driver to take them to Pindaya where they would board a boat to their resort hotel on Inle Lake. As they rode across the verdant mountain range down into the Inle Valley, they had a thousand questions about this magical place. The driver stopped at the Hot Springs on the lake as they were nearing the hotel. He told them they might want to return to the hot spring for a luxuriant soak with the locals. They would have a chance to chat with the Shan people bathing there. When they arrived at the Inle Lake View Resort, it was everything they imagined. After seeing the impressive lobby with all its teakwood accents and gold leaf decorations, they couldn't wait to see the room they had booked. It was a magnificent suite, decorated in soft tropical hues, bamboo shades and more teak wood just like the lobby had. The resort was on a huge twelve acre parcel of land, so they knew there would be plenty of activities for them to do. Myine had her eye on the leaflet on the check-in desk that advertised a traditional massage in your room by a local villager masseuse. She nudged Khin to make sure he saw it as well. They checked out the restaurant and that, too, was to their liking. Their goal was not to spend too much time in their hotel room, although they planned on enjoying all it offered when they were in it. They freshened up and went down for lunch. The Bougainvillaca Restaurant seemed to have a wonderful, friendly staff with both an international and Asian cuisine. When they stopped at the desk the Maitre'D greeted them with much attention and warmth. Myine commented how much she already liked their stay there. Khin was glad because he always wanted to please his wife.

Even though they were born and raised in Myanmar, neither of them had ever traveled to Inle Lake. They wanted to enjoy every minute of this trip.

"What makes your city so special?" Khin asked the waiter. "We have heard many splendid things about it back in Yangon where we are from."

"I think my city is very special for many reasons, but the best way to find out is to venture out and see it for yourselves. Your best bet is to talk to the concierge and let him give you some pointers on where to start, where to go and what to see. But I will tell you one thing; do not miss the Floating Market City. It is a wonder to behold! It is also the home of the *Inthas*, the "Natives of the Lake. You will see why many people find them amusing. Ask him to set you up for a day-long cruise on the lake. It is the only way to see the Intha habitat, the beautiful landscape and the villages and monasteries on stilts."

"Thank you, my good man," Khin said, "we will take your advice and see where it leads us. We already like the cool green lands of your

Shan State. It is so different from the rest of Myanmar. People always told us about it but you cannot appreciate it until you experience it for yourself."

"First thing tomorrow morning I will meet with the concierge as you recommended. Thank you for your help."

After enjoying a luscious dinner and an evening of lounging around, Khin called it a night. They wanted to get up early and start the next phase of their vacation and search for Mrs. Win. Myine spent about a half hour on the veranda enjoying the moonlight over the lake before she retired for the night. She knew the cool breeze would give her a pleasant night's sleep.

Rising at a reasonably early hour, they made their way downstairs to the dining room to have a good breakfast before they departed for the lake region. They did want to ask the concierge a few things first. As soon as breakfast was finished they found the concierge at his desk, not seeming too busy. They were glad for that because they wanted his undivided attention.

"Good Morning!" Khin said with Myine uttering the same. "We are visiting here from Yangon for a little business and mostly pleasure. Can you tell us what the most important things are that we should see? We only have a few days so we would like to see what the best is here at Inle Lake. Our driver told us you might be able to book us on a day-long excursion to the floating market."

"Good Morning to you!" the concierge said. "I am happy to meet you fine people. You will have a glorious time here if you plan it well. Inle Lake, our famous natural inland lake has outstanding natural beauty. It is almost like a jewel that is encircled by a ring of mountains. The lake itself is 2,900 feet above sea level and is very famous for its leg rowers, floating markets and prolific birdlife. While cruising on the lake in a motorized sampan you will be surprised when you see that in these wetlands, whole villages, built on stilts, sit near floating gardens on the lake. It is a spectacular sight! You will see a very traditional way of life among these people. The hill tribes live in the surrounding valleys and on the mountaintops that seem covered by forest land, where they weave their silk by hand from the peelings of the lotus stem. They make the most magnificent longyis. Your wife would very much want to own one when she sees them. They are just so colorful and well-made."

Khin replied with a positive tone in his voice, "Well, please arrange a trip for us. We are anxious to see this natural spectacle."

"You are correct in calling it a spectacle of sorts. It is quite a unique place, especially with the *kyunpaw*, the "floating gardens. Then there is the floating marketplace where the people gather to sell their wares."

"What are they?" Myine asked curiously.

"You must see for yourself. But I will tell you this much, they are the most colorful things I have ever seen. The assortment of flowers, different vegetables and the clothing worn by the people blend in to the most magnificent aura of colors, more beautiful than an artist's pallet of multi-colored paints."

Khin said, "I think we should get going as I cannot wait another minute to see this place. Are there any tour guides there at the lake?"

"As a matter of fact there are some native people who like to do that, but if you would like; I have several tour guides in my employ that I can send with you for the day. There is an additional fee, but it is well worth it."

"Please set us up with one of your guides. I think we would enjoy that very much." Khin said. "We want to be sure to cover everything we possibly can on our short stay."

They met their guide at the desk in the lobby. He explained that he was born right here in Inle Lake in one of the quaint houses that were nestled into the side of the mountains that surrounded the lake. There are several hundred villages on or around the lake. His family was involved in the floating markets. He told them to follow him over to a dock on the lake where he had a motorboat waiting and he would take them on a wonderful excursion.

When they reached the dock they saw numerous sampans, one painted more beautifully than the other. Each one had different kinds of cushioned seats. The boats were all next to each other in a row. The smooth ride out to the Lake region was pleasant and scenic. They arrived at the main lake town called Nyaung Shwe. Along the western side of the lake they saw the thousands of stupas surrounding the main pagoda, the Indaing Pagoda. As they entered the long corridors of the Pagoda they found numerous vendors selling their wares. Khin thought that might be a good place to inquire about Mr. Win's wife. He approached several vendors, one selling clothing, another selling lacquerware, others selling household items. He asked the sellers if they had ever heard of Kyi Lin Win or his wife, Daw Thiri Thuza. No one was able to help and they didn't recognize the names. Khin had entered another dead end street. They returned to the boat and continued on.

The guide continued to explain, "We are entering the area of the Floating Gardens. This is the Nanland Canal which is very shallow. It is here that many people have their floating gardens and reclaimed land. It is so heavily trafficked that the waterway looks more like a network of canals than a lake. The people use their boats as stores and the lake looks like a floating market. These floating gardens are built up from strips of water hyacinth and mud that is dredged from the lake bed. Over the years it becomes a very rich humus soil. The floating gardens are anchored to the bottom of the lake with bamboo poles. This is one way land is reclaimed by the people as their own place and the lake is sort of divided into plots around the maze of canals. Most of the produce grown is vegetables, mainly tomatoes and beans and the *codia leaf,* which is used to roll tobacco and make cheroots (cigars). They fill the boats up daily with their foods or wares and row out to the spot where they all meet to buy and sell. Everything is so colorful that it is a rainbow to behold! The produce is so fresh and ripe that you can't resist buying it. There is a lot of wildlife here. Ducks, swine and water buffalo hang around everywhere. These people are accomplished fishermen and market gardeners. The goods that are sold are of the highest quality. In a sense, they really do give you your money's worth."

Khin said, "This is so fascinating. I have heard of the floating market but have never seen it. I can now see what people mean when they describe it as an unusual marketplace. I can't get over how many boats are in this lake, all sizes and yet no one bumps into the other. Look, Myine, some have those gorgeous umbrellas you like. I think you might want one of those cone hats they wear, too."

"I am so astounded by this display of colors. The fresh vegetables, fruits and flowers are one masterpiece of natural beauty; but the clothing of the people adds to the colorful presentation as well. Oh look, Khin," Myine said, "A young family with their children is going to do some shopping. They are in their own little sampan. That is so cute!"

Myine asked, "Would we be able to stop for lunch now at that wonderful restaurant I see over there?"

"Of course we can. The Inn Thar Lay Restaurant has a lot of local delicacies if you would like to try some. I think you would enjoy it there."

"Will you join us?' Khin asked the driver.

"I would be happy to. Thank you!"

"Before we dock for lunch, I will stop here by the lakeside so you can observe the 'one-legged fishermen'. They are skillful at rowing with one leg while balancing their sampan with the other leg. Their hands are free to drop their conical nets over passing fish, which are easy to see in the shallow lake water. Fishing is a big part of their lives. These people, the Inthas, build most of their homes on stilts near the bank of the lake which is their lifeline. That makes it easier for them to tend their floating gardens in their sampans and then get their produce to the floating market area."

Khin asked, "Where do they learn to do this one-legged rowing?"

"It is taught to them at an early age. They must practice it and become precise before they are allowed to venture out onto the lake. The men that fish actually use smaller sampans so that they can maneuver their boats easier."

"I cannot understand how the sampan doesn't tip over. They stand right on the edge of it," Khin said in wonder.

Myine asked, "I have heard that they use the lake for almost everything. Is that true?"

"Yes, it is, they not only fish in it, but bathe in it and even wash their animals in it as well. Almost everything they do centers around the lake."

"Let me pull up the boat so that we can get our lunch and then we will be on our way," the guide said.

Lunch was just as delicious as he said it would be. They knew they were eating some of the finest vegetables and fruits from the area. Everything looked so lush and fresh. They returned to the boat where the man ferried them across the narrow waterway to visit some sacred places. As they approached the pagoda they saw a beautifully landscaped pagoda with a very clean dock all around it.

"This is the *Phaung Daw Oo Pagoda*, famous for its five small gold Buddhas which they consider to be the lake's guardians."

"It is magnificent." Khin said. "I especially like the red roofs with the gold adornments. It is a grand pagoda! We have stupendous ones in Yangon as you must know, but each pagoda has some specific beauty about it that makes it unique. This one is just a work of art!"

The tour guide continued on past the floating weaving factory where there were a lot of people engaged in a lot of different things like making colored turbans and black costumes with red and blue piping. "Now I will show you the entire Floating Market where they all congregate at once." When he arrived at the spot in the lake where the extensive *Floating Gardens* were, Khin and Myine gasped from surprise. They were unbelievable to see. They looked like little green floating islands of vegetation. Beyond the garden islands they could see the Floating Market, a "town" of sampans all close together selling just about everything. Each sampan had one or two people in it and all were selling something different. One was more colorful than the other. The driver rode along slowly and Myine and Khin bought several items for themselves. They were thinking that if they didn't have to travel back home they would buy a lot more of the fresh vegetables, fruits and flowers.

When they left the Floating Market, the tour guide showed them the unique bridge built in the middle of the lake that the boats rode under when passing by. It was just a sort of arch in the middle of the lake with no sides. It made for a unique attraction. The panoramic view of the lake with the mountains in the distance made for a great picture.

The guide told them he wouldn't want them to miss the jumping cats so he stopped at the Nge Hpe Chuank Monastery which is famous for its jumping cats. The Buddhist monks there teach the cats to jump through hoops as a form of entertainment. They are a very big attraction for our visitors. He said the cats have a rather good life with the monks.

As Khin and Myine walked through the porticos of the pagoda they passed several rooms where the monks were engaged in entertaining people with their cats. "Look at that cat jump through that narrow hoop, Khin," Myine said. "They are adorable to watch!"

Khin said, "I know, I especially like the colorful coats of fur on these cats. You could tell they are specially bred and wonderfully cared for. They certainly seem content. Isn't it strange how they are not distracted by visitors?"

The guide said, "The monks work long and hard with their cats. So one doesn't expect any of the cats to misbehave or not respond to their commands."

It was getting near dusk, so the guide told Khin and Myine he would have to start heading back to their hotel. They would have to dine at their hotel because after dusk none of the longboats run on the lake. They didn't have a problem with that and were getting kind of tired, so they were happy to call it a day. The guide dropped them off at the hotel dock and they offered their gracious thanks. He told them he would see them in the morning and they would go on a land tour in the mountains.

That night after a delightful dinner, Khin and Myine walked around the grounds that were lighted by tropical torches. Khin said, "You know, Myine, it is easy to forget part of the reason we came here. This place is so beautiful and peaceful that it makes one forget all one's troubles. I mean, of course, that I have been so engrossed in this unusual place that I completely forgot about looking for Mrs. Win or her son. I don't want to disappoint my friend in America."

"Don't fret, Khin," Myine said, "We will get back to that part of our trip. Don't forget you did say that we were making this our annual vacation too. I'm sure your friend wouldn't object to you having some fun on your vacation."

"Yes, you're right. We need to rest and enjoy ourselves a bit as well. There will be ample time to do some inquiring about the Wins or Thiri Thuza, as she calls herself."

The next morning, the guide arrived around nine o'clock just after they had finished breakfast. Khin was anxious to see how they would travel today. As he looked out toward the lake, the sun's rays were glistening over the top of it. He saw the wildlife enjoying themselves before the onrush of sampans pushed them out of the way.

"Good morning," Khin said. "How do we get around today, my good friend? I know we must go by sampan to the lake's edge, but what happens there?"

"Well, we will go by motorboat and dock at the shore of southern Shan state. Then we will proceed by jeep into some of the villages. We will be visiting the city of Taunggyi which lies on a plateau. It is in an atmosphere conducive to good health from the mountain air. You will breathe in some of the freshest mountain air. You will get a good view of the land as we zigzag through the roads that wind up the mountain. It is more of a modern city that still holds to some tradition. We will be passing a hospital, department store, the market, cinemas, shops, stores, restaurants and residential buildings. It is as you say a typical town. The busiest part of Taunggyi is the *Myoma Market*, which has become a very busy market that is always crowded with people. They sell a lot of things here from dresses, farm implements, and paintings, to sculptures, and arts and crafts. You can get just about anything here."

Khin answered, "That might be very important for me. Besides vacationing here I am also looking for someone. I am thinking that this may be the place to inquire about her."

"I will leave you two alone to go about your business today. I am going to visit a friend. I will meet you back here in town in the late afternoon and we will go back to Inle Lake before dark. Is that suitable to you?" the guide asked.

"That would be fine. My wife and I would like to shop and look around for awhile. Just give us about two hours. We will meet you later then."

Khin and Myine sauntered casually along the main road in town, stopping in some of the smaller shops. They weren't interested in the tall buildings or business offices. Though Myine was on a shopping spree, Khin, on the other hand, was on his inquiry mission. He asked a lot of proprietors if they ever heard of the Wins, Kyi Lin and Thiri Thuza, or their son, Sanei Win, but no one here could offer him any suitable answers. Khin suspected that this place might be too far from Yangon for Mrs. Win to have ventured out after her husband died. But he thought maybe Mr. Win's son might live out this way. No one, however, ever heard of them. As it was getting late, they decided to head to the center of town to meet the guide for the return trip to Inle Lake.

Khin, Myine and their guide rode down the twisting roads again and arrived at the lake where their boat was waiting for them. Before they knew it they were back in Inle Lake at the Resort. The guide told them he would meet them in the morning in the lobby for the return trip to Heho Airport.

Myine was glad the touring was finished. As much as she enjoyed seeing new things or visiting places she hadn't seen, she always liked to relax a bit on her vacations. Besides, she wanted to take advantage of some of the hotel's luxuries. She told Khin that she wanted to get a massage before dinner. Khin thought that would be fine and he simply went about walking around the grounds and enjoying nature's beauty. When he returned to the room, Myine was finished with her masseuse and she was getting ready for a special dinner with Khin. Two hours later they were showered, dressed and dining in the fine restaurant. They couldn't wait to sample the fresh fish of the Inle Lake that was offered on the menu and of course, the fresh vegetables. The meal turned out to be delicious and they were happy with their choices. After enjoying their tea and dessert, they were both quite tired and ready to call it a day. They went to their room to retire for the night.

The next morning, they were off to Heho Airport where they would catch their flight back to Mandalay. They had to stay for one night more in Mandalay and retrieve the rest of their luggage before heading back home to Yangon.

Chapter Thirteen
High Bridge, New Jersey

Nick was busy preparing a brief for one of his court cases when the phone broke his train of thought. He actually welcomed the interruption as he had hit a snag in his writing.

"Gardina Law Office, Good Afternoon." Nick said politely.

"Good Morning, Nick," Charlie Ling said. "I know it has been a while since I spoke to you, but I finally heard again from my friend, Khin in Myanmar. He just returned from a vacation in Mandalay and a few other cities and wanted me to know how things went. The trip was wonderful but he didn't find out too much more about Mr. Win or his family. He did, however, come up with some additional information that may hold a clue for us. The wife, Thiri Thuza, was a talented woman as well as her husband. She sold lacquerware in the husband's store and also liked to paint and sew designs on material she made into decorative pillows. In addition, I found out from a former school chum that their son was interested in sculpture and metals. That may be a lead for us to pursue next."

"I'll tell you what, Charlie," Nick said, "I am going to pass this information on to my wife and her friend, Krystyna and see what they can do with it. I'll tell them to keep Dena informed as well. Thank you for the follow-up. I hope it is helpful, to all of us."

"I still may want to take another trip out to Myanmar in the very near future, this time with my wife, as a pleasure trip. They are getting around to their good season, when the weather is the best and the festivals are going on. Then maybe I can do my own snooping around first hand with my friend, Khin. Somehow I feel the son would be enormously helpful, if we could only locate him."

"Well, let me know if and when you decide to take that trip, Charlie. Meanwhile have a good day."

"Give that wife of mine my love," Charlie answered. "Don't overwork her!"

After another successful workday, Nick's Volvo pulled into the driveway around six-thirty that evening. Stefan and Francesca were playing on the swings in the side yard, waiting for dinner hour to come. Nick pressed the garage door opener and he parked the car on his side of the double garage. Giovanna heard the car door and opened the door to the garage. She always liked to welcome Nick home when she could.

"I'm glad you're home early for a change," she said with a happy lilt in her voice. "I made a delicious white clam sauce for you and I have a beautiful piece of red snapper waiting to get into my oven."

"I know, my dear, I can smell it way out here. It is beckoning me to come in," Nick laughed. "And I know you must have a side order of broccoli rabe and fresh semolina bread for me."

As they sat and had their usual evening glass of Merlot together, they sat in the living room by the stone fireplace and exchanged their happenings of the day.

"I heard from Charlie Ling this afternoon. He had some news from Myanmar. His friend Khin and his wife took their vacation to some other cities in Myanmar. Aside from having a good time, they tried to ask about the Wins but they didn't get any leads as to the whereabouts of the Win family. They did find out that the wife went by her birth name as most Myanmar women do. He at least had another name to use, not that it helped any. The wife was involved with lacquerware for a while but she also dabbled in painting of some sort and sewing designs of some kind or other."

Giovanna asked, "How did they find that out?"

"Khin explained to me that he and his wife asked an awful lot of questions while they shopped and toured. In their own city, Yangon, they came across one store owner, a younger man, who remembered the Win Family and their business. He also went to school with the only son the Wins had."

"Well that was a favorable lead, wasn't it? Giovanna asked.

"I guess so. But they did manage to get the son's name, Sanei Win. That may be the lead we needed. Charlie Ling said he and his wife may take a trip to Myanmar. So maybe if we can gather some more information here by our own research, we can be of some help to him when he goes there."

"I'll explain everything to Krystyna and we will see what we can come up with. So now, let's go and eat my delicious meal. Please call Francesca in for me. She is playing in the yard with Stefan. Those two would stay out all night if we let them."

"I know I saw them together when I pulled in. Those two play so great together."

The next day as Giovanna and Krystyna were straightening up the store for the days group of visitors, Giovanna told her everything she had learned from Nick via Charlie Ling.

"So where do we go from here?" Krystyna asked with a confused tone in her voice.

Charlie Ling told Nick that Mrs. Win went by a different name. It is a Myanmar custom for the wife to keep her own name after marriage. So Mrs. Win went by her birth name, Thiri Thuza. The names mean "golden angel" and it seems the husband named his store after his wife's names. Charlie told Nick it was called the *Golden Angel Fine Gems and Teak Woodcraft Store.* Some young storeowner in Yangon knew of the Win Family having gone to school with the Win son, Sanei. The young man gave Khin a lot of information about the Win family, their skills, their talents and things like that. It seems the wife was involved with a small lacquerware business while the husband ran his teak and gem business. But the wife had other talents, one was painting and the other was sewing designs on material. The son, Sanei, may be a sculptor or involved in bronze casting because he likes to work with metals."

"I think maybe we should do some research into the sort of trades the people of Myanmar do. Then maybe we can focus in on the specific interests of Mrs. Win and her son. At least we can give Charlie a little help for when he goes there."

"That's a good idea. I think you and I should go back to the library one day and see what we can find out about the trades and businesses there, Krys. I don't know how you feel, but I just have this desire to do something more to help."

"Okay, then tonight when I go home I am going to try and find out what the predominant trades are that the people make their lives with over there in Myanmar. I'll search the web and see what I come up with. Nick said that Charlie's friend, Khin, in Yangon wasn't able to find out much in Mandalay, Bagan, Inle Lake and other cities where they vacationed recently. So I think we should focus in more on Yangon where the Wins actually lived years ago and ran their business. Sooner or later, one of us will stumble onto something I'm sure."

When they finished for the day, and locked up the store they headed home.

That evening after dinner, Krystyna went on her computer and began checking out sites about Myanmar, specifically focusing in on Yangon, the capital city. She found quite a bit of information which she printed out. She would share her information with Giovanna tomorrow at the store, where they always seemed to have their best conversations.

Mornings in High Bridge were usually quiet with the usual people trekking along to their jobs and businesses. Krystyna and Giovanna were among the routine pedestrians making their way to their locations. They opened up at ten and got their coffee urn turned on for their morning brew. As they sat and sipped their coffee they munched on the homemade apple walnut muffins that Krystyna baked the night before.

"I must say I had a bit of luck last night. I found out the names of several trades that the people of Yangon have. I listed them as such: (1) *pabu* – sculpture; (2) *pantain* – the art of gold and silver smithy; (3) *padin* – the art of bronze casting; (4) *pantarot* – the art of making floral designs using masonry; (5) *payan* – bricklaying; (6) *pabe* – blacksmith; (7) *pantamault* – sculpting with stone; (8) *panpoot* – the art of turning designs on the lathe; (9) *Bochi* – painting; and (10) *panyun* – lacquerware. How is that for a list to start with?"

"I think that will take us a while but it sure sounds interesting. I just hope it leads somewhere beneficial to our cause. Maybe we should divide it in half; you take the first five and I'll work with the second five. Pick out the trades you feel are pertinent to our "case" meaning what you think the wife or son might have been into, and I will do the same. I think we can eliminate the trades that don't pertain to the ones the family was involved with. That way we will get done faster," Giovanna said.

"That sounds like a good game plan to me," Krystyna answered. "Do you want to go over to the library on our way home for a while to see if we can get started? It is opened late tonight. We can call our husbands and tell them we'll be a little late tonight."

"I think so. I am so into this that I want to delve right into the research," Giovanna said.

At day's end the two "sleuths" found themselves in the High Bridge Library. They roamed over to the history section and chose a nice secluded spot in the corner where they could talk without disturbing anyone with their chatter. They were beginning to feel like the Snoop Sisters of mystery fame.

After about an hour of research, opening musty old books, and pushing around volumes of large books, they put their two heads together and tried to come to some kind of conclusion.

Giovanna said, "I researched the *panbu* trade, sculpture, but didn't think the son would be into that because it was done on a larger scale with figures made of wood or ivory. Then I almost thought the son might be into *pantain*, working with gold and silver, making bowls, belts, earrings, pendants and such. But supposedly the man that knew him in Myanmar said he was more into sculpture or casting. So I am going with my third choice and my intuition and saying that I think he was into *padin*, bronze casting. I say that simply because it is still a thriving type of business there in Myanmar. They use copper, bronze or brass to make gongs, brass bowls for the monks, trays, pots, cymbals, and jingle bells; all items they use profusely there in their pagodas, on their buildings, in their stores and in their homes. I read that the gongs are struck there to tell the people of good deeds done. And since they are big on traditional practices, I feel that maybe he is a bronze caster. Are you with me so far?"

"I am following your train of thought. Now listen to my deduction from what I've found. I eliminated *pantarot*, the art of making floral designs using masonry because I don't think the son would be into that and it would also be too complicated for the wife. Knowing what we know about the son, that he was into sculpting, I, for a moment or two considered that his art was *pantamault*, which is when artisans make Buddha images, stone sculptures and such. Stone sculpture is a significant feature of Myanmar fine arts and it is the pride of the people there. There are many sculpting studios throughout Yangon and Mandalay. But since the majority of them are in Mandalay, I discounted my theory that the son might be into that art. It's possible that he liked to sculpt, but I don't think it became his trade for some reason."

"Well that makes good sense. I agree with you there," Giovanna said. "Perhaps your intuition is right."

Krystyna continued babbling on and on, "I came to what I believe is a very good conclusion. I think our Mrs. Win, Thiri Thuza, is still into the lacquerware. That is the art the Mayanmar man said she was interested in. *Panyun*, the lacquerware handicraft is a process one learns over the years, almost like a trade. She must have been good at it if she had a small store of her own. I don't think she would abandon her business especially now that she was a widow. She probably needed the income and needed to keep busy."

"Is it a complicated process, Krys?" Giovanna asked. "What did you learn about it?

"The process involves using materials from bamboo, wood and thick black varnish. They use finely cut strips of bamboo, mixtures of *thit-see* resin with clay and ash. These materials are built up, styled into shapes they want to make, and then polished with the ash of fossil wood. Then they etch designs they want on them by hand."

"That sounds like something the wife would be doing especially since she also liked to design or paint, Krys," Giovanna said. "Didn't Charlie tell Nick that she liked to sew designs on material or something? Maybe we ought to consider the sewing angle a bit more. Hmmmm!"

Krystyna continued with her explanation, "The traditional lacquerware is a unique terracotta color with Buddha scenes etched in them and then filled with a green pigment. The more modern designs are deep black velvet, with gold leaf designs etched into them. I have seen a lot of them around, various kinds of boxes, vases, trays. Pier One Imports has some of them as do stores in Chinatown in New York. Yes, I think we are on to something here and we should pursue it. I'm going to get in touch with Charlie Ling and see if he will be going to Myanmar anytime soon."

"Let me know what happens after you talk to him," Giovanna answered. "I think we should head home and explain our theories to our husbands. Let's see if they agree with us."

When they arrived home at Krystyna's house, the husbands had everything under control; the kids were fed and playing and the men were watching a ballgame. Seeing they were engrossed in what they were doing, they just said hello and went into the kitchen. Krys whipped up a quick sandwich and a cup of coffee for the both of them. Afterwards Krystyna put in a call to Charlie Ling.

Luckily Charlie was home early from work. He was surprised to hear Krystyna's voice when he answered the phone. "Hi there, did you find out anything new?"

"Well, yes and no," Krystyna said. We did some research on the arts and trades of Myanmar and came to a few conclusions. One, we feel the son is into what they call *padin* or bronze casting. That's an art where they use copper, bronze or brass to make things like bowls, bells, gongs and such. It's a trade that is still very useful there and we feel that maybe the son might be making and selling them. Sculpting might be a side hobby. Of course, we aren't sure of that deduction. However, we are taking a long shot in the dark with that theory. So we are not positive about that idea but we feel it is worth pursuing. Then regarding the wife, we deduced that she is still into lacquerware with the possibility that she is designing by painting on her wares or sewing designs, maybe like tapestries. We don't think she would give that trade up because she had to have an income after her husband died. If she had a successful business going then and enjoyed the artistic part of it, designing and etching, she probably kept it up. What do you think of our theories?"

"You two are amazing! You manage to find information very fast. I know you are merely guessing at things but your theories sound rather solid. I think the only way we are going to get farther with this at this point is to go to Myanmar ourselves and do some investigating. My friend Khin has done a lot for us and has found out some things, but I think it's time for me to go there myself. I was planning to take Dena there on a vacation anyway. So maybe I will ask for time off and plan a trip very soon."

Krystyna said, "Let us know when you are going. Meanwhile I will fax you our notes as a reminder for when you do go. Keep in touch now; say hi to Dena for us."

"I'll do that," Charlie said.

Several weeks later Giovanna heard from Dena. She explained that she and Charlie would be leaving for Myanmar in a few days. Charlie wanted to go at this time of year because the climate was best there. They would have very little or no rain to contend with. So Charlie booked them on their flights to Myanmar via London.

Dena said, "I know it is going to be a long trip and I am not looking forward to that. I really don't like flying. I just go because there is no other way to get there. But I will make the best of it and think of all the nice things Charlie always tells me about Myanmar. And I am sure he is going to keep me occupied with conversation and other activities. He always does."

"I envy you, Dena," Giovanna said. "I would love to go there, especially now with this turtle situation we are faced with. You are lucky to have this opportunity. I'm sure Charlie will show you a fabulous time, especially with the new friends he made there. You will probably see more than the average tourist because you will have a first hand guide. I assume Charlie will be asking Khin to accompany you wherever you go."

Dena answered, "Khin is supposed to come along to a few places with us, but at others we will be on our own; which should be quite interesting."

"That's true," Giovanna said. "I know Khin has a gem store to run. Let us know when you return; and I hope you bring home good news for us. Have a great time and wish Charlie the same."

Chapter Fourteen

Charlie and Dena Ling got picked up early by Limo and were anxious to get to JFK International Airport. Their teenagers would be staying with their grandparents for the duration so they wouldn't have to worry about them. They were responsible, but when they were out of town, the grandparents always helped out.

While waiting for their flight on British Air to London, then on to Yangon in Myanmar, Charlie was making sure they had everything they needed. Dena was holding the portfolio with their passports and entry Visa which was required for all visitors. Health wise Charlie knew that they didn't need any vaccinations going into Myanmar from the States. But he wanted to reassure Dena.

"I hope I took the proper clothing for this trip, Charlie," Dena said. "I know we have to dress modestly in Myanmar. I remember you telling me they don't allow shorts and tank tops, so I didn't even take shorts. I tried to bring shoes that were easy to slip on and off as well, because you said we have to take our shoes off when entering religious pagodas."

"Yes, we have to remove our shoes and socks too if we enter a pagoda. It is also a custom there to remove your shoes when you enter someone's home. That's why I told you to bring only shoes that were easy to slip on and off. The Mayanmar people wear thong-style sandals as they are most convenient to get on and off."

"I won't have any trouble with my shoes. I always wear easy style shoes; and I did bring several pairs of thong sandals."

"Did you bring the beautiful longyi I bought you on one of my trips? Now is your chance to wear it and in grand style. You will look lovely in it."

"I did pack it and I was planning on wearing it one evening for dinner. If I find it comfortable I may wear it more often." Dena smiled and gave Charlie one of her flirty looks.

"Dena asked, "Do we have to change planes a lot, Charlie?"

"Only a few times; we will fly to London and then on to Yangon. It shouldn't be too much of a hassle. I think you will enjoy our trip. Just try to relax; I can feel your tense vibes from here," Charlie joshed.

"Maybe you can fill me in on some of the places we will visit in Myanmar since this flight is rather long," Dena said. "I already know a lot about the country from all the things you always tell me about it, but there is nothing like seeing it for yourself."

"Dena, you are going to love it there. It has a lot of romantic charm. The swaying palm trees, the wide streets, sparkling lakes and gilded shrines make it a very special place. It is a country that is unspoiled by the modern world. At times you will feel like you are stepping back in time to another era. They still have the old British colonial horse carriages in a few places and you hear the clip clop of the horses now and then. The marketplaces are on a sensory overload of spices and exotic vegetables. Hundreds of Buddhist monks walk around in the early morning hours with their alms bowls. There is lot to do and see. You will be asking me to slow down and take a rest; you'll see."

"Where will we be staying in Yangon?" Dena asked.

"This time I chose the Traders Hotel which is about thirty minutes from the airport. It's close to key attractions like Chinatown, the Bogyoke Aung San Market and a lot of other places I want to show you. If we don't go to the Myanmar informal Chinatown our trip won't be complete. You are going to love it there. The streets are lined with four-story brick townhouses that are white-washed in pastel colors and decorated with ornamental scrollwork. It is a bustling place until two in the morning with people eating Chinese food, enjoying barbecue, and drinking beer and liquor. There are lots of shops which should be right up your alley; gold shops with plenty of jewelry, and fruits and vegetable vendors. Fruit is very plentiful out here, so you will have your choice of many like mandarin oranges, apples, watermelons, bananas, guava, pomelo, grapes, and mango, among many others. I know how much you enjoy your fruit. You may as well buy it and enjoy it while you are here because we cannot take it home."

Dena asked, "Will we be able to dine on the sidewalk like we do in New York? Do the people do that in Yangon?"

"Of course, and you'll smell the delicious dishes of egg and wheat noodles, grilled meats, and deep-fried spring rolls. That should wet your appetite. You'll be pleading to eat." Charlie laughed.

Within thirty minutes they arrived at the hotel. The beautiful white hotel stood out. It had a sophisticated elegance about it and seemed to be in a prime location, close to town and everything of importance. They received warm hospitality from the moment they exited their limo.

"I love the appearance of this hotel, Charlie. Its warmth is beckoning me. Don't you feel it?" Dena asked.

"I can appreciate the excited feeling you are experiencing. I have had it when I came here on past trips. Myanmar has a magnetic pull to it; one seems to love it the minute one comes here. Because of our little turtle, we finally have a good reason to vacation here. Maybe the turtle's secret gift to us is drawing us to its roots." Charlie couldn't help but chuckle at his comment.

"I agree with you. I like this place very much already." Dena said excitedly.

After checking in they were escorted up to the top floor as Charlie requested the suite at the top. He wanted Dena to enjoy the beauty of Yangon from above; the awe-inspiring view of golden topped pagodas and the Yangon River and Sule Pagoda. *There was so much to appreciate here, he thought.*

Their room was tastefully decorated in pastels and accented with teak fixtures and gold adornments. The furniture was done up in beautiful brocade material and the walls were graced with colorful scenic tapestries of various sizes. Charlie took over the executive writing desk with his laptop computer and his briefcase. Dena didn't seem to mind as she was enjoying the elegance of the room and the breathtaking view of the lush green palm trees swaying in the breeze from the enormous glass windows.

"What are you daydreaming about, my dear?"

"I was just thinking of one of the sayings of Confucius that says *everything has beauty, but not everyone sees it.* The more you observe, the more you see."

"Not everyone is fortunate enough to see such beauty, Dena. Now, would you like to make this first day memorable by dining in the hotel restaurant this evening?" Charlie asked. "They are supposed to have an Asian & International Restaurant with spectacular views of the city. They are recognized for their traditional Cantonese cuisine and their mouth-watering desserts."

"I would like that, darling," Dena said. You know how I love to fine dine. I hope they have some type of Myanmar music playing. That would top off the evening."

"You are such a romantic, Dena, my love; another reason why I love you so much."

Dena and Charlie had a delicious dinner that evening and enjoyed one of the delicious desserts along with their tea. It was a cream of wheat cake which was custard with a raisin center and lightly browned on the top. Dena remarked about how tasty it was. When they returned to their room Charlie said he was going to call Khin to tell him they were in town. It wasn't too late yet so he knew he was probably still in the store.

The phone rang in the Zeya Gem Store and Khin picked up the phone very promptly. "Mingalarbar," Khin said loudly. "Zeya Gem Store, how may I help you?"

"Mingalarbar, Khin; it's Charlie Ling. Dena and I arrived early today and got settled in. The hotel, Traders, we are staying in is wonderful. I showed Dena around a bit and before we knew it, evening overshadowed us. We just finished dinner and I thought I would call to let you `know that we are finally here. At last I found an opportunity to bring my wife to Myanmar. I can hardly wait to show her some of its beautiful places. You will finally meet my sweetheart."

"Welcome, my friend, I am so glad you are here. Myine and I would like to see you tomorrow. After all, our wives have never met and I have never met your wife. I think our getting acquainted is way overdue."

Charlie answered, "Before I set out on my business, slash pleasure trip, I do think we should meet. How about if I bring Dena to the store tomorrow and you ask Myine to be there? At least we will meet and then maybe make plans for a dinner during our stay here."

"That's a great idea. Myine and I will be waiting for you in the store. How does eleven o'clock sound?"

Charlie answered, "That sounds perfect to me."

"Oh, and Charlie, don't eat breakfast," Khin said. "Myine and I will prepare a nice brunch for us in my plush little office. Have a pleasant night."

"See you tomorrow. Thank you, Khin. Thwame naw! (Good Bye)."

Mornings in Myanmar are so refreshing and uplifting, Charlie thought as he hopped off the king sized bed. He drew the bamboo blind and took in the rapturous view of the lake and its surroundings. Dena stirred, arose and then joined Charlie by the huge window.

"My, oh My, what beauty I behold! You are right, dear, this place is captivating! I cannot wait to see more of this city and maybe some others."

The Traders Hotel wasn't too far from town so Charlie told Dena they would take a leisurely walk over to Khin's store. They had enough time before Khin and Myine expected them. As they walked they were getting a perfect picture of how life worked in Myanmar, specifically in Yangon, the capital. People were scurrying about their business, yet they weren't in a mad frenzy like New Yorkers appeared to be, running up and down streets. Everyone seemed to be casually walking to wherever they wanted to be. Some were hanging out at the local cafes.

As they walked, Dena said, "I see what you mean about the Mayanmar people using a lot of gold to accent their homes and businesses. The doorways especially are decorated with gold leafs and other ornaments. They are so pretty."

Charlie said, "Khin told me one time that if the people can't afford to buy the gold leafs to place on their homes or wherever they want them, they use gold paint instead. Gold leaf making is one of the big businesses out here. The Mayanmar people like to place them everywhere."

Charlie pointed out the Sule Pagoda in the distance and other stately buildings like the court buildings, the post office with its arched entrance and other city hotels as they walked along. As they got further into the downtown, Dena noticed the increase in noise, like any city would have. A lot of trucks were riding by along with basic morning traffic. They saw the Railway Station to the west side of town and were nearing the famous Bogyoke Aung San Market Building and the Holy Trinity Cathedral in the same area.

Dena commented, "I can see the English colonial style in these buildings because they used red very dominantly in their architecture. Some of the buildings have wide yellow-trimmed arches and looming turrets also. You can definitely detect the British influence from years past. Some of those aging colonial mansions have moss growing out of the faded and peeling stucco of their facades."

Lastly on their jaunt, Charlie pointed out the Secretariat Government Offices which occupied an entire city block. They were grand elegant buildings, ones that the Mayanmar government seemed to take pride in upkeeping. They were approaching the Zeya Gem Store area so Charlie nudged Dena to cross the street.

When they entered the Zeya Gem Store, Dena smiled at hearing the pleasant sounding chimes in the doorway. You could tell she thought the store was as lovely as Charlie always told her it was.

"Good afternoon," Khin said as he immediately approached his American friend. "And Dena, I am so pleased to meet you finally," as he extended his hand. Dena returned the handshake with the warmth of her hand.

Khin continued, "This is my wife, Myine. We have been so anxious about this visit. We are both so glad to meet you and we hope you enjoy your stay."

"It is so wonderful to meet you both," Dena commented in her bubbly sort of way.

Khin said, "Myine has prepared a wonderful brunch for us in my office dining area. Please come and enjoy our food and drink."

Charlie and Dena followed Khin to the back office as Myine scurried ahead to prepare to serve. As they sat at the rattan table and cushioned chairs, Dena commented that something smelled absolutely delicious.

I hope you enjoy the Asian luncheon I have prepared for you," Myine offered. I made a homemade poo poo platter with some wonderful fried fish and I have Lobster Cantonese as our main dish."

"What a treat this is, Myine," Charlie said. "I'm sure both Dena and I will enjoy this meal, especially since it was homemade by you.

Thank you for a warm Myanmar welcome. We feel very much at home already."

"That is what we intended our reception to do; make you feel at home in our city. Now, please eat before it gets cold. While we dine you can fill me in on your plans."

Charlie began to tell Khin about his plan to look for Mrs. Win, Thiri Thuza. He would try both names and see where it led. His plan was to look first in Yangon very intently. "I know you have inquired a lot about her in many places. But perhaps there are some places we have overlooked, thinking they wouldn't pertain to her."

"I'll help as much as I can," Khin said, "but I think you might be better off on your own with your wife. See how you do. I am always here to assist if you need me."

After lunch and a repeated thank you, Charlie and Dena said their so longs and left the store. With Khin's reassurance in the background, Charlie knew he would do alright with his search.

When Dena and Charlie got back to the hotel, Dena decided to take advantage of the spa facilities. She wanted to use the sauna and relax a bit. Charlie told her to go and enjoy the spa, but he was going to finalize the plans for their little trip away from Yangon.

Charlie was deep in his paperwork when Dena returned. "I hope you are making good plans for us, Charlie my dear."

"I certainly am and I want you to get a good night's sleep because we are starting out early for the airport. I want to get to Ngapali Beach on the Bay of Bengal. I figured we should enjoy some R & R before we come back to Yangon to do some intense searching for Mrs. Win."

"Oh, we're going to fly? I thought you wanted to drive."

"I was considering it at first, but it is too far. It would take us fourteen hours to drive there. The flight only takes about an hour, so we will be going via Air Mandalay since it flies two times a day in season. We will be flying into a town called Thandwe. So let's get some rest. I wish you pleasant dreams, Dena."

Dena was up and getting ready way before Charlie. He was glad though because Dena always took long to pack and get ready when they were going somewhere.

They packed their belongings for a four day trip to Ngapali Beach. Charlie had limo pick up waiting for them when they exited the elevator in the hotel lobby.

170

"Okay, we are finally en route to Mingaladon Airport. We should be there shortly."

The limo made it in no time flat, and Charlie and Dena entered the airport and hurried to get to their plane. They were to take off in a half hour.

After an hour flight, which seemed very short to Dena, they arrived at the airport in Thandwe. It was a small airport and not too crowded. It appeared to be undergoing a lot of construction and road work. Charlie got a cab to take them to their hotel. The driver told them it was seven kilometers to Ngapali Beach. He said," You folks will like this beach. We refer to it as our "Naples, Italy."

"Why is that?" Charlie asked.

"It is said to have been named that by a homesick Italian who stayed here."

Dena laughed and said, "Well, from what I see so far, it sure looks a lot like coastal Italy. I can see the unspoiled beauty. The beach sand looks like white powder and I'll bet it feels as soft. I can hardly wait to sink my feet into it."

"There is a lot to do here, if you choose to," the driver added. There is cycling, motor boat rides, golf and much more. But, of course, if you wish to be laid back and do next to nothing like sunbathe or stroll on the beach, you will see that it is a rather peaceful place in which to do just that. You won't have to contend with beach hawkers either who try to persuade you to buy things. All you have to do is enjoy the cobalt blue sea, our white sand and tranquil, transparent water. Even our marine life is clean and far from dangerous."

"It certainly seems serene and calm as we are riding along the coast," Dena chimed in. "It seems like an awfully long coast."

The driver answered, "Oh, this is not one beach, but a series of beaches that are interspersed with fishing villages all along this vast coastline. This small winding tarmac road snakes along the whole coast for about twelve miles from the town of Mazin to the town of Lontha. You will see what I mean as we continue to ride and when you tour around while you are staying here. Well, here we are at your hotel, the Ngapali Beach Hotel. You should like it here as this is one of our recently refurbished hotels. We are doing a lot of rebuilding and reconstruction, as you can see."

"Thank you, my good man," Charlie said. You were most helpful. We will keep in mind all of your advice about our visit here."

Charlie and Dena followed the bell hop who was taking their luggage on the carrier. They met him at the main desk and proceeded to check in.

"What a beautiful hotel, Charlie," Dena exclaimed. "I know I am going to enjoy this fine place. Even if I do nothing but sit on the beach and admire this beauty of nature, I will be content."

As Charlie was finishing up checking in, Dena busied herself by checking out the Ngapali Beach Hotel lobby from one end to the other, including the restaurants. She was in awe of the newly renovated lobby with its warm variegated brown and beige color scheme and the teak furniture. The thing that caught her eye was the abundance of fresh flowers everywhere. There was a huge bouquet in the center of the lobby right beneath a huge round skylight. The sun's rays were penetrating through and creating a kaleidoscope effect. The floral fragrance permeated everywhere she turned. She felt as if the flowers were putting on an aromatic performance of some sort. *What a stupendous lobby, she thought.* She was completely enthralled by the aviaries with beautiful exotic birds and colorful parrots. One was a blue macaw that seemed to be eating pine nuts. All she could think about was that there was a lot going on here and she didn't know where to look first. She presumed that was the idea for the décor; to captivate one's attention in all directions. She had traveled with Charlie before, to other island locations, other cities; but this was truly a paradise.

Charlie sauntered over to where Dena was standing in the middle of the lobby. He saw how mesmerized she was with this unique lobby.

"We are ready to go up to our room, Dena. We can always come down here and look around some more later on or tomorrow."

"I'm ready to go up. I was just in awe of all the color and beautiful things I see. Before we go I want to show you the plaque I found hanging on the wall over there. Look what it says. *Mind is the forerunner of all good condition. Mind is their chief and they are mind-made. If, with a pure mind, one speaks and acts, then happiness follows one. Like a never-departing shadow.* It says at the bottom that this excerpt is taken from the opening lines of the Dhammapada – they illustrate the central theme of Buddhist teaching. Isn't that a profound thought, Charlie?"

Charlie replied, "It certainly gives you a lot of food for thought. You may find a lot of such surprises here in Myanmar. Now let's make our way up to our room."

Upon entering their two-room suite, Dena gasped. She didn't quite expect Charlie to get such an extravagant room. One room would have been sufficient. Nevertheless, she was appreciative of the extra sitting room with satellite TV and a wet bar. When Charlie pulled back the huge bamboo shade, they both saw the most beautiful inland lake that was cradled by low lying hills.

Charlie said, "It says in this brochure I grabbed at the front desk that this is a reservoir here behind the hotel. They certainly keep it in good shape. Look at the landscaping on those hills! Everything is so perfectly terraced. You could see how much work they have put into this place."

"I would love to see that lake a little closer. This place is beginning to inspire me to write one of my poems. You know it doesn't take much to inspire me. You know, something, Charlie, we are actually between a magnificent man-made oasis and the majestic blue of the Bay of Bengal. What a word picture that conjures up in my mind! I must say, if it was not for that turtle of ours, you probably would have never brought me here. That turtle is both causing a lot of trouble for all of us and at the same time bringing us an abundance of joy and reflection. Yes, this definitely warrants me writing a poem that will be a perfect souvenir and memento of this place, Ngapali Beach."

Charlie said, "I hope you do write that poem so that we can both have a memory of our trip and reminisce about it when we are old and gray." They looked at each other and laughed heartily.

"Since it is early in the day yet, I think we should take a tour of the small fishing villages along the coast. When I checked in, I rented a jeep for our use while we are here." Charlie said. "That way we can leisurely drive and stop when and where we want to."

As they drove along they saw that each little village had its own charm and mode of activity. Dena bought several souvenir items for their kids. While she shopped Charlie took advantage of these opportunities to ask the locals about Mrs. Win and her son. He knew he was grasping at straws here, but he also knew it wouldn't hurt to ask. His probing was to no avail though. No one out there ever heard of them.

When they returned to their hotel grounds, they sauntered through the lobby making their way to the elevator. Dena stopped in her tracks when she saw the gift shop in the far corner. She went in to browse with Charlie tailing behind. Shopping was not his cup of tea, but there were things Dena did with him that she didn't much care for either. So he tagged along and patiently let her look around. While Dena was engrossed in the dainty things, Charlie decided to go over by some large lacquerware pieces he spied on one side. He picked up several of the pieces to examine them closely. He was admiring the etchings and designs on them when suddenly he looked stunned. Dena saw him staring and walked over to see what had her husband, the "shopper's," attention.

"Dena, look at this!" Charlie uttered in a nervous tone. "What do you make of this? The name *Thiri Thuza* is etched on the side of several of these bigger pieces. That's the name Mrs. Win uses. I never dreamed I would find anything relating to her way out here in Ngapali Beach. Khin and his wife were to so many other places in Myanmar on their vacation and never found anything at all. I came all the way from America and low and behold a breaking point! What do you make of this?"

"I think we should go over to the counter and ask to speak to the manager. Maybe he can give us some answers to our questions. He seems to be free now; let's go over there. Now keep calm because we don't want to alarm the man."

They approached the man behind the counter. "Are you the manager of this shop?" Dena asked.

The man looked up and saw two tourists staring at him. He wondered what this was all about. *I hope they didn't break anything, he thought to himself.* "Yes, how may I help you? Is anything wrong; you look apprehensive about something?"

"We were wondering if you could tell us anything about the artisan who made these lacquerware pieces that you have for sale in your shop. There seems to be a name etched on the side of each one in fine gold lettering that says, *Thiri Thuza*. Do you know this person?" Charlie asked.

"I do not know the artisan personally, but I can tell you that I buy all of my lacquerware pieces from her. I love her work. She makes unique pieces but I especially love the etchings and designs she creates. She is quite talented. I have seen lacquerware all over Myanmar, but hers is the finest. I happened to buy one from her store years ago in my travels and I tracked her down when I opened this store in the hotel. I wanted to have some of her work displayed in my store because I know they will sell and make business for me."

Dena asked, "Can you tell me where she lives or where she works? We are looking for a woman with that name, Thiri Thuza, who was married to a Mr. Kyi Lin Win back in Yangon."

Well, I use to buy some pieces from a store in Mandalay and other pieces from a store in Yangon and my last purchase was almost a year ago. I don't know if the woman you are looking for is still in Mandalay or Yangon, but I will give you the last address that I used to purchase my pieces."

"That would be so helpful to us. I would like to speak to her and see more of her work," Charlie said. He didn't want to give the man more information than he had to.

The man wrote out the name and last known address of Thiri Thuza on a small note pad and handed it to Charlie. Charlie was so grateful that he bought two of her pieces, a small jewelry box for his daughter, Carla and a beautiful vase for his wife. They left the store feeling very good about the day's happenings.

When they returned to their suite to get ready for dinner that night they talked about where they would go next. Charlie told Dena he felt that they should go to Kyaiktiyo tomorrow to see the Golden Rock. He told her it was a must to see while they were in Myanmar. Dena was agreeable to Charlie's suggestion.

After dinner that evening they went over to the main desk to inquire as to how long a trip might take to see the Golden Rock. The desk clerk explained that it would take them about two and a half hour to get to Kyaiktiyo and then another forty-five minutes to reach the Golden Rock site and then a slow trek up to the Golden Rock itself. He told them most people make it a two day trip. There are a few hotels up there at the base of the site. He advised them to make a reservation. They were satisfied with the information and retired to their room for a good night's sleep. They knew they were going to need a good rest before this pilgrimage.

The next morning after breakfast Charlie and Dena headed out for The Golden Rock. The beginning of the trek wasn't too bad as they passed various creeks and paddy fields. But as they neared the area of the Golden Rock the road narrowed between lush green foliage and trees. They were in a line of vehicles making their way slowly up the mountain. When they finally reached the base camp, where cars and other vehicles had to be parked, they saw hundreds of tourists and local people congregated in the square. Some were getting refreshments that were offered of sticky rice and boiled beans, and, of course, a drink. Now they had to join the hundreds of others who would make the last leg of the journey on foot up the hill. So they fell in line for the long walk upward.

Charlie interrupted the silence of the moment when he said, "You know, Dena, this site is very appealing to all Chinese people. They feel it is associated with financial good fortune. Isn't it spectacular?"

"I'm so glad we are going to make the walk up the hill to the Golden Rock. It will be exhausting but rewarding. Let's get in the line that is starting up the hill now. It looks like it is going to take us a while."

They walked along with all the other pilgrims making their way upward. As they walked they noticed the bronze bells strewn along the fences that guided the pilgrims up to the top. As they walked they saw a few tourists being carried up on stretcher type chairs because they were too lazy or too weak to walk up of their own volition. They looked kind of weird being carried by four young men. *They must be paying handsomely for that privilege, Dena thought.*

This trek took quite a while because it was exhausting walking up a winding steep hill. When they finally reached the top, they beheld the Golden Rock. They found it to be breathtaking. They heard the guide say that legend suggests that the Golden Rock which is a giant boulder, maintains its balance on the edge of the cliff due to a precisely place Buddha hair within the pagoda. It is covered in gilded gold leaf which is plentiful in Myanmar. Everyone seemed to be in deep thought as this was a very good place for meditation. Charlie and Dena joined in the quiet of the moment as they approached the Rock. Unfortunately they found out that only men can approach the Golden Rock close up in order to place gold leaves on the rock as an offering.

"I cannot believe the crowds of people that come here, especially since it is not an easy climb," Dena said. "Everyone is very respectful of each other and no one is boisterous. They seem to have great respect."

After a while Charlie said, "I think it is time for us to descend now, Dena, and get to our Golden Rock Hotel for the night. I arranged a room for us back in Ngapali so we could be assured of a room. The desk clerk said it gets very crowded up here with all the tourists visiting. I thought it would be nice to spend one night in this peaceful haven. Besides I am tired from this jaunt and will be happy to crash in my room for a rest before dinner."

The hotel proved to be very inspiring. It was situated in a beautifully landscaped area that had a peaceful ambience. Charlie said, "You know, Dena, this is a perfect place for meditation. This tropical setting is very conducive for it; age-old rocks and breathtaking views surely add to the moment."

That evening they enjoyed a nice quiet dinner in this peaceful place and retired early to get some rest.

Dena enjoyed the hotel and the relaxation that it offered. But she was ready to move on. So they got up early and made their way down the road. The jeep was handling the bumps of the road very well. Dena couldn't wait to get back down to the city of Thandwe. Their plan was to spend another relaxing day on Ngapali's fabulous beach and enjoy the gorgeous weather and views and to have a delightful dinner the evening before they left. The day at the beach proved to be everything they said it would be; white soft sand, clear blue water and peace and quiet. The evening topped off their trip with a delightful dinner of island delicacies.

Early the next morning before they left they paid one more visit to the hotel gift shop. Charlie wanted to ask the manager a few more questions about Mrs. Win. He and Dena looked around the store a little more to make sure there was nothing they missed that may have been important to their search. As Dena moved along she spied a beautiful tapestry depicting elephants on parade in colors of royal blue, silver and gold. She knew it would fit in with her den décor back home and she did have her eye out for a special souvenir for her and Charlie to take home as a memento of this charming seaside place. She asked the store manager what the price was. He checked and told her it was valued at four hundred and fifty dollars.

"That doesn't seem too unreasonable, Charlie; I think I will take it." Charlie liked it as well and told her he was happy with her choice."

They arrived back in Yangon several hours later and returned to their Traders hotel. Being rather exhausted they decided to make use of the hotel's facilities. Charlie went to the pool while Dena made her way to the sauna first. They spent the rest of the day relaxing and again topped off their evening with a nice quiet dinner.

When they returned to their room, Dena took the tapestry she purchased, and unrolled it carefully. She wanted to get another and even a better look at it. As she meticulously studied it she noticed at the very bottom in very minute letters, a name of some kind. She wished she had a magnifying glass or something to see it more clearly. Charlie came over to see what she was doing.

"You certainly chose a beautiful tapestry, Dena," he said. "It looks even better here out of the lights of the store. The colors are more vivid and the complicated pictorial design is extraordinary. I think it is going to look beautiful on the wall in our den at home."

"I'm glad you like it, too. It is such an exquisite work of art! Look here, darling, does this seem like a name at the bottom to you? I seem to think it might be the name of the artisan. It is so tiny that I cannot make it out. I wish I had something to magnify it."

"Your wish is my command." He went over to the desk where his briefcase was and took out his jeweler's loupe. "Here you are, my dear; try this out. It's a little small but it should help."

Dena took the loupe, held it to her eye, and took a very close look at the name. She was elated when she raised her head and looked at Charlie.

"You are not going to believe this, but I think the name is Thiri Thuza. Here, take a look; you are better trained at looking through this little instrument. What do you think?"

Charlie put the loop to his trained eye and was convinced without the shadow of a doubt, that the name was Thiri Thuza. What a stroke of luck again!

"I can't believe this, Dena! Two strokes of good luck in our search. Mrs. Win must have also been a tapestry artisan."

Dena said, "Well, it certainly makes sense since she is so skillful at etchings on lacquerware, it stands to reason that she could be skillful at embroidering tapestries. Maybe we have stumbled onto something very significant at last, Charlie."

"I sure hope so. Now all we have to do is find out if she is in Yangon and if so, where exactly she works or lives. Maybe Khin Zeya or his wife can help out here now that we have a providential lead. I'll call Khin in the morning to see what he thinks of all our findings.'

"That is a very good idea, Charlie. Maybe we should go over there to ask Khin whereabout we should start our search in Yangon."

Chapter Fifteen

When Charlie phoned Khin he told him to come over to the store at anytime. Charlie and Dena told Khin they would be there in an hour or so. Khin was waiting for Charlie and Dena at the door of his store, anxious to hear what they had found out. He greeted them very hospitably and they all exchanged warm hellos.

Khin looked at Charlie and asked, "So, what did you learn, my friend? You sounded very positive on the phone."

Charlie answered, "We actually had two strokes of good luck for a change. In Thandwe when we went to our hotel gift shop, we stumbled on some lacquerware made by none other than Thiri Thuza, Mrs. Win. How lucky was that?"

"I'd say that was very lucky, indeed," Khin said. You are doing better than I did and I am the native of Myanmar who is supposed to know his country and its culture."

"Don't feel badly Khin," Dena said, "we were just fortunate to be in the right place at the right time. It wasn't really luck, maybe just good fortune."

"That's one way of looking at it, Dena," Khin replied. "And what was the second good thing you found out?"

Charlie answered with an assurance in his voice, "Dena happened to buy a tapestry when we went back to the gift shop before we left for home. She chose a beautiful tapestry depicting a parade of elephants and their place here in Myanmar. It is simply gorgeous. Guess whose name was on the bottom of it in very small letters? Thiri Thuza, Mrs. Win! How do you explain such a discovery?"

"I'd say it was a very interesting find," Khin said, "especially since you weren't really looking for tapestries."

Dena asked, "Khin, do you think Mrs. Win could be in the tapestry business or working for a shop that sells them?"

Khin answered, "I know that here in Myanmar there are about a dozen tapestry shops, scattered in different towns or cities. They specialize in embroidering the finest quality tapestries that are all handmade. Here tapestries are better known as "kalaga" which are unique to Myanmar alone. Kalaga are the finest made tapestries in all of Southeast Asia."

"Is there one main company or a big business that is the top of the line tapestry shop in Myanmar, like in a particular city?" Charlie asked.

Khin replied, "Actually the center for making them is in Mandalay and the top shop for tapestries, in my opinion, happens to be the Mon Swe Gon handicraft shop. It employs the most talented tapestry artisans."

Dena asked, "Do they make more than one of a kind?"

"Not really," Khin replied, "I was told once that they are all individually drawn by hand without a pattern or a template, and then they are hand-stitched with decorative threads sequins, and other materials. I know for a fact, from an old friend of mine that the Mon Swe Gon shop employs an elite group of artisans, highly skilled in their craft."

"Do you know how long it takes to make a tapestry?" Dena asked.

Khin said, "From what I know about tapestries, I would think it depends on how intricate the design is. You know, our Myanmar heritage is to illustrate things of a cultural or philosophical importance. Our culture, as I am sure you know Charlie, after having been here a few times, is very diverse. Some designs capture the feeling of palaces and pagodas. I remember seeing one in a hotel that described the five hundred fifty lives of Buddha. That was quite intricate."

"That is so interesting and is opening a whole new world to me," Dena said with interest. "As a matter of fact in my short stay here I did notice a lot of tapestries on the walls of hotels and restaurants rather than pictures."

"Yes Dena," Khin said, "We hang them with great dignity in our hotels, restaurants, in our businesses and even in our nicer homes. Some of their designs reflect a Myanmar region's spiritual life that often depicts a religious or superstitious tale. And artisans are always creating new patterns that can be found nowhere else in the world. That is something we are very proud of. In a way, we take tapestries as a matter of fact here in Myanmar because they are hanging in a lot of our buildings. To have a tapestry in one's house is almost a status symbol here. I'm surprised that you haven't noticed the ones I have on my store walls here depicting the astrological signs."

"Oh, but I have, Khin and I am going to be much more observant of the décor in places I visit from now on," Dena said enthusiastically. After finding all of this out, I may just buy another tapestry. I simply love the intricacy of the work in each one and the variations in themes."

"Oh boy," Charlie said, "my wife is going to spend more of my money." Charlie and Khin laughed at the quip.

Khin asked, "Do you want to make a trip to Mandalay? My wife and I were there but we didn't inquire about tapestries."

Charlie said, "No, I don't think I want to go there but maybe you can make some calls for us and find out more about the tapestry business. Perhaps someone there may know of Thiri Thuza since she is considered to be a fine artisan at tapestry making."

"I could do that," Khin replied, "I have a few connections. I will make some calls and see what I can find out. Meanwhile, you two go about your business and do your own inquiring here in Yangon. See where it leads you."

"Yes, I think we will scout around Yangon and check out some of the tapestries in the stores here. Who knows, we may be able to locate Mrs. Win sooner than we think," Charlie said.

Dena added, "We had better get to it because we only have a few more days to spend here in Myanmar."

༄

Thiri Thuza moved to Mandalay after her husband died and she established herself as an artisan of making fine tapestries. She could have remained in the lacquerware business but it reminded her to much of her late husband. She felt badly about leaving her dear son and his

182

family back in Yangon but she had to move on for a while. Mandalay was where she grew up and where she met her husband, Kyi Lin Win many years ago. Fortunate for her, many people in the area of the city where she lived had remembered her and her family. So that was a good fortune for her. It made it easier to get re-established in the community.

When she arrived in Mandalay back then she first got a job designing etchings on lacquerware items for several vendors. That way she was able to make a living and acquire some money with which to venture out into other areas of design. Eventually her etchings and designs were noticed by prominent artisans in the tapestry industry. She was approached by several business owners to consider going to work for them. She hesitated when first approached as she felt inadequate in the tapestry field. It took several attempts to get her to consider coming aboard the tapestry making business. Finally a dear friend of her family from years back won her over. He owned and operated the Mon Swe Gon handicraft shop. That was the beginning of a new life interest for Thiri Thuza, Mrs. Win.

Thiri Thuza learned all of the secrets and styles of tapestry making that she could absorb. In no time, she became one of the finest artisans, in fact, an artisan that some considered the best. She became renowned and famous for her designs that were quite unique. She never made two of a kind. Her past interests and skills at etching designs had come in very handy. In no time at all she ventured out and established her own shop with a small staff of employees. Since most of the work was done by hand, she employed several people skilled at sewing and stitching, a few designers whom she trained to suit her style and a business manager. All transactions, especially final decisions, were overseen by Thiri herself. Most of the time she preferred to remain in the background, simply sewing her tapestries of a phenomenal magnitude. Her little shop was popular among the local people, but her work was recognized by people far and wide. Many of her tapestries were in Yangon and other cities of Myanmar. Word of mouth spread about the fine work of Thiri Thuza.

Thiri Thuza was beginning to feel her age so she decided to return to Yangon. She sold her business to her head artisan and business manager with the reassurance that she would still design for them, but at her own pace. She would design and make only special order tapestries now, ones that required intricate and precise work that only she seemed to be able to complete. It was time for her to once again go to Yangon to be near her family. In the back of her mind she thought she might want to teach her trade to her granddaughter who seemed to have artistic abilities. She promised herself that she would be open-minded about that so as not to force her interest in design on anyone else. But she would, however, encourage the child to try it out.

Her son, Sanei, was glad to have his mother back home. He had a thriving business selling his bronze and metal wares and his store was big enough to include his mother's business. She didn't require a lot of space to work in. Feeling the comforts of home and family made it easier for Thiri to continue her tapestry designs. She actually had several on display in her son's store. Most of her tapestries, however, were special orders from businesses in Mandalay for their clients. So she had enough work to keep herself busy and creative juices flowing. Her son was very proud of his mother and never let a day go by without telling her so. It was at those special moments when she realized how much she missed by being away from her family for several years.

Sanei Win was a skillful bronze caster and made a name for himself in the trade. He built up his business over the years and was now recognized for his fine work. Myanmar had thousands of pagodas and buildings in which his products were used; the gongs and bells were needed in many places. His bronze work was exceptional because he had special designs emblazoned on them depicting things in Myanmar culture. People from all over the country of Myanmar sought out his pieces. He made gorgeous bowls, trays and other smaller jewelry holders as well. His trademark was to put a symbol of an *ingyin* on the bottom of every piece he made. The ingyin is a flower, whether pink, white or yellow that grows on some of the trees in Yangon. Sanei's wife loved flowers and she always had the ingyin flower in her hair. He loved to see her wearing that colorful blossom so it wasn't difficult to choose that as a sort of trademark. He always thought, *what is more beautiful than a woman in a beautiful longyi, with thanaka on her face and a blossom in her hair.* He felt that his wife brought him the luck in his business.

The store on Pyay Road was always busy with tourists and regular customers stopping by. It was considered to be quite large especially with the bronze making being done on the premises in the long warehouse in the back. Sanei Win had a full staff of people most of which he personally trained to produce his wares. It made for a good livelihood for him and his family. Many businesses in Myanmar bought from him regularly so that he had an even flow of production and profit. There weren't many tradesmen of his caliber in Myanmar so his work was very much in demand. He even branched out to neighboring countries with his merchandise. Word of mouth spread about his special touch at the bronze making trade especially when he added extra etchings to his wares. The artistry talents he had seemed to be inherited from both of his parents.

One day his friend from downtown Yangon that he went to school with came by to purchase a few things for his own store. He always like to keep a supply of all kinds of bells, cups, bowls, trays and small sculptures on hand as tourists were always looking for such items when they came into his shop. He hadn't seen Sanei for a long time because he usually sent his sons to pick up the merchandise he wanted. This time though he decided to come himself as he thought maybe Sanei was making some new things. When he entered the store, he asked the store employee at the counter if Sanei was in today.

"Mingalarbar!" ("Good Morning!") I am here to buy but I was wondering if perhaps I might speak to the owner, Sanei Win. I am a friend of his from years ago and I just wanted to say hello to him."

"One moment, please. I will call him from the back. I believe he is in his office."

Several minutes passed and Sanei came to the front of the store. He smiled and greeted his classmate of years ago. "So your sons have been fired I take it," Sanei quipped.

"Oh no, I just wanted to make a personal trip for a change to see if you are making anything new. You know I keep a good account with you even though I rely on my sons to do my running around. It is so good to see you, Sanei; it has been way too long."

"I know, Lin, but we are both always so busy with our work. Maybe we should set some time aside for some social meeting, and very soon. We should not let the days go by and forget about each other again."

Lin said, "You know something, some time ago someone was inquiring about your parents. I didn't give them too much information as I didn't feel it was my business to do so."

"Who was asking about my parents? That is rather odd."

It was a gem dealer from Yangon over by the Bogyoke Market. He said he was inquiring for a friend from America that had traveled here a year or so ago."

"I wonder what that is all about. No one ever looks for a member of my family. We are not very important people nor are we a politically involved family. I hope this isn't a problem or something. I don't want any trouble from the government or anyone else."

"Oh, I don't think it is anything too serious. He just seemed interested in finding out about your father, but even more so about your mother. I got the feeling that they knew your father was deceased but that your mother wasn't. I can't imagine where they would get that information."

Sanei said, "I can't fathom how they are even interested in us and why. Do you happen to know the name of the gem dealer? Maybe I should call on him and find out what this is all about. I would not want to alarm my dear mother."

"It might be the wisest thing to do," Lin said to his friend. I'm sure he would be kind enough to tell you what this is all about. His store is over by the Bogyoke Market and from what he told me he is quite reputable. It is worth it to try, my friend."

"Can I ask you for a favor, Lin? Would you go there for me first and feel the people out; see if you can find out what it is they want of me and my family. I want to protect my mother in case this is a dangerous situation."

Lin answered, "I will do that for you gladly, my friend. I will be in touch with you in a little while."

"Thank you, Lin," Sanei said feeling somewhat relieved; "I will owe you a debt of gratitude for this favor."

"Do not mention it, Sanei that is what friends are for."

Chapter Sixteen

Dena and Charlie went back to Khin's store early the next day to fill him in on what they had done. They told him they went back to the Bogyoke Market and inquired more about the Win family, in particular Thiri Thuza or her son, Sanei Win. Since it was a dead end, they told Khin they were going to head over to the friend that knew of the Win family and its business years ago. They told Khin they would question the friend again and perhaps find out something that Khin missed in the conversation.

Before they could even think of leaving the Zeya Gem store, a young man walked in. Charlie, Dena and Khin all turned toward the man and thought he looked a bit puzzled. Khin walked over to him and asked if he could help him.

"I am looking for a Mr. U Khin Zeya, the gem dealer."

"You are speaking to him, Mr.?????" Khin tried to subtly find out his name.

"I am Lin Nyat, owner of the White Elephant Craft Shop here in Yangon; I am an artisan skilled in the pantamault trade, which is sculpturing in stone. Have you ever been in my store?"

Khin replied rather quickly, "Why yes, I have been in your store and I admired your Buddha sculptures as well as the fine elephants you create. In fact I was there recently inquiring about the whereabouts of a family with the surname Win. Do you remember me being there?"

"Now that I am looking at you a little longer I do remember that it was you, Mr. Zeya, who I was speaking to. Now you can help me with some information. Yesterday, I stopped by to see a Mr. U Sanei Win, a friend from my younger days. I believe he is the son of the woman you were inquiring about."

"Yes, yes, please come and sit with me and my friend from America. We are both interested in what you have to say. In fact, we are extremely interested."

Lin followed them with a little hesitation in his gait but continued, "Well, I stopped in to buy some merchandise from Sanei Win's bronze casting store and we got to talking about many things. In the course of our conversation I mentioned to Sanei that you were inquiring about his mother. He became quite upset at the mention of this and is worried that his mother is in some kind of danger."

Khin replied with immediacy, "Oh no, it is nothing of that nature. There is no danger involved, just some intrigue and confusion. Let me explain, if you have the time."

Lin answered abruptly, "I would rather you talk to Sanei Win himself. Would it be alright if I went and asked him to come back here with me? I know he would feel better if I was with him for moral support. Would that be okay?"

Khin turned to Charlie and Dena and asked if they minded waiting for the return of the two men. He said it wouldn't take long as Sanei's store wasn't too far away.

Charlie and Dena nodded their approval and said they would await his return with Sanei Win.

After Lin left, Khin said, "I can't believe the people we are looking for were right under our noses all the time. We have a saying of Buddha that reads *Right focus brings about reality*. I think we can apply that thought here, don't you?"

Charlie said, "That is so true. If we had concentrated a little better we might have found her ourselves. But I am still happy with the way things are turning out. Now I just hope Sanei Win cooperates with us to the fullest."

"I hope we get to meet and speak with Thiri Thuza, Sanei's mother, too," Dena added.

Lin rushed back to the store and found Sanei sitting and waiting anxiously to find out about this matter. He was overjoyed to see Lin return so quickly.

"So, what is this all about, Lin?" Sanei asked. "Is my family's safety in jeopardy for some reason? Or is someone out to make trouble for us? Please tell me what you found out."

Lin answered immediately so as not to keep Sanei in the dark and in a bundle of nerves. "Neither you nor your family is in any danger; that much I found out. However, I told them I would bring you back to the Zeya Gem Store with me. They want to talk to you. I will go with you so you will feel more comfortable."

"Alright, I will go with you; I must get to the bottom of this, not only for my mother's sake but for my own satisfaction as well."

Lin asked, "You didn't mention this to your wife or mother did you?"

"Definitely not," Sanei said, "I thought I should wait until I know more about this before I bring it to their attention. Why upset everyone?"

"Okay, let's go over there, as they are waiting for us."

Sanei stopped for a moment and turned to look at Lin, "What do you mean, THEY are waiting for us? Who else is there?"

"Khin Zeya has a friend and his wife visiting from America and they are the ones interested in you and your family."

"Okay, let's go and see what this is about," Sanei said with a skeptical tone to his voice.

Within minutes Sanei and Lin were at the gem store door. When they entered amidst the sound of faintly sounding door chimes, Khin walked over to greet them and make them feel welcome. Charlie and Dena stood up and offered greetings as well. That seemed to make the two gentlemen visitors feel calmer.

Sanei spoke first out of anxiety. "I am U Sanei Win, son of U Kyi Lin Win and Daw Thiri Thuza. I understand you are looking for me and my family. For what purpose, may I ask?"

Khin jumped right in with a quick reply, "I am U Khin Zeya the owner of this store and these are my friends from America, Charlie and Dena Ling. Mr. Ling is a gemologist from New York."

"I am pleased to meet you," Sanei said. May I ask why you are so interested in my family?" Sanei added.

"Let me take over here, Khin," Charlie offered. "This is quite a long story, but I will try to make it as brief as I can. A few years ago I was here in Myanmar to purchase gems for my company. I became acquainted with Khin Zeya because we had gems in common. We traveled all the way to Mogok to obtain many precious gemstones. While in Mogok at Khin's friend's gem store I noticed some teak products he had for sale. One item that caught my eye was a teak turtle of very rare beauty and fine craftsmanship. It had wonderful carvings on it and it was rather heavy. It intrigued me so much that I had to buy it for my wife for many reasons. So I bought it and had it shipped home with my gems. Naturally the government did not know about how we sent it to the United States. To make a long story short, for now, I purchased it for my wife as a present. Over the course of time it was stolen along with other things from my wife's place of business. We had a thorough investigation with our city police department and it led nowhere. Several months later my wife Dena and I attended a Grand Opening of an antique store. The store owners were Dena's boss's wife, Giovanna Gardina and a friend of hers, Krystyna Safenski. During the celebration of the opening of the store, my wife, Dena noticed her turtle on one of the store shelves. One thing led to another and it turned out to be the teak turtle I originally purchased here in Myanmar, the one that was stolen from Dena's office."

"This is quite a story, my good people. It is almost unbelievable. I'm glad you found your stolen turtle, but what does this have to do with me?" Sanei asked.

Charlie continued his explanation, "I'm afraid it has more to do with you than you may think. You see, my friend, your father is the original owner of that turtle."

"And what makes you think that?" Sanei asked with a sarcastic tone in his voice.

Charlie replied in a calm tone, "We have done a lot of investigating and researching about this teak turtle for months; more than you realize. Our three families are involved in this search for the owner of the turtle. Our wives have been busy researching; we have even been traveling a lot to find out different things."

Sanei interrupted, "Alright, so you found out information about it, maybe how it is made, what it is made of, who made it and so forth. I still do not see what all of this means, and more so how it all connects to my family."

Khin interjected here, "In time you will understand all about this, Sanei. We will explain every detail of it to you. There is a lot to tell. Our story and inquisitiveness does not end only with this turtle. There is much more to this story. Please allow us to explain the whole thing to you. Then you will see why you and your mother are so important to us now."

Charlie said, "We found out that a man in Bangkok, Mr. Nicro, a friend of your father, made the turtle as a gift for your father many years ago. He owns a company there that specializes in the making of fine teak pieces. Khin went to Bangkok to see Mr. Nicro personally to obtain that information. It so happens that after your father died, your mother sent the turtle back to Mr. Nicro to keep it in his memory since he was the one who gave it to him. Your mother must have felt that the turtle had more meaning to Mr. Nicro than it did to her."

"I do remember that turtle now that you are relating this story," Sanei said. "My father always kept it in his room in a secure spot. He would not let us play with it or even touch it too much. He showed it to us a lot but never allowed us to handle it. We always thought that was kind of odd, but we respected his wishes and his privacy. I remember seeing him carve something on it now and then. When I saw him carving one time, he tried to show me what he was doing and explain to me what it meant. I was very young though and what my father was actually carving on the turtle did not interest me. I do remember this much, that what he was carving was strange. I might have even remarked to my mother that my father was carving words on his turtle; maybe I even asked her why he was doing that."

"Would we be able to talk with your mother, Thiri Thuza, at some time?" Dena asked, trying to make Sanei feel more at ease with them. "Do you think she would mind meeting with us? I'm sure she would have a lot to tell us about this."

"Let me go home now and talk to my mother. I have a lot to explain to her so that she will understand and not misinterpret any of this. She is a wise and intelligent woman so I think she will cooperate with us.

The only thing that might stand in our way is if she is very busy with a tapestry that needs to be finished by some deadline. But I will talk to her and see."

"Before you leave let me tell you that my wife and I have been here on a vacation while we continued our search for your family's whereabouts," Charlie said. "While we were at Ngapali Beach we happened to be shopping in the hotel gift shop. We purchased several lacquerware pieces and found your mother's name on them. Before we left to return to Yangon we made another stop in the gift shop and my wife found a beautiful tapestry that she purchased for our home in New York. When we got back to our hotel in Yangon, we unrolled the tapestry to take a better look at it and my wife noticed your mother's name on the bottom in very small letters. That led us in another direction to look for your mother. We always thought she might have still been in the lacquerware business. We never dreamed of her being a tapestry artisan and one of the finest quality and craftsmanship."

"Yes, my mother is a multi-talented woman," Sanei added. "After my father died she grew disheartened and decided to move back to Mandalay where her roots were for a while. It was there that friends of hers got her interested in the tapestry industry. I was glad that she had finally found something to keep her mind occupied. My family is very proud of my mother for all she has accomplished".

"From the work I have seen," Dena said, "she is a gifted person indeed. Her designs are exceptionally exquisite. I told my husband that I must buy a few more of her tapestries for our home."

"I will tell her everything that you have all related to me. Give me a day and I will get back to you. I'm sure we can arrange a meeting with my mother. Besides you did say that there was more to this story, didn't you?"

There is much more to tell you indeed," Khin said. Please let us know when and where we can meet you again; and thank you for all your help and for being understanding and patient with us."

Charlie and Dena said good night to Khin and returned to their hotel. The stress of the day led them to take advantage of the state of the art spa. The Traders Hotel sauna was a truly soothing place in which to relax. Following their time spent in the sauna they both went for a massage.

"It is amazing what a few hours in a spa can do for your body and your mind, isn't it?" Dena asked. "I am feeling so much calmer now."

"I certainly feel revitalized, Dena," Charlie replied. "Now I am ready to enjoy a nice quiet dinner in the hotel dining room. My appetite is ravenous; so let's go up to our suite and shower and dress for a pleasant evening."

At dinner Charlie and Dena rehashed the events of the day. They both felt a sense of relief upon locating the Win family. Charlie said, "I don't know how Thiri Thuza is going to react to all of this but I hope she is open to discussion with us at least. I know she will undoubtedly have the answers to a lot of our questions."

How are we going to go about this, Charlie?" Dena asked. "What is the best way to tell her about the turtle's secret code and its unusual contents? Where do we even begin to explain this? Will Mrs. Win trust us; will she even believe us?"

"Well, the best way to tackle any problem is head on," Charlie said. "I was reassured by the son, Sanei's reaction. I think they will be open and helpful. Once her son breaks the ice and starts telling her what he already learned from us, resolving this may be easier than we think."

"I wonder if Thiri Thuza even knows that her husband made that turtle into a secret little vault with all those special codes. I can't imagine her not knowing, but then again if she knew about the codes and that he placed the ruby in there, why would she give it away?" Dena wondered out loud.

"I'm sure we will get all of the answers we seek when we get a chance to speak with her ourselves," Charlie replied. "I have a feeling she will be very understanding, at least I'm hoping she is. If she is anything like her son, she should be open to discussion."

Dena said, "When we go back upstairs I think I am going to call Krystyna and fill her in. I'm sure they are sitting on pins and needles, especially since we haven't called them yet. They probably think we aren't getting anywhere in our search. They'll be rather surprised at how our discovery came about. I know they will agree with me when I say that our trip here to Myanmar was vital and beneficial in more ways than one."

When the Lings got back to their suite, Dena changed her clothes and got herself comfortable in a reclining chair over by the window. She got the switchboard and asked to have her call placed to New Jersey, U.S.A.

The phone in the Safenski household never rang for a long time. Krystyna usually answered promptly, if possible, because she didn't like to keep people waiting. She also wanted to know who it was. When she picked up the phone, she was pleasantly surprised to hear Dena's voice.

"Hello, Krystyna, it is Dena calling from Yangon in Myanmar."

"Oh my goodness, Dena," Krystyna said happily. It is so wonderful to hear from you. We didn't expect you to call because we know how far away Myanmar is. But, I must tell you, the suspense is killing us here back home. We talk about you and Charlie everyday. Your ears must be ringing."

"Our trip has been just grand and we have made great progress in our search," Dena said. "We have so much to tell you. I won't go into it in detail since we will be home in a few more days. Our vacation is winding down but, I must add, winding down with an astonishing twist."

"What kind of twist, Dena? Did you find the woman we are looking for; at least tell me that much. I can't stand not knowing. I am driving Kaz crazy with my anxiety over this whole situation. Please tell me something?"

"Okay, I know you are sitting on pins and needles," Dena said. "We've located Mrs. Win, Thiri Thuza as she is called and also her son, Sanei Win. When we tell you how it came about, you'll find it hard to believe that fate was on our side somehow. I'll have to save that part of the story for when we get home because it is too lengthy to relate now. Suffice it to say that we have already made contact with the son, spoken to him at length and he is arranging a meeting with his mother, Mrs. Win as we speak."

"That is fantastic, Dena! I cannot wait until you return home now, not that I am wishing your vacation away from you; we are all anxious to hear about what you've found out. I'll be sure to tell Giovanna, Kaz and Nick that you've called with good news; very good news indeed. Meanwhile, enjoy the rest of your trip and call us when you get home. Give our regards to Charlie and Khin Zeya."

Dena hung up feeling delightful and content and a lot less anxious than she had been. She was overjoyed to be able to share good news with her friends. *I hope the rest of the story materializes as easily,* she thought.

Charlie interrupted Dena's pensiveness with a hug and said, "I can see you are feeling happy and relieved at the way this is unfolding so far."

"Yes, my dear, the load on my mind is lightened by the way this turn of events is happening. I am just so glad that we have found out something. Now maybe we can resolve this whole situation and my turtle can come home where he belongs. *The poor little fellow has been tossed about, all around and can't seem to find his home,* Dena thought again with a smile on her face.

Charlie noticed his wife's sly smile and said, "You will have your turtle back in the clutches of your tender heart very soon, Dena; just be patient and continue to believe in fate."

"Yes, and a little bit of luck would help as well," Dena added.

They retired for the night knowing that they had a very busy day tomorrow.

Chapter Seventeen

Morning came fast and Charlie and Dena arose early so as not miss a minute of its loveliness. They were both athletic-minded and decided to go for an early jog around the hotel grounds. They headed downstairs and had a good one hour run. When they returned to their room to shower, they noticed that their phone had a message flashing on it. Charlie retrieved the message; it was Khin who called to say that Thiri Thuza agreed to meet with them today around eleven o'clock at her store. The son, Sanei, said his mother was very happy to help. Khin asked them to meet him at his store around ten and then they would all head over to Pyay Road to the Win store. Charlie and Dena showered, ate some room service breakfast and headed for the Zeya Gem Store. Khin was there prepping his two employees for the day's work.

In a matter of moments, Khin, Dena and Charlie were on their way. Khin's jeep jostled its way through the late morning traffic in downtown Yangon. They had to get to the other side of town. When Khin saw that they passed the People's Park he knew they would be nearing the Win store.

"There it is," Khin said. I'll pull over there to the right; I think we can park on the street in front of the store. There aren't any signs indicating that we cannot."

When they entered the store, an employee looked up from the counter. She asked how she could help them. Khin told her they were there to meet with Mr. Win and his mother, Thiri Thuza. The woman phoned Sanei in the back and he immediately came out.

"Mingalarbar (Good Morning)," Sanei said. "Welcome to my store and home. My mother will join us shortly. Would you please come with me to my office? I am about to have my midday tea. Can I offer you some?"

Dena answered first. "I would love a cup of tea, Sanei. Thank you!"

They followed Sanei into his office which turned out to be quite a cozy room. It was in the back and it overlooked the beautiful park in the distance. Of course he had some of his mother's fine work hanging on the walls. Dena couldn't help but admire them. The room appeared to have all the comforts of home. It certainly had the appearance of more than just an office. It looked like a little apartment with its comfortable looking chairs and small kitchen area.

After they all got comfortable, a woman appeared in the doorway of the office. Sanei rose and went to greet and welcome his mother into the room. It was obvious that he loved his mother very much by the attention he was paying to her. But that was the Myanmar way; love and deep respect for one's parents.

Thiri Thuza was a woman of medium height, slender and had lovely gray hair. She was wearing a soft colored longyi and thongs to match. She even had a fresh flower pinned on her longyi. Yes, this woman had an aged beauty as well as class. Dena, Charlie and Khin got up and walked over to Mrs. Win. They wanted to greet her properly.

"Mingalarbar, Mrs. Win," Khin said. Dena and Charlie chimed in with a Good Morning as well. They were surprised at what a gracious woman she appeared to be at first sight.

"Hello my dear people, I am happy to meet you," Thiri Thuza said warmly. "You are most welcome in our home and we hope you are feeling at home while you are visiting us in Myanmar. My son tells me you want to talk to me about a turtle my husband once owned."

"Yes, we are interested in finding out about that particular turtle," Charlie said. "It has come into our lives in a most unusual way, left us for a while for various reasons which we will explain, and then returned to us unexpectedly."

"I must say, this sounds very disconcerting right now," Mrs. Win said. "I think you had better explain from the beginning; otherwise I am afraid I will not understand."

"Oh, we intend to tell you the whole story; in fact, we MUST tell you all the details because I am afraid we desperately need your input and help," Dena said. "I think we should begin from the beginning, with Charlie's trip last year to Myanmar. What do you think Charlie?"

Charlie replied, "Yes, I think that would be fine."

"Let me say Mrs. Win…" Dena's words were interrupted by Mrs. Win.

"Please call me Thiri as I do not use the title Mrs. Win. As you know here in Mayanmar women use their birth names all of their lives. I have always gone by the name, Thiri Thuza so please feel comfortable in calling me Thiri."

"I thank you for that, Thiri," Dena answered. "That certainly makes me feel more at ease. And you may call me Dena."

Thiri said, "How are you enjoying our wonderful country set aside from most of the outside world?"

"I am in awe of its history and beauty," Dena said. "It is too bad that it is so far from the United States. More people should have the opportunity to travel here and see the pristine beauty of your country."

"I often told Dena about Myanmar because I have been here several times before on business," Charlie said. "I am intrigued by the Buddhist spirituality of your country and how it is upheld and practiced by almost everyone."

"How are your accommodations?" Thiri asked. "Where are you staying, if I may ask?"

"We are at the Traders Hotel," Charlie replied, "I wanted to be near downtown so that I could show my wife a lot more without having to travel too much. I did take her on a few day excursions to Ngapali Beach though."

"I'm sure that was a wonderful time for you. I know Ngapali beach is a relaxed, yet blissful place. The views of the Bay of Bengal are incredible and the beaches themselves are very clean with their soothing, soft, white sand. Did you get a chance to enjoy the beach and the warm water?" Thiri asked.

"Oh, I assure you, Charlie and I soaked in that sun as much as we could and lounged in the cool, azure water," Dena said. "I even tried out the *thanaka* face treatment that the Myanmar people use. I am definitely taking some of that home for myself and my daughter. It works far better than our sunscreens do. I'm very much surprised that our American manufacturers have not discovered this secret ingredient yet." Dena chuckled a bit.

"I'm happy to hear that you enjoyed yourself there and I also hope the rest of your stay here is equally satisfactory and to your liking," Thiri said. "I understand that at Ngapali is where you discovered my whereabouts; is that so? My son tells me you have been on a quest to find and meet with me."

Charlie said, "Yes, we were shopping in the hotel gift shop and we noticed your lacquerware pieces and bought several of them. Then before we left we stopped in again for another quick browse and Dena found one of your magnificent tapestries."

"I see," Thiri said. "But how did you exactly find out where I was?"

"Well, with a little persuasion, the shop keeper gave us your address here in Yangon," Dena added. "He was reluctant at first for fear that we might cause you trouble. It took a lot of convincing on our part to reassure him that we were no threat to you or your family. After a while, he provided us with the name of your son's store. So upon our return to Yangon, we contacted Khin Zeya and we proceeded to make contact with your son, Sanei. I must say you have raised a fine man as he was very gracious to us when we approached him about your family. After all, we were total strangers to him and visitors from a far away nation."

"My son opened this store in this part of town after I left for Mandalay a few years ago. I advised him to do that so that he would be on the cultural part of town by the National Museum and foreign embassies," Thiri explained. "His store, *Win Bronze and Brass Handicrafts*, has been doing very well here. There are a lot of foreign visitors who come here to see our main attraction, the Sule Pagoda. Have you seen it yet? It is two thousand years old and the sacred relic hair of Buddha is enshrined in it."

Dena said, "No, we have not been inside but we could not help but notice it as we approached your store. It stands out very distinctly in the center of the town it seems. Its golden sheen glistens in the sunlight. I find the sight of it to be quite beautiful."

"Yes, it is very often overlooked by visitors because it is so visible and central and the town revolves around it. But its high golden dome is recognized for its octagon shape that spirals up toward the sky," Thiri added. "We like to compare it somewhat to the Arc de Triomphe in Paris because of its central location. It is a focal point for our part of the city. Our military government continues to keep it intact for its religious significance and also for its artistic beauty. We are proud if it."

"I noticed a lot of small shops that surround the base of the pagoda. They all seem to be doing a thriving business. At least they seemed busy with shoppers as we passed by on our way here."

"That is one reason why I wanted Sanei to move his store here. If you get a chance, take a walk around the Sule Pagoda and you will observe people praying beads and doing other everyday things. And if you can make the time, do not leave here without going inside the pagoda and making your way to the top as far as they let you go. I would want you to enjoy the view of our entire area. You will see the Independence Pillar in Maha Bandoola Park, which is one of our monuments, Immanuel Church, a mosque and our town Hall of actual Myanmar architectural design. You will see how our thoroughfares all branch out from the pagoda in all directions as if it is always casting a blessing upon us. I just love that view and that thought," Thiri added.

Sanei chimed in with his comment, "You know the Buddha saying goes that, *an idea that is developed and put into action is more important than an idea that exists only as an idea.*" I, for one, am glad our government keeps up the idea and plans that our ancestors had in mind for this pagoda."

"Well, my son and my dear new friends," Thiri interjected, "I have another saying of Buddha for you, which is, *Do not dwell in the past, do not dream of the future, concentrate on the present moment.*" I think I have talked on and on enough about our part of town. Maybe we should get back to the reason why you are here; not that I am not enjoying relating wonderful things to you about my beloved country."

Khin decided to begin the exchange of facts and opinions between the four of them. "Let me ask you, Thiri, if you don't mind telling us, how you got involved in tapestry making? We have much to discuss but we are curious as to how this came about for you since it was mainly instrumental in how we found you."

"You should know, Khin, as you are a native of Myanmar that the tapestry industry became a booming money-making trade here. It gave women who had the talent of designing and embroidering free hand a chance to get their creative juices flowing. Many women here are very talented at etching and sewing tapestry designs. I found that out in Mandalay when my friends got me involved in tapestry making. I was thrilled to be able to create and complete my own designs to finished products. It is such a pleasure to be able to just let your creativity flow and then see a beautiful work of art as a result."

"I think tapestry art gave my mother her life back," Sanei said. "Thiri was in a depressed state after my father died and this gave her a reason to go on. And I must add that I am quite happy she is home here with her family. I, for one, missed her a great deal. And she has brought a prosperous boost to my business with the demand for her tapestries growing."

"Before we move on, Khin, please let Thiri tell us how the tapestry art works," Dena asked. "I want to be able to explain all about it to my family and friends in New York when I proudly display my extraordinary tapestries on my walls at home."

"Oh sure, Dena, I'm sure Thiri will not mind giving you some background about her art. We have time to talk about other things later. Maybe we men can get a tour of Sanei's store and see if there is something we may want to purchase. So take your time and let us know when you are finished."

Dena then continued, "So, Thiri, just where do you get your ideas from? Do you design what you want or do you fulfill people's requests?"

"Most of the time I create delicate pictures and patterns of my own choosing as it allows me to be very creative and try innovative styles and new materials. But very often I make one exactly as someone may describe a scene or an idea to me."

"What are the materials that you actually use, if I may be a little nosy?"

"I mainly sew with gold thread as that makes my embroidery look highly decorative. Here in Myanmar we call the art of tapestry, *Swhe Chi Hto,* which means 'gold embroidery'. But I have progressed to more complicated designs that require new materials and varied colored threads. Besides gold thread, I now use silver and colored threads as well as tinsel, beads, sequins, seed pearls, and even semi-precious gems.

The ones with the gems are much more expensive because they are harder to work with."

Dena asked, "I saw some tapestries done on velvet and satin in a few places. Do you do those kinds?"

"I do just about anything now. I am skillful enough to even try more challenging designs. I just love what I do. Making etchings on my lacquerware pieces was interesting but this is far more challenging. I wish I had lived in the past sometimes. Our Myanmar history tells us that royal ceremonial robes known as *Mahalatta* were worn by kings and queens. They were heavily embroidered in gold and encrusted with gems. The Mahalatta worn by King Thibaw and Queen Suphyalatt in centuries past are on display at the National Museum here in Yangon. I have gone there many times to see it and study its work and design. I would have loved to make one of those robes."

"I saw in some pictures that Charlie showed me of other tribal people in other parts of Myanmar that the people still wear ceremonial garbs for their festivals and special occasions. Their garment and headgear seemed to be gold embroidered."

"You are correct, Dena. The Mon, Rakhine, Shan, Palaung, Kachin and many other groups are into heavily traditional embroidered clothing and headwear and some of them are really gorgeous." Thiri was digging in her little box she brought out with her. "I want to give you this written description of how to make embroidery. Take it home with you and compare it to your American way of embroidering. I give it to you as a gift and I don't believe I am giving away any secrets. I can see how much you appreciate my fine work and I want you to have this from me."

"Thank you so very much, Thiri," Dena said. "I will always keep it and share it with my daughter and people I know will appreciate this fine art."

Thiri said, "Maybe it is time to call the men back up here. I am getting anxious to know what it is you want to know from me." Thiri got on the phone and told her son to come back to the front of the office.

Dena got the feeling that Thiri Thuza was getting relaxed with their presence. She didn't seem to mind all the questioning.

The small group sat around a lovely table with soft cushioned chairs and started their discussion. While they talked, a person brought out a serving of hot tea and some golden patties of yellow split peas which were crispy on the outside and cakey inside. They enjoyed the peculiarly tasting lunch while they chatted.

Thiri asked, "What is it you want to ask me about my husband and his work?"

Charlie started, "When I was out here a year or so ago, I purchased a teak turtle with unusual markings on it over in the town of Mogok. I was attracted to it because of its significance for me and my wife, since we are Chinese, and I was fascinated by the complexity of the designs on the bottom of it. The woodwork was exquisite, in my opinion. I found the turtle to be unusual and mysteriously heavy in weight as well. So I purchased it and had it sent home with the gem delivery I mailed to my company in New York. I didn't intend to smuggle anything out of Mayanmar or be secretive. However, my friend told me the Mayanmar government frowns on anyone taking any antiques pieces out of the country. So I was advised to send it home packed in my gem delivery."

"I am following you so far, but how does this involve me or my family?" Thiri asked.

Charlie continued patiently relating the story. "The turtle made it to the states safe and sound. I then presented it to my wife, Dena. She loved the gift and decided to keep it in her place of business on an office credenza. Several months passed and unfortunately there was a robbery at the law office where she works. A number of things were stolen and the turtle along with them. Why anyone wanted that turtle was beyond us at the time. Several months later we were invited to the Grand Opening of an antique store in New Jersey. Dena's friend Giovanna and her friend Krystyna were the owners of the shop. While browsing through the new store and enjoying the festivities of the day, Dena had the shock of her life. There sitting on a special shelf in the store was her turtle! She couldn't believe her eyes, gasped deeply and yelled out! Everyone came running to see what happened. Dena told them about the turtle belonging to her and that it was stolen from her office. She asked to see it closely and upon examining it carefully with Charlie's help, was sure it was the same teak turtle."

Sanei asked, "But how did the women happen to acquire it for their store?"

Dena said, "My two friends happen to be antique dealers. While shopping at a market one day they discovered the turtle on a vendor's table and ended up buying it. They had a feeling when they purchased it that it was worth far more than the vendor was selling it for. My friend, Krystyna took it home and cherished it in her home as a wonderful antique find. When it came time for them to open the business that they have today in High Bridge, New Jersey, they placed the turtle in their store for good luck. It was not an item that was for sale, but used only for display and good fortune.

"You are right in saying that this is quite a story," Thiri said. "This is quite amazing to listen to. I can't imagine where else you are going to take me with this story."

"That is only a third of this story," Charlie added eagerly. "You see, once we learned that the turtle belonged to Dena, we all got together so that we could discuss its origin and markings, among other things. We all studied the carvings on the turtle and decided that we had to know more about them. We spent many hours researching foreign languages of South East Asia, in particular, Mayanmar and Thailand, since that is where we knew that turtle originated."

Thiri asked, "How did you know it was from this part of the world?"

"For several reasons," Khin offered his viewpoint. "It was bought in Mogok here in Myanmar. With my help and the help of others we determined that it was originally made in Bangkok, Thailand by the Unique Asian Wood Products Company owned by a Mr. Nicro. We learned that Mr. Nicro was your husband's friend and that he had it made for your husband, his best friend, as a token of friendship."

"I cannot believe this!" Thiri Thuza finally replied. "Then you must also know that I sent the turtle back to Mr. Nicro soon after my husband, U Kyi Lin Win died. I thought it would be something he would want to have back and hold in his memory. Now you have me wondering how it got away from Mr. Nicro's possession. This is most unbelievable!"

Khin continued to explain, "It so happened that Mr. Nicro's main store was robbed and a lot of teak items were taken, among them the turtle in question. Mr. Nicro was shocked to learn that I knew the whereabouts of his turtle. He indirectly admitted to me that he had his own company people looking for it and trying to track it down, simply because it had sentimental value for him. When he learned from me that it was now in America, he didn't appear too surprised. Somehow I felt that he already knew that."

Charlie added, "We, in fact, thought that his people, who were looking for it, tracked it to New York and perhaps were the ones responsible for it being taken from Dena's office. But we never pursued that with our local police. You know something, Khin, now that we are reiterating this story, it makes me think that maybe it WAS his people who robbed Dena's office and stole the turtle," Charlie said. "Heaven only knows how it escaped from their grasp and ended up in the flea market that Krystyna and Giovanna went to. This would make for one great mystery story. Maybe we should write a book later on." Everyone laughed at his far out idea.

Dena said, "We even had an attempted robbery in our own home some time before the office was robbed. Nothing was taken from our house. The turtle was already in my office. This is all beginning to fit together the more we talk about it. This all seems to tie in with those people from Bangkok, who were on a mission from Mr. Nicro. They didn't find the turtle in our home so they trailed its path to my place of business."

Sanei said, "Well you said that was one third of the story. What in the world is the second part? I can't wait to hear this, please continue."

Charlie began to explain, "While we were having a meeting at one of our homes, Krystyna and Kaz' son, Stefan, and Giovanna and Nick's daughter, Francesca were playing in the family room of their home and happened to take the turtle as part of their playtime. They were pushing it, pressing it and all the other things small children do with toys. When Kaz noticed that his son was using the turtle as a toy he went over to him and was going to scold him for taking it. But his son interrupted his train of thought when he told his father that something in the turtle made a clicking noise. Kaz thought his son had maybe dropped the turtle and broke it in some way. When the son explained that neither he nor Francesca dropped it or broke it, Kaz took the turtle away from him."

"We continued to meet on other occasions to study the turtle and compare our notes and findings from our research of it," Dena continued on. "One day Kaz remembered that when Stefan handed the turtle to him they heard something click. So Kaz took it back to the grownups who started to look at it and touch it, press it and probe it. This went on for weeks until we decided to decipher the carvings on the bottom and the unusual word that was carved on the top."

"And what did you find out, if I may ask?" Sanei said.

Charlie said, "After a long time and a lot of calling back and forth to Khin in Myanmar along with lots of researching on our part, we finally cracked the code of the symbols your husband carved on the bottom and by the neck of the turtle. The symbols stand for the date of your Mayanmar Independence Day, January 4, 1948. It took us a while to decode this after we figured out that they were Myanmar symbols and not Thai ones. I must tell you that was quite a challenge for us!"

"I am in awe of your determination," Thiri Thuza said. "I know my husband carved symbols on the turtle, I saw them when I cleaned his room. But I never questioned him about it because I thought it was just one of his casual pastimes. I always admired it and my son knew never to touch it or remove it from his father's room. We respected his privacy and request. I do, however, question why he carved the date of our Independence. I don't understand the significance of that at all. Perhaps he felt that we had achieved a bit of freedom. Who knows what was on his mind? I didn't know him to be such a patriot."

Sanei was growing impatient with this long discussion when he asked, "What does this all mean to us, my mother and me? It really wasn't ours any longer, the minute my mother gave it back to Mr. Nicro."

Charlie and Dena both said together, "Wait; there's more to this story."

"What do you mean?" Sanei asked, showing his anxiety.

Dena said, "Once we knew the date we tried to see if it meant anything, especially after our children heard a lot of noise from it by pressing the symbols your father carved on the bottom. After a long time and many frustrating days and moments, we finally were able to figure out why he used those numerals in the date and in what sequence he used them."

"Why would you have to know that?" Thiri asked with a frown on her face.

"As it turned out, our mysterious turtle was magical indeed," Charlie added knowing he was getting the Wins confused. They were looking at him with skepticism on their faces and beginning to fidget in their seats.

"Allow me to explain," Charlie continued with certainty in his voice. "We spent many more hours trying to figure out what sequence your husband, Kyi Lin used for the turtle. When we solved the sequence he used, we almost totally solved the turtle puzzle."

"Puzzle?" Sanei questioned apprehensively. "What do you mean?"

"We had to learn by trial and error and all of us putting our heads together, as we say in America," Dena said. "We had to figure out a code your father used. When we found the correct sequence which was 04 for the day of the week, 01 for the month of the year and 1-9-4-8 for the actual year, we started to press the symbols in that exact sequential order. When we did that, we heard a lot of clicking going on and movement happening within the turtle. At one point, our manipulating the turtle's bottom, pressing on the right symbols, we saw something strange happen and heard it pop open like the hood or a trunk on a car opening once it was unlocked. Then we still could not get it all the way open until Charlie reminded us what Khin told him about the symbolic word by the neck of the turtle on the top by its head…**hpwin,** which we learned means OPEN. So we pressed down hard on **hpwin** and we were all in a state of shock. We were all so wired from this occurrence that we broke out in laughter from our nervousness."

"You mean the turtle actually opened up?" Thiri asked in total amazement. "How could that happen? My husband never said anything about it opening up. Well, it is no matter now. It seems there was a lot my husband failed to tell me." Thiri Thuza seemed to have a slight annoyance in her voice.

Khin added here, "When I spoke to Mr. Nicro in Bangkok myself he never mentioned anything about it opening up, so I don't think he knew anything about that part of his turtle's life." Khin gave out a nervous laugh.

Thiri spontaneously blurted out, "I knew my husband was a fine artisan and a skilled craftsman but I never knew him to be a magician of sorts. Am I to believe that my husband, Kyi Lin Win, was a master at disguise and secret coding? If this wasn't sounding so real I would think you are making it up. What did my husband have in mind to do such a thing to his turtle antique? And why did he not ever tell me or Sanei about it?

Now they all started fidgeting and Charlie and Dena saw that this was becoming an unnerving situation for the Wins. But they had to go on with the story now.

Charlie finally broke through the nervousness in the room with his next comment, "Perhaps if you let us continue you will have your answers, which may or may not complicate this whole situation. We'll see. Now we must continue with the third part of the story which is going to make your hair stand on end."

Dena started in a low tone of voice so as not to alarm Thiri and Sanei. Khin sat back and let Dena explain. "When we finally got the turtle to pop open we had another surprise to deal with. Inside the turtle was a hollowed out cavity. Placed in that cavity was a black velvet bag tied with gold braided cord. It was so delicate looking that we were proceeding very cautiously to open it. When we finally untied the bag what we beheld was beyond words to describe."

"What was it?" Sanei asked not wanting to wait for long explanations any longer.

Charlie said with a lot of excitement in his voice, "It was a brilliant pigeon blood **ruby** the size of a baseball! It just glistened in all its majesty as we stared at it in awe. We could not speak for a while after discovering the ruby. I always wondered why the turtle had so much weight to it. Then I knew why."

"Are you telling me a ruby of that size and brilliance was inside the turtle my husband created to open up by a code?" Thiri questioned with much apprehension in her voice and a lot of worry on her face.

"Yes we are," Khin said, knowing this was a bit upsetting for Thiri Thuza and her son. He wanted to soothe them and put them at ease somehow, but there was no getting around a shock of this magnitude.

"We are wondering if you can fill in the cracks so that we can make sense of this." Charlie said. "Did you ever see your husband working on the turtle?"

"Not really," Thiri said. "I know he was a very skillful craftsman and that he could very well have done this. I could see why maybe he tried to make it into an antique that opened. Perhaps he was attempting to start a new style of antique. Maybe he made others of the same style with latches on them. However, this one must have been very specially made and with a lot of thought by Kyi Lin because he even put something very precious in it. I am in awe of his ingenuity. I am also baffled because how could I live with a man all those years and not know what he did? Was I that withdrawn from his life?"

"What about the ruby, mother?" Sanei questioned with a very thoughtful expression on his face. "What are we to make of that? Did our family have such a rare heirloom like some other Myanmar families have? I know we were not extremely wealthy like other families even though we were considered to be quite well off."

"Not that I know of, Sanei, but I always had my suspicions about some gems of our culture and historical background. Let me tell you all a true story that I am sure our American friends will find most fascinating. The story goes that *the famous fabulous royal jewels of King Thebaw's reign in the eighteen hundreds, the years of skirmishes with the British, a lot of their jewels were stolen, lost or misplaced. The story continues that the Queen's ladies were allowed to roam about the palace unnoticed or ignored by the British. Many people feel that it was at that time that the precious royal jewels disappeared, never to be found even until today.*"

"No one ever found any of those jewels?" Dena asked.

"No, my dear, our government thinks they are lost forever or may be somewhere in today's England. Who knows?" Thiri answered. "We have a saying that says, *a genuine ruby won't sink and disappear in mud.* That makes me believe that the jewels were probably right under the noses of the palace guards who never really noticed them gradually disappearing. Those jewels didn't just vanish into thin air. They were so brilliant that they would have stood out and a person couldn't help but notice them. Whoever confiscated those centuries ago was really very clever indeed."

Khin asked, "Thiri, do you now where your husband might have gotten the ruby?"

"You know," Thiri said, "this is very overwhelming almost to the point of being upsetting. I am completely surprised by this action of my husband and I'm sure my son is as well. If my husband, Kyi Lin had this gem in his possession all of our married life, I certainly never knew it. I have no idea where he got it or when he obtained it. We definitely will never know what his intentions were for that ruby. We certainly can't ask him."

Thiri hesitated for a moment, turned very pensive, looked at her son and asked, "Sanei, do you know anything about this gem? Did your father ever take you into his confidence?"

"No, mother, father never told me anything about any gems or heirlooms. And as I already said earlier, he never even let me touch the turtle or play with it or even show it to my friends. Sometimes I use to think that was rather odd because he always wanted me to show them other things he made. Perhaps it is very special or part of someone's valuable gem collection that he once knew. He certainly had some reason for not telling us about it. Otherwise he would have, wouldn't he?"

"I really don't know what to say, Sanei," Thiri said. "I am just as bewildered about all of this as you are. In fact, I feel worse than you do I think as he was my husband and we should have shared everything. I always thought we did."

Charlie asked, "Do you think he might have been protecting you from something or someone? Maybe he didn't want to put you both in harm's way, as we say. You do have a family, Sanei, don't you?"

"Yes, I am married and have two children. They loved their grandfather dearly and he affectionately loved them in return. My wife is from a reputable family here in Yangon; they are law abiding and do not cause any problems."

Thiri said, "If I knew that turtle of his had that ruby inside of it, I never would have sent it back to Mr. Nicro in Bangkok to cherish it as a keepsake in Kyi Lin's memory. And I also believe that if Mr. Nicro knew about the gem he would have had it in a safer place than in his store office. I'm sure of one thing; my husband probably never thought I would part with the turtle or anything that was precious to him. Otherwise he never would have hidden the ruby inside of it. I don't know what more to say other than that I will turn my house upside down after you leave to see if I can find anything that might give us a clue as to why he did this. Maybe he wrote something down somewhere. I'll check his old business books and ledgers to see if he left any notes around."

Sanei added, "I know father traveled a lot to Mogok to buy gems from all the vendors there many times. I went with him on many occasions. Do you remember, mother?"

"Yes, I do recall him going there on business trips," Thiri said. "He used to say they were the most bone-jarring trips he ever made. The roads were bad, especially back in the old days. After all, that was a seven hour trip from here. Oh yes, it was scenic, but very hazardous and grueling. He told me on several occasions, that if it wasn't so nice when he got there, it would never have been worth the trip. He often went to the Panchan-tar-pwe, the outdoor market in Mogok because it was an enormously large market for buying and selling gems. He described it as a place where assorted-colored beach-sized umbrellas were scattered all over the area to give it a festive sight for people coming to buy and sell."

Khin added, "I know that to be so true, as I myself have been to the market and have seen those umbrellas. But I also remember that a lot of owners of gem collections were there to show off their collections rather than to sell them. They seemed to get a lot of enjoyment out of displaying their gems. Not too many parted with them. You had to really barter a lot to get an owner to sell you a gem of sizable interest. That I remember very well because I have bartered with the toughest. One thing that was good about the place was that it had a vast number of markets, so if you didn't do well at the Panchan-tar-pwe, for example, there was always another to go to. Such is the life of a gem dealer here in Myanmar."

Sanei said, "My father gossiped and traded and wheeled and dealed with the best of them. I use to sit back in awe and watch him buy and sell. We always came home with some good deals though. That much I remember. Now that I am thinking more about this maybe that is when he purchased the ruby he put into the turtle. Maybe it was a hot stolen one."

"Oh Sanei, don't say such a thing," Thiri said. "I don't think your father had a crooked bone in his body. I would be apt to say that maybe someone gave it to him for safe keeping. That would be more like Kyi Lin."

"Well," Charlie said looking a little haggard, "after listening to all of you talk about this, I feel that we should let Thiri and her son do some checking around for themselves. Let's see if they turn up anything more. We are all quite fatigued and need some rest."

Chapter Eighteen

Thiri Thuza and her son had their work cut out for them. *Where will I ever start looking?* She wondered. Thiri decided to go through the box that contained all of her husband's personal papers. She had never destroyed them because of his former business accounts; and they had a type of sentimental meaning for her. She sat down at her desk and began one of the most tedious tasks of her lifetime. She had a distant look on her face as she paged through old invoices and read copies of orders filled over the years by Kyi Lin. Hours later she was still at a loss. Nothing she saw indicated that her husband made any major deals with anyone of significant wealth.

Thiri went over to talk to her son. Sanei could not understand how or why his father did what he did. He said, "You know, mother, I went on trips with father many times. I don't remember him making any huge gem exchanges or purchases. But, then again, I was very young and not much interested in what he was talking about most of the time. I never even really paid attention to who he talked to either. Don't forget there are hundreds of dealers at those market sales. You could never keep track of all of them."

Thiri asked, "Did he ever take you into his confidence when you were older? You aren't keeping anything from me, are you, Sanei?"

"Of course not, mother. How could you doubt me? I would never do something like that to you. I have too much respect for you just as I always held my father up on a pedestal. I do not blame him for anything he did even though this is causing us some anxiety. I am reminded of the opening lines of the Dhammapada which illustrates the central theme of Buddhist teaching, *Mind is the forerunner of all good condition. Mind is their chief and they are mind-made. If, with a pure mind, one speaks and acts, then happiness follows one, like a never-departing shadow.* I try to live by that rule, mother. I only want to think good thoughts about my father. I have no reason to think ill of him. He was always a fair man in business and an understanding father to me. I saw the way he always treated you, my mother. That is enough for me to remember about him. I will always think the best of him and forever admire his work. That is the kind of happiness I want to hold on to in my father's memory."

"Oh Sanei, I did not wish to accuse you or upset you. I am just so confused and do not know where to turn. What do you think I should do about this?"

Sanei answered, "These are my thoughts on this, mother. One scenario is that we never had such a gem of this quality in our family. We have done without it all our lives, so why should we need it now? Even if it had been in our possession, we probably could never do anything with it for fear the government would question us about it. What if it belonged to the crown jewels stolen years ago? Furthermore, how could we deal with it among gem dealers without calling attention to ourselves and our father's past? We couldn't even have it cut or whatever it is those gemologists do with gems. I think this might cause a huge problem for us. People would talk and would want to know where we got it? How could we explain this? My second scenario would be to take it back from the Americans and just keep it under lock and key as father did, although I think that was his fear for himself and for us. That's why he hid the ruby in the turtle. Perhaps that is why he never told us about it. Who knows, maybe in his mind he thought it would pass down in our family for generations and eventually be found by some future family member. I'm sure if he knew you would have given the turtle back to the man in Bangkok, he never would have put a ruby in it. There are too many ifs here, mother. The third option is to let the Americans keep it and do what they want with it. I don't think we will ever know where father got it, or how he came upon it. It is my opinion that we will never know why father did this. I think it is best to tell the Americans that they may keep the turtle and the ruby and do what they think is best. It probably would be easier for them to hide it, have it cut into smaller rubies by lapidaries or have it placed somewhere special. I think we should leave it up to them to maneuver this situation and tell them we do not want to be involved any longer with the turtle and its secret. Besides I do not want to involve my wife and children in this escapade. I have made a good life for myself and my family and I think I will leave them with an upstanding legacy to be proud of in my own right. I want them also to remember their grandfather as they knew him before. Why shake up a family's unity and trust? That is how I feel, mother."

"Well my son, after listening to you and your wise thoughts, I think I might agree with you. But now, I still must decide which route to take. I will weigh everything you've told me and add my own thoughts. Then I will invite the Americans back before they leave for home, and give them my decision. They will only be here one more day they said. Now I will retire to my room to ponder this and resolve it."

Thiri went to her room and recapitulated all of the facts. She felt in her heart that the turtle was never really hers to begin with. It was an object that was given to her husband from a friend and it technically held no meaning for her. If it had any purpose at all for her personally she would never have parted with it in the first place. *I feel that the inspiration of Buddha led me to give it away.* She thought to herself. Another thought crossed her mind. *If I ask the Americans to give it back to me, what would I do with it? Do I want this burden in my life?* She was already into her own phase of a career in her personal life and one that she enjoyed and was making a great success at. Her son was well off with a thriving business and had a wholesome family life. Their family enjoyed a phenomenal reputation in the city. Why change things now? That would only call attention to their family and their lives. Thiri was trying to think as her husband did now. If he wanted me or Sanei to have that gem in our lives, he would have told us about it. *He did not reveal it to us, so my answer to that is, so be it.* She thought again. Her mind was racing but she was coming to fast conclusions. She was kind of glad things were falling into place rapidly because she wasn't the kind of person to dwell on something for long spans of time. She preferred to live in the present moment, enjoy it, and live it well.

Finally she concluded that she would tell the Americans that she could not find out anything about the ruby. It was a mystery to her and would remain a mystery as far as she was concerned. Her family would be in total agreement as to whatever decision she made regarding the ruby. She would assure them that the ruby was theirs to deal with and that she would not want any further contact regarding it. With that decided Thiri retired for the night and was able to rest peacefully that a problem such as this was leaving her hands.

In the morning Sanei noticed a happy air about his mother. *Mother must have made her decision, he thought.* Sanei didn't probe or ask his mother anything. He knew she would bring it up in due time. They had their morning tea and breakfast food and then sat looking at each other. Thiri looked affectionately at Sanei and said, "My dear son, you know I would do anything for you to make your life easier. I do not feel you need my help or anyone's at this time in your life. Your business is successful, you are happy at your work, you have many friends and you have a loving and closely-knit family. To change that wonderful life in a way that might bring you into harm's way or cause you anxiety or bring your business to a downfall would cause me great pain. And I do not think your father would have wanted that for you. To keep the ruby in our family I feel would do all those things. It would only cause us a lot of stress, maybe even ruin our family. Besides I also thought about how the authorities might view us and the situation of a sudden newly-found wealth. The cons far outweigh the pros in this dilemma, I'm afraid. So I have decided to tell the Americans that I do not want anything more to do with the gem. Do you agree with my way of thinking, Sanei?"

"I was, in fact, hoping you did just that, mother. We certainly have a very good life now and I wouldn't want it spoiled for us or my family. I think your decision is wise and I support you. Let us do what we have to do to conclude this situation. I just have one suggestion to offer you. Maybe we should put something in writing indicating that we sign this gem over to the Americans. I feel that would be prudent and officially seal this deal."

Thiri added, "So it shall be. Then I will call Khin and ask him to bring them over again. Thank you, Sanei; you are not only a devoted son, but a very wise one too. Someday I hope your family members return to you the love and trust that you have given your mother."

When Khin answered the phone and heard Thiri's voice, he felt relieved. From the sound of her voice he felt that things might work out for the best. Thiri told Khin to bring Charlie and Dena and come over to her home for lunch. He thanked her and said he would try to be there with the Lings in about an hour.

A while later, Charlie and Dena found themselves sitting at the dinner table with Thiri Thuza, Sanei and Khin. To Charlie, Thiri appeared to look content and peaceful. He was hoping this saga would have a favorable turnout. They ate a wonderfully prepared lunch and enjoyed some small talk. Afterwards Thiri started to explain her outcome of the situation, as she called it.

"My dear new friends from America, Charlie and Dena, I know you are not alone in this situation we have found ourselves included in. I realize you have others at home involved who are awaiting some answers. I do not wish to drag this on and on and I realize that you will be going home tomorrow, so I have reached a quick solution. I imagine it will still cause problems or a lot of decision-making for all of you in America, but at least you won't have to worry about us here in Myanmar any longer. Furthermore, I do not want this to materialize into a complicated situation, one that will cause many problems for us here in Mayanmar or for you as well. I think it is best to choose a safe maneuver and simply allow you to keep the ruby and do with it what you feel is best for all concerned. My family has no need of this gem, nor do we want it in our possession for reasons that I will let Khin explain to you. We hope that the ruby brings you good fortune or at least brings you some kind of happiness or satisfaction. Maybe in the future someday you can inform me of its whereabouts or what became of it. I wish you a safe trip home and would hope that you keep in touch with us now and then. We do consider you friends, especially since we share a precious secret. However, as a final gesture of good will I wish to give you this document in my own handwriting, indicating that I freely gave this ruby to you. My son and I feel this should make the deal final and official. We kindly ask, you, Khin Zeya to witness this statement for all concerned."

Khin replied, "I am happy to do this for all of you."

Dena and Charlie did not know how to show their gratitude to Thiri Thuza and Sanei for this, but they tried by simply saying a thank you. They reassured Thiri that the turtle would always be cherished, more than likely by Dena, if the rest of the group allowed her to have it back. As far as the ruby was concerned, that was another story. They had a lot of discussing and thinking to do when they got home and met with the others involved and some important decisions would have to be made regarding the ruby. Charlie told Thiri that he would keep her informed of all the decisions made regarding the ruby.

Charlie spoke up with a feeling of wanting to compensate the Wins somehow. "Would you accept a monetary gift from us if or when we sell the ruby in America? We somehow feel you should benefit somehow from this gemstone."

"Oh no, Charlie, we cannot accept any money for this gem. We feel that might compromise the situation and cause us problems," Thiri answered. "Be at peace with our decision and know that we too will have peace knowing good people will be in possession of something dear to us. We have faith that you will use the gem wisely to the benefit of all."

Dena said, "I promise to keep you informed as to what happens to the ruby and somehow I feel that we will stay in touch. How can we not?"

They thanked Thiri and Sanei and left with Khin to enjoy their last night in Myanmar. Khin had some plans for their last night together.

When Khin dropped Charlie and Dena off at their hotel he told them he would return in about two hours to take them to a farewell dinner at a special place. Dena and Charlie were grateful and said they would be waiting for him.

Later that evening Khin arrived with his wife, Myine. They entered the lobby and approached the desk and asked the clerk to ring the Ling room to tell them they were waiting downstairs. Myine and Khin made themselves comfortable in the lobby sitting area. After a few minutes passed Khin noticed Dena and Charlie getting off the elevator in the center of the lobby. Charlie and Dena walked over to where Khin and Myine were waiting.

"So, are you ready to go out for a while?" Khin asked.

"I think we are going to enjoy this last evening here in Myanmar for more reasons than one," Charlie answered. "Our trip here was worthwhile because we have made new friends and visited with old ones."

Dena added, "I am glad also that we were able to resolve our situation without too much hassle and inconvenience to anyone. I think our friends at home are going to be pleasantly surprised at all we have to tell them. Now, what do you have in store for us Khin, if I may ask?"

"Myine and I thought we would take you to the Pandovar Restaurant on Inya Road. It is a newly renovated colonial style house and has some beautiful friezes of Bagan carvings and a 'trompe l'oeil' masterpiece that we think you might enjoy seeing," Khin said.

"But the best part is the delicious food we will have," Myine interjected with a tone of glee in her voice. "We are personal friends with the owner, Sonny Tun. He creates the most delectable dishes!"

The restaurant décor was black ebony furniture with vases of purple and white orchids placed at strategic places to catch one's eye on entering the dining room. The party of four was seated in the center of the room so as to take in the aura of the whole room. Khin particularly asked for the table to be sure his friends would see all he had described to them.

After a luscious dinner of 'balhchaung' which was fried dried shrimp in garlic, onion and chili and of course, noodles in a fresh tomato sauce, banana cake and a sweet cake called *sanwin-ma-kin* and tea, Dena asked, "What is that music we are listening to, Myine?"

It is from the *ou:zi* drum. If you look to your right you will see that a dance is being performed by the ou:zi drum players to the accompaniment of Myanmar folk music. The group consists of four instrumentalists: an ou:zi drum player, an oboe player, a cymbal player and a bamboo clapper."

"It certainly is a very different sound but one that is quite pleasing to the ear," Dena said. "What is the extra sound I hear in the background though?"

"That is the chanting of *Thangja*, an antiphonal style chant and its meaning is usually amusing, but oftentimes satirical. Are you enjoying it?" Myine asked.

"It is most entertaining," Dena added. "Your culture includes a lot of entertainment as far as I have noticed while I was here."

Khin interrupted the flow of conversation. "Now, my two friends, Myine and I would like you to come back to our store. I have something special I want to give you. So let us be on our way."

When they got to the store, Khin asked Dena and Charlie to have a seat at the pearl display case. Dena was mesmerized by the glow of the south sea pearls. Khin left them for a moment but when he returned he had several gold jewelry boxes. He placed them on the counter in front of Dena and Charlie.

"What is this all about, Khin?" Dena asked.

"Myine and I wanted you to have a very special remembrance of your visit here and of our meeting. After careful discussion as to what to give you as a souvenir and memento of us, we decided on these."

Khin handed the glittering gold boxes to Dena and Charlie and asked them to open the ones with their names on them first. Charlie couldn't help but notice that there was more than one gift there in front of them.

Dena actually had two boxes. When she opened the larger one her eyes beheld the most magnificent lustrous pearl and diamond necklace. She was gasping with delight. "Oh my," she uttered. "This is exquisite! Charlie will have to take me to a grand ball or a very festive party where I can show this off." Everyone laughed at her insinuation.

Khin said, "Dena, always remember that a pearl's beauty is lit from within. It has a deep inner glow which shimmers like moonlight upon a deep blue sea. It gives the pearl what we call luminescence."

Myine added, "One should always look for a pearl's lustre rather than dimples or imperfections. Lustre is what gives it value and distinction among gems. Its thick nacre coating helps it keep its natural color and beauty for many years."

"Most of our Myanmar oysters are gold-lipped, which makes our golden pearls very famous in international markets. Please enjoy wearing them."

The second box a bit smaller contained the most beautiful tear drop diamond and pearl earrings to match the necklace. Dena said, "My daughter will be in awe of these."

Charlie opened his next. He always wore a tie to work and everywhere he went at home. So when he saw the pearl and diamond tie bar with its golden chain, he was quite overcome. "You are spoiling us U Khin Zeya and Daw Myine. How will we ever thank you?"

"Seeing our friends happy is all the thanks we need," Khin said.

"Those other boxes are for your children, Carla and Daniel. I will tell you what they are but you can let them open them when you arrive home," Khin explained. "For your daughter there is a single pearl of considerable size surrounded by diamond baguettes; for your son, a pearl and diamond tie tack. It is our hope and wish that they wear and enjoy them for a long time."

"Where did you get such huge and gorgeous pearls, Khin?" Charlie asked.

"That's one item we didn't discuss on all of your trips here," Khin answered. "Our pearls are from the Mergui Archipelago where our giant oysters are found. They were valued for centuries by our people who dove for them and treasured them. Our sea beds are rich with them. Our own Myanmar biologists have learned to seed the oysters so that we obtain rather large pearls and ones of great value. Myanmar pearls are sold at the Myanmar Gems, Jade and Pearl Emporium and are able to fulfill the demands of connoisseurs from all over the world. You did not express an interest in pearls when you came to me so I didn't push them too much with you."

Myine proudly added, "We presently have three foreign and two joint venture companies in Myanmar conducting pearl culturing as well as running an oyster hatchery. Our production is thriving and our pearl industry is expected to offer us a good financial year. We certainly hope so, as it enhances our jewelry business as well."

"We are overjoyed with your precious gifts and we shall cherish them and think of you whenever we wear them. We thank you also for our children's gifts," Charlie said. "There is just one thing I want to ask of you, Khin. I would like to bring my friends back home a gift from Myanmar as well. What can I purchase from you that would be a happy remembrance?"

Khin moved over to the display case where Charlie was standing. "How about bringing them pearls as well to remind them of our beautiful turquoise water here in South East Asia? I have a large selection of earrings that the ladies might like and several men's pinky rings with a pronounced pearl in the center on a back of onyx. What do you think? Would that do for you?"

"I'm sure I can select a few gifts from your collection, Khin," Charlie said as he continued to look the case over and select gifts for his friends back home. He even bought two smaller pearls for Francesca and Stefan so as not to leave anyone out.

Khin and Charlie settled their account for the gifts and returned to the women at the center of the store.

Dena said, "Before we depart we want to tell you that if you ever happen to travel to the United States, please come and stay with us. We would like that very much. Who knows? The way people travel today, anything is possible. Keep that thought in the back of your minds. Now we really must go and pack up our belongings as we are leaving very early tomorrow."

Khin asked, "Would you be so kind as to send me a fax when you arrive home. Myine and I will both sleep better when we know you are home safe and sound."

Charlie said, "Thank you for everything you have done to help us out and make our trip one worth remembering. We could never have been successful without all of your help. We will keep in touch with you, one way or another. Good bye for now, Khin and Myine."

Dena and Charlie left feeling much satisfaction and very uplifted. They couldn't wait to get home now and see their children and talk to Krystyna, Kaz, Nick and Giovanna. They had a lot to tell them.

Chapter Nineteen

A day or two after Charlie and Dena returned from Myanmar and they had rested from their long flight, Dena placed a call to Giovanna. The phone didn't ring for long before Dena heard Giovanna's voice.

"We are home, my dear friend. We left Mayanmar with a lot of memories and with some wonderful news for all of us," Dena said. "Oh, and we also have a few surprises for you."

"Welcome home, Dena," Giovanna said. "We are so glad you are back. Did you have a good trip?"

"It was more than I could have hoped for. Everything Charlie always told me about Myanmar is so true. I have so much to tell you and Krystyna. Perhaps we should get together as soon as we can all make time."

"First tell me if you are rested up from the tedious traveling," Giovanna said with friendly concern.

"Oh, we're fine and we're ready to meet with all of you whenever you give us the word to come over," Dena said. "Just give us a call when you want us. We aren't that far away so we can be there in forty-five minutes or so. Just do me one favor before we meet. Ask Krystyna to look up some information about the Ngamauk Ruby on her computer or in the library. It may have some bearing on what we are about to tell you. And if not, it will be very helpful to us, to say the least."

"That sounds very intriguing and exciting, Dena. You certainly peaked my interest with your request and I want you to know that we are all waiting patiently to hear about your trip and its outcome. Let me talk to Krystyna and I will let you know when we can all get together."

"Okay, I'll talk to you soon, but don't wait too long. I am bursting with information and wonderful things to tell you!" Dena said with joy in her voice.

"You will hear from me later this evening. Say hello to Charlie, too," Giovanna said.

The Ling's were just finished with dinner when the phone rang. Charlie said he'd get it as Dena was cleaning up the dishes.

"Hello, you've reached the Lings," Charlie said.

"Hello, Charlie, it is so good to hear your voice," Giovanna said. Dena told me you have a lot of wonderful things to share with us. I can hardly wait. That's why we can't delay and we want you to come over tomorrow. It is Saturday and we are all off from work so that should work out for all of us. Can we count on you to come around eleven o'clock?"

"Yes, Giovanna, that sounds perfect. Will we meet at your house or the Safenski's?"

"Come to our home, Charlie. Nick and I will tell Krystyna and Kaz to meet us there also. They are just as excited as we are. I hope you are ready to get bombarded with a lot of questions," Giovanna said.

"We'll be there with bells on," Charlie said as he laughed out loud.

Charlie and Dena were punctual people so they arrived almost at the stroke of eleven. Nick, Giovanna, Kaz and Krystyna were in the comfortable Gardina den having cocktails when the doorbell rang. Little Francesca ran to get the door while her father called out to her to look out the window first before opening.

"How is the little princess today? Charlie asked when he saw Francesca. He was a softie for cute little girls. My but you have grown since I last saw you." Charlie was dangling a little bag in front of the child.

Francesca was glowing with satisfaction and pride from this attention. She loved her compliments. "What do you have there?" she asked Charlie. "Is it something for me?"

"How did you guess that this present was for you? Here take it and open it. I know you are going to like it very much. Maybe you can put the gift on your bicycle. Let me know if you like the gift. I also have one for Stefan. Would you give it to him for me?"

"Yes, Mr. Ling. Thank you very much. I'll give Stefan his, too."

"Now may we come in and visit with your parents and our friends?" Dena asked.

"Come in Mr. Ling and you, too, Mrs. Ling," Francesca said politely. "My parents are in the den waiting for you."

"I think we can find our way there. Thank you, Francesca," Dena added.

Everyone stood up and hugged each other warmly. They all loved each other like family. There was no phoniness in their words and actions.

"It seems like forever since we've been in contact with each other, doesn't it?" Krystyna asked. "I am so anxious to hear about everything you've found out. Shall we get right to it?"

Charlie said, "I guess that would be okay, if you all agree. You don't want to eat first do you? I know how you girls cook and prepare so I know something special is waiting for us in the wings."

Nick added, "No, let's talk first, at least to find out the important things."

They all agreed that their appetites could certainly wait. They had more important things on their minds.

Dena asked, "Krystyna, did you manage to find out about the Ngamauk Ruby? Did you have time to research it?"

"Yes I did and it is quite interesting. But why did you want to know about that ruby?"

"It might give more meaning to what we have to relate to you," Dena answered. "I understand that there is quite a story to tell about the ruby and other Myanmar jewels of the former royal family of Myanmar."

Krystyna began, "From all my earlier reading and from what I discovered yesterday, I can tell you that the Ngamauk Ruby is very special and its whereabouts is still unknown."

"What do you mean, Krys?" Giovanna asked.

"Let me relate the story to you and you tell me what you think of it. What I found out by researching is that when the British seized Mandalay in November of eighteen eighty-five, the Ngamauk Royal

Ruby was kept in the Royal Treasury. A Colonel Sladen of the British army ordered the Royal Treasurer to make a list of all royal gems. Included in that list was the famous Ngamauk Ruby which was over 90 rati (carats) and several other priceless royal gems such as the Sinmataw Ruby of 10 rati, the San Kyauk taw of 6 rati and many others. The colonel ordered the palace people to pack up everything as they were making them vacate the palace. They were being exiled. The article I read explained that there was said to be an eyewitness account of Myanmar Queen Su Phaya Lat in her palace chamber with her maid of honor, Princess Thiri Sanda Wadi, packing away the royal gems into gold boxes, lacquerware boxes and velvet bags."

Giovanna interrupted and jumped of her seat with a look of joy, "Velvet Bags! Are you thinking what I'm thinking?"

"Don't jump the gun yet, Giovanna, let me continue."

Krystyna went on, "When this Colonel Sladen saw them packing up the jewels and gems he requested to see the Ngamauk Ruby. The story went on to say that he thoroughly looked at it against the sunlight and even showed it to two of his captains that were with him."

"Sounds like the guy knew how to look at gems, huh?" Charlie offered. "Go on, Krys, I'm sorry for interrupting you." Dena gave Charlie a look to be quiet.

Krystyna continued, "The shrewd colonel took out his handkerchief from his trousers and pretended to wipe sweat from his brow. He then, unobtrusively wrapped the ring with his handkerchief and put it into his pocket. The princess happened to see him do that and was waiting with the opened gold box. When the queen asked why the princess didn't close the box she told the queen she was waiting for the colonel to give the ruby back to her. The colonel suddenly got flushed and gave it back pretending his action was unintentional. That same night when King Thibaw and Queen Su Phaya Lat boarded their ship to depart from Mandalay, Colonel Sladen came to the ship at night on the twenty-ninth of November in 1885. He took back the gold box and Royal Treasure saying that he would keep it for safety. When the ship left the next morning, the Colonel was not on board. The dethroned King, his Queen and royal family sailed from Mandalay and arrived in Yangon on the fifth of December in 1885. From there they sailed in a canning ship from Mandalay to Madras, India, arriving on the fifteenth of

December in 1885 where they lived until the ninth of April, 1886. The King tried to inform the authorities that the royal treasure, including the Ngamauk Ruby, were kept by Colonel Sladen. The authorities made inquiries but Colonel Sladen denied that he had any involvement in the missing jewels. The imprisoned king tried to get the royal jewels back but, eventually over time, the theft of the jewels was forgotten. There is a theory that the relatives of Colonel Sladen presented the Padamya Ngamauk Ruby to Queen Victoria in England after his death. Keep in mind though that this is all a matter of opinion and nothing has ever been solidly proven."

Listening to all of this, Nick got curious and asked, "Was that the end of the search for the ruby and jewels? Are we to assume that they have never been found? Is that where this is all leading?"

"Patience, please, Nick, let me finish," Krys said. "As I read on, it said that twenty six years later, when King Thibaw died in 1916, Queen Su Phaya Lat and her two daughters returned to Myanmar and lived in Yangon. When asked by a reporter about the ruby, the Queen was supposed to have said that Sladen took it. Nine years later on the twenty-fourth of November in 1925, the queen died. Her youngest daughter took up the cause for several years and contacted the British government on the fifteenth of December in 1935. She requested that the royal jewels be returned and also sent a letter to the then League of Nations, now the United Nations. Because of her pursuit and letters and questioning she was sent to live in Mawlamyine and placed under restriction until she died in 1936. The story still did not end there. Her two sons continued to ask the British for the Ruby and royal jewels until 1959. The British refused to acknowledge this affair and said the request was denied. It has been many years since Mayanmar got its independence from Britain and nothing more was ever heard of the ruby or the royal jewels."

"Whew! What a story!" Giovanna said. The date that Mr. Kyi Lin Win used as the code for his turtle, January 4, 1948, holds a lot of significance for the Myanmar people then; especially in regard to the royal jewels. Maybe that's why Kyi Lin used that date. He probably was a great Mayanmar patriot and was proud of his country's independence."

"Could the ruby we now have in our possession be the Ngamauk Ruby?" Kaz asked with wonder on his face. "Or maybe it is one of the other ones from the royal jewels. Hmmmm!"

"My goodness! What a situation for us to be in!" Nick added. "What in the world are we going to do now? I must say this worries me a little, maybe even a lot!"

Charlie chimed in, "Wait a minute, everybody, let us tell you what we've learned when we were in Mayanmar before we all jump to false conclusions."

"Oh sure, Charlie, Dena, please tell us about your trip and the interesting things you did and what you found out. We didn't mean to ignore you," Krystyna said. "You told me to tell you about the Ngamauk Ruby, so I did."

"Okay," Dena said with a determined sound to her voice. "Let me tell you now who we met. We were able to talk with the wife of Kyi Lin Win the creator of our secret turtle with its surprise inside. She goes by her birth name, Daw Thiri Thuza, as all Myanmar women do. That is why it was a little more difficult to find her. Charlie and I traveled around a bit. One of the places we went to was the Ngapali Beach area on the coast of the Bay of Bengal. Besides the natural beauty of the place we also shopped a lot and made a lot of inquiries about Mrs. Win or "Thiri." We found some lacquerware made by her and knew it was hers because she had her name etched on all of her pieces. But the real breakthrough came when I bought a tapestry. When we returned to our hotel room in Yangon from the beach area, I unrolled the tapestry to admire it a little more. Upon examining the fine work and enjoying the gorgeous blends of color in it, I noticed a name sewn at the very bottom. It was so minute that Charlie had to use his loupe so that we could make it out. It turned out to be that of Thiri Thuza."

"Wow! That was pure luck, Dena," Krystyna said. "So what did you and Charlie do with that information?"

"Well, it was not an easy task, but with the help of Charlie's friend, Mr. Khin Zeya, we were able to track down a friend of Mrs. Win's son who owned a store in Yangon. It happened that he knew the son, Sanei Win and knew exactly where they lived. Khin remembered meeting the son earlier."

Charlie continued because Dena was out of breath from being overly excited with telling their story. "So first we met with the friend who paved the way for us to meet the Wins. The friend came to Khin's store and we briefed him on the fact that we were looking for Thiri Thuza. We got him to trust us enough to take our message to Thiri Thuza and Sanei Win. In a day's time we were in touch with them. They invited us to their store for a visit and to discuss what we wanted of them and why we were looking for them. That visit proved to be very beneficial and rewarding for us."

"In what way was it beneficial?" Krystyna asked.

"Thiri Thuza told us her husband was the owner of the turtle and the artisan of the turtle's code. But she was not aware that he had turned it into a secret cache with a coded mechanism for opening it or sealing something into it. In fact, she was enthralled over how her husband created it right under her nose."

"What about the ruby?" Giovanna asked.

"That discovery completely astonished Thiri and her son, Sanei," Charlie said. "You could visibly see by her quick reaction that she had no idea there was anything in the turtle, let alone a gem of that size and weight. I think our information overwhelmed them."

Nick being the lawyer in the group was troubled at the legal ramifications of all of this and asked, "If this ruby is her family heirloom, will she want it back? If that is the case, we will have a real problem on our hands."

Charlie quickly replied, "No, Nick, it is nothing like that. Don't get excited. Thiri had a long talk with her son after she carefully thought about the whole situation we threw in her lap. She decided that we should keep the turtle and its contents, the ruby."

"They gave it to us gratis?" Nick asked.

Giovanna shouted loudly, "That's incredible!" Most people would never do that. They certainly wouldn't give away a gem, namely a ruby of that size and value so readily. I am curious as to why she doesn't want it."

Dena said, "She gave several reasons why she made her decision. One, she felt that her family never had such a gem and they still thrived and were considered to be quite comfortable; two, she feared that the military authorities might cause a problem for her family if they found out she had come into a sudden unexplained wealth from somewhere; and third, she did not want to place her family in harm's way for various reasons. We didn't question her too much because we didn't want to upset her and we wanted to show her that we respected her wishes and decision. She and her son assured us that they gave the situation a lot of thought."

"Was her son in agreement of this?" Nick asked.

"Yes, he was and told us he would do whatever his mother wanted," Dena answered.

"Did she happen to mention her husband in the conversation?" Kaz asked. "I mean, did she allude to the fact of where he might have obtained such a gem?"

Charlie said, "The way Khin explained it to Dena and me after we left the Wins, was that Thiri Thuza did not really know why her husband had this ruby, or where he bought it. He said he thought she might have been somewhat upset with her husband keeping such a secret from her and her son. He said maybe she thought he was protecting them from undue harm and a complicated interrogation or involvement. Khin said there was and still is a lot of hoopla going on about the missing gems and royal treasure from years ago. He said perhaps Thiri didn't want to open Pandora's Box. Khin advised us to accept her decision and go home with a free conscience and an open heart."

"Thiri did want a few things from all of us though," Dena added. "She wanted us to not worry any longer about her and Sanei in Myanmar, she wished us good fortune with the ruby with whatever we choose to do with it and lastly she asked us to sign a document she had handwritten signing the gem over to us. Khin witnessed the paper." Dena opened her pocketbook and took out the document and laid it on the table in front of everyone.

"This sounds too easy to me," Nick said apprehensively. "Who in today's world is so outright generous?"

Charlie said, "It doesn't sound too far out when you remember that Mayanmar is a third world country where there is some amount of danger still around and a lot of uncertainty in the air. Thiri and Sanei do not want any trouble. She made special note of the fact that if her husband wanted them to have the responsibility he would have told them about the gem. He said nothing to them so she takes that to mean he never wanted them to know about it, for whatever his reasons were. Now I think WE have the problem to decide what to do about this ruby."

"I have a suggestion as to what we should do with the teak turtle," Krystyna said. "I would like to give it back to Dena and Charlie. After all, it was hers from the very beginning. How could we deprive her of possessing it?"

Everyone nodded in agreement and said yes unanimously. There was no doubt in their minds that the turtle should be returned to Dena. That was a definite!

Dena started to cry from happiness and Charlie hugged her in consolation. They had truly found true friends in their lifetime, people that were totally unselfish. That thought made them feel great! They thanked the other two couples, their friends, and said they would always remember that the turtle truly brought them good luck in their lifetime.

Krystyna wanted to get her two cents in before she lost her train of thought and she blurted out, "Let me tell you all something else that I found out while I was in the library."

"I knew you'd go the extra mile, Krys," Giovanna said. "What else did you find out?"

"Well, this is a rather current bit of information but it may prove to be very helpful to us in some way. Listen to this, if you would bear with me a bit longer. You all know that the Smithsonian National Museum of Natural History is dedicated to understanding the natural world and our place in it. Well I decided to research the Smithsonian's gem background and information. Listen to what I found out. *The "Carmen Lucia Ruby is on view there indefinitely. This spectacular Burmese Ruby was donated to the museum by philanthropist and businessman, Dr. Peter Buck in memory of his late wife, Carmen Lucia Buck. The article states that the ruby was mined from the fabled Mogok Region of Burma in the 1930's. The ruby possesses a richly saturated homogenous red color combined with an exceptional degree of transparency. It has been on view in the museum since October 16, 2004. It is set in a platinum ring with two brilliant-cut diamonds.* They say that Burmese rubies larger than twenty carats are exceedingly rare. What do you think of that story?"

Kaz knew this was important to Krystyna so he added, "I was actually thinking along those lines in regard to our newly-obtained ruby. It's funny that you discovered that, Krys. I was tossing around the idea of us giving our ruby to the Smithsonian."

Charlie finally stood up and had something to say. "That is absolutely amazing! Kaz, I, too, thought about that, but I couldn't decide in my own mind if that was the route for us to take. This is a very complex situation we are in. Think about it. We are three different families who now possess a rare ruby of sizable proportion and great value. We have a lot to think about and to tell you the truth; I really don't know where to turn now."

Nick, sensing the anxiety building said, "Maybe our next step is to once again put our heads together, evaluate all possibilities, weigh all the information and then make a decision we can all live with. That "togetherness" worked for us before. Why shouldn't it work for us now?"

Wanting to keep things flowing, Kaz added, "You're absolutely right, Nick. That group interaction worked for us in the past, so why shouldn't it now? I agree with you. I think we need to talk this out in great detail."

Charlie said, "I'm sure we all have our own thoughts and ideas about the ruby. So why not take a few days to think about it, rehash the situation with our spouses and then meet again in a few days. We are all intelligent people and we do care for one another. So I feel we should take time to study our own thoughts and research what we think we would do with the ruby if it was our own. Then we will meet and try to arrive at a conclusion that will benefit all of us."

Dena interrupted with excitement, "We almost forgot, Charlie! What about our gifts?"

"Yes, I got so engrossed in our plight that I totally forgot that we have some special things for all of you. We bought some precious gifts from Khin Zeya. All of these little gold boxes have special treasured gifts for you. Dena put your names on them. There is even something for the kids. We wanted you to have mementos of Mayanmar as we do. We hope you like what we have chosen for you."

Everyone let out a shout of joy in their own personal way. They all said their thank you and offered their hugs as well. There were a lot of oohs and ahhs going on. They spent the next several minutes admiring their pearls of great price.

Charlie added, "I also gave the kids a special bell for their bicycles. The Myanmar people make some beautiful sounding bells. I thought the kids might like them. I gave them to Francesca when we first came just in case you are wondering where they came from."

Krystyna was full of her bubbly excitement and Giovanna and Dena chimed in with their added exuberance. They immediately agreed to do just what Charlie, Kaz and Nick suggested. They were going on a special mission again; this time to resolve the predicament with the ruby.

Chapter Twenty

Krystyna, Dena and Giovanna agreed to meet the following weekend at Giovanna's house. They had a lot to talk about and even more to think about. They knew they had their work cut out for them but they had to try to determine what to do with their ruby. Everyone's fate was resting on the decision the six of them would make.

The weekend came faster than they all thought it would. Dena drove in from the city and met with Krys and Giovanna at the Gardina house. As always, there were refreshments to share and goodies to keep their minds accurate and open.

"I can really understand why Thiri Thuza didn't want to get involved with the ruby and its consequences," Krystyna said with much sensitivity in her voice. "This is truly a problem of great magnitude and complexity. I hardly know where to begin thinking what to do with this ruby. I know it is ours to do with it as we will, but how do we make the outcome benefit all of us?"

Giovanna answered sympathetically, "We will do the best that we can. That's all we can expect from ourselves. Let's face it, we are only human and this is definitely not our line of work. So let's simply start from the beginning as we see it."

"You are both correct in your thinking," Dena added wisely. "Let's talk about a few things first, make some notes and start from those ideas. Who knows, maybe we will get an unforeseen brainstorm! I was also thinking that maybe more research is not the way to deal with this at this time. We have done a lot of delving into books, more than I care to think about. You two, in fact, did more research than all of us since this began. Let's do some plain old-fashioned talking. Maybe we will come up with a good solution."

"That's a wise idea, Dena," Krystyna answered. "I still have a lot of notes and information from our other jaunts to the library and checking out websites on the computer. I'm sure there is something we missed, so it certainly won't hurt to look over the notes again and maybe again and again." Krystyna smiled broadly. The other women chuckled as well.

Giovanna, wanting to get the discussion going on a favorable note said, "I read somewhere that according to Buddha, *the three essential elements for a successful life are luck, wisdom and diligence. Without proper effort nobody can achieve their goals.* I think we have had a lot of luck since the day we discovered the turtle with its treasure inside. It allowed us to meet Charlie and Dena, brought success to our store and is still bringing us ongoing happiness and luck. We have been applying ourselves very industriously to finding out all about the turtle and its contents. In the process of searching we have learned a lot about the third world country, Myanmar, which certainly sounds like it is a beautiful place in the world. Now all that is left for us to add to the success of our lives is to apply a lot of our steady and earnest energy into coming to a conclusion that will benefit all of us and make us all happy."

Dena added, "I agree with that train of thought. We have bent over backwards to resolve this issue without hurting anyone's feelings, keeping in mind not to offend our foreign friends as well. Surely this situation must have a happy ending. I, for one, will not settle for less."

"Well then, my dear friends," Krystyna interjected, "let's roll up our sleeves, as they say, and get started. We have a Polish saying that says *Gdie zgoda tam i sila*, which means, with unity there is strength."

"Charlie told me that the miners in the Mogok region of Myanmar work long hours and many years, and still never find that one precious gem that could make them rich or even famous," Dena said. "They say it all depends on luck. Some people find a valuable gem after only a few weeks of mining and reap the reward of owning a ruby worth millions. Those people feel that their fate is sealed. Mining for gems is a grueling business for those people over there. I appreciate our good fortune all the more after hearing about the hard lives of the miners."

Krystyna said, "Some of the royal rubies worn by the Myanmar royalty were so valuable that it said in one book I read that a Chinese emperor is said to have offered a city in his own country in exchange for one of the prized gemstones." Krystyna pause in thought, and then continued. "If you will bear with me I have a few more notes here to share with you. Rubies were used in ceremonies and to adorn royal regalia. It seems that the choicest items were reserved for the court. A lot of the Myanmar gems were dedicated to the Buddhist religion and I imagine a lot of them are in safe keeping in the major pagodas. A lot of the gems were not used for personal reasons but rather they were encased in the relic chambers of the pagodas and stupas. History books explain that the search for these riches was one reason why more than one thousand pagodas were desecrated and destroyed by British troops during the Third Anglo-Burmese War."

"Where are you going with this Krys? Giovanna asked getting antsy.

"Allow me to finish my train of thought," Krys answered. "It is my opinion and that of many in the history books that a lot of the royal gems and some of considerable size and value that had been confiscated during the wars in Myanmar, have led to the loss of many of them. I am somehow feeling that the ruby that has come into our possession might just be one of those precious gems lost in the shuffle of war and mayhem. This is why I think Mr. Kyi Lin Win put the gem into the turtle. He must have obtained it somehow either illegally or under a suspicious exchange. Even his wife didn't know about it. That tells me that it certainly is a HOT gem, if you will follow me. He was even protecting his loved ones from any undue complications or danger."

"That makes a lot of sense, Krys," Dena said. "I'll go along with you so far. Kyi Lin Win was actually very smart. Instead of cashing in on the wealth of that ruby, he hid it for future generations to discover, or so he thought. He probably figured that eventually someone in his household would discover his secret cache and reap the rewards of possessing a gem of great value. I also think he knew that the government sponsored auctions are dominated by local dealers who pay extremely high prices in their local currency. Perhaps he thought he would not get what it was really worth if he attempted to sell it. And, of course, there were also the government rules and regulations to consider. So I think all was against him. He just decided to hold on to the ruby for his family; and then he died suddenly."

Giovanna asked with a puzzled look on her face, "Just how much are these rubies and gems of considerable size worth?"

Krystyna continued to read and ad lib from her notes. "In one article it said that the auctions held at the Gem Emporium in Myanmar net around twenty-three million dollars in United States currency, and that is just from the locally produced gems through competitive bidding. That is a LOT of money girls! I know the famous rubies known to us are worth a fortune. We'll soon find out what ours is worth. We have to let the gemologists of Charlie's company do their work."

Giovanna added, "I also found out that a company founded in 1967 called Stoneworthy International, is one of America's great colored stone houses. It is a direct source for the finest gemstones. Their staff makes several trips a year to the world's major gem-producing centers. Their motto is *"the only way to obtain quality is to purchase it."* The article said that they assure satisfaction. Places like Tiffany's, Neiman Marcus, the Smithsonian Institution and the American Museum of Natural History have bought gemstones from Stoneworthy. Maybe we can contact Stoneworthy International and ask their advice about our ruby."

Dena interrupted, "I thought we were going to let Charlie's company in New York investigate things for us. They are quite reputable in their own right. I would like to give them a chance to study the ruby, evaluate it, scrutinize it and do whatever else it takes to tell us everything about it. For one thing, I know they can be trusted to be truthful with us and honest."

Krystyna answered, "Oh sure, Dena, we will definitely let Charlie and his colleagues do what they have to do for us first. But we have to be prepared with other avenues and also have some knowledge ourselves to know what we are talking about and to ask the proper questions. We don't want to appear inadequate."

"There are a lot of quacks out there in the world of jewels and gems who have no regard whatsoever for theory, methodology and above all their clients," Giovanna said, "and we have to be careful who we talk to. Don't you agree?"

The three women nodded in agreement of Giovanna's statement. While they continued their discussion the husbands arrived to join in. The women informed of them of their ideas so far and they were surprised how systematic and orderly the women were handling things.

After listening intently to what their wives had to say, Kaz asked, "How about getting in touch with a professional appraiser?"

Nick said, "Appraising is a good profession if the appraiser is on the up and up."

"What do you mean, honey?" Giovanna asked her husband.

"Well, I've dealt with a few jewelry cases in my law practice and had the opportunity to meet and speak with some appraisers. I learned from experience that a good appraiser should be well educated and tested in the field. A professional appraiser should have a high level of education backed by a high level of experience and knowledge. If a person is a real professional appraiser he or she will have good credentials, be involved in a healthy business practice and live and work by good ethics and standards."

"But how are we supposed to know if an appraiser has all those qualities?" Krystyna asked. "Do we just come out and ask the person?"

Nick replied, "As far as I know in my own professional experience with appraisers, a true appraiser will hold a membership within a professional appraisal organization. I found that out from a few of my clients. Being a member is a good indication of an appraiser's genuine commitment to his client. The best thing to do is just outright ask the appraiser a few questions. It is your right to inquire."

"What would we ask?" Dena inquired. "We would not want to appear too forward."

Nick replied, "Oh, a truly professional appraiser will welcome questions to qualm any doubts you may have. They won't be defensive or appear edgy. We are all good judges of character so we shouldn't have any trouble distinguishing between a quack and the real McCoy. You could ask what kind of membership they are in and how they earned it; you could ask how often they retest to keep abreast of changes in their professions. We have to be careful because some organizations "grandfather" their member which means that they only have to pass one test and they are lifetime members never having to be tested again. Those are the kind of appraisers you want to avoid. They would do us more harm than good. In my opinion, a good appraiser should be retested about every five years to stay current and updated in regard to changes in appraising."

"I think we will leave the appraisal business up to you men; in fact, we are assigning that chore to you three," Krystyna said. The women all snickered. "Let us know what you come up with and if we have to meet with one, we'll decide what to do."

Charlie said, "I already mentioned the ruby to my staff. They know it is in the company vault but they don't know why it's there or where it came from. I'll have to fill them in on how we came to acquire it. They probably will find it very hard to believe but with my boss backing me up it will eventually become believable. I'll let you know how things progress. Give me about a week."

Charlie was in his office earlier than usual on Monday morning. Even his boss was shocked to see him at his desk. Charlie was so engrossed in what he had to say to all of his staff that he didn't even hear his boss, Lee Chang walk in.

"What are you doing here so early, Charlie? You are so preoccupied with your thoughts that you didn't even hear me come in. Is everything alright?"

"Everything is fine, Lee. I was just gathering my thoughts because I would like to speak to our staff today about the ruby I brought in for examining. They deserve to know where it came from and what this is all about. Besides, my friends are anxious to resolve this issue as am I. We have to check out all possibilities and then make a decision that will benefit all of us. I already told you about the ruby, didn't I?"

"Yes, you did, Charlie, and it is my opinion and advice that you sell it to us and let us deal with it and handle it," Lee said.

Charlie answered with deep creases in his forehead as he frowned, "I respect your decision and judgment, Lee, but I must respect the wishes of my other friends and my wife who are also the main players in this gemstone drama. After we have exhausted all possibilities that we know about, we will be in touch with you with our answer. Until then, I ask you to be patient with us and help me out with the examination of the ruby. I value your expertise, you know that."

Later that morning Charlie met in the lab with the lapidaries and gem experts. He saw that they had taken the ruby out of the vault and had it beneath the overhead skylight with many lamps focusing on it.

One gemologist said, "Charlie, you have got yourself one fine gem here. This ruby is extraordinary, especially because it is in its uncut state. We have placed it on the dop which is holding it in the machine. That way we can view its symmetry more accurately as we turn it."

"I don't want it cut, at least not yet," Charlie said with urgency in his voice. I have other people's opinions to consider."

"We have no intention of doing anything to it without your permission. We want to study it and examine it as closely as we can. We have to view the ruby in the correct direction of the crystal since its color changes with the direction."

"I know we have to consider its color, luster, weight, size and its fire, if you will," Charlie said. "Our stone seems to be in the round shape family. What do you think?"

"Yes, it appears to seem round," another man said. "We have a lot of work to do with it. So, let's get organized and begin our study gentlemen."

Chapter Twenty-one

Lee Chang had a very amicable staff working for him at his Chan Continental Gem Export Company. He had a diversified personnel roster with varied ethnic backgrounds. He had an equal number of male and female lapidaries in his employ. Some had been with him from the early days of the company while others had several years of experience. But all were undyingly loyal to Lee and his principles.

One senior staff member was Jin Cho, who, if it wasn't for his white hair one would think he was in his fifties. He had many years of experience as a lapidary and was also skilled in other aspects of the gem business. Lee relied on him for advice and always trusted that he would make the right decision for his company. Jin Cho's experiences in the gem trade put him at the top of the list in Lee Chang's opinion. To him, Jin was irreplaceable. Jin was a member of several noteworthy gem federations and clubs and had outstanding credentials. Jin's own personal staff that he had in his charge was equally as qualified. He only worked with the best, as was his unattested opinion.

Jia Li Kwan had the perfect name for her profession. Her name meant good and beautiful and Jin admired her for her excellent work. He could trust her to carry out his decisions to the letter. Once she donned her vision visor there was no stopping her. She loved to get down to the nitty gritty and examine those sparkling gemstones for Jin Cho. Her white vinyl apron always looked clean and dustless. He wondered how she managed to do that. Perhaps it was an innate trait that she possessed.

Her partner, Lili Wong was another lapidary that blossomed under the tutelage of Jin Cho. From the first day she took her loupe out of its leather case and put it to her eye, Jin knew they would bond. He could see that Lili was a natural and was willing to learn his techniques. But he also allowed her to grow with her own abilities as well. Jin Cho enjoyed training and working with his prodigies especially when he saw that they had great potential. Jin relied on the judgment of these two special women to give him accurate findings and precise conclusions.

Others on his staff were also quite proficient at their jobs. Jim Zhao and Ben Wu were at their best when using their lapidary skills. Jin Cho could not be more pleased. Those two men kept his section running very smoothly. After the gemstones were passed over to them they took charge of the sawing, grinding, sanding, lapping, polishing or whatever other procedure had to be done to the stone. Behind their filter masks you wouldn't think they could see what they were doing; but on the contrary, they excelled at their jobs. They knew how to use the grinding wheels to shape gemstones to their desired rough forms and they had strong control over the coolant used to prevent overheating of the machines. When they were at the sanding stage, they used finer abrasives to remove any deep scratches left by the grinding process. Jin always watched his men at work and was in awe of their accuracy and precision. He enjoyed watching his team use the lap, a rotating flat disk, to make the flat surfaces on one side of a stone.

When the time came for the polishing process, Jia Lin and Lili always liked to join in. They all got the gemstone down to a mirror-like finish and delighted in admiring the gem in the light. But when it came to the tumbling process whereby the gems are tumbled or turned at a slow speed in a rotating barrel to gradually make them even smoother and polished to a very attractive shape, the women left the men to themselves.

Lee Chang relied on Jin Cho to keep his business running smoothly. He didn't make Jin his CEO for nothing. He had complete trust and confidence in his abilities. His successful company was proof enough for Lee that Jin was the right choice he made years ago.

Lee Chang's staff was indeed highly qualified. They knew the four C's of gemology: color, clarity, cut and carat weight and never ceased to amaze Lee with their ingenuity. They loved tackling a challenge. They had done it time and time again for Lee and always with a favorable outcome. That's why he paid them so well. So Lee knew that Charlie Ling's gemstone situation would certainly be a welcomed task.

Lee convened his staff in the conference room of his offices on the fifth floor of his ten story building. He liked having his main conference room and main offices at this strategic part of the building. He secured a lot of special memorabilia that he had acquired over the years here on this special floor. This was a very secure floor and had special security guards who monitored the floor with a very intricate security system. Lee had too many valuable items here that needed watching and he had this system installed years ago when he started his collection. It was his personal collection and he had to preserve it. He had a lot to explain to them about Charlie Ling's gem and he didn't want anyone to be misinformed about it or jump to any conclusions. In fact, he was going to leave it up to Charlie to explain the situation. Lee wanted to remain neutral, at least for now. He did not want to influence anyone's decision even though he believed he had at least a part of the perfect solution for Charlie and his friends.

"Good day my dear friends," Lee began. "You all know that our profession as lapidaries is an art and a craft. You are all artists who know your specific crafts and you have enough experience to convey your feelings and opinions to others honestly and professionally. You know how to use the tools of your trade to present original observations to arrive at accurate conclusions. I always tell you at our meetings that your work is art when it is fresh and original and done with skilled craftsmanship. Artisans such us we convey our feelings of awe, wonder, understanding and curiosity to others who watch us. I've convened this meeting so that one member of our staff might explain his plight to you. He is in need of our services in a big way. I know there has been a buzz around the building about the secret gemstone that we have in our vault. None of you have seen it in great detail yet, but I assure you, you will in time. First I will allow Charlie Ling to give you some background about this gemstone and then we will open the floor to your questions. Is that suitable to all of you?"

Everyone nodded in agreement as they usually trusted Lee Chang's judgment without questioning him. Lee had their undivided attention and he was grateful. He didn't want Charlie Ling to feel inhibited in any way.

Lee said, "Okay, Charlie, the floor is yours! Take it away!"

Charlie stood up at the far end of the long conference table opposite to Lee Chang. He noticed Lee staring at him, but Lee always did that so it didn't upset Charlie. Charlie, with a bit of nervousness in his voice, began his lengthy explanation. "I have decided to share my story with you, my co-workers and friends; because somehow I feel that its outcome will have an indirect effect on you as well. On my recent trip to Myanmar in South East Asia, I had purchased a teak turtle antique for my wife. As some of you know, it was stolen from her office and we thought it was lost forever. But that was not to be so. You see my wife's friend, Giovanna Gardina and her friend Krystyna Safenski, proprietors of an antique store in High Bridge, New Jersey, purchased it at a flea market and had it in their newly opened store. At the Grand Opening of their new store, they had the turtle enshrined on a special shelf for luck because it was so unusual. As luck would have it, Dena and I went to the Grand Opening of the store and Dena spied the turtle. One thing led to another and we were certain that it was the same turtle that I bought for Dena in Mayanmar and that was stolen from her office. It was too unique for there to be another one like it."

"What does this have to do with the gemstone in the vault, Charlie?" Jin Cho asked.

"Have patience, my friend. If you allow me some time, I will get to that. I want you to understand this story in its totality. It is a rather complex story and has its twists and turns. As I relate it to you, try to imagine all the anxiety, mistrust, doubts and so forth that my friends and I have gone through and are still faced with."

"Go on, Charlie," Lili said. "We are following you so far. Let's see where this is leading us and how it will involve us."

Charlie continued to explain. "After carefully looking over the teak turtle we were positive that it was Dena's. Our friends in High Bridge have been so very gracious about all of this. They have been bending over backwards to help us resolve this issue. Anyway, without going off on a tangent, let me tell you that this turtle is most definitely unique. While the Gardina and Safenski children were playing with the turtle one evening when we were visiting, they heard a clicking sound when they pressed the bottom of the turtle. To make a long story short, the bottom of the turtle had carvings of symbols on it that we found out after long searches were Mayanmar symbols for a certain date."

"What date was that and is it significant in any way to your story, Charlie?" Ben Wu asked.

"As a matter of fact, Ben, the date was significant in a few ways. The symbols stood for January 4, 1948, the date of Myanmar's independence from British rule. The man who created the code was from Myanmar and he did it for a reason known only to him. The important thing for you to know is that the date's symbols were important for us because it solved the puzzle as to why the turtle was making a clicking sound. It turned out to be like a Rubik Cube puzzle. By that I mean when we deciphered the date and then discovered in what sequence to press the symbols, the turtle actually opened up like a hood on a car would pop up when pressed to open."

"Are you telling us that the turtle opened up?" Jim Zhao asked in amazement. "What does this mean, Charlie? This sounds almost like an impossibility. I cannot believe what I am hearing."

Charlie answered quickly, "Can you imagine how WE felt after figuring this all out and then watching the turtle open before our eyes? We were in awe! There was a lot of gasping and oooing and aaahing going on!"

"Go on, Charlie," Lee Chang said. "Let us hear the rest of your story."

"Hold to your seats, because what I am about to tell you now will blow your mind away! When we proceeded to open up the turtle, we found a treasure inside. In the cavity of the turtle below the top raised shell was a black velvet bag tied with golden cord and inside of the bag was the gemstone, the gem that is now in our vault! How is that for a story?"

There was a lot of mumbling going on in that conference room. Everyone present had a comment and all were speaking at the same time to each other. Charlie was thinking, *I'll bet I know just how they are feeling right about now. The questions will start any moment.*

Ben Wu spoke first, "Charlie, what a find that was! You people must have gone crazy with excitement! I know I sure would have."

Charlie said, "When we opened that black velvet bag and beheld that fabulous ruby, you can't imagine the feeling we experienced!"

Jin Cho asked, "Have you any idea how the ruby got into the turtle?"

Charlie replied, "Yes, Jin, we finally know all about our turtle friend and its secret; at least we know who made the turtle, who owned it and who put the gem inside. What we don't know is where this special ruby originated. We don't know if it was part of the Ancient Burmese royal jewels that were lost during the many wars; or if it was purchased by the man who put it in the turtle. The man's family knew nothing about the ruby or about the turtle's secret compartment. So that's where we stand right now.

Lili asked, "Can we assume that we are going to help you with your ruby from this point on?"

Charlie answered, "It is my hope that you will all use your special talents and help us out with this. My other friends trust me with this next important phase in our ruby's life span. I do not want to let them down. It was agreed among all of us that my job right now is to study the ruby, evaluate it and price it accurately, with all of your assistance that is. So, are you all willing to lend a hand?"

Again there was a lot of low-toned chattering going on, but this time it had a pleasant sound to it. Charlie somehow knew his friends and colleagues would come through. These special people were elated with the task entrusted to them. Charlie could see it in their faces. He knew that if anyone could help him resolve this issue, they certainly were the group to do it.

Jin Cho spoke for the group when he said, "Charlie, you have nothing to worry about. We thank you for your trust and confidence in us. We would like nothing more than to study this fine specimen of nature. My goodness, a ruby from the Mogok Tract in Mayanmar; that is a dream come true for us. Give us a few hours to get organized and then we will fill you in on what we plan to do."

"I want to know every step you take, Jin," Charlie said, "not because I don't trust you, but because I want to know everything about this gem. I want to be able to explain the whole procedure you take, no matter how complicated, to my friends."

Jia Li chimed in with her sweet little voice, "Charlie, you have seen us at work as we worked along with you, side by side, many times. So put your mind at ease and all your trust in our expertise. You know the outcome will be favorable. Have no doubt about it. We will make this a priority item and I don't think Lee would mind. Would you Lee?"

Lee was at a loss for words as he knew he was outnumbered. He said, "Go to it, my friends. This is quite an undertaking for us. And it is also a feather in my cap if it is a famous ruby, whether we really find that out or not. I will not stand in anyone's way. Just keep me informed, as Charlie asked you to do as well."

Charlie let out a loud sigh and wiped his brow with his handkerchief. Then he had the widest smile on his face that his friends had ever seen. Charlie was indeed satisfied with his friends' reactions. He thanked each one individually; the men with a firm handshake and the women with a warm hug.

As the staff left the conference room and proceeded to the lab to get underway with this important task, Lee tapped Charlie on the shoulder and asked him to remain behind for a few minutes. When the room was empty and quiet, Lee asked Charlie to sit a moment.

"Charlie, I just wanted to ask you again, that when we are all done with our research and your friends are finished with their probing, would you give me first dibs on the ruby if it goes up for sale?"

Trying to put Lee at ease, Charlie said, "Lee, we have been friends a long time and you have always been very good to me. You know the answer to that question and you should not lose any sleep over it. Rest easy, and wish us luck. I'll keep you abreast of every detail that I learn as we move along with this. And Lee, I want to thank you for allowing me to use the staff and your work time for this."

Lee replied, "Don't thank me, Charlie. I consider this to be one of the fine points in my career in gemology. It is not many companies that get such an opportunity to study a gem of this caliber and rarity. I trust my staff implicitly and I trust and admire your judgment when it comes to gems. I am grateful that you came to me with this."

"Thanks Lee," Charlie said, "I really appreciate that vote of confidence and your trust. Now I must contact my friends and fill them in on where we stand. I'll talk to you later, Lee."

Chapter Twenty-two

The first call Charlie made was to his dear Dena. "Hello darling, I just wanted to check in with you and let you know how the first meeting with my colleagues went."

"I'm so glad you called, honey. Krystyna and Giovanna have called me a few times wondering how things were going. Do you have any news to relate yet?"

"As a matter of fact, I do," Charlie replied. "Tell the others that the first meeting went extremely well and we have embarked on the road to a solution of one kind or another. Lee Chang, Jin Cho, Jia Li, Lili, Jim and Ben are all excited about our ruby. I wish you all could have witnessed the enthusiasm that I saw exuding from them. They are all excited and ready to tackle both our gemstone's assets and secrets. They all have an open mind about our situation and are willing to bend over backwards to help us all out. I got the impression that they are going to treat our ruby not as a component of jewelry but rather as a piece of art."

"I'm glad to hear that, Charlie. The ruby should be treasured for its unusual nature, its discovery and for the craftsmanship of the artisans who shaped it, handled it and even hid it, if you will," Dena added. "I will call the others and fill them in. I know Krystyna and Giovanna are still tossing around many ideas. We were all going over the notes yesterday in fine detail. They have some great ideas which we will have to consider later on."

Charlie said, "Just tell them what we are doing right now and that we will keep them informed. I have to go and join the others in the lab, so I will talk more with you about this when I get home tonight."

Charlie hung up the phone and was whistling as he sauntered down the hall to the elevator that would take him to the lab floor. He was feeling quite good about things right now.

When Charlie entered the lab his friends were busy at work. He saw his precious ruby on the study table sitting in the dop to hold it in place in front of Jin Cho. The others were gathered around in a semi circle poking their heads between each other to get a good look at the gem.

Jin looked up and gave Charlie a nod and a motion to come in closer. He said, "Charlie, you have quite a rare one on your hands. As we all know, all rubies have imperfections and the fewer the imperfections, the more valuable it is. From first sight, this ruby appears to have very few flaws."

Ben Wu had a comment he wanted to share with the group. "I remember back in my school days a saying from the noted English writer of centuries ago, William Blake that said; *to see the world in a grain of sand, and to see heaven in a wild flower, hold infinity in the palm of your hand, and eternity in an hour.* Some interpret his thought as meaning he may well have been talking about rubies. I personally think you can certainly lose yourself inside the beauty of the ruby's soft glowing inner world and experience something as ancient as our earth itself. Being able to actually hold and touch a ruby of such rarity makes me feel in touch with past ages."

Jia Li said," That is quite a profound thought, Ben. I kind of like that and will keep that in my information bank for future seminars. Thanks for sharing that with us. It sheds a lot of light on the value of a ruby."

"You are all full of intelligent data from your backgrounds," Jin Cho added. "You all know that gems permeate our history. If you recall some of your studies, you'll remember the *lapis lazak* and the treasures of the Egyptian pharaohs, the jades of ancient China, turquoise of the Native Americans and of course, the rubies, emeralds and sapphires of India and South East Asia. Every royal family in history had its treasured gems and jewels many of which were family heirlooms."

Jim Zhao added, "Look at our museums. They contain vast collections of uncut gems, loose gemstones and precious metal jewelry set with faceted stones. You have all been in museums at one time or another in your lives. Don't you remember seeing those things?"

Charlie said, "My wife's friends have been doing nothing else but talking about gems lately. They have been saying how husbands and wives exchange jewelry, how people carry lucky stones around with them or wear amulets around their necks for luck. They pointed out that even our children, young and old, have school rings from graduations or those given as signet rings on special occasions in their lives."

"In our society we learn about birthstones at an early age. Don't most families give their children rings and necklaces with their birthstones?" Lili asked not wanting to feel left out of the conversation. She always came up with a quip or a saying that amused everyone. The group usually referred to her as *Miss Quote.* "You also all know the old adage, *Diamonds are forever.* Maybe that should apply to rubies as well."

"Okay let's not get too far away from the matter at hand," Jin said; "go back to the examination of our ruby. You all know that gems of deep colors are more highly prized than others. A ruby should be intensely red from across the room as you all know from experience. Let's check this one out from a distance. Before we do though, keep in mind that in our modern society many rubies and emeralds are poorly cut in order to maximize weight. Unfortunately that action is done at the expense of appearance. Many rubies are cheapened by such thoughtless work.

Charlie said, "As you all know this ruby is most definitely from the Mogok Tract in Upper Myanmar. That small tract has produced the best stones of the finest color for years. Some people say that there is always one aspect of a thing that stands out in every region or area. By way of comparison I mean that just as a single section of a vineyard can produce grapes for a wine of delicate and rare bouquet which no other vineyard in the same area can; so it is with the ruby. In the gem world, the best of the best rubies have always been found in the Mogok Valley."

Jin Cho added, "I must tell you that the Mogok Valley is quite an awesome place to visit. I myself have been there once. I was taken there by a friend who showed me all the aspects of how the people mine for the rubies. One thing that interested me was why the valley had such a snow like effect to its land. My friend told me that the local women wait along the perimeter of the mining area for the miners to come out with the large rubies they found. The women then gather the rocks of white marble that are left behind by the miners and pack it into their buckets. They take the buckets home and carefully re-sift them for smaller stones left unnoticed or unwanted. When they are done sorting, the remaining white marble gravel is thrown outdoors. Because of this daily routine, the entire village looks as though it was sprinkled with crystalline snow. In the daylight it sparkles. What an awesome valley it is!"

Charlie continued, "I know what Jin is talking about. It is just something to behold! In the former days of Burma, the Kings of Burma were called the 'Lords of the Rubies.' Mother Nature has blessed this land with incredible natural gemstones. This area has remained the world's premier source of rubies for more than eight hundred years. You can tell that this ruby is from that tract by its pure red color and strong fluorescence when exposed to ultraviolet rays like those in sunlight. The sunlight seems to bring out the deep shade of red. I would like you all to view it in the direct light of the sun also. Then you will see what I mean. When I was at the tract on one of my trips I stood in awe of the natural sparkling red gemstones that were shining in my face. It was an unbelievable experience; one which I will never forget. "

Ben added, "I know you can obtain some fine rubies from other places like Thailand, Sri Lanka and Vietnam, to name a few. I have traveled enough myself to know that fact. But I am also quite aware that Myanmar remains the largest and best source for high quality stones. They actually have fewer inclusions than stones from other places. So, Charlie, I have to agree with you that the rubies of Myanmar hold their glow in all lighting conditions, but are best viewed in direct sunlight."

Jia Lin was anxious to add what she knew. "When you mentioned the red glow of the rubies of Myanmar it reminded of some research I did. I learned that the intense glowing color is important to a rare and beautiful ruby because it covers up the dark areas of the stone caused by extinction when a stone is cut. When facets are cut too deep in stones the light exits through the side instead of returning to the eye creating darker areas known as extinction. And, my dear friends, although all stones possess extinction to a certain degree, fine rubies have a strong crimson fluorescence that masks these darker areas. A top quality ruby has a spectral hue with not too many overtones of brown or blue color."

"I think color is of paramount importance when judging the value of a ruby," Lili Wong added with great interest. "You've all heard the term "pigeon blood" when referring to rubies. Well, the ideal stone displays a very intense, rich crimson without being too light or too dark. If the stones are too dark, they are less highly valued. It is no wonder our ancestors ascribed magical powers to the fiery glows of nature's rubies. They never seemed to extinguish. A quality ruby appears lively and attractive."

"A lot of jewelers don't overlook the slightly less intense shades of color in gems," Jim Zhao explained. "Some even feel that less intense stones look better in low lighting and use them in their pieces of jewelry. It is my opinion as well that like all things that are beautiful in the world, rubies come in many shades and preference is simply a matter of taste."

Everyone looked at Jim with scowling foreheads but they didn't say anything. They all knew that Jim was always the contrary member of the group and would naturally come up with some opposing opinion.

Jin Cho took over the discussion not wanting things to get out of hand and lead to a heated argument. He knew when the group was together there was always a chance to disagree at something. "Let me add that microscopic inclusions called "silk" are normal characteristics of rubies. I also believe that the intensity of the red color determines the price of the ruby. Even though the ruby is considered to be the toughest gem, the kind of light source one observes it in is important to its evaluation. So let us not be too hasty or too indifferent when examining the ruby very closely in all phases and sources of lighting."

After about a half hour of examining the ruby in light sources, Charlie said, "I'd like to shift gears now, if you all don't mind, and talk about the hardness aspect. We all know that on the Mohs scale of hardness, ruby ranks 9, actually sharing that status with the sapphire as the highest in the gem world after the diamond. Quite a prestigious spot to be in the gem world! It is quite durable and a favorite choice for rings and bracelets because it can withstand a lot of nicks and knocks. Looking at my ruby I would say that it will most definitely resist scratching. What do you think?"

Jin answered Charlie with assertiveness, "I believe that to be very true in this case. We have a ruby of spectacular hardness, as I see it. But allow me to point out to you one very special quality this ruby has. Notice the three-ray, six point star. All the legs of the star are intact and smooth. This is one of the best because it has a sharp star very visible against an intense crimson body color. Our ruby has the asterism effect which is caused by light reflecting off tiny rutile needles called *silk*, which are oriented along the crystal faces. The intensity and attractiveness of the body color and the strength and sharpness of the star is what gives this ruby great value, great value indeed. Observe closely, my friends, this ruby has all six legs straight and equally prominent. This ruby is quite valuable and is extremely expensive."

Everyone offered their approval as well. They knew they had a most unusual ruby before them and were getting quite excited about it.

Jia Li was bursting with enthusiasm and couldn't resist her comment. "Let's not overlook the vitreous luster this ruby is emitting. Just look at its glasslike appearance; it is peculiar but also very reflective. The rays it shoots off have such intensity! I'd give anything to own such a gem! This ruby definitely has its true luster coming from within itself."

"Miss Quote," Lili, blurted out another favorite saying from her memory bank.... "William Shakespeare in his Midsummer Night's Dream states, *those be rubies, fairy favors.* In my opinion this ruby is a favor that was dropped on our doorstep."

Everyone laughed at Lili's ideas. She always managed to lighten up a tense situation. Feeling more confident in their work and more light-hearted, the group continued on with more assurance.

"It is time to move on to the clarity of our gem," Ben announced with interest. "Since this is my area of expertise, allow me to bend your ears a bit. We all know that the less inclusions a gem has the more valuable it is. Any ordinary person might know that much. But let me remind you that most faceted stones are cut so that light will enter, reflect and come back toward the eye. So, let me say that upon examining this aspect of this ruby, I believe it to have very little inclusions. That's why it glows with such brilliance."

"What a precise observation and I must add, a very definitive one at that," Jin Cho said to his colleague. I saw such clarity that you describe, Ben, when you turned the ruby in all directions, rocking it back and forth while looking for specks or spots. Even looking at it from the "pavilion" or bottom, it still showed intense clarity. I know that in gem examination inclusions are either easy to see or difficult to see. That's why we have to check it out in all directions; to make certain."

"Are we interested in cutting such a gem?" Jia Li asked.

Charlie answered almost immediately, "I am of the opinion that we should not cut it but leave it as it is, as we found it. It is far too rare and unusual to spoil its natural state. I am even more convinced of that idea because we do not really know where it is actually from and cannot find out about its origination. Why alter a genuine specimen of nature such as this rare beauty!"

Jim Zhao took a little offense at Charlie's statements and said, "Do you not trust that we can cut this gemstone into a finely faceted gem, Charlie?"

"I do not mean to insinuate that your cutting expertise is inferior, Jim," Charlie answered. "I simply mean that I would rather leave this ruby in its original form and not change it in any way."

For the first time Lee Chang spoke up. Usually he stayed out of his staff's work procedure. "I am leaning toward Charlie's suggestion that we leave the ruby alone. Who wouldn't want to own such a fine ruby in its original state? Look people, I know I have in my employ some of the best craftsmen in the lapidary field. That statement also means you women as well. You hold your own place among the men here, too. You are all the top of the line in your fields. I don't want any of you to feel that what you have to offer is insignificant or trivial or unimportant."

Charlie knew how much Lee wanted to own the ruby. In the back of his mind he remembered his first statements to him when he spoke to him about the ruby when he returned from Myanmar. Charlie thought, *I think I have the best possible solution to this problem, but I cannot say anything yet until I speak to my other friends. I have to see what solutions they came up with as well before I offer my opinion.*

Charlie's momentary dreaming was interrupted by Jin Cho's question. "Shall we move on to the carat weight of our ruby? I think we are all anxious to know its weight and what price it holds."

Everyone in the room stood up to stretch and offer their interest in the value of the ruby that was resting in all its glowing beauty before them. They most definitely wanted to know its worth.

Jin started the evaluation. "If we had to explain this to the common man, a person outside of our industry, we would tell them that one carat equals one hundred points. So a twenty-five point stone would be a quarter carat. The carat weight affects a stone's value in several ways. For example, a two-carat stone will cost more than a one-carat stone. That is simple mathematics. And that is simply because there is twice as much of it. It is really simple logic."

Charlie added, "Some stones are rarely found in sizes over a few carats. In Mayanmar I saw a 12.15 carats oval star ruby selling for $6,083.00 per carat which put its worth at $73,908.00. Another one, a 4.63 carat star ruby from Burma sold for $19,990.00."

Jia Li was excited about this phase of the evaluation. This was her area. "Listen up, my friends," Jia Lin said. "I have some interesting facts for you. It might interest you to know, or maybe for you to recall, that rubies are today still more valuable and rare than even the top quality colorless diamonds. For instance, a sixteen-carat ruby sold at auction at Sotheby's in 1988 for $227,301 per carat. Another sale of a 27.37 carat Burmese ruby ring sold for four million dollars at Sotheby's in Geneva in 1995, or $146,145 per carat. How about the 32 carat ruby sold at Sotheby's in 1989? Those figures are nothing to sneeze at, as the saying goes!"

Lili chimed in to give Jia Lin some support with her factual information. "As a matter of fact, in contrast, I read about eight internally flawless diamonds over fifty carats that were sold in the past few years and the largest which was a pear-shaped diamond of 102 carats, fetched a mere $125,000 per carat. You all know that top rubies are so rare that even the world's top gem dealers must incessantly comb estate sales and auctions to find them. Sizes above five carats are particularly rare."

Charlie added, "This information should make it clearer for all of you to see that we, indeed, have a very rare ruby in our possession. Not many people are fortunate to travel to faraway Myanmar and see the best rubies in the world first hand, Burmese rubies. Perhaps Lee Chang will allow all of you someday to have the privilege I had of traveling to South East Asia and view the Mogok Tract and even newer tracts that are being mined."

Lee Chang was busting inside and was so thrilled with the way this was going that he said to his staff, "If you will all bear with me for a moment, I will share with you an excerpt that I cherish from the works of Ralph Waldo Emerson. The poem reads as follows: *Rubies, the Crimson Marvels of the World, They brought me rubies from the mine, and held them to the sun; I said, "They are drops of frozen wine from Eden's vats that run. I looked again" I thought them hearts of friends, to friends unknown; Tides that should warm each neighboring life are locked in sparkling stone. But fire to thaw that ruddy snow, to break enchanted ice, and give love's scarlet tides to flow – When shall that sun arise?* Doesn't this say it all? I have read this over many times. In the world we live in today there are many marvels that surround us. We have numerous innovations in technology and even extraordinary individuals who do some marvelous deeds. But, my friends, there are few of nature's creations that are more breathtaking or beautiful than the ruby."

"That is so profound, Lee," Jin Cho said. "Thank you for sharing it with us. I didn't know you were such a literary enthusiast. Now I think we should review all our findings and meet tomorrow with a conclusion."

"I would like to place a value on the ruby also," Charlie said, "because I would want something substantial to say to my friends. They are waiting patiently for an outcome of your evaluation and I want to be accurate with what I tell them."

Lee Chang had a big smile and satisfactory look on his face when he said, "Thank you for a job well done. I'm sure the results when compiled by all of you, will produce a favorable result for all concerned. So I will meet you all here tomorrow at mid-morning, around ten thirty."

After the members of the staff took what they thought would be a long last look at the rare ruby, they placed the valuable stone back into the vault for safe keeping. This "lord of gems," "king of precious stones," or "leader of precious gemstones," was holding up to its many names.

Chapter Twenty-three

After a very strenuous day's work, one which was at times filled with apprehensive moments, Charlie went home to finalize his notes as well. He couldn't wait to tell his friends how his staff pulled together to help resolve their concerns and issues for the ruby.

Dena was glad to see Charlie come home early for a change and immediately asked how things went. "Am I to understand that things went very well since you are home at a decent hour?"

"I think our evaluation proceeded rather quickly and quite efficiently. Everyone pitched in with their knowledge and skills and now they are all re-evaluating their findings to give Lee a final report."

"Have you any idea what the ruby is worth yet?" Dena asked.

"We have some idea, but we will know more definitively after we all review our notes."

"We suspect that our ruby may be around fifty or more carats in weight," Charlie said. "I've decided to leave the final conclusion up to the others. I will know for certain tomorrow at mid-morning when we meet. Maybe I should call Giovanna and Krystyna and fill them in a bit."

"That is a very good idea," Dena said, "they are all very anxious and I can understand why. So give Giovanna a call."

Giovanna picked up the phone on the first ring.

"Are you sitting right next to the phone?" Charlie asked.

"Wouldn't you be, Charlie?" Giovanna answered.

"Yes, I would, Giovanna. At least I have some very good news to share with you."

"Pray tell, please tell me, Charlie," Giovanna blurted out getting impatient. She could hardly contain herself. She almost fell off her kitchen stool where she was having her afternoon cup of latte.

I'll fill you in but just briefly for now because we are all finalizing our notes from the evaluation today. We will convene tomorrow morning and then after that I should have more definite results for all of you, so, please bear with me, okay?"

"Oh, I'm so sorry for being so jumpy, Charlie. It is just nervous energy. Now, tell me what you can for now so I can satisfy the others' curiosities as well."

Charlie related what he and his colleagues did throughout the day. Giovanna was excited with what Charlie had to tell her, and couldn't wait to fill in the others.

"In my wildest dreams I never would have thought we could be in the possession of such a rare gem," Giovanna said. "Have we been blessed or what, Charlie? What a gift fell into our laps and so unexpectedly! We have you to thank for that! It is hard to imagine what the outcome will be for all of us. But I won't badger you for more information at this time. I know you must be exhausted yourself from all of this anxiety."

Charlie replied, "I'll be in touch tomorrow sometime and we'll set up a time to meet together. Meanwhile, I hope you all are doing your part of the project. We must decide what to do with our ruby once we know its worth. So gather your notes. And tell the others to be prepared to offer their ideas when we meet. I'll call you as soon as I know anything final. Oh and give my regards to all."

A visibly happy Giovanna left the kitchen with her cell phone in hand and found a comfortable spot where she could talk with Krystyna. The Safenski phone was ringing off the wall. *Where is that girl? Now when I need her she decides to go out?*

"Hello?" Krystyna said in a jovial tone.

"Where were you?" Giovanna asked nervously. "I have news for you."

"Okay, okay, take it easy. I was just indisposed for a moment. Don't bite my head off."

Giovanna apologized for her rude tone. "Forgive my nervousness, Krys, I am just so excited. I heard from Charlie and want to talk to you. Can you come over?"

"Yes, this is actually a very good time because Kaz took Stefan to a local soccer game. I'll be right over."

Oh, and Krys, bring your recent notes."

It was only minutes before Krystyna was at the Gardina back door ringing the bell. Giovanna, of course was right there waiting.

"Come in, Krys, make yourself comfortable. I'm making us some coffee."

As the two friends sat at the dining room table with the notes, they simultaneously looked at each other with satisfaction. In their hearts they both knew they were lucky, very lucky indeed. Finally things seemed to be falling into place for them, in more ways than one.

Giovanna began, "Charlie and his co-workers worked most of the day on our ruby. They are finalizing their notes and will produce their concluding results tomorrow morning. I can hardly wait, can you?"

"Are you kidding?" Krystyna answered with a sly look on her face. "I am ecstatic that this is all happening and so quickly at that. I am so anxious to see what the ruby is worth."

"Have you any idea about what we should do with it?" Giovanna asked.

Krystyna replied, "If it is worth a lot, which I think it will be; I feel that maybe we should auction it at Sotheby's here in New York. That is one possibility I was tossing around. That way we could all benefit from it equally. How about your thoughts on the matter? Have you come to any conclusions?"

Giovanna said, "Nick and I have discussed this so much, we are totally exhausted. One idea Nick came up with was maybe to sell it to a big jewelry store like Tiffany's. I'm sure if they knew of our ruby there would be some bidding going on or at least a lot of interest shown. The other idea Nick suggested was to keep our situation as quiet as possible from the public, for several reasons. Sometimes it is better to keep silent with such a windfall. We have been tossing around so many ifs, ands and buts that I think we have almost exhausted all of our ideas. I even thought about the Smithsonian Institution. They probably would be interested even though it is not a novel thing for them. They already have several famous rubies like the one on display, the 137-carat Rosser-Reeves Ruby."

Krystyna replied, "I haven't asked Dena what her uptake is on all of this, but I would imagine she has her own views. When we all get together we can decide. That togetherness idea always works for us.

"I know Dena was researching various ways gems are used," Giovanna said. "She told me that gems are used in a lot of things, for example, in all kinds of jewelry, for displays, as keepsakes or heirlooms, as investments, and so forth. She said many people are simply collectors of fine and rare gemstones. Maybe when we talk with her we will get an insight that we have been overlooking."

That evening after the dinner hour, Dena placed a call to Krystyna. Krystyna was thrilled to hear from her. She thought maybe Dena was reading her mind.

"You must have mental telepathy," Krystyna said. "Giovanna and I were talking about you a few minutes ago. We have to get together as soon as Charlie gets the results of his company's findings."

"That is actually why I am calling," Dena said. "Charlie should have the result tomorrow or the next day sometime. Then we can schedule a time to meet. Where do you want to meet?"

Krystyna answered, "It would be easier for you to come here because we wouldn't have to worry about our children. So as soon as you know something definite, call me and I'll arrange the meeting. Is that alright with you?"

"That would be fine, Krys. Charlie and I are looking forward to seeing you again. Like you and Giovanna, I have been busy at work, thinking, planning and trying to find a perfect solution that will suit all of us. I might, in fact, have the perfect solution, if you'll all go along with me. But I'll save my thoughts for later."

"Now you have me feeling extremely curious, Dena. I look forward to seeing you and Charlie. Don't forget; try to hasten Charlie to get after his staff people. Ciao!"

When Kaz got home Krystyna was just bubbling over with information. "Kaz, I heard from Giovanna and then I got a call from Dena."

"So what's going on, my love?" Kaz asked.

"Well, Charlie told Giovanna that his colleagues are finished with their evaluation and are preparing a statement for us. As soon as Charlie calls we will be meeting here at our house. Then from what Charlie tells us, we will have to start discussing what exactly we want to do with our gemstone. In reality, there is not much new for now. But I'm sure things will explode soon enough!"

"Okay," Kaz said, "then we will just have to wait patiently a little while longer. I would rather see Charlie's colleagues taking their time to make a proper evaluation and judgment for us. That way we will know it is as close to accurate as we can get. So when they call, make a time to meet. My schedule is flexible and I am available at almost any time. Did Giovanna check with Nick, too?"

"I'm sure she will, as I always do with you," Krystyna said. "I am getting so anxious about this. Dena mentioned to me on the phone that she may have the perfect solution for us. She wouldn't go into detail but it must be something worthwhile and solid for her to make mention of it. She has been tossing all kinds of ideas around just as we all have. We'll just have to wait another day or two."

"You know something, Kaz?" Krystyna continued, "I was looking over my notes as I do frequently and I read about a legend from the fifteenth century. The Myanmar people have a lot of legends as Charlie repeatedly told us"

"What did it say?" Kaz asked.

"It explained that back then any rubies found in Mogok were officially the property of the King or the government. This official decree resulted in the disappearance of many large rubies that were either broken into smaller pieces in order to avoid the decree and punishment for taking the rubies or the rubies were hidden for generations."

"So what are you trying to get at?"

Krystyna answered, "Maybe our ruby is one of those from the fifteenth century. If that is so, it would be worth millions."

Kaz replied, "I seriously doubt if we will ever find that out. That would be pushing it a bit, don't you think?"

"You are probably right, but it doesn't hurt to toss these ideas around. By looking at all aspects we'll find we may come to an easier solution; at least I think it helps."

"This is turning out to be one daunting task! I hope we are not out of our league," Kaz replied feeling very concerned about the whole situation.

"What a difference with the way gems are handled today!" Krystyna said. "Now gemstones are delivered by armored couriers in packages that are waxed and sealed closed under the watchful eyes of the buyer, the seller and even the customs officials. You should be aware of such procedures, Kaz. It is your line of work. Have you ever seen such packages sent that way?"

"I certainly have, dear, but back in the ancient days of Mayanmar I don't think that kind of scrutiny went on. Maybe today in Myanmar they have strict government rules, procedures, and regulations, but not back then."

"This can get very complicated if we are not prudent and careful. I really can't wait till this is all over so that we can go on with some normalcy in our lives. Our antique store is being a bit neglected because of all of this other stuff."

"Well, let's wait and see what happens next. Be patient, my dear."

Chapter Twenty-four

Four days went by and now Krystyna and Giovanna were getting nervous. They knew Charlie said it would take a day or two for his company's staff to finalize their data. This waiting game was becoming unnerving.

Krystyna was up bright and early this Friday morning. As she sat in her breakfast nook by the bay window sipping her morning brew she saw Giovanna at her back door. "Good morning," Krystyna said cheerily as she opened the door for her friend.

Giovanna's voice was calm and collected but Krystyna sensed urgency. "Good Morning to you, too," Giovanna answered. "Are you as nervous as I am, Krys? I can't stand this waiting, especially for something of this magnitude. Do you think we should call Dena and see what the holdup is? I don't want to pester her but I can't stand this waiting."

Krystyna offered her thoughts, "Well, the New York experts have had the last four days to make a decision. Since today is Friday I am hoping we hear from Charlie and Dena. Then we can spend the weekend finalizing our end of the situation. I am just as antsy as you are, Gi, but let's think positive."

"Yes, you're right, Krys. We must be patient. How can we expect our windfall to materialize at a quick pace? But that thought still doesn't calm my nerves."

"I know what you are feeling, Giovanna. You're not the only one wondering and wishing and hoping. We all want an outcome that will hearten our enthusiasm and reward us generously."

"You always know the right thing to say, Krys; thanks for the uplift of my spirits."

Amidst this mode of conversation between the two friends, the phone in the Safenski household was ringing loudly. Krystyna grabbed the phone on the second ring. When she heard Dena's voice she covered her phone with her hand and mouthed to Giovanna, *It's Dena*! Giovanna showed her delight by motioning her hands in a silent clap.

"Dena, your ears must have been ringing. We were just talking about you and Charlie," Krystyna said. "Your voice is a breath of fresh air right now. So what information do you have for us?"

Dena began her pleasant refrain, "I think you are going to like this outcome, my friends. When and where can we meet? Charlie has a lot to tell us and we must do it in person. Let me at least ease your minds by saying you are going to be totally blown away with the results of their findings. I was quite flabbergasted myself."

"Hold on one minute, Dena," Krys said. "Giovanna is sitting right here with me. Let me see what she wants to do."

Krystyna asked Giovanna what she preferred to do and where to meet and so forth. After several seconds, Krystyna was back on the phone with Dena.

"We've decided to meet at my house tomorrow morning, Saturday around ten o'clock. Is that alright with you and Charlie?"

"Charlie left it up to me to make the arrangements, so that will be fine, Krys. Please don't fuss with meals. I'm sure we will be too excited to be hungry. If we do feel the need to eat we'll order pizza or some take-out. Is that alright with you?"

"That sounds like a perfect plan. We will be waiting for you with open arms and open minds as well. We'll see you tomorrow then," Krystyna said as she placed the phone in its cradle.

Krystyna and Giovanna hugged each other with heartfelt warmth that only true friends can elicit. Things were winding down now or coming to a head, whichever way you'd like to look at it. Nevertheless the solution to their anticipation was near at hand, nearer than they ever dreamed it would be.

Saturday morning couldn't come fast enough for all concerned. Giovanna hardly slept a wink. Her living room rug probably formed a path where she paced most of the night. Nick awoke several times and went down to check on her. Krystyna was in just about the same shape. She sat in the kitchen most of the night looking over her notes and jotting down more of her latest thoughts. Kaz sat with Krys for a while but then he succumbed to some sound sleep in his roomy king-sized bed. Dena and Charlie sat up till very late, almost till two A.M.; then they sauntered upstairs, fell into bed and snored soundly until the alarm went off at seven A.M. Needless to say, they were all quite tired by the time morning rolled around, but that didn't stop them from hurrying with breakfasts. By the time ten A.M. gonged on the grandfather clock in the Safenski household's foyer, the doorbell was ringing as well. No one was going to be late for this date!

Kaz approached the front door with a two-step gait. He was surely exhibiting his enthusiastic joviality. When he opened the door everyone on his doorstep was in the same mode. Each one was smiling widely and all began talking at once. But they were use to such behavior, as they often all talked at the same time. It was funny how they all heard what each of the others were saying even though they were all speaking at the same time.

Nick broke the gibberish and said, "Are we excited or what?" He felt that he was speaking for everyone.

Everyone made their way into the Safenski living room and got themselves comfortable. Since it was still early morning Krystyna decided to offer everyone some coffee and miniature cinnamon muffins. That wouldn't take up too much time. After a cup or two of caffeine they would be able to stay focused better.

While Krystyna tidied up the area, Dena and Giovanna went over to help. Dena pulled her two friends over to the corner of the room and was whispering something. From the looks on their faces, the friendly banter seemed quite serious, very serious indeed. After several minutes Krystyna, Giovanna and Dena joined the loves of their lives in the living room and asked Charlie to take the floor. Everyone was waiting in anticipation long enough. Now it was time to find out the results of the study.

Charlie began the discussion with the written notes in front of him. "My colleagues did a fine and thorough study for us. I think you will agree with me after you hear what I have to report. My company employs some of the best craftsmen in the lapidary field. Our cutters are innovators and will be copied for generations and recognized for their work for years to come as well. Their skillful work is art indeed! The carvers we employ are producing meaningful work in hard material, which equal many masterpieces of the past done in marble or other soft material. I think you are all aware that lapidaries who work with gem materials are privileged to handle the most colorful and beautiful bits of this earth. I can attest to that beauty from what I saw of the Mogok Valley in Myanmar and other places as well when I traveled there. So many people don't recognize lapidary work as an art possibly because they are outnumbered by other art forms that dominate the art world".

Nick said, "Charlie, I think I can speak for everyone here when I say that we have no doubts about the skillfulness and knowledge of your colleagues."

Charlie went on, "Our ruby is indeed a star ruby with very few flaws or inclusions as they like to say. The ruby, a gemstone composed of the mineral corundum, is a crystal structure composed of aluminum oxide. Now that may sound too scientific to you or like a very ordinary statement, but I think it is important for all of us to know everything there is to know about the ruby so that we better and totally appreciate its value. Keep in mind also that <u>red</u> corundum is classified as rubies while other corundum colors are classified as sapphires. Due to their scarcity, the ruby is considered to be the most valuable variety of corundum."

"I think ours is the most vivid red color I have ever seen in a gem or in anything," Giovanna said. "For that reason alone, I feel that it must be of great value."

Charlie continued, "My team members informed that they know that high quality Burmese rubies larger than twenty carats are exceedingly rare. When they calculated the weight of ours, they deduced that it is in the range of 50.75 carats."

Everyone let out a huge sigh that seemed to release a lot of pent up energy. The comments started flowing. They all flopped backward into their seats and breathed deeply.

Charlie dispelled the sighing and deep breathing sounds with his next comment. "The highest price per carat ever paid for a ruby was

Alan Caplan's Mogok Ruby, a 15.97-carat faceted stone that sold at Sotheby's in New York in October of 1988 for $3,630,000. As you can see, I've done my own research as well."

"How much is that a carat?" Nick asked.

"From what they told me, that is about $227,301 per carat," Charlie answered very assuredly.

Nick's fingers were busy tapping his calculator. "Wow, if that's true, our ruby is worth in the range of twelve million dollars, $11, 545, 525 and 75 cents to be exact! That is nothing to sneeze at!"

Krystyna, Giovanna and Dena jumped out of their seats and began laughing in excitement and yelling their comments and hugging each other in a circle. It sounded like they were at a pep rally.

"Is this for real?" Dena asked. "Did we hear you gentlemen correctly?"

Nick replied with assurance, "You did, indeed. We are about to become very wealthy people and I hope we are all ready for this new venture and style of living."

"Oh I will make myself ready and learn to adjust to living comfortably, I assure you," Krystyna uttered with a shaky voice. "Do you realize how much money that is? This is quite a surprise and one that is quite overwhelming!"

"Being rich and spending our wealth is the least of our problems," Charlie added. "What in the world are we going to do with this ruby? Who is going to pay that kind of money to us for it?"

Dena said, "Look, we have all been tossing stories around in our minds. We all have our own theory as to what to do with the ruby. We have already shared many of our ideas with each other and exchanged views. I think it is time to get serious about this gem."

"I've researched prominent current day jewelry stores," Giovanna said. "Any one of them would be more than willing to purchase our ruby. But will they give us the asking price? That remains to be seen if we go that route."

Kaz said, "I'm sure all of our solutions are appropriate or might prove beneficial to all of us. We just have to decide among us which one is the most perfect of all. And that, my friends, is going to be a difficult decision, I'm afraid."

"Maybe not as difficult as we think," Dena added. "If we come up with the perfect solution that is satisfying and pleasing to all of us, the outcome will be easy."

"There goes my wife, the optimist again," Charlie said with a chuckle. "She always leans toward the brighter sides of things. There is not a person I know that has a more positive outlook on life than Dena. Of course I am not prejudiced, you understand."

Nick offered his two cents worth. "If you all recall, we thought about just leaving the ruby in the vault in Charlie's company where it is for awhile. Maybe after time we will come up with a good idea. I'm usually not that passive about things but I must admit I am quite overwhelmed by all of this."

Dena was holding back her thoughts as she compiled them and organized them in her mind. She was listening intently to everyone's opinion and usually chimed right in with the others. But she was somewhat preoccupied with her own solution. She finally spoke up. "We all have the greatest ideas for our ruby and I'm sure they would bring us satisfaction. But when I tell you what I've cooked up in this brain of mine, you will either think I am crazy or you will think it is unique."

Giovanna could hardly contain her interest and said, "Alright Dena, let's hear what you came up with, that is if all the rest of you are in agreement."

Everyone nodded their approval and prodded Dena to go on.

"Now bear with me as I try to explain my idea to you," Dena continued. "First of all, Charlie said his boss – Lee Chang is very much interested in our ruby and would purchase it in a heartbeat. Why not give him first crack at it, as they say? That would free us up from worrying about the ruby and what to do with it; yet we would make a substantial profit from the sale. I'm sure Lee will give us the asking price because he definitely wants to own it. However, the second part of my idea MUST include the ruby, so we will have to really negotiate with Lee Chang."

Kaz asked, "Dena, you are confusing me a bit. You say to sell the ruby to Lee, yet you say we need to keep it. How can we do that? Let's make some better sense of this."

Krystyna intervened in Dena's defense. "Kaz, give Dena a chance to explain and you will see that she has a truly perfect solution to our dilemma; one I think we will all like and agree with. She gave me a quick insight as to what it is in the kitchen before. Dena's idea totally overwhelmed me! So listen now and let her explain."

Dena graciously continued. "Let me be more specific to get my idea across to all of you. What do you all think about having a tapestry made for the main lobby on the fifth floor of Charlie's company and having the ruby placed in the center of it or in a strategic spot in the tapestry that would give it prominence, meaning and prestige?"

At first the group of friends was at a loss for words. That thought caught them totally off guard! No one could speak for a moment or two. Finally, Giovanna clapped with delight. "Bravo, Dena, I love that idea! That certainly would become a perfect solution if we could manipulate it properly and safely to its fruition. But we have to convince Lee Chang, that as part of the deal we want him to keep the ruby in his company in that very special place and let it be the crowning purchase of his lifetime career. Besides, I don't think Lee Chang is going to purchase the ruby just to resell it. It is much too valuable to him not to keep it in his possession."

Krystyna added, "It is of the utmost importance that Lee understands where we are coming from; what our deepest feelings are about this ruby. We must convince him that the ruby remains in the company, but we will make sure it has a place of honor to be marveled at by everyone who enters his building. This attraction should boost his business in the gem world and make gemologists from all over the world want to visit his company. Now, my dearest friends in the world, what do you think of our suggestions?"

Charlie's chest was bursting with delight that his wife came up with such an extraordinary idea. "Honey, you are unbelievable! What an idea!"

Krystyna was thrilled and bursting with joy at the thought of a tapestry. She said, "I am simply elated about your idea, Dena."

Dena continued, "If you will all bear with me, I have something further to add to our plan. Do you think it would be possible to make this project even more intriguing by asking Thiri Thuza to design and create our tapestry, to our specifications and ideas, of course? Is that a great idea or is it too far fetched?"

Charlie blurted in, "What a fascinating and appealing thought!"

"I think that is the most profound tribute we can pay to her and her husband," Krystyna answered. "It surely is a perfect way to say thank you to her for being so generous to us. And it is the perfect way to show Thiri Thuza that we acknowledge the genius of her husband."

Nick added, "We could pay her handsomely for her creation. In fact, we SHOULD pay her well for the tapestry because I'm sure it is going to be magnificent."

Krystyna said, "I think we should come up with the theme of the design we want her to create though. Once she has an idea what we want we will let her take off with her creativity."

"I have no doubt that it will be an original masterpiece," Giovanna added. That tapestry will be a living mosaic or pietre dure like some of the fine Italian artists in Italy."

Dena couldn't contain herself at this point. Tapestries were something she learned to appreciate when she traveled to Myanmar with Charlie. She said, "You can be sure that a tapestry made by Thiri Thuza would be made almost entirely by hand. Her years of living and experiences have developed her mind set. We can be assured of a valuable masterpiece that we probably will find it hard to put a price on. We would have to make it quite large to get the effect of the scene."

Charlie said, "Fortunately there is a lot of wall space in our lobby."

Nick asked, "Do you think Lee Chang will go for our idea, Charlie?"

Charlie answered, "I think we all have to sit down with him and explain our idea. Let me set up an appointment with him for Monday and we can all meet with him."

Giovanna added, "You know something, I cannot believe how well our thoughts come together to perfection when the six of us share our individual ideas. We have a special charisma for solving things when we work as one unit. That, dear friends, is a special gift!"

Now that things are falling into place, I am feeling more relaxed," Krystyna said. "How about if I order us some of High Bridge's finest pizza now and we can relax a bit with a beer or soda? I know I could eat a slice or two, or maybe three of pizza right about now."

"That's a great idea," Nick said. "Then we can all meet in New York on Monday, if Charlie sets up an appointment."

Charlie said, "When Lee hears that we want to see him, I know he is going to give us an immediate appointment at any time we ask for. So what if I set one up for about eleven o'clock Monday morning? Is that suitable to all of you?"

All were in agreement as they joined their hands together in a circle of friendship and squeezed each other with reassurance and hope.

Chapter Twenty-five

Charlie left his house at the crack of dawn. By the time Dena awoke, he was long gone, on his way to work. He arrived at the building so early that, Matt, the night security guard was still on duty.

"Hey, good morning, Mr. Ling," the guard said with a yawn. "What brings you to work so early? When we see you here at such an hour, we suspect something spectacular is going on."

"Wish me luck, Matt; I have some great things happening! You will learn about them in due time, if they become a reality."

Well, good luck to you then, Mr. Ling. I hope the day proves to be a happy and rewarding one for you."

"Thank you, Matt; you are always so cordial, even at this early hour."

Charlie rushed to the elevator and proceeded to the fifth floor. He wanted to check out the wall space before he spoke to Lee. He became elated when he spied the perfect wall for the tapestry. It was directly across from the elevator as one entered the lobby of the fifth floor. He thought *what a perfect place to hang such a masterpiece! The lighting would work out just perfectly too. We could even add more spotlight action on the tapestry.* Charlie could hardly contain his enthusiasm. Just as he stood there in the lobby staring at the wall, Lee Chang got off the elevator.

"Good morning, Charlie," Lee said. "What in the world are you staring at? And why are you here so early? I thought I was an early riser."

"Oh Lee, I have such good news for you; at least I hope you find it to be good news," Charlie said. "Can we talk privately?"

"Right now, Charlie, before we even had our morning coffee?" Lee asked.

"When you hear what I have to say, you'll forget about your morning brew," Charlie answered. "Come on now; let's go to your office."

Lee was an easy man to get along with and a great boss. He suspected that if Charlie felt urgency then what he had to say must be vitally important. They went inside and closed the door behind them.

The two men got comfortable in the leather chairs and felt at ease; they were always peaceful in each other's company. All through the years that Charlie worked for Lee Chang, they never once uttered a harsh word to each other.

Lee began, "So, Charlie, what is so important that it brought you to work so early?"

Charlie smiled as he was always known to do and began, "Lee, I am about to help you make your lifetime dream come true; at least I hope I do."

Lee sat up taller; Charlie had his interest more than peaked. "What is it, Charlie?"

"I have several things to explain to you but first of all, what would you say if my friends and I offered you first dibs at purchasing our Mogok ruby? Would you be interested?"

Lee's jaw dropped, he jumped out of his chair, picked Charlie up out of his chair, and hugged him as he slapped his back affectionately. He then stepped back and said, "Wow, Charlie, you are a man of surprises. Over the years, as you traveled, you always brought me good news and many special gemstones for my collection and company use. But you've topped them all with this offer! Am I interested? You bet I am; I appreciate you considering me first above all others, even some of the more prestigious companies and jewelers of the world."

Charlie replied, "Well, then, before I go any further, I want my other friends in on all phases of this project. So they have asked me to set up an appointment with you for today at eleven o'clock. Can you fit us in at that time?"

"Can I fit you in, you ask," Lee said, "I am canceling all of my appointments for the day as soon as my secretary comes in. Call your friends and tell them to come in for eleven or sooner if they want. I am extremely anxious to meet with them."

"I want you to know, Lee, that there is much more involved with the outcome and final resting place of this ruby. But we want to be together to explain it to you. We have a lot to ask of you also."

Lee answered, "This is mind-boggling, my friend. I am so elated that I'd probably give you whatever else it is you people are going to ask of me; especially how I feel right now. Does the other part of this have anything to do with why you were staring at the lobby wall?"

"You will know in due time. I want the others to help me explain our sale of the ruby and other requests to you, so we will all meet about eleven."

Since it was only 6:00 A.M., Lee said, "I'll try to control my emotions and keep busy, but I know I am going to have a hard time. You sure know how to rattle a guy, Charlie Ling!"

"All good things come to those who wait," Charlie quoted an old adage. "So have a little patience and the eleventh hour will be here before you blink your eyes."

Both men laughed heartily and shook hands.

Charlie unlocked his office, pushed his large leather chair away from his desk and immediately phoned Dena. "Hello, Dena, my love, our appointment is set for eleven. Please tell the others."

Dena answered, "I wondered where you had gone to when I awoke and found you missing. I guess you slept as restless as I did. I will phone the others as soon as we hang up. Before I do, tell me though, did Lee look interested?"

"Interested? He was frothing at the mouth!" Now hurry and make those calls. I'll see you later!"

Charlie went to his office to make some final notes. He wanted to keep busy so that the time would fly by. At ten thirty he made his way down the elevator to the bottom floor to await the arrival of his wife and friends. As he paced he noticed Nick's suburban van pull up in front of the building. As they all filed out of the van, Charlie was there waiting with open arms. He led them into the first floor lobby and toward the elevator. Not too much conversation was going on as everyone in the group appeared to be visibly nervous and in deep thought. The women huddled together to one side while the men just waited for the elevator to reach the fifth floor. Finally the deafening ping of the elevator bell announced their arrival and broke the silence. As they exited a lot of chatter started. Charlie showed them to Lee's conference room. Lee got up from his desk and greeted the group warmly.

"Good morning, everyone," Lee said, "it is so good to finally meet you all. Charlie and Dena have spoken about their friends from New Jersey many times. I almost feel that I know you very well. Come in; please sit down anywhere you wish. There certainly is enough room for all of you."

Charlie spoke first. "Well, Lee, now that we are all here, let me start by saying that my friends and I would like to honor you with the first chance at buying our Mogok ruby. What do you think of that?"

Lee was almost at a loss for words but he replied quickly, "I am, indeed, honored by this proposal and offer. To obtain and own a Mogok ruby, especially one of your caliber, is a gem connoisseur's dream. I am aware that while Mogok in Myanmar is the traditional source of the world's finest rubies, good stones are rare even from Mogok. Mogok rubies have a rare fluorescence and a unique crimson glow. I must tell you that to own such a ruby is to own a source of strength for my heart that will over time give me increased energy. This ruby will promote my independence, give me great insights and enhance my powers in the gem industry. As it was the gem of kings, it will surely make me feel like a king, in more ways than one."

Charlie said, "Gosh, Lee, that is quite a statement! We are glad you are so honored."

"I am aware of the worth of your ruby after hearing the study results of my staff. Its value does not scare me away; it, in fact, makes me want it more. So tell me dear people, if you are sincerely offering me this gem. I am DEFINITELY interested in buying it and owning it. The price is not a problem."

"We're glad to hear that," Nick said, feeling somewhat relieved. "But maybe you should hear what further conditions we have placed on the sale of our ruby, before you accept our offer."

Lee replied, "Charlie already hinted that you people have more than the sale of the ruby on your minds. So go ahead and explain yourselves."

Dena took over at this point. "They say that every great room has a focal point that gives it valuable beauty and makes it a topic of conversation for hours on end. We would like to make your fifth floor lobby such a place. Our idea is to have a tapestry made for that long high wall and make the ruby a focal point part of the tapestry."

Lee sat quiet for several moments and then he stood up and walked out to the lobby. They all followed him wondering where he was going, especially without saying a word. He stood staring at the wall just as he saw Charlie doing earlier for a minute or two. He paced and thought and thought and paced. Finally he stood still, looked them all in the face and said, "It's a deal, my friends, and I am deeply overwhelmed with the honor that you have proposed for my place of business and the culmination of my life's work. Yes, indeed, it is the deal of a lifetime for me and I thank you!"

They all laughed out loud from nervous energy and their laughter echoed off the walls of the hallowed halls of the lobby. The women hugged Lee warmly and the men shook his hand with a gratuitous feeling. They had not expected things to move along so fast, but they were relieved with the way things were materializing.

Charlie said, "Lee, we thank you for accepting our offer; actually for going along with our gem sale and with the making of the tapestry. You won't be sorry, I can assure you."

"I am not one bit worried about the outcome of this deal, Charlie," Lee answered. "I look forward to transacting this business deal with all of you and I want to be involved in the creation of this tapestry as well. Just how are you going to get this tapestry made? Where will you get it made?"

Kaz said, "Dena, Krystyna and Giovanna have that well under control. Dena actually thought of the idea and the three of them ran with it. You can be assured, Lee, that they will do a fine job with the project and see it through to its completion."

"Allow me to explain another idea we had in mind, Lee," Dena said. "We know it is an intricate process to create a tapestry. I personally learned that on my trip to Mayanmar. The picture or design has to be incorporated with a lot of dexterity for a distinct picture to emerge. The color of the threads, the design, the background and even the room it is to be hung in, must all be preplanned and taken into consideration. The artist must actually weave her magic into the fabric. You want your wall to come alive, if you will, and appear very realistic."

Krystyna added, "Let me add that many tapestries are made by machinery in the modern world. You can expect to see almost anything in a modern day tapestry such as dolls sewn into the tapestry to depict figures. Tapestry is an art form that has grown and evolved through the centuries. They were used profusely to display the artistic talents of people and they depicted many stories, religion, history and nature on the material used. The skill and artistry of the artisan would certainly be noticed by the magnificent end result."

Dena added, "What Krys is saying is true. I can attest to that from my own experience with seeing the tapestries in Myanmar. Love and warmth exude from wall tapestries made by skilled artisans. That is why we want to share the next part of our project with you, Lee."

"So far I am very inspired by what I am hearing," Lee answered with a positive tone in his voice. "I want to hear more, so please continue."

Giovanna could hardly wait to share the news. She blurted out, "We were thinking of asking Thiri Thuza, the woman who gave us the ruby that her husband hid in the turtle, to design and create the tapestry for us to hang in your lobby, Lee. What do you think of that?"

Lee asked, "Why do you want her to make it? I'm sure there are many places here in the states where we can get it made."

Dena replied, "We have several reasons for wanting to ask her, Lee. First, it would be a way for us to thank her for her generosity. You know she would not take any money or anything from us. Second, we would be able to repay her financially somehow, because we would let her make it only if we could pay her for her work. And third, we would have an authentic handmade tapestry, one of a kind, made by an artisan of unique and rare abilities and style."

Charlie added, "We, of course, want to design the tapestry to our own specifications, you included, Lee. We might have to travel there to make this come about."

Lee said, "As I sat here listening to you all, the one thought that kept coming to me was that you all should take a trip there, meet with the woman and get her started on the tapestry. I will pay for half of the trip for all of you to go. That will be my additional participation in the project."

Kaz said in disbelief, "Lee, that is so generous of you; even after you buy our gem from us. That would be a trip of a lifetime for us, especially the four of us who have never been there."

The women were delighted with such a proposal and they just beamed with happiness. They never dreamed that they could ever make such a trip.

Lee added, "Allow me to make the travel arrangements for the six of you. I know the best place to stay and the easiest way to travel there. Having Charlie and Dena with you will make it even easier to travel so far away to the South East since they have already been there."

Dena answered, "Thank you, Lee, from all of us. I think I will have to call Thiri Thuza to inform her of our request and to let her know when we will be there. As soon as you have the final plans made, let me know."

Before they concluded Nick asked, "Lee, would you want me to draw up the necessary papers for the sale of the gem to you since I am the attorney in the group? If you want to use your own attorney though, let me know. Otherwise I will proceed with the process."

"Go right ahead and do what you have to do, Nick. That will save me time and trouble. Let me add a request here, if I may. I would like to take you all out for dinner this evening to celebrate the event of the day. So please meet me here around seven o'clock this evening and we will enjoy a dinner at a fine restaurant in the city."

Krystyna said, "I think we can do that as our children are being well taken care of by our parents. I am all for celebrating now that the pressure is off."

Everyone agreed with the invitation and decided to remain in the city until evening. Dena and Charlie offered their house as a place to unwind and relax in while they waited.

Chapter Twenty-six
Myanmar

Arriving in Myanmar was the highlight of the trip for Krystyna, Giovanna, Kaz and Nick. Charlie and Dena spent a lot of the long travel time trying to fill them in on the beauty of Myanmar. They managed to give them a lot of background information so that they could enjoy what they were about to see. They were going to travel a bit to show them around, but a few days of the two-week trip would be spent with Thiri Thuza planning and discussing their tapestry. If there were other side trips of importance, they would make arrangements when they got there.

Charlie arranged for Khin Zeya and his wife, Myine to pick them up at the airport. He wanted them to meet the others and to be in on the making of the tapestry as well. It would make for a perfect reunion for Charlie and Dena and a pleasant visit with everyone else.

Khin and Myine were at the airport awaiting the arrival of their American friends. They were delighted to meet the other members of the American entourage as well. They greeted each other warmly and were off to their hotel in Yangon. They were having such great conversation with each other that they hardly noticed that they were in Yangon pulling up to their hotel. Since they were weary from traveling they all decided that after check-in they would have an informal dinner at one of the hotel casual dining rooms. That evening during dinner Khin told everyone that he set up an appointment with Daw Thiri

Thuza for one o'clock the next day. He figured it would be best to get the tapestry project out of the way.

Dena's exuberance was showing when she asked, "Do you think Thiri will go along with our request? Last time we met with her she seemed to want to have everything over with. I don't know if it was out of a sense of fear or just that she felt it was over for her and her family."

Khin answered, "Thiri Thuza and her family are warm and friendly people. Do not feel apprehensive about meeting with her. When I called to tell her you were all here, I kind of got the impression that she felt honored that you returned to see them, making such a long trip and that you had a special request to ask of her."

"I cannot wait to meet this wonderful woman and her son and family," Krystyna added. "I've listened to Charlie and Dena talk about her many times and they had nothing but pleasant things to say about her. I think I speak for all of us when I say we are very anxious to meet this special person, Thiri Thuza."

With that said, Khin and Myine rose from the round table and told their friends from America that they would meet them here at the hotel around twelve noon and then they would make their way over to Thiri Thuza's home. Everyone bid each other a pleasant good night and expressed gratitude for a warm reception and dinner.

The next morning couldn't come fast enough for Krystyna and Giovanna. They were up and about very early and decided to go down to the restaurant for an early cup of coffee. When Kaz and Nick got up and were ready to go downstairs, they walked out of their rooms at the same time and laughed.

"It's no use asking where our wives are, is it?" Nick asked. "I'm sure they are already in the restaurant, if I know Giovanna."

"You can bet on it," Kaz replied. "Krystyna didn't sleep very much last night. Between my grogginess all night I saw her looking out the window and making some notes. Those two never cease to amaze me. I don't know where they get their energy."

"Yes, Giovanna was pacing a lot also. She was actually keeping me up all night as well."

"Kaz said, "Well, let's go find the two wanderers."

When they found their wives they were sitting at a corner table by the window, taking in the early morning view. They were sipping their coffee and chatting away with Charlie and Dena who were also up early.

Nick interrupted their idle chatter. "Good morning, girls. I see you beat us downstairs. I hope you ordered some breakfast for us. I'm quite hungry. This place is giving me a ravenous appetite. It must be the air."

Charlie said, "This place will do that to you. Take it from me. I am always famished when I visit here."

Giovanna said to Nick, "As a matter of fact, my dear, we did order you a very wholesome breakfast which should be coming shortly. We figured you two would get down here sooner or later. At least we allowed you to sleep a little since we kept you up most of the night."

After a delicious ordinary breakfast of bacon and eggs and toast, the three couples toured the grounds a bit before going back up to their rooms to freshen up for the arrival of Khin and Myine. They were in awe of the beauty of the grounds. But Charlie explained to them that the entire city is not as beautiful. Parts of it show the result of former wars, insurrections and other problems. He told them that each town or city in Myanmar has its own beauty and specialty to offer, each in its own unique way. He told them to breathe in the clear South East air and to find the beauty in the place. He wanted them to like it as much as he and Dena did.

A while later, the six travelers found themselves waiting in the lobby for their Myanmar friends. They didn't have to wait long because Khin and Myine were right on time. They made their way to Khin's jeep and off they went to see Thiri Thuza. The day was perfect and they were feeling good about things. Somehow they knew everything was going to work out in their favor.

Thiri Thuza was waiting anxiously for the people from America to arrive. While sipping her tea she said to her son, "What do you think they want of me now, Sanei? I thought we would be free of this situation, my son. I hope there are no developing problems over this ruby your father hid in the turtle. We certainly don't want any trouble for our family. I often wonder what your father would have said or did under these unusual circumstances. I ponder often over why he had the ruby, why he hid it in the way that he did and so forth. It is truly puzzling to me. Sometimes I drive myself crazy thinking about it."

Sanei answered his mother affectionately, "Do not worry, mother, I'm sure the Americans mean us no harm. According to what Khin Zeya said when he called, they simply have a proposal to make to you or a favor to ask of you. So let's wait and see. They should be here any moment now. And do not fret over the choices father made or the reason why he hid the ruby. We will never know the answers, so why dwell on it."

Thiri answered her son, "You are right, Sanei. I will try to forget what your father did. I will find comfort in remembering that he must have had a very good reason to do what he did."

A few seconds later, the outside bells hanging by the door were ringing pleasantly. Sanei went to welcome everyone to their home. He was surprised when he opened the door and eight people were standing there. He didn't realize that they all came to Myanmar. He led them into the room where his mother, Thiri was seated in her cushioned wicker chair. Everyone was delighted to make her acquaintance especially after hearing so much about her from Dena and Charlie.

"Come, come in, please," Thiri said. "Sit with me and my son will see to it that refreshments are brought out. I am so happy to meet you all at last. It was so wonderful that you were all able to travel so far to come here to Myanmar. I am honored!"

Krystyna could not wait to speak to Thiri. She said, "No, we are the ones who are delighted to finally meet you. Charlie and Dena have spoken about you and your wonderful country to us many times. In fact, we had a lengthy conversation on the very long flight here."

Thiri answered with glee in her voice, "So, how do you like it here in Myanmar so far? Have you had a chance to see anything of importance yet?"

Khin said, "Oh, we are trying our best to show them around, but we felt it was most important to speak with you first, Daw Thiri Thuza. These people have a wonderful request to ask of you so I will let them talk with you."

Dena started by saying, "Daw Thiri Thuza, we have thought long and hard about the ruby you have so graciously given to us. We finally unanimously came to a decision as to what to do with it. So if you will bear with us, we would like to explain our plan to you."

Thiri asked with a curious expression on her face, "And what is YOUR PLAN, my friend?"

Dena continued, "My husband Charlie's boss from his company decided to purchase the ruby from us for his company and as a lifetime acquisition that any gemologist might desire. We knew he really wanted to own it, so we asked him first before presenting to any other jeweler or gem dealer or museum. He is willing to pay us top dollar for it as it is worth millions, as you must know. However, as part of the sale to Mr. Lee Chang though we have requested that he keep it on display somewhere for all to see who enter his company building. A lot of American and foreign visitors come to do business with him and it certainly will be viewed by many and much appreciated."

'What a wonderful idea!" Thiri said. "I am glad you have found such a unique way in which to enthrone this precious ruby. This Mr. Chang must be a fine gentleman and a lucky man as well to buy and possess a Mayanmar ruby of such value and beauty."

Sanei, looking puzzled and wanting to look out for his mother and family asked, "What more can we possibly do for you?"

Charlie, trying to put Sanei at ease answered, "Sanei, your mother, in fact, can do a lot more for us at this time. Please allow us to explain."

Dena said, "It is our wish to have a huge oversized tapestry made of the Mogok Valley and have our ruby become the focal point of the scene. We are all in agreement of this request. Also, it is our specific wish that you, Thiri Thuza, design and create this tapestry for us."

Thiri's eyes lit up brightly, she stood up and said, "That would be a creation of a lifetime. I am deeply honored that you ask this of me. I would be happy to make it for you. But I have certain requests to ask of you before I do."

There was a little gasping going on in the group. They didn't want to overwhelm Thiri and make her afraid to make the tapestry for them.

Charlie got up, paced a little, and said, "We want to include you in all phases of our planning and we want your valuable input as well before we begin to create this masterpiece."

Thiri immediately said, "I would like to take you all to the Mogok Valley on a day's excursion, to see for yourself the beauty of the valley. Then you will appreciate my suggestions and the media I would like to use to design and create your tapestry."

Giovanna was just bubbling over with happiness and said, "That is a marvelous idea. We would all like to go there; in fact, I think we MUST go there. Will you take us there, Thiri? Would you be our guide along with Khin and Myine? I cannot think of anyone else who could better explain the Mogok Valley to us."

"I will definitely arrange for this to happen. Sanei will help me, I'm sure. Would you be able to go as soon as tomorrow morning? I know you are only visiting here for a short time."

"Nick spoke for the group when he said, "We will be ready. Just tell us when, where, and how; we'll be there."

Charlie added, "I will add some advice that I received from a friend when I went there." He looked over at Khin and smiled. "Dress casually, comfortably, and bring binoculars and cameras and sketching pads. The terrain that we will travel will be rough at times but at the same time you will find beauty in the landscapes you see and delight in the uniqueness of the valley and countryside."

Kaz said, "Before we set out on our trip and finalize our tapestry plans, we want you to know that we will not let you make this tapestry for nothing. You must allow us to pay you for your work. We will be generous and we want it to be our gift to you for all you have done for us."

Nick added, "We want to make an agreement with you for a substantial price. We also want you to know that we will pay for any extra incurred expenses that you will need if you want to purchase various media to bring this work to completion."

Thiri rose from her seat and looked at all of them and said, "My dear people, I don't expect a lot of payment for my work. I am happy to have this opportunity to please you with my expert work."

Krystyna said, "We would like to offer you $50,000 for the tapestry. Does that sound fair?"

"Oh my," Thiri said as Sanei gasped in the background. "I am completely surprised with that offer. That is so very generous of you. I would never expect such a large amount of payment for my work."

"Well, we want it to be very large and decorative with delicate details and extra jewels if need be," Giovanna said. "We want it to take up a huge section of the wall in Lee Chang's lobby on the main floor of his building. We will show you the dimensions on one of your son's walls in his warehouse to give you an idea of the size we expect it to be."

Thiri asked, "Do you want this made in a hurry or do I have some time to devote to it?"

Nick said, "We would like it done as quickly as possible. However we want you to enjoy making it for us. We know it involves a lot of tedious work so please don't worry about time. We know we can count on you to make it as fast as you can. We understand that you need time to design it and then gather your media to create it."

"Take all the time you need, Thiri," Dena said. "We just want the reassurance that we have your total commitment to our tapestry and total devotion to our project."

Thiri looked at them all graciously with her warm brown eyes and said, "My dear friends from America, I feel that I have known you all for ages. You make me feel like family. First, thank you for including me in the final phases of your ruby's journey. I am happy to be able to maneuver my schedule to accommodate your request. I will be delighted to make your tapestry. I am deeply honored because it will be my lifetime work of art. But, as I said, I want all of your input before I design or create the tapestry. That is why I feel it is important for all of us to go to Mogok together. So before we talk further, we will make the trip. Then when we return, we will have another session to discuss the media and exact design and specifications. Is that suitable to all of you?"

Dena, being the tapestry expert of the American group said, "Yes, Thiri, we must travel there and see Mogok Valley for ourselves. Then we can more adequately tell you our ideas and alter them if need be to create our tapestry. We are aware that we will most likely then have to maneuver our frame of mind into another realm – one of completion and satisfaction. We have a lot of confidence in you or else we never would have asked you to be the artisan. I hope you know how much we care about you and your family and that we always will."

Sanei stood up and walked over to his mother putting his arm around her shoulders. He said, "Thank you for honoring my mother with such a magnificent project and generous offer. My family will assist her however we can to help her complete this tapestry in a reasonable amount of time."

Thiri looked up at her son with much pride. *He was definitely his father's son, she thought.*

Thiri had a few added thoughts for her friends. She said, "The Mogok is a magnificent valley and I look forward to visiting it with all of you. You will be amazed at what you see there. Hard working people will greet you and picturesque scenery awaits you. It will be wonderful for me to go back there also to see how it has changed. I have not been there for many years. So now, I will look forward to tomorrow. My son and Khin will arrange transportation and anything we will need to travel."

With that said, the group said their good byes and left Thiri and her family. They were looking forward to their visit to the Mogok Valley of Rubies.

Chapter Twenty-seven
The Mogok Valley

The next morning couldn't come fast enough for Kaz, Giovanna and Dena. They wanted to get underway as quickly as possible. After they got ready they hustled to the hotel lobby to wait for the Zeyas and Thiri Thuza. They weren't kept waiting for long because Thiri was just as anxious to get an early start. The group managed to squeeze into Khin's large jeep which would make for great conversation exchange. In a matter of moments they were on their way. The day couldn't have been better with bright sunshine and mild breezes.

As they rode along they chatted about everything and anything. Kaz said, "Charlie, you have seen the Mogok Valley. So why don't you give us your thoughts on the scene and what you think we should include in it."

Charlie was quick to answer as he loved talking about Mogok and especially its rubies. "The Mogok is a valley of color. The towering mountains overshadow the lush green valley below that sparkles with the pure white powdery crystal residue of rubies left behind. Rubies have been there for centuries and the hundreds of white-topped pagodas that dot the valley and its surrounding hills appear to be watching over the valley."

Khin asked, "May I speak for a moment?"

Khin continued with confidence, "Everyone knows how important the mines are to Mogok. Why not include the mines as well somehow.

They are a large part of the valley. Without them there wouldn't be a story to tell about Mogok. They are what brought the people to settle here and make a living."

As she was taking notes Thiri said, "That would be easy to do. I may place the mining area of Mogok as the center of the tapestry scene and leave a place to encase the actual ruby in the lower part of the valley, almost in the center as a focal point. I want the ruby to stand out. I will have to try various ways. Leave it to me."

Krystyna was so excited with this journey to Mogok. She said, "I can already picture this! It sounds glorious and picturesque beyond words! I am expecting a lot. I hope I am not disappointed."

Charlie added, "Oh, you won't be, not by a long shot."

While they chatted, Thiri kept jotting her own thoughts down and she even did some sketching. By the time they arrived in Mogok, she had a very detailed sketch of the Mogok Valley drawn on her pad. The women kept peeking over their shoulders to see what she was drawing and writing.

As their 600 kilometer trip from Yangon was winding down they approached the entrance to the Mogok Valley. They passed under a colorful archway that said *Welcome to Ruby Land*. Khin explained to the group that the government was allowing more visitors to visit Mogok with special permission since nineteen ninety. The remote land was truly a city in the clouds as the high mountains stood looking over the valley. The whole town appeared to reflect off the mirrored lake below with the mountains in the background. As they rode along they saw a few old two-story teak buildings along the narrow streets. Women with straw hats sat by an outdoor vegetable and fruit market. The thanaka covered faces of the women selling the produce under colorful umbrellas showed that they were enjoying their jobs. They had their merchandise arranged very neatly in baskets and bowls in front of them on low tables. As they rode on they passed through a crowded part of town where Khin explained the people were selling and buying gems. As they proceeded to drive from street to street making their way to the mine area, they saw men inspecting gemstones and women washing the *byon*, gem-bearing stones.

Khin told them that Mogok had a lot of legends and folklore besides being the land of rubies. Every family had a lot of stories to tell. The

Mogok Valley towns were home to many ethnic groups who settled there over the centuries. He told them Mogok was a land of diversity and sharing. It is not in too many places in the world where Buddhist pagodas, Christian churches, Muslim Mosques and Hindu temples co-exist in a harmony so rare. Being surrounded by lush thickly jungled hills, one had to expect to see animals such as elephants, tigers, bears and leopards once in a while in the mountains. Khin tried to explain what a diverse magical land Mogok was. He had his group of friends enraptured by his knowledge.

Charlie said, "I think we are getting close to my friend Shein's gem store. We definitely must stop there to see him because that is where I purchased our beloved teak turtle that started this whole story. He would be very unhappy if he found out we were here and didn't stop in to see him."

Khin agreed with Charlie as he, too, wanted to see Shein again. He didn't get out here to Mogok too often anymore. So it would indeed be a treat to visit his friend.

They pulled up to Shein's store just as Shein happened to step outside his door. He couldn't believe his eyes! His friends had come back to visit and brought others with them. He was so glad to meet the group, the husbands and the wives. He insisted they stay for lunch before moving on toward the mines.

After a delightful noon lunch they left for the mining area to get a quick look at the opencast mines where the people were hard at work. They were amazed at the organized way in which the mining was done. Of course they only saw the surface mining. They could not go down into the deep mines as that would have been too dangerous. Besides most outside visitors were not permitted to go down there.

Nick and Kaz were amazed at Mogok and its treasures. Nick said, "Maybe our ruby came from the alluvial beds of the valley bottoms. In a way it is sad that we will never know that part of its life."

Kaz added, "Maybe it came from the depths of the mines below. What a mystery our ruby presented us with! I guess we will have to be content simply to own it."

They stopped and parked for a few moments half way up to the top of a huge mountain that overlooked the whole valley. Their eyes beheld a magnificent view of the valley below. As they enjoyed the panoramic scenery they saw that Thiri was sketching intensely and smiling as she did so. Everyone was indeed glad that they came to see the Mogok Valley. With all the wonderful pictures they were taking in their minds they knew the tapestry was going to be an exquisite work of art, like none other. The natural colors of the valley were overwhelmingly beautiful. Words do not do them justice.

Giovanna said, "There is so much to take in as we stand here in awe! I truly hope that our tapestry does the valley justice."

Thiri answered, "I will do my best to bring out the beauty as closely as I can with the media I will use. I certainly have my work cut out for me. But now that I have seen the valley with my own eyes, I can more accurately portray it on canvas. It will be a joy for me to create this tapestry."

Charlie said, "We have been here for a while. Let's take a closer look at the valley below as we drive down the mountain. I think we all want to remember this magical place for the rest of our lives since it has touched our lives in such a mysterious and generous way."

Krystyna said, "Yes, I want to remember this place forever as the place that brought unfathomable secrets to our lives and immense joy and happiness."

After a few more hours of touring the valley and stopping to talk with some of the people, they decided it was time for them to head back to Yangon. They had a lot to discuss with Thiri. They said farewell to Shein and offered gratitude for his time and help while they visited Mogok. They left for Yangon with a lot to think about and a lot to be grateful for.

After several hours of driving the winding roads they were happy to get back to Yangon. Since it was very late, they all decided to call it a day. After they dropped Thiri and Sanei off at their home they all went back to their hotel. They all agreed to meet the next day at Thiri's house to complete the plans for the tapestry. There was a lot they had to do yet.

Yangon Mayanmar

Thiri was up very early preparing herself for the visitors from America. She was up half of the night arranging her notes and finalizing her sketches. She was definitely organized now and ready for her friends to arrive. She knew she first had a lot to explain to them about tapestries before she even began to design or work on it. She wanted them to really understand the value and worth of the art so that they would fully appreciate its beauty.

Charlie, Dena, Kaz, Krystyna, Nick and Giovanna were on Thiri's doorstep almost at eleven o'clock that morning. They, too, were anxious to get the project underway. After that was completely settled their plan was to spend the last few days of their trip touring a few more places of interest. Having come so far from home they wanted to take in all they could.

Thiri answered the door herself as Sanei prepared a comfortable seating arrangement for the group. Thiri wanted everyone to take part in the planning and decision making. *After all, they were paying for it, she thought.* She welcomed them warmly when she said, "Come in, my dear friends, I have so much to tell you."

As they made their way in to the house, they followed Thiri down the hallway to the most beautiful solarium. Bouquets of flowers accented every corner of the room. The sun was beating down through the glass windows on the inside greenery as they looked out over the lush floral garden outside. Even Thiri's home and gardens were delightful.

After everyone was seated, Thiri began, "It is my wish to explain tapestry making to you a little because I want you to know something about the process I use and how an actual tapestry is made. So if you will bear with me, I will tell you about this ancient technique. Perhaps you already even know a lot about tapestries after doing your research. But I would ask you to indulge me as I try to explain my art to you."

Dena said, "Thiri, feel free to explain anything you want to. I'm sure this will be a learning experience for all of us; one that we will never forget. We want to be well versed in tapestry making so that we can more easily explain ours to the public if we have to."

Thiri continued, "A tapestry is a kind of fabric with trimmings and figures. Each country that makes them has its own distinctive techniques and features. Some depict historical events, others reveal colloquial happenings; all showing deep meaning. Many tapestries down through the centuries are treasured as family heirlooms and accentuate the décor of the home. An old and treasured tapestry will not only bring out the interior of a room but it will also create a sense of history. I want your tapestry to do that for all of you, including and especially Mr. Lee Chang, in whose place of business this tapestry will hang. I want the tapestry to give you warmth, satisfaction and happiness each time you look upon it. I would like to think it will always remind you of your friends here in Myanmar who have become parts of your family in America."

Krystyna said, "I don't think we have to sell Mr. Chang on our tapestry idea. He is one hundred per cent committed to our project, especially since he will be the owner of the tapestry and the gem around which it is being created."

"We could never forget you and your family, Thiri. You are truly amazing people who are unselfish and most generous. Each time we look upon the tapestry we will be reminded of that fact."

"Let me continue," Thiri uttered. "I have sketched what I think will be the ideal setting for your scene," she said as she unrolled her drawing. "As you see, I have chosen the view from the midway point of the mountain in Mogok that overlooks the valley below. That way I can capture the mining area as well as the white-topped pagodas and stupas and the snow-like ruby dust effect scattered throughout the area. I would also like to include some people figures in various ways to add the extra human touch to the tapestry. If you give me free reign I would like to interweave my own mind pictures into the tapestry as well."

Nick said, "I think I can speak for everyone when I say that you have our permission to use your artistic abilities anyway you wish. We have unconditional faith in your expertise."

"You had mentioned earlier that you want me to use various media, Thiri said. "Is that still your desire; that I use many media regardless of price?"

"Charlie said, "Yes, that is our wish."

"We want you to even use some fine gems in various sizes besides the usual forms usually used," Kaz added.

Thiri said, "Oh, I plan on using a lot of threads of all colors including a lot of gold and silver. A tapestry of that size will require a lot of it. Anyone who does needlepoint is certainly aware of how tedious this project will be for me and can appreciate the work that will go into it. I will most likely use vivid appliqués as well, where needed."

Dena said, "We want you to use any media you deem necessary to make this tapestry a work of art. Please remember, Thiri that we are not experts at tapestry making, but you are. Whatever you decide to create will be fine I'm sure. We trust you to make this as if you were making it for yourself. I think my friends will all agree with me when I say that you do not have to go into the fine details of how you will make this a finished product. We all know you have your own technique and that you will make it in the stages that are necessary to get it finished."

Krystyna added, "All we want is for our tapestry to tell a marvelous unfolding story, OUR story. We want you to make it "come alive". This tapestry will be around for a long time and it will pass down from generation to generation. Let it reveal our subtle secrets through your artistic talents and the media you choose to make that effective. And of course, we want people who look upon it to see a part of beautiful Myanmar in South East Asia."

"I can see you have been reading a lot about tapestries, Krystyna," Thiri said. You are well-versed in the makings of them. I will not disappoint all of you."

Giovanna asked, "Will you do any three-dimensional effects, Thiri?"

"Oh yes, that is a definite, the tapestry calls for it. This tapestry will reflect your story, an unbelievable one. I will make your tapestry appear real and alive, I assure you. When I interweave the gold threads and gems the embroidery will be so fine and intricate that it will defy the imagination of any unskilled person. All of my time from today on will be spent on the tapestry. First I will sketch the scene which is the easy part. Then the stitching begins at a slow and persevering pace. After all the stitching is complete I will proceed to sew on the three-dimensional media, such as stars, sequins, gems, beads, pearls and whatever else it calls for. That part of the tapestry making is called 'laying down the figure.' I must be careful to leave a special place of honor for the ruby itself which you will have to insert after it is hung on the wall. I will use all of the artistry and skills I know to make this beautiful and eye-catching."

Charlie said, "In the long run, our Mogok Valley will not only be the work of a single fine artisan but it will be a cooperative effort. We have been working together on this from the beginning as a group. It seems that even at its end, our project is a team effort."

Nick, wanting to get on with the rest of the vacation, said, "I think we have just about covered every phase of this project. Now it is in your hands, Thiri. Do you have any idea how long it will take you to finish it?"

"Maybe six months if all goes well," Thiri answered. "I will let you know as soon as I complete it. I don't want to rush with it as I will be trying to make it as near to perfect as I possibly can."

"We are going give you half of the payment in case you have to buy things for its completion. Then we will send you the rest of our gift to you after Lee Chang purchases the ruby from us officially," Charlie said.

Thiri said, "Oh, don't worry about paying me. I am not worried about such things."

Dena replied, "We know you are not worried about payment, Thiri, but we want to offer you our help in that way, by our financial participation. Besides, you truly deserve some remuneration for your hard work."

After a light lunch prepared by Thiri's daughter-in-law, everyone said their good-byes with promises to keep in touch for many years to come. The three couples returned to the city to plan out the last few days of their vacation before heading back home.

Chapter Twenty-eight

The flight back to JFK International Airport in New York was long but the three couples didn't seem to notice. The only reminder they had of the trip's length was their fatigue. Jet lag had set in upon them big time and they knew they had traveled far and long. None of them regretted the long plane ride as they had so much to discuss. Dena, Giovanna and Krystyna were tireless in their exchange of ideas. They hardly came up for air except maybe when some food arrived at their seats. Before they all knew it they were landing and the trip was one they would remember for a long time, undoubtedly forever.

After customs inspection and gathering their luggage they all headed back to Charlie's Gem Company to meet with Lee Chang. They had been in phone touch with Lee and he was expecting them and anxiously awaiting their return. Charlie called Lee from the limo to let him know they were en route.

When they pulled up to the company entrance, Lee's doorman warmly greeted them and told them that Mr. Chang was waiting for them in his office suite. They left their luggage in the care of the doorman and headed to the elevator. In a matter of seconds they were out of the elevator and making their way to Lee's office. The way they were all hurrying and chattering, one wondered who was more excited, Lee Chang or them.

"Welcome home, my dear friends," Lee shouted exuberantly. "Tell me now; do we have a solid deal with Daw Thiri Thuza? Is our tapestry in the works?"

"Easy now, Lee," Charlie said, "let us sit down first so that we can explain every detail to you as we know it. We have a lot to tell you."

Krystyna started the explanation with her comment. "Lee, the tapestry is being made as we speak. Thiri is giving it her undivided attention and will be working on it feverishly."

Lee asked, "So how long do I have to wait for the finished product, if I may so boldly ask?"

Giovanna answered, "Not too long, Lee. Thiri said it may take her about six months, give or take a few months. She is so overjoyed with the commission to make it and intends to make it her life's work of art. It has a lot of sentimental value and meaning for her as it does for us. We can expect nothing short of perfection from her."

Dena added, "We told her not to rush as we want it to be as flawless as possible."

Lee said, "I guess you are all right. We must allow Thiri to work carefully and accurately. After all it will be gracing my lobby wall and it will reflect an epical story. I know we will be proud of her work."

"You can count on that, Lee," Charlie said. "We left the project in her hands. All we have to do now is wait patiently for the result. We have had to practice a lot of patience since this began so a few more months should not upset us."

"You are so right," Lee answered. "We will let Daw Thiri Thuza make our masterpiece. When it is complete we will have reason to celebrate big time!"

Everyone clapped their approval. They were a team after all, one that stuck together through thick and thin. Their unity brought the project about and it was now bringing it to completion."

Before leaving, Giovanna asked, clearing her throat, "Don't you think we should decide how we will hang this tapestry, discuss the lighting and so forth before we disperse? Being an interior decorator expert I know a few things about hanging tapestries. At least I know I did some thorough research about them. What do you think?"

Nick answered quickly, "Oh I know you are just bursting with enthusiasm to show YOUR expertise, my dear. Why don't you fill us in with the info you have; that is, if the others have the time and are not too tired to listen."

They all nodded their approval and wanted to hear what Giovanna had to offer, especially Lee Chang. This was his wall in his building that was going to be turned into a piece of South East Asia.

"Okay, listen up," Giovanna began. "This is what I've found out about hanging tapestries before we left for Myanmar. There are different methods of hanging tapestries just as there are hanging draperies. One way is to use rods and brackets to keep the tapestry close to the wall. "Feather" finials are used because they are unique. Tassels can be hung on the bottom corners. This is a good way; however, it shows a lot of shadows. I don't think we want to see shadows; they distract from the tapestry. The finials and tassels might be okay to add for beauty sake."

Krystyna asked, "What are finials, Giovanna?"

"Oh, they are foliated ornaments that form an upper extremity in architecture; in other words, they are crowning ornaments that add beauty to the hanging."

Krystyna replied, "I kind of like those as added attachments; they might look rather unique and pretty."

Giovanna continued, "Another popular way to hang is the European style, flat to the wall with finials exclusively designed for the piece. This method prevents waving and curtaining of the tapestry and eliminates any shadows cast behind the tapestry. With this method we will never have mildew or mold to worry about because about an eighth of an inch of space is between the wall and the tapestry. It will *breathe*, as they say."

"It sounds to me like we should go with the European method," Dena said. "After all they have been hanging tapestries for centuries in those old castles and stone buildings. Their tapestries have withheld the sands of time; let's learn from their experience. We are only going to do this once, so let's do it right."

Kaz said, "I hope our tapestry turns out well. How do we know if it will be of the best quality?"

"Have no fear, Kaz," Giovanna offered, "we will know our tapestry is a great one by the weave, the thread density, the detail in the design and the quality of the fiber content. After speaking ourselves in person with Thiri Thuza, I have no fear that it will turn out perfectly. I firmly believe that we can trust her to turn out the best of the best for us."

"I agree," Dena added, "our tapestry will be so unique that its design will be unmatched. After Thiri puts her fine details in it with all the subtle color ranges that she spoke about our tapestry will have an inviting thickness that will be tangible to the eye and to the touch."

Charlie backed Dena's confidence in Thiri up with his comments. "I have no doubt that the tapestry that Thiri creates for us will have a sophisticated look coupled by a regal mystique. It will indeed fascinate all who view it. She is going to use some of Myanmar's finest gemstones in it along with other media. It has to turn out as a magnificent piece of artistry."

Giovanna said with enthusiasm, "Our special tapestry will be easily authenticated because as you will see when it is finished, you will be able to view it from the reverse side as well. That is how well that tapestry will be made. I know this because of the ones I purchased for myself when I was there with Charlie. They are exquisitely and finely made and can be viewed from the reverse side as well. You will see what I mean when you see ours."

Krystyna said, "This is all as exciting for me as I know it must be for all of you. I cannot wait to see our tapestry. I for one will be sitting on pins and needles awaiting its completion. I'll try not to drive all of you crazy with my nervousness."

"You will just have to keep busy in the antique store, my dear," Kaz said to his wife. "Time will pass faster than you think; you'll see."

Lee Chang broke everyone's thoughts with his suggestion. "How about having a quick dinner here in the city before you head back to Jersey? I think you all must be hungry in spite of your fatigue. Besides, I would like to treat you."

Charlie said, "That sounds great! Let's go. I know a great little place, home style, where we can talk loud and not have anyone look at us cross-eyed."

So they all went downtown and finished the day off with warm friendship and a hearty meal. Afterwards the two groups from New Jersey and New York split up and made their way home. They all knew in their hearts that they would have to wind down from this magnificent trip. Time was needed now to get this project finished. They desperately needed to get back to some normalcy in their lives. The discovery of the ruby turned their worlds upside down. Now it was a waiting game they needed to play.

Chapter Twenty-nine

The telephone was ringing off the wall in the Ling household. The months flew by so fast that Dena could hardly believe she was hearing Thiri Thuza's voice at last. "Hello, Thiri. It is so good to hear from you. I assure you, we have never stopped thinking about you; not for one single moment. What news do you have for us?"

Thiri began, "I have completed your "shwe-chi-doe"; your gold-threaded tapestry. I am certain that you will be pleased with it. I have used numerous media from sequins, velvet, wool, glass, beads, and of course the jewels that you requested. The jewels make it a rare piece of art and very expensive at that."

"Oh, Thiri, my friends will be so pleased that it is completed. When do you think you will ship it to us?"

My son, Sanei is having it shipped as we speak. It will arrive directly at your New York Company. Please let me know when you get it."

Dena replied, "I surely will call you. I know we will all want to talk with you after we see it. I am so excited, Thiri."

"First view it on the wall, properly hung, before you give me your evaluations and comments. Also, please let me know how you hang it."

Dena answered, "We will be sending you many photos, Thiri. You will see it as we hang it, and photos for the final unveiling. We are actually planning to have a special day to dedicate it. We are supposed to have a video made of the whole process. You will definitely get a copy.

Of that be assured. Please know that we will also be forwarding you the balance of payment that we wish you to have for your work plus an added stipend for your son, Sanei and his family. I will make sure that Charlie informs you when it will be arriving and how we will send it to you. Until then, Thiri, thank you so very much and tell your family we all ask for them. I'm sure we will all want to keep in touch with you. So you can be assured that we will call you from time to time and we hope that you feel that you can do the same."

After the phone connection ended, Dena went running downstairs to tell Charlie the good news. Then she phoned Krystyna and Giovanna as well. Finally everything was falling into place.

Once Giovanna heard the news she immediately got in touch with the company that would be hanging their tapestry for them. The company she was using was quite reputable as it was known to do a lot of work for European clients.

Everyone again pitched in to do their share and get things in motion for the arrival of the tapestry. Charlie and Dena worked closely with Lee Chang to prepare the lobby for the tapestry. Spotlights and recessed lighting were installed. Lee saw to it that a teak floor was installed in front of where the tapestry would hang. He wanted to make the lobby portray the land of Myanmar as much as possible so as to fit in with the theme of South East Asia. He asked Dena to purchase an appropriate area rug with an exotic design for in front of the wall.

Meanwhile, Krystyna and Giovanna were busy ordering floral pieces for the lobby and the dais where they would all be sitting. They were trying hard to create a South East Asian atmosphere. They knew the media would be there so they were preparing for a gala occasion. Along with Lee Chang's approval and input they finalized the invitations, some of which would be sent to notable figures of the city. The idea was to create a festive atmosphere. The last item on the agenda was the cocktail hour which was going to include various food stations and almost every finger food available. Plans were finally in place to make this day one unforgettable enchantment for everyone; one to be remembered for a long time.

After several days the tapestry had arrived in Charlie Ling's name. Lee Chang instructed his staff to help Charlie in unpacking it and getting it ready for hanging. While this was being done, the other work crews were quite busy. Before they knew it the lobby was ready. All that was left now was to call the installers to do their job of hanging the tapestry in place. This was a tedious part of the project. Everyone was just holding their breath that everything went smoothly.

It actually took the installer three days to get the tapestry hung properly with the lighting focused in the perfect spots. Once that was done there was only one more thing to do, set the ruby in its place. When Lee and Charlie looked at the tapestry on the lobby wall they saw for the first time the innate creativity of the artisan, Thiri Thuza. She provided an ornately detailed spot for where the ruby would be placed on a teak pedestal. The spot around the ruby was stitched with diamonds and emeralds interwoven with the golden thread from the golden land.

Everyone, indeed, was going to be pleased with this! Charlie thought as he sat meditating on the tapestry scene. They will not believe the intricacy of this masterpiece. Thiri put a lot of personal perception into this work. Those of us who were actually there in the Mogok Valley can truly appreciate what Thiri has created here.

The public dedication of the tapestry was set for the following weekend. As the guests arrived, they were seated by ushers hired by Lee Chang for the occasion. Soft South Eastern music was playing from the CD that Charlie and Dena brought back with them. It was going to be a grand day!

As Krystyna, Kaz, Nick and Giovanna sat on the dais next to Charlie and Dena and Lee Chang and his wife, May Lee, they looked silently in awe for a few moments at the crowd facing them. The guests were sitting with looks of admiration and happiness on their faces. They could tell that the guests were pointing them out and continually pointing to things in the tapestry. And they all knew that the focal point of it all was the ruby; the precious gem from Myanmar. They knew in their hearts what excitement the people were feeling looking at the tapestry, especially with the ruby as the focal point of it. They, too, were at a loss for words when they saw it for the first time. It was far more than they had expected. Thiri outdid herself. They all felt one regret among themselves; that Thiri could not be here for the dedication. They would keep their promise to her though, of having the whole day videotaped and sent to her from beginning to end.

The short program began with a warm welcome from Mr. Lee Chang. Certain noted guests were recognized before Lee introduced the people on the dais. As he mentioned each of their names they stood to accept their acknowledgement. Lee gave a brief account of how and why the tapestry came to be. He gave a short biographical description of Daw Thiri Thuza, the artisan of the tapestry and explained how they happened to find and choose her. The group was grateful that the media present were not too interested in the finer details of the whole story. They wanted to keep their entire story low key. Lee explained to the guests that he had purchased the ruby from the six couples who had acquired it in a strange way. It was his purchase of a lifetime as a gemologist. Of course he had to explain about the teak turtle and how the women inadvertently bought it at a flea market. He told the guests to shop carefully when they do shop because one never knows what will cross one's path in life. Everyone smiled at the thought.

The day's festivities were topped off with a gala cocktail hour that lasted for several hours in the conference hall. Everyone had a jubilant time and would remember this day for a long time. There were a lot of questions and comments for the couples and Lee Chang. But they were able to handle them and satisfy the curiosity of all.

After everyone left, the three couples and Lee Chang took some final looks at the tapestry. They studied it more intensely now that everyone else had gone. They wanted to enjoy the details and appreciate all of Thiri's artistry and talent. As they stared at the tapestry each one noticed something significant. The ruby had been placed on the top of the main pagoda in the center of the tapestry. Upon closer inspection, they saw that Thiri in her unique artisan way was able to superimpose the outline of a turtle on the lake in the bottom center of the tapestry. Her embroidery work was magnificent. They had not seen the turtle outline earlier. The tapestry had portrayed every part of their story from beginning to end. What a masterpiece!

Conclusion

"A generous heart is good for the right sort of people." Saying of Buddha

Though the people in this book are all fictional, we can relate to all of them. They are ordinary people living ordinary lives doing everyday things. Their lives all came together in a unique way which proves that people can get along when they give and take ideas and accept each other for who they are. True friends do not try to change each other, but rather they help each other to grow in knowledge and holiness. People are the same all over the world. Their cultures, customs and languages may be different, but their family ideals and lifetime goals seem to be the same. The characters in my book had their defining moments when they showed their generosity to each other. They were the right sort of people who deserved the generosity that each extended to the other.

"Right focus brings about reality." Saying of Buddha

It is important to keep yourself focused on the important things in life. Outside influences of the world try to make you stray from the goals you set for yourself. Keep your focus. You know what you want out of life. Go for it, strive for it, and don't let obstacles stand in your way. You can achieve anything you want to if you put your mind to it. Your lifetime goals will be achieved and become your reality if you persistently focus on what is important and wholesome.

"An idea that is developed and put into action is more important than an idea that exists only as an idea." Saying of Buddha

Everyone is gifted with ideas of one kind or another and they have the necessary talents to make them become realities. Take your idea and run with it. You can do anything if you apply yourself and stick to your dreams. If you have setbacks, don't give up. *"Rome wasn't built in a day,"* as they say. Put your idea into motion and make it worthwhile. Let it work for the good of others.

"When the student is ready, the Master appears." Saying of Buddha

About The Author

Ruth A. Manieri was an elementary school teacher for twenty years. She is presently in a second career as a church secretary and organist. Last year Ruth published her first book, "Pounding Down...One Day at a Time." Having caught the writing bug, Ruth decided to venture into the realm of fiction. The Myanmar Maneuver is her first attempt at writing a novel, an adventure story.

Ruth's hobbies include writing poetry and composing sacred music pieces. Writing The Myanmar Maneuver has enhanced Ruth's wealth of knowledge and peaked her desire to continue writing.

A graduate of Seton Hall University in South Orange, New Jersey, Ruth holds a Bachelor's degree in Education. She resides with her husband, William in Sayreville, New Jersey.

Printed in the United States
50509LVS00002B/106-234